THE Apocalypse Waltz

For a color map of Ythedra
based on Danny Ramirez's notes,
go to www.ninthplanetpress.com/maps

THE Apocalypse Waltz

A Memoir

by Bruce McCandless

From Notes by

Danny Ramirez

For Jeanette E. Doyle

Copyright 2017 Danny Ramirez and Bruce McCandless
Ninth Planet Press, Inc.
Austin, Texas
All Rights Reserved

Cover Photo by Kelly Lynn James
Cover Design by Shaun Venish
and Meggie Weirich

ISBN-10: 0615413862
EAN-13: 9780615413860

Esteban Daniel Ramirez disappeared from his Manhattan apartment in October of 2005. No reliable sighting of the man has been recorded since. In 2012, however, I received in the mail a banker's box full of notes, maps, and sketches. While the box had no return address, the documents were clearly in Danny's hand. I know. I grew up with Danny in southeast Texas. I was his first and most enthusiastic fan.

I'm grateful to the people who helped me decipher Danny's disjointed manuscript over the course of the last sixteen months. It wasn't easy. We didn't always agree on references, or translations, or even on the chronology of events recorded in that rat's nest of narratives and confessions Danny sent me. But one thing is certain: publication of this account of Danny Ramirez's disappearance would have been impossible without the efforts of Billy Wicker, Caroline Fuller, Dewey Brackin, Jeff Burrus, Jack Wilkinson, and the men and women of the New York City Police Department. They have my heartfelt thanks.

Danny, I speak for all of us when I say you have not been forgotten. We hope we got it right. Wherever you are, *compadre*, we wish you peace. BMcC

Fallen! Fallen is Babylon the Great!
She has become a home for demons
And a haunt for every evil spirit.

Revelations 18:2

I've been walkin' forty miles of bad road.
If the Bible's right, the world will explode.
I've been tryin' to get as far away from myself
as I can.

Bob Dylan

The Apocalypse Waltz

1

Laser Turns

They did a lousy job of killing me.

And here's the kicker. I could have saved them the trip. It was a typical Thursday and I had just about squeezed myself into a bottle of single malt scotch. I was thinking about Rachel Chen again. I was eyeing sharp objects. I was wondering how many bandanas I'd need to make a decent noose. That's when Edward stepped out of my closet to give me the news.

Dark Lord.

Unhappy.

Something about my head.

I coughed up a couple bucks' worth of whiskey. Most of it landed on my coffee table, where I could lick it up later. But still. The indignity. Edward stood four-feet-seven. He'd gathered his shoulder-length hair in a red velveteen band, and he sported a princess-cut diamond on one flange of his nose. It wasn't a look that inspired confidence. It was a look that inspired ridicule. One of my specialties.

"He's turned the Laser," Edward continued, "and—"

"Not *the* Laser," I said. "Just *Laser.*"

"Whatever. Pack yer things. We're gettin' outta here."

I've always had trouble following orders. This one was no exception. It was two-thirty in the a.m. and I figured enough was enough with the muttering dwarf. In fact I was just about ready to do the obvious thing—*keep drinking*—when the glass of my Broadway-side window shattered in a thousand airborne blades. I turned to find the homicidal cyborg Laser standing like a statue inside my apartment. He was all of six and a half feet in his combat boots, and he weighed three hundred and sixty-three pounds when his magazines were full, though most of that weight was Kevlar KM2 plating around his ribs and spine. I could hear the optic sensors implanted in his skull whirring as they transmitted data to his central processing unit. His dirty cape curled like a purple breeze around the contours of his anodized body armor.

"Bang," said the cyborg.

I was about to say something pithy when Laser gave me that *screw you* squint he'd employed in lieu of any sort of meaningful dialogue in the last several issues of his very own comic book. Then he aimed the twenty-millimeter plasma cannon fused to the bones of his right forearm at the obvious target, my mouth, and it was at this pregnant moment that Edward rolled a grenade across my parquet floor. The sound it made was like one of those little white balls rattling around beneath the table when you make a goal in foosball. It fetched up just a few inches from Laser's left boot. Maybe the cyborg was as puzzled as I was. Maybe he was just stoned out of his mind. He watched the spheroid rotate twice on its horizontal axis. This was a mistake. The grenade exploded with a noise like the end of the world.

Light. Heat.

Plaster. More glass.

I found myself flat on my back. I saw swathes of burnt ceiling. A full moon of face.

"Odds are," Edward hissed, "the toaster's right. You ready to travel, smart-ass?"

I looked around. Laser was gone—along with most of one exterior wall of my apartment. The night sky beckoned.

"Can I bring my bottle?" I said. Or maybe I shouted. My ears were ringing and I can't be certain. The only thing I know for sure is this: the little dude threw a helluva punch.

Wasn't expecting it.

Caught me square on the chin.

It was the classic knock-out formula. Head snaps around, brain tries to follow. Movement of head arrested by tendon and muscle. Gray matter crashes into skull, and several million neurotransmitters fire at once. Instant overload. Knees give way. Floor has to sign for the cargo.

So I lay there a couple of seconds, semi-paralyzed, wondering why Edward was upside down. That's when forever reached out and grabbed me.

2

On the Move

I was thirty-four when it happened. I lived on Manhattan's Upper West Side and got by on what was left of a rapidly diminishing severance package from my ex-employer, Empire Media Arts. The severance wasn't a king's ransom. I probably could have done better if I'd stayed sober during the arbitration. But then again I wasn't exactly collecting cans. I owned a two-bedroom apartment smack-dab in the middle of the priciest real estate in America. I had a TV as big as a Smart car and a sweet pair of Knicks season tickets. I also had a formidable cache of my favorite libations and, this being Manhattan and all, access to a steady stream of recreational pharmaceutical products. Fentanyl. Oxycontin. Diazepam.

As Laser himself might have said, "Dude, who's complainin'?"

Actually, Laser hadn't said anything so philosophical in months. These days the half-man, half-missile mostly just capped people—good people, bad people—and let his microprocessors do the talk-ing. In fact he was rapidly losing the little bit of organic "mind" he had left, though he was still gaining readers. Laser was one of my first creations for Empire Comics. He could kill in eighteen lan-guages and a handful of Chinese dialects. He had the moral sense of a monitor lizard, and he liked to wile away the hours by making origami swans out of strips of human skin—typically the soles of the feet, which are most resistant to tearing. As you can imagine, I was expecting my call from the Pulitzer people any day. Although on this particular night I was also expecting confinement in a psychiatric facility, Bellevue maybe, on account of when I regained my senses I found Edward dragging me by one ankle through what had to be the filthiest alley in New York City. By means of sounds somewhere the far side of sentences and just shy of actual grunts, the little man led me to understand that the world was in mortal danger due to the fact that Satan wanted my imagination—and was prepared to cut a few ethical corners to get it.

"It ain't just *yers*," Edward said. He stopped in the middle of the alley to catch his breath. Saliva flecked the corners of his mouth. Twin channels of dried blood made a Roman numeral II beneath his nose. "There are forces at work tonight that I can't even describe in your tongue. Might as well try to spread a star on a sandwich. If we're not pretty goddamned lucky, pretty goddamned *soon*, there ain't gonna be no more heroes. No more upholders. Only rapists, cannibals, demons, and slaves."

"Whoa. Hold on. Can I make one observation? Maybe raise a question or two? From what I can recall—and I admit I've had a few snorts, so correct me if I'm wrong—a comic book I invented a decade or so ago just smashed a bay window, hopped into my condo and aimed his plasma cannon straight at my face. I had the distinct impression he was about to kill me when you...*you know*. Blew him up. Then savagely attacked me."

The dwarf held my glance for several seconds. I could tell he wanted to slug me again. I showed him my palms. Shrugged.

"I didn't *blow him up*. I blew him outta yer place. He fell twelve stories and landed on a bus. He wasn't moving. Mighta been the PCP he's been tankin' up on lately. Or maybe I knocked his transponders out of sync. Whatever it was, we ain't seen the last a' Laser. It's yer own fault."

"My fault?"

"Creating heroes who ain't no different than what they're supposed to be fighting. It's no wonder Laser was one of the first to turn."

"Turn what? I hate to tell you this, *vato*, but Laser is a fictional character. He's a figment of the collective imagination of some massively immature and possibly emotionally disturbed middle-aged men. Including me. He doesn't exist."

"For most people he don't exist. You have trouble remembering that fact. Yer what we call a *bridge*. And they're plannin' to cross you tonight."

"Cross me?" I said. "Cross me how? And who the hell *are* you, anyway?"

Edward mopped the grime from his cheeks with one sleeve of his smoking jacket. A rat went scurrying along the wall behind him. He whirled to watch it pass.

"The mechanics can vary," he said. "But death is generally part of the process. In fact, it's one of the more pleasant parts of the process. And all you need to know about me is that my name is Edward and I'm here to keep you alive."

"Good luck with that. I'm not even going to ask you what you were doing in my closet. My name's Ramirez."

"Esteban Daniel Ramirez. I know who you are. One-time comic book publishing prodigy. Made a million."

"More like ten million, when you throw in the back-end stuff."

"Made ten million. Noted purveyor of necrophilia and assorted other sexual fetishes to the nation's twelve-year-olds. Developed a nasty drinking problem and proceeded to make powerful enemies, including his friends, most of his co-workers, and a significant portion of his readership. Now a lonely, disillusioned has-been with serious substance abuse issues and a not-so-latent death wish."

"I see you got my resume. Different question. Who's planning to *cross me*, as you put it? Laser? And where's he trying to go?"

"Laser's one of 'em," said the dwarf. "No question. Along with the Blaster, Casimir, and Mr. Large, not to mention a crapload of other funny-book freaks, a couple dozen demons, ghouls, creatures with teeth but no eyes and a nasty little shit bucket named Baal who's been worshiped by the worst of your kind for thirty-six thousand years. Where Laser wants to get to, Ramirez, is here."

"Manhattan?"

"Earth, Einstein. What you probably consider to be the real world."

"Oh. But you know better, right?"

Edward shrugged. "I know we got maybe twenty minutes to get you into a transfer duct and out of this sector before all hell breaks loose. That duct's about to close—if it hasn't already. Now, if only... *good*. They're here. Late, as usual. But they're here."

Three long shadows bobbed toward us along the brick walls of the alley. Absurd as it seemed, I felt a wave of genuine panic. I had no idea who was coming. But if Laser was back to finish what he'd started, the odds were pretty good I was about to look like something that falls through the grill at a backyard barbecue. I tried to wedge myself behind the nearest dumpster. A moment later I found myself staring up at an elephant. He stood on his massive hind legs. He wore a gold crown studded with walnut-sized emeralds, and in his trunk he carried a platinum scepter the length of a javelin. His tusks were tipped with steel spikes.

"Mr...Mason?" I stammered. "The Elephant Prince?"

The pachyderm inclined his boulder-like head. His voice was a rich, chuckling baritone, a sonic cocktail of earthquake and asphalt. "Delighted to meet you, Ramirez. You were one of my favorite readers when I was a calf. But I'm not alone. May I introduce Elwer the Wandering Elf, Lord of Il-Istirkhan on the Violet Bay; and Barney, a Faithful Black Lab?"

I had no clue who the elf was. But as I stared at the dog, a handsome hundred-pound brute with a chocolate-colored coat and amber eyes, a substantial piece of my childhood came tumbling toward me. It hit me so hard it almost knocked me down.

"Barney? I remember Barney! From the old Indigo series, *Song of the West*! I used to ride my bike to the U-Tote-'Em every third Thursday to wait for the comic book truck to roll in. Where's the

Lonesome Rider, pal? And Jesus, who's next? Gary, Larry, and Harry?"

I was talking about the Beaver Brothers, comic book faves of my youth who went on to star in a genuinely awful Saturday morning cartoon series and a number of straight-to-video features. But Edward turned his back on me. He yanked a nylon gym bag out from underneath one of the dumpsters and opened it to reveal a military-issue Mossberg 590A-1, a twelve-gauge scattergun with a fourteen-inch barrel, a dual-action bar pump and a battered, duct-taped pistol stock. The little man glanced up as he thumbed green plastic shells into the magazine.

"Gary and Larry are dead. Harry's been missing three weeks. You got some more cracks you wanna make, funny man?"

"Possibly. What are you loading in that thing? Those don't look like any shotgun shells I've ever seen."

"On account a' they ain't. Special formula. Mostly Willie Pete."

"Say again?"

"White phosphorous," said Mr. Mason. I turned to find the pachyderm looming over me. "Used extensively in Vietnam. Nasty stuff. Burns on contact. Straight down to the bone—or whatever else it can get to."

Elwer's pale features hardened. The sickle-shaped pupils of his eyes glowed like tiny moons. "Enough talk. We have to *move*. The Park may already be taken."

"You're right," said the elephant. "Barney, you take point. I'll lead our guest. Edward and Elwer, you flank us, a few steps behind. We'll cut into Central Park at 73rd Street and make for Belvedere Castle. We'll deposit Mr. Ramirez in the transfer duct there and stand by for evac. Agreed?"

My companions considered each other's grim faces.

"Gentlemen," said Edward, nodding at me, "this is it. Believe it or not, the boss says this bottle jockey could make a difference."

"I always thought I could make a difference."

Edward chuckled, though he didn't sound amused. He chambered a shell.

CHIK-CHUK, said the shotgun.

"Get caught tonight," said Edward, glancing over his shoulder, "and you might make someone a pretty nice belt."

3

Belvedere Castle

Call me a liar.

I don't blame you. I had trouble with it myself. I wondered when I'd finally wake up and like, *get a grip*. Not that I'm going to bore you with the endless ellipses and bullshit dithering you typically get with inexplicable sagas. I've edited out most of the sheer stunned disorientation I felt, especially in those first few days after Laser showed up in my living room with patricide at the top of his To-Do list.

It's not that the shock didn't happen. It's just that it's not an important part of the story. Because let's face it. Despite what I think I saw and felt, I know it's possible I simply never emerged from whatever millennial fever dream climbed up on top of me one night and jammed its tongue down my throat. And the corollary is that a different version of me—quite possibly, the *real* me—is currently lying tits-up on a hospital bed with a respirator tube jammed up his nose and his cerebral cortex functioning on the level of the average cranberry. He's a victim of some mental malfunction, traumatic or endemic, that has left *this me* stranded in the dismal precincts of my own delusions. Has left *this me*, in other words, well and truly screwed.

I admit this.

I know it.

But somehow I think it all happened. And because this is the case, I'll stick to telling you what I experienced, and you can judge for yourself how real it was. In other words, forget my reactions. Check out what I was reacting to.

———+———

There are plenty of ways to see Central Park.

You can ride in a carriage. You can ride in a cab. You can ride in the back of a squad car on your way to the 24th Precinct to answer a few questions about that meth lab in the apartment next door. But you're probably not going to see the Park the way I did: from just behind the butt of the best-educated two-ton ungulate ever to strap on a diadem.

We crossed Central Park West between 73rd and 74th Streets, then ducked into the tangled trails of the Ramble, heading uptown. The woods were deserted. We reached Belvedere Castle in just under ten minutes. The Castle is a crazy little architectural wet dream that stands on a ridge of granite just south of the Park's Great Lawn. It's one of my favorite spots in the city. But just as I was starting to feel pretty good about things—my temporary insanity; the crisp autumn air—Barney stopped in his tracks. He growled at the snap of a branch in the trees to our left. I heard the trill of metal on metal as Elwer's scimitar flashed in the murky lamplight. I took a step backward, stumbled as something cold slammed into my shoulder.

"FROGS!" Edward said.

But *bigger*. These things were the size of Adirondack chairs. Still, it was only when I caught a glimpse of one frog's face that I started to scream. The creature had dead black eyes, like a shark, and teeth that looked like scaling knives. It scrambled up on my chest. I flailed with both my arms but it bore in just the same. The frog pinned me flat on my spine. Just as I felt its breath on my throat, I heard a sickening, meaty slap, like raw hamburger thrown against a cinder block wall. The frog slumped to one side of me, its long legs thrashing. The top of its skull landed ten yards away.

I rolled away from the carcass and looked up to see Elwer the Wandering Elf. His sword dripped brains and dark blood.

"Down," he said.

The blade whirred past my head and another amphibian hit the ground, sliced nearly in half by the stroke. Edward fired the Mossberg and two more figures fell, their bellies erupting in flame. Around me I heard Barney's furious snarls, the gasps of the frogs, Mr. Mason's ear-splitting roar.

Then, almost as quickly as they'd attacked, the frogs drew back.

The elf yanked me to my feet.

"The castle!" he spat.

We scrambled another ten steps toward the gray stone edifice before the electric lights along the sidewalk flickered and went dark. Elwer pulled a slender cylinder from the pouch on his belt and scratched it hard, like a match, on the cement. The blue glow lit up everything nearby. I recognized most of those who barred our way. Laser, for one. His left arm glistened with synthetic blood, and a flap of skin drooped from his titanium skull like wallpaper in a cheap hotel. Beside Laser stood Casimir the Black Magician, a trafficker in arcane spells and contraband souls, and Anarkiss, the Nubian Vampire Queen. You may remember Anarkiss from her stint in *Hellraiders* #9-16. Angelic face. Acidic saliva. A predilection for arterial blood. To their left squatted the skull-crushing nitwit Mr. Large, a North Korean genetic experiment gone six kinds of wrong. He clucked to himself as he gnawed on a bone. *Femur*, from the looks of it.

Beyond the others stood a fifth figure, shrouded in darkness. A *part of it*, somehow. Him I didn't know. And wasn't eager to meet.

Around us, nightmare figments—leering gargoyles, carnivorous amphibians—watched from the shadows. Though some of them, I realized, *were* shadows. We were hemmed in.

Surrounded.

Trapped.

"Hand over the fuck stick," said Laser.

"Fuck stick?" The Elephant Prince made a quick survey of the forces ranked against us.

"You know who I mean. Give us the human, you freak, or I'm gonna rip those tusks out your head and shove 'em up your ass."

Mr. Mason sighed. "Ah, yes. Bombast. Another thing I dislike about the lackeys of evil. What was it Milton said? *He who overcomes by force hath overcome but half his foe.* If you'll excuse us, friends, we have business inside the castle."

The shrouded figure emitted a hollow laugh. Holy smoking hell broke loose at roughly the same time. Mr. Mason was first to be hit. Laser shattered his shoulder with a plasma blast and I smelled burnt flesh in the air. But the elephant stayed on his feet. Edward side-armed a grenade at the figures who barred our way and the world erupted in sound and flame. We piled along behind Mr. Mason as he lumbered toward the castle. Barney thrashed and snapped. Elwer's bright blade preached death to the resurgent frogs. The Elephant Prince slammed into the stout wooden door of the castle and left it in splinters and somehow Edward found me in the pile of struggling bodies. He was missing a piece of his neck and he was bleeding like a stuck pig, but the dwarf wrestled me out of the crush of flesh and hauled me by my collar up a set of winding stone steps. Twice he turned and fired one-handed blasts from the Mossberg. The second time I turned too and saw Anarkiss take a face full of phosphorous pellets. The Vampire Queen shrieked as her head exploded in white flame. She lost her grip on the ceiling and crashed to the floor, her limbs doing some spastic dance of disaffection as her brain began to bake inside her head. A frog sprang over her body toward us. It flew backward just as fast, propelled by a point-blank blast to the chest.

Edward shouldered me forward. At the top of the stairs stood another door. *Open*, this time. We burst into a candle-lit room that was bare but for a single chair. And, in the corner, a washing machine.

White.

Whirlpool, I think.

"In!" said Edward.

Before I could even think to resist, the dwarf shoved me into the machine. A shadow fell over the room, and the portholed door of the washer slammed shut behind me with the weight of Edward's body. I heard the Mossberg roar, and a scabrous, birdlike claw scraped against what couldn't have been the mere glass of the window. The machine clicked on. Blood streaked the portal as I started to tumble. Then a face appeared at the window, and I'll never forget the long teeth and black tongue that pressed close. *It was Baal*, I realized. It was the figure who'd stood in the darkness outside the castle. The last thing I witnessed that night was the demon holding Edward's severed head like a grape above its ugly mouth. The creature glanced sideways toward me, and what I saw in its glittering eyes wasn't malice. It was *worse* than malice. What I saw looked a lot like amusement. Then the world danced away like a chorus girl on crack and I fell oh I fell and I fell.

4

Ancient History

A whole lot of South Texas looks like it was shot at point-blank range with a high-caliber crap gun. Pasadena has the typical sprawl of strip malls and car lots on a scrubby, treeless landscape. But it's also humid, and six degrees hotter than hell, and it *stinks*. A byproduct of the hulking petrochemical refineries along the Houston Ship Channel, this little loaf of perdition is one of a handful of places in the United States where death by mesothelioma is considered "natural causes." I know. I grew up in Pasadena. At night I watched hydrogen sulfide burn-offs from my bedroom window and dreamed that God was angry with the world. I have more heavy metals in my veins than a Chinese spray paint. The first time I ever gave blood, I was mistaken for a Chevy Impala.

My foster parents, Reuben and Inez, were petty and strict and way too fond of *barbacoa*. But they meant well. They kept me fed. They bought me my first sketchbook. In fact, they bought me a hundred sketchbooks over the years, though they grew uneasy with what I chose to fill them with—chiefly, variants on themes from Alan Moore and Robert Crumb. I was saddened but not particularly surprised when Reuben and Inez died of natural causes within a month of each other. I was twenty-two at the time. I swear to God

I would have gotten them out of that place if I'd had the means. They died too soon. I miss them.

But not Pasadena. I bolted as soon as I could. Sporting parachute pants and hair to my lumbar vertebrae, I arrived in New York City after spending what felt like a month on a Greyhound bus. My first years in the city tasted like warm beer and stale tortillas. They smelled like the F train in August. My poverty wasn't entirely the President's fault. I was an artist. I wanted to do literary illustrations—intricate, suitable-for-framing jobs like the ones by Beardsley, Parrish, and Frank Frazetta. But Gotham has a way of abasing ambition. My first job was printing flyers for Sal's Famous Pizza at 102nd and Broadway in Manhattan. I moved up to flyers for Chinese food, hot dogs, and unfinished furniture, and I did a fair amount of graffiti in the Bronx. But I couldn't get in the door at Marvel, and DC wouldn't even look at my drawings. So I worked days as a bicycle courier. I donated blood at thirty-six dollars a pop. Finally, in frustration, despair, and a basement apartment in Brooklyn, I dreamt up an entire comic book. And that, as a dead guy once said, has made all the difference.

———+———

I joined Empire Comics on the strength of my first few sketches of *Warriors of Ythedra*, the thirty-two page book on which I lavished everything I knew about *chiaroscuro*, perspective, and barbarian witchcraft. At the time, Empire's founder, John K. Y. ("Junky") Chen, was struggling to keep his artists in inks and his writers in trousers. We had nineteen metal desks, a transvestite receptionist named Ray, and a four-book retail list. We were wallowing in more red ink than the bullpen could slop onto the pages of *The Punishment Squad*. Our landlord hated us. But *Warriors of Ythedra* had what Junky Chen lovingly referred to as the four Ms: Monsters, Magic, Mayhem and, most importantly, additional Mayhem. After only a little consideration, the boss asked me to make *Warriors* a series. This was easy. In fact, for a while I couldn't seem to *stop* drawing the story. I saw Ythedra when I was sleeping. I saw the land and its people in the shower, on the subway—even in the elevators, on those rare occasions when the elevators in our building actually worked. It was as if a conceptual levee had cracked inside my brain. The images started pouring out of my hand whether I wanted them to or not.

Commercial success was another matter. That first issue of *Warriors* sold just over nineteen hundred copies. The sixteenth and final installment, "The Spiders of Dred Siryat," in which the valiant and pathetic Ban Lohannon manages to jam a dagger into the neck of the sorcerer Aln Adrackt and shove him into a pit of giant arachnids, sold slightly fewer than three thousand. These were tiny numbers even by Empire's standards. Still, Junky Chen liked my style. With the possible exception of his daughter Rachel, he liked it more than anyone else in the world. When *Warriors* ended, he put me in charge of outlining stories for the company's more contemporary titles. I dug the work. I was good at it. And eventually I created a few titles of my own: *Laser Kill. Yesterday City. The Eel and I.* To populate the dirty back streets of these worlds, I invented characters like Casimir and Mr. Large. I figured out how they moved and ate and smelled, and I spent a lot of time thinking about how best to depict their random acts of horrific violence. A few years earlier Frank Miller had reinvigorated the genre with his work on the new but not necessarily improved Batman, one of the first crime fighters with bad breath and a hard-on for shattered cartilage. Sales jumped for everyone. The lesson was obvious. Nihilism was big business—especially if you could give it some decent dialogue. The race to the bottom was on, and we did our level best to get there first. Our stories grew darker. Our protagonists got uglier. And somehow, through a combination of canny hiring decisions and sheer dumb luck, Junky Chen managed to assemble the most depraved and imaginative group of artists and writers in the industry.

You know the story. Empire soared through several years of unexpected triumph and carefully orchestrated controversy. John K.Y. Chen grinned from the cover of *Newsweek*. He spoke puckishly in *Forbes, Fortune,* and *The Wall Street Journal,* and sales kept climbing. Congressmen sputtered. There was talk of a hearing. "Where Have All the Heroes Gone?" bleated one banner headline. At Empire we knew exactly where the heroes had gone. The heroes were sitting in one of our shitters, shooting smack and comparing tattoos. They'd pooled their cash to purchase the services of a woman named Wanda, who had two gold teeth and a mouth like a Jersey landfill. The heroes slept till four p.m. The heroes were getting to be a real pain in the ass.

———+———

But Empire's profits attracted predators. Seeking content for its video games, a Japanese electronics company engineered a hostile take-over of the company a year after its initial listing on NASDAQ. Junky Chen retired to Flushing with his many millions, his barely post-pubescent Russian wife, and a growing fondness for Gulfstream jets. When he grew restless he started all over again, with an outfit called Chaos Comics and worse luck this time. Chaos called it quits two years later, just a month before Junky Chen dropped dead from a massive cerebral aneurysm. But Empire kept expanding.

Metastasizing, we called it.

At the behest of the Atsushiro Capital Group, Empire's new *jefes*, I eventually gave up my pens altogether and concentrated on editing and story-line development. I even worked on movie tie-ins and toy distribution, especially as our books grew grimmer. Our Japanese overlords were simply continuing a long-time tradition. Their *manga*, or graphic books, had been astonishingly violent for decades. In the U.S., the stuff was still something of a shock. But shocks wear off. Folks got used to the Empire style, which certain critics began to compare to the style of other American originals. Charles Whitman, for example. Soon we found ourselves on the cutting edge of what industry analysts, those joyless clods in the scarlet suspenders, call "dark comics." In dark comics, people like me denounce the brutality and ugliness of the world with holy disillusioned fury. Then we kick off our britches, get down on our bellies and wallow around in the spit and the sweat like a tweaker on a speedball slip 'n slide. Women are raped. Children get killed. Unattractive people die in awful, extremely graphic ways and no one really gives a shit. When you read editorials in those days about the unfortunate effects of gratuitous violence and equivocal protagonists on American youth, you were reading about us. The company's name changed from Empire Comics to Empire Media Arts to reflect our focus on gaming. EMA, we were called. Maybe you've seen our first-person shooters. You know. The ones with the secret but easily accessed scenes of nudity and gang rape? Highly unsuitable for kids! Not sure how they got there!

We were vilified, fined, picketed, sued.

Business was awesome.

———+———

But even as Empire prospered, my mental health began to deteriorate. I'd always had the ability to dream my work, to see the images in my head as if they were really there. The vision was never stronger than when I drew *Warriors of Ythedra*. That mountainous green world—Ythedra, I mean; the Emerald of the Ninelands—opened up in front of me so vividly that I could smell the salt of its southern seas and taste the chalky water in its high-country creeks. I was never able to re-create the elegance and intricacy I brought to those drawings. Various fan sites spent a fair amount of time reminding me of that fact, but trust me, I *knew*. And my disappointment in myself didn't help when things started getting strange in the sinkhole that was my personal life. Maybe it was the alcohol that caused the visions. Maybe it was the visions that made me drink. Maybe when you're puking your guts up in the back of a Fox news van parked outside of Comic-Con, it doesn't matter anymore. The point is, like goddamned Ebenezer Scrooge on Christmas Eve, I'd started to see things move that shouldn't have moved. Furniture. Photographs. Architectural details. I had foul dreams that made my edgiest books look like *Dora the Explorer*. Over the course of eleven months I lost my job, my nerve, and the only woman who ever loved me—my foster mother excepted. I drank myself to sleep most nights I could remember and God only knows what happened on the nights I couldn't. Slowly but surely I managed to alienate the very few people who still claimed to care about me. They said I "rambled." Or maybe it was "raved." Hell. Even I was aware that I had developed an unfortunate tendency to spray spit as I lectured whoever happened to be sitting on the barstool next to mine. Let's just say I didn't have many social commitments anymore.

Then I met Edward, the dwarf in my closet, who saved me from flesh-eating frogs. Or maybe from *worse*.

But first I kept falling.

From the Annals of Ythedra

*M*any *centuries ago, the realm called Dar-Annon stretched from the scarlet sands of Emerkest to the turf-crowned cliffs of Sidhara. In those days, Dar-Annon was the mightiest kingdom in the Ninelands—the center of the circle, Darannan priests proclaimed. It was ruled from the White Cities by the warrior king An Karabekian, a vigorous soldier and canny judge who nevertheless made the mistake of siring three sons by three different wives. And that's where our story begins.*

One of them, anyway.

An Karabekian was a tall, iron-eyed man who knew better than to believe the legends that surrounded him. It wasn't easy. His people called him An the Devourer. The Dragon of the Ivory Cave. Flame of Man. It was true that An and his Darannan armies never lost a campaign. But An knew that he'd had more than his fair share of good luck and able officers on the battlefield, and he retained a sense of perspective rare in the histories of empire. In the end, this humility served him well. A fall while hunting left him partially paralyzed at the age of forty-nine, and he died of pneumonia four months later. Though in the end he lost even the ability to speak, he was never bitter. He was blessed to know nothing of what was to come for his kingdom.

An's eldest son succeeded him on the throne. Ridwen was brisk, forth-right, and prematurely bald. Immune to flattery and blandishment, he took a special interest in the practical arts of fortification and bridge building. In many ways he was an ideal prince. Though he was never his father's equal as a warrior, he was amiable and curious, and he desperately wanted to be a capable king. The people of Dar-Annon suspected he would lead them well. They were probably right. But fate was not so kind.

King An's middle son, Varun, second in line for the throne, fell ill shortly after his father's cremation. Varun grew pale. He coughed up blood. The court physicians couldn't treat, or even diagnose, Varun's affliction, which even-tually left the prince so weak he couldn't pull on his own boots. Ridwen sent riders to every corner of Dar-Annon, summoning healers to tend to his brother. A few of the leeches who answered the call brought temporary relief, but none could fully restore the young man. People started whispering that Varun would soon follow his father on dark roads unknown to the living.

But one bitterly cold day in February, an emaciated man appeared out of the east and made his way through the White Cities to the gates of Kaer Rhygat, the imperial palace. The man stood well over six feet tall, with jet-black hair and dark, close-set eyes. Though his clothes were ragged, he had a commanding voice, and his manner bordered on impudence. The castellan had heard it all before. A score of potion vendors had appeared in the past few weeks, each promising miraculous cures, none actually able to deliver. How was this one any different? But King Ridwen was increasingly desperate to help his brother. When he received word of the foreign healer waiting at the gate, he invited the stranger in.

The stranger went immediately to Varun's chamber. He swept the assort-ment of blue and green bottles from the table beside the Prince's bed. He chased two nursemaids out of the room and slammed the chamber's oak door behind them so hard that one of the palace's most elaborate tapestries, a depiction of King An's defeat of the cannibals of Niyarr, crashed to the floor.

For three weeks, no one saw the old man leave the room. Food and drink were left outside the chamber each evening, but they went untouched. The only evidence that the prince was even alive came in the form of a series of notes. Each was written in the prince's elegant hand and slipped under the door, saying all was well and that he wished to be left alone with his physician. But eavesdroppers——and there were spies in this court, as there are in any other——reported hearing garbled chanting from inside Varun's room at hours when a sick man should have been asleep. Others went further. They claimed the chamber gave off the smell of putrefaction. It was as if death itself was a beast that had followed the physician in off the desert to make its home in the palace.

At last even King Ridwen grew alarmed by the rumors. Gathering a dozen of his fiercest soldiers, lancers of the Palace Guard, he marched to Varun's room and pounded at the door. When no one answered, the King stepped aside and nodded to his captain. But just as the men of the Guard were about to break it down, the door was flung open from inside. Prince Varun stepped into the hallway and bowed to his older brother, who dropped to his knees in gladness, thanksgiving, and——he couldn't hide it——shock. Varun was standing. He was moving around. But he looked ten years older.

Of course there were feasts in honor of the miraculous healing. Idiots danced. Troubadours sang. But not everyone was thrilled by the sight of the revivified prince. Skeptics pointed out that Varun seemed different since his recovery. The prince was blonde and slightly built, with one leg a little longer than the other. He was an accomplished swordsman, and much given to music. It was a pleasure to have him back. And yet, though he walked and talked like the young man everyone remembered, he grew paler by the day, and he refused to eat anything except what his doctor prepared for him. The slender prince no longer rode out falconing with the nobles of Ridwen's court. Indeed Varun absented himself altogether from the balls and pageants that brightened life in Kaer Rhygat. He shut himself up for days at a time with the physician from the east, poring over ancient texts the healer had carried with him out of the wasteland.

And the physician himself inspired suspicion. For if, as everyone said, Prince Varun looked a decade older since his illness, was it not also true that his healer looked a dozen years younger? It was an ugly question. It turned out that the answer was uglier.

One morning that summer——an unusually cool summer, according to the chronicles——King Ridwen was found dead in his chamber. Again the whispers went around. The king had expired in his bed, it was said. But not in his sleep. In death his mouth was open to scream, his eyes wide with horror. Pieces of the royal torso occupied various portions of the marble floor. Murder was the obvious conclusion. But what mortal could have slipped past the men of the Palace Guard stationed outside the king's door? And who——or what——could have butchered Ridwen without disturbing the wives who slept only a few feet from the king? Lacking answers, the people of the White Cities did the only things they knew to do. The battlements of Kaer Rhygat were draped in black. Veiled women sang dirges in the streets, and dutiful citizens prostrated themselves each evening for a month, mourning the loss of another ruler. Alas, Dar-Annon! Alas, King Ridwen!

That's when Varun made his first mistake.

5

Dislocation

Next thing I heard was the drip of water on stone. From closer came the steady breathing of livestock. I felt a sharp pain in my shoulder and a sharper throbbing in my head, but I'd washed up on the far shore of a nightmare and I was content to know my heart still hammered the idiot backbeat of life. I flexed my fingers and found something that felt like wet grass. A flame flared in the darkness. In the wreath of light I saw a scarred face. It was made uglier by the radiance casting shadows upward on its features.

"Told 'em you wasn't dead," said the face. Speaking perfectly plainly. Not speaking English, exactly. Not speaking *English* at all. But something else. Something I recognized. It took me a minute to find the words to respond. The words felt strange in my mouth. It was like trying to throw a baseball left-handed.

"Not yet," I said.

"So you *can* talk. You must be feelin' better."

"Better...than what?"

The face snorted. "A philosopher," it said. "I shoulda known. Place is crawlin' with 'em."

"What place?" *Kor velamet?* is what I actually said. "Where am I?"

"Where are you? You was lyin' on the floor last time I checked."

"Whose floor?" I persisted.

The flame guttered and died. The voice seemed puzzled. "Bryd Drennen's floor. His jail, ain't it?"

"Bryd Drennen," I said.

"Where'd you think you were?"

"I don't know. McSorley's? What happened to my clothes? My *pants*. It feels like I'm wearing a bathrobe."

"If you're speaking the Tongue, you've got the strangest accent I've ever heard. I only caught the first part of that. But I can tell you what happened to your clothes. Dredyat's work. Little weasel traded with you before lock-down last night. You were still out cold. You can settle up with him this afternoon, after we eat."

"Great. Does Dredyat know he has fleas?"

Someone nearby laughed, or coughed, and I realized that what I had thought were cattle surrounding me were actually slumbering men. I heard soft curses. Muttered complaints. From above me came the clank of machinery, then the clack of a door latch being turned.

"Another deep thinker," said the voice beside me. "Ajin Wyrill. Yard boss. Hard-ass in chief."

As if on cue, a fat little man holding a candle appeared at the foot of a set of stone steps. He chuckled to himself as he used the candle to light the torches mounted on the wall opposite where I lay. When he had completed this task, he plucked one of the torches from its stanchion and strolled along the line of cells. Spotting a shirtless man sleeping in the cell beside mine, the jailor stopped, opened his robe, and pissed on the man's forehead. The man didn't sleep much longer.

"How's the new meat?" Wyrill demanded, glancing at me as he refolded his cassock. He had a weak chin and a wattle of soft flesh beneath it, wide-set pale eyes and a sloping forehead. Ajin Wyrill had a face only a mother could love. A mother that lays *eggs*.

"Stranger? Hey. You sober?"

"Christ," I said. I winced at the torchlight. "I hope not. All I know is, I'm cold as hell, my head hurts, and I'd like to make my one phone call now. If someone could spot me lend me their cell."

"Gibberish, huh? Splendid. Sounds like you're ready for the straps. Especially as you've gone and swiped poor Dredyat's clothes."

"He's a thief!" someone shouted. "Cut off his hands!"

The jailor allowed himself a sad little smile. "Tempting. He looks like a screamer. But it's river work today—direct orders from the Duke—and we need every hand we can get. Maybe next time. You know the drill. Line the fuck up!"

At this point, half a dozen figures appeared at the foot of the steps. They were soldiers, equipped with blue capes, leather helmets, and brass-tipped cudgels. As my eyes adjusted to the half-light, I saw a score of barred cells in the vast dungeon. The furthest from me was barely visible in the gloom. The soldiers stepped from cell to cell, unlocking the doors. The men who emerged from the cages arranged themselves in a sloppy double file. Rolled their necks. Hawked. Spat.

"Name's Gowen," said my cellmate. He was big, with matted blond hair and a beginner's beard. "You might want to slip them huaraches on." He nodded at a pair of mismatched sandals on the floor. "Gotta be better than nothing. Now we just fall in and march. You know what they say. Unless you're the lead dog, the view never changes."

"Thanks. I'm Ramirez."

"Ramirez?" said Gowen.

"Danny Ramirez. You're gonna have to bear with me."

"Had a couple drinks too many, huh?"

"Something like that."

"Word is, a goatherd found you passed out in one of the Duke's pastures yesterday evening. Constable——. What?"

"Slower, please."

"Sure. Constable went to take a look. He smelled the liquor on your breath and threw you in here to teach you a lesson. Public drunkenness is illegal in these parts. It's been explained to me several times."

We climbed three flights of narrow steps, then plodded along a straw-strewn corridor toward a narrow doorway. The guard who led the way stopped and leaned his torch against the stone wall. I heard keys jingling.

I leaned closer to my companion.

"This may sound strange," I said. "In fact, I *know* it's gonna sound strange. But could you tell me what country I'm in? Like, what *world*?"

Gowen chuckled as the guard pulled the door.

"I've felt like that a few times myself," he said. "Can't say I miss the sensation. Welcome, my friend, to the wonders of Ythedra."

The sun hit my eyes like a hammer.

6

Work Detail

We walked twenty minutes before I opened my mouth. It was some kind of record.

"Ythedra," I said. "The Emerald, right?"

"Some people still call it that."

"South of the Sea of Clouds?"

"Unless they moved it."

Just then one of our guards shouted, "Gowen! You and the new meat work upstream today. Stay near that cottonwood where I can keep an eye on you. I want to see a hundred stones out of you two by noon."

The big man spat. "YESSIR! You miserable HUNDRED STONES, EASY! crap slurpin' horse nut."

After we had picked our way fifty yards upstream along the bank of a shallow river, Gowen and I bent and began gathering rocks. There wasn't anything better to do. From long experience dealing with hangovers, I knew to pace myself—and to drink as much of the cold water as I could. I took a sip after every stone. After an hour of work, I rinsed my face and scalp and paused to look around. It was a brilliant morning: sunny and dry, maybe seventy degrees. The sky was an ocean of blue, with a single paisley of cloud hanging motionless overhead. Swallows skimmed the shallows for insects. Every few minutes we heard the splash of a trout rising to hit a fly.

Several pairs of shaggy men foraged just as Gowen and I did along the near bank. A few of them had already stripped to the waist, and their pale flesh glowed in the early sunshine. I envied their options. I didn't have anything to take off anymore. Courtesy of Dredyat, my only garment resembled a soiled hospital gown. It smelled a lot worse, which—*which was Dredyat right there, dammit!* He was a wiry man with close-cropped hair and a skinny little Popsicle stick of a neck. Sort of like mine. He stood laughing at me from the distance of a decent pop fly. He was wearing blue jeans, sneakers, and a faded Houston Oilers t-shirt.

"Hold on," said Gowen. "Not now. You'll just get a kick in the throat for your trouble. Dredyat has friends in here."

"Dude, that's my shirt he's wearing. And it happens to be the only one I haven't thrown up on."

"Later."

"Forget later. I'm not wearing a dress all day."

"*Later*," Gowen said. His hand was the size of an oven mitt. "You get me crossways with the guards today and they'll throw me in the hole for a month. And if that happens, brother, I'm gonna make your life hell as soon as I'm out. You understand what I'm saying?"

The big man tightened his grasp. I felt my collarbone start to warp.

"Later," I conceded.

———+———

Half a mile upstream and a mile to the east, a squat sandstone castle perched on a bluff overlooking the river I was wading in. Even from this distance, I could make out the blue and yellow pennants that fluttered from its spires. Gowen had informed me as we marched that the structure was called *Kaer Rhennet*. Its curtain walls were twenty-four feet high and eight feet thick, shielded at each gate by a scaffolding of heavy oak timbers. This made the castle's perimeter almost impossible to breach. Tunneling wouldn't work either, since the castle stood on rocky ground that was denser than the walls themselves. I nodded. I acted interested. But I knew this stuff already. I knew all about the impregnable Kaer Rhennet: its fields and fortifications; its throne room and antechambers; its oblong, two-tiered chamber for meetings of the Council of Farmers and Tradesmen. After all, I was the one who had cobbled Kaer Rhennet together in the first place. I, Danny Ramirez, the promising young author of *Warriors of Ythedra*. An up-and-comer. Certified Range Rover owner. And now, evidently, the unwilling peg boy of an addled God.

As I wrestled another rock out of the riverbed, Gowen stared at the highlands beyond the castle. He lifted the coarse blonde hair off his brow with one hand and shielded his eyes against the midmorning glare.

"Something wrong?"

"Hmm?" He shook his head. "Guess not. Thought I saw a flash of metal up in the hills. You know. Like weapons. Or a mirror. Could be Marshal Quin's brigade—the Outriders—coming home from the north. Or it could be a trick of the light. Big sun today."

I looked where he pointed, but I couldn't see anything other than the scrubby highlands themselves—a portion of the limestone escarpment called the Step that stretched like a standing wave across central Ythedra. Instead I turned back to Gowen. He was a big man, over six feet tall, with a full head of strawberry blonde hair and a slightly darker beard. I guessed he was in his early twenties. Powerfully built, he had the generally swollen appearance of an athlete gone to seed. He had thick, even features, including a prominent brow and a nose that had to have been broken more than once. I figured maybe a deviated septum accounted for the whistling sound he made when he breathed.

"So," I began. "What are you in for?"

I had always wanted to say the words. Even if they were in another language.

"Drunk and disorderly." My companion rolled his head around on his neck like a boxer waiting for the bell. "I reckon it's my specialty. A while back, I guzzled a bottle or two of mezcal and punched out a platoon of the Duke's best cavalry. *Outriders*, like I said. Not that they didn't punch back. Someone broke a table over my head and next thing I know, I got chains on my ankles. Municipal judge said he was sick of seeing my face in his court-room. I offered to show him my ass instead, which was when he gave me the choice of six months in a cell or two years in the infantry. I've tried army life a couple of times and never had much luck with it. It wasn't all bad. I learned how to fight. I'm just not much good at kissing butts and polishing boots. So I said no thanks to the military, and here I am. Anyhow, it ain't like I'm suffering. I've seen prisons all over Ythedra. Kaer Rhennet's is the best of a sorry lot."

"Yeah?" I said. "How so?"

"Not much abuse, for one thing—despite what you probably think of that maggot Wyrill. He'll yank out a fingernail or two, maybe have the bulls break a few of your ribs if you give him an excuse. Nothing gruesome. And now Bryd Drennen—the Duke—puts us to work stacking stones. For my money, if I had any money, it's a damn sight healthier than sitting in a hole strangling rats for your supper. Even the food ain't bad. At least, I've had worse."

The big man stretched, arching his spine. He hadn't missed many meals.

"Food?"

Gowen glanced over at me. "Oh. Right. You didn't get any breakfast. None of us does. That's so we don't feel so good when we're sent out to work. Less likely to hightail it. There's tortillas and water at noon, but the big meal's post-meridian, which gives a man reason to stick around. 'Course by then we're back in the cells, so there's no *choice* but to stick around. Bryd Drennen's got it figured out. You might think he'd spent time in a few dungeons himself. Threatened to slit his own throat and got locked up for sedition. But what about—Get it? *Sedition?*—what about you? What's your story? You speak the Tongue, though I can't say I recognize the accent. I'm a rover myself. Got three women in two cities and a dozen creditors you might say at large. Some of them just *large*. So I keep moving."

I pointed at the tattoo on Gowen's right bicep. "That one of 'em?"

"One of what?"

"One of your women?"

Gowen blushed. "That's my mother. What's it to you?"

"Just wondering."

"Yeah, well. *Stop.* Where are you from, anyhow?"

"I know this is going to sound funny, but I'm not sure I know where I'm from. I think I must have lost a good chunk of my memory. I have this lump on my skull the size of a plum and—well, things are a little hazy, to tell you the truth."

I wasn't really amnesic. I just figured, *Why call attention to myself? Why say I'm from Texas by way of New York City?* I've read a few of these stories. Dudes who wake up in other dimensions are always bulging their eyeballs and wailing non-sequiturs at unsettled bystanders. I figured shouting wasn't going to help me here. For lack of anything better to do, I let my delusions drift where they wanted. It wasn't bad. I liked feeling the sun on my scalp. The river gurgled around a boulder just upstream, and a breeze rattled the leaves of the cottonwood trees along the bank. I couldn't hear a single siren. There wasn't a taxi or a trash can in sight. Ythedra, I decided, was a lot like Vermont.

"Not those," said Gowen. He shook his head at the armful of stones I'd gathered. "Too small. These rocks have gotta have enough heft to crack a Syrtian skull. Twenty pounds oughta do it."

"Crack a skull? What, they're weapons?"

My companion mopped the sweat from his face with a grimy sleeve. For the first time I noticed the bracelet he wore on his left wrist. It was a smudged silver, the color of old nickels. A miniature copper key dangled from it.

"Family thing," he said, noticing my interest. His face darkened. "It ain't for sale. But to get back to your question: Yeah. They're weapons. This character down south—the so-called Emperor of Emerkest—has got his Syrtian followers thinking they're just the folks to rule the world. There's rumors of magic, and demons, and all kinda horse shit. The part that scares Bryd Drennen, though, is the part about the swords. The Syrtian Army has 'em. *Lots* of 'em. Right now the Syrtians are busy chasin' the Surb cavalry around Emerkest, but—"

"But nothing," said a voice behind me. "That's no longer the case."

A thin man in rough traveling gear stood on the bank just a few feet away from us. He was a picture of desperation. Close-set gray eyes gazed out over a hawk-like nose. Sweat salt lined his cheeks and throat, and his feet and the hem of his cloak were caked with mud. The man wore a circular silver pendant on a chain around his neck. As he stepped toward us, the pendant glittered in the green light reflected off the stream.

"The Surb confederacy is destroyed," the stranger announced. "Its cities are gutted and its fields are in flame. The Syrtians have a new ally."

"Yeah?" said Gowen. "Who?"

The man glanced beyond us.

"Urzeks," he answered.

I saw the whites beneath Gowen's pupils. "Urzeks," he repeated. "And who the hell are you?"

The stranger ignored the question. He surveyed my tattered shift and dirty feet. He studied my face. Finally he grabbed my left arm. I have a dragon on that forearm. It's your basic pissed-off Chinese basilisk in red, blue, and green, courtesy of Lenny Youtsakis at Lenny's Liquid Skin on West 14th. This seemed to mean something to the stranger. "You'll come with me, Ramirez. We have business elsewhere."

"Hold it!" Gowen barked, drawing himself up to his full height. He shook his blonde hair out of his face and stole a quick glance back toward the guards. "You ain't taking no one *nowhere*. I got nine days left of——"

The move was so fast that I hardly saw it. The stranger brought his left palm to his mouth and blew into it. Brown dust flew into Gowen's eyes. Gowen reflexively brought both hands to his face, at which point the stranger struck him on the side of the head with his staff. The big man crumpled as if he'd been shot. The slap of wood on flesh echoed like a gunshot off the river.

"Strong," said the stranger, giving Gowen an appraising glance. "But stupid. Come. They'll be here soon, and we're all in danger."

"They? They who? Not that thing that ate Edward's head?"

No response. I tried again.

"In Belvedere Castle. Back on Earth. He held it up so I could see it. It was Edward's *head*, man. I swear. And maybe——I don't know—— part of his trachea."

"You speak the Tongue," said the stranger. "How——?"

"I do," I said. "The Tongue. The Common Tongue. Don't ask me where I picked it up."

"Explain later. For now, we move."

"I think I might just stick around," I said. "If it's all the same to you."

The stranger pulled a length of leather cord from a pouch he wore on his belt. "It's not," he replied, his lips pursed with annoyance. "But if you want to be tied like an animal…"

I shrugged. It wasn't that I wanted to be tied. It was just that I'd seen something the stranger hadn't. It was Gowen. He was bleeding from one ear and holding a slab of limestone the size of a manhole cover. The outlander must have seen my eyes shift, because at the last second he lunged to one side and the stone only clipped his shoulder. Even this glancing blow would have finished me, but the stranger responded by kicking Gowen square in the ribs. Gowen stunned the outlander with a looping right hook. I heard shouts.

Guards and prisoners alike were hustling toward us, roused by the prospect of bloodshed.

The stranger slipped under Gowen's next swing, then took a step back and delivered a kick to the big man's left knee. Gowen lost his footing and slid down the bank. The stranger's face was flushed with exertion and anger.

"Idiots!" he hissed. "The noose is tightening!"

With this, the outlander leapt into the shallow stream and headed for a stand of cedar elms on the far bank. Once he got there, he disappeared into the trees.

But not for long.

7

Betrayal

So we told the truth. We had no idea who our visitor was. All we knew was that he wanted to kidnap me because of my dragon tattoo and that he claimed to have news about the Syrtian war against the Surbs. *Bad news*, as it turned out, which we dutifully divulged. Invigorated by the prospect of a chase, several sentries forded the river. For half an hour they thrashed around in the woods on the far bank, where they claimed to find several footprints but no coherent trail. We prisoners were herded together while this was going on. Gowen welcomed the break in routine. It gave him a chance to describe how he'd have broken the stranger's head if the fight had lasted a little longer. Cracked his skull. Stomped on his throat. By the time he finished, I was the only one listening.

"Gowen," I asked, when we got back to work, "was I imagining things, or did that guy mention urzeks?"

"That's right. Flesh-eaters. Lizard-spawn. If it's true that urzeks fight in league with the Syrtians, then the Syrtians have sold themselves to the devil. And they've delivered Ythedra to hell into the bargain."

"But that's ridiculous. I know what the urzeks are, or were. They lived in a place called Gilmolok, north of Emerkest, where fortune hunters journeyed in search of silver. The urzeks weren't allies of men. They were *creatures*. Freaks. They killed anything that moved."

"They're still freaks. But some people claim they're here in Ythedra. They say they do the bidding of Aln Adrackt, the Emperor of Emerkest, and walk under protection of his evil."

I examined one of my broken fingernails.

"Whoa," I said. "Wait a minute. Aln Adrackt is dead. Killed by his own spiders in the dungeons beneath the Red Cities. How could he be Emperor of anything?"

Gowen scratched the skin beneath his beard. "I haven't heard that one in a while. Ban Lohannon, right? And the Autumn Prince. Varun? That his name? They're the ones who fed Aln Adrackt to his spiders. Your memory's comin' back. So maybe tomorrow you'll dredge up the nine hundred years years or so since all that crap went down. Or supposedly went down." My companion twisted at the hips to loosen up. "Though I don't know why you'd bother. No one else does."

"Nine hundred *years?*"

The big man stooped to cup a handful of river to his mouth. "Don't panic. I can fill you in later. There's the bell."

I listened as the solemn peals filled the valley. High overhead, a hawk made slow circles in the sky. The swallows had disappeared.

"Bell for what?"

"Town assembly," said Gowen.

"We're allowed to go?"

"Required to go. And we're supposed to cheer like idiots at whatever the Duke has to say—which ain't a whole lot these days. Should be a good show today, though. The Syrtian Border Guard is bringin' in a Naztali for beheading."

"The Naztali tribes are enemies of the Duke?"

"You ever gonna stop asking questions, Ramirez?"

I shrugged, tapped my temple.

"Oh. Right. Well, the Naztali are touchy. Difficult to deal with. But their real beef isn't with Bryd Drennen, it's with the Syrtians, who are killing the game and pushin' the tribes off the southern half of the Greensea. The Naztali reckon the Duke is in bed with the Syrtians, and maybe they got a point. But he don't have a lot of choice in the matter. The Syrtians control just about every square mile south of here, so the Duke has to humor 'em. He lets the Syrtian Border Guard buy provisions in Kaer Rhennet for their raids to the north. Food. Tack. Whatever. And he lets them execute the occasional Naztali brave they manage to capture. I reckon Bryd Drennen would just as soon piss on the Syrtian flag, but without an alliance with the Naztali or—I don't know—Sidhara, he has to put up with the crap. Just like the rest of us do."

Gowen stared at the calluses on his hands as if he'd never seen them. He was roused by the calls of our guards.

"Come on. Toss them last stones on the pile. Provost'll send his ox teams around this afternoon to haul the whole load up to the city."

I dumped my last stones as instructed. Unfortunately, they were a little too big, and the whole pile collapsed. It was probably an omen. At the time, though, I didn't believe in omens. I was already walking away.

———————+———————

Gowen told me not to be surprised by our relative freedom. The men on our work detail were mostly drunkards and petty thieves. The real scum languished in the castle's sub-dungeons. They only saw the light of day long enough to remember what they were missing. Besides, he said. Even if one of us wanted to run, where could we go? There wasn't much of Ythedra fit to escape to anymore. You could try to make your way south, to the Free Cities along the coast. But these days the Free Cities were free in name only, allowed to govern themselves only as long as they cooperated with the Empire and its extensive network of flunkies and spies. Besides, the Syrtian Border Guard patrolled the roads to the south. They had a nasty habit of seizing refugees from the Cities and sending them off to work in the mines of Gilmolok—a death sentence, really, since no one ever returned from that dark region. Copper-skinned

Naztalis rode the grasslands to the north—the *Greensea*, they called it. The horse warriors would just as soon gut a white man as look at him. To the west, beyond the Duke's farmlands, stood the Big Thicket, uncharted and uninviting. Eastward lay black moors and the marshlands surrounding the haunted city of Crag Glzhak. They weren't exactly destinations to set a prisoner's heart thumping. The lands beyond the sea were said to be worse. Ravaged for decades by drought and disease, they were now the dominions of nomadic scavengers oath-bound to the Emperor of Emerkest.

Anyway, Gowen concluded, life at Kaer Rhennet wasn't so bad. Certainly our walk back to the castle was pleasant enough. The road was mostly dirt, peppered with gravel and occasional bright spots where river sand had been used to level the ruts. It wound around a sprawling village of tile-roofed adobe houses with gables and shutters painted gold and green. The residents mostly ignored us. If they were worried about an attack from the south, they didn't show it. They seemed to be busy doing the work of any town, small or large: making a living, tending their children, steering clear of the incarcerated. We passed a flourmill, four farms, and a furniture-making shop. We moved to the side of the road to accommodate a caravan of wagons loaded with sweet-smelling hay. Jays screamed from the elms as we crossed a creek that tumbled gin-clear toward the river, and our guards stopped to count us again. Then we got back in line and climbed through acres of orchards. Yellow pears hung fat on the trees, and a gang of adolescent boys was kind enough to hurl a few samples at the backs of our heads.

The road widened. The limestone walls of the fortress I'd seen from the river rose up in front of us, and soon we passed beneath an iron portcullis. Fifty yards further on, we entered Kaer Rhennet's central courtyard. Gowen and I and the rest of the work detail were herded to a spot just a few feet from a wooden platform that extended into the square from the base of the keep. Our guards passed out stale tortillas and warm cheese to all hands. It was a poor excuse for lunch, but I was starving. I ate as much as I could.

As my fellow inmates stared at passing women, I studied the smoke-smeared walls of the keep. I counted the crenellated parapets on the walls around us and the huge Darannan pennants flapping from a score of staffs. The pennants were horizontal bands of river blue and hayfield yellow, fronted by the solitary white tower of Kaer Rhennet. It was the same flag Prince An-Nashayel, the youngest heir of Dar-Annon, had carried into war against the sorcerer Aln Adrackt in my comic book epic *Warriors of Ythedra*. *Warriors* chronicled the Years of Iron, when Aln Adrackt's Kirikite and Tazgat riders brought the torch to Ythedra, and men fell like wheat at harvest. When the wannabe outlaw Ban Lohannon wandered lonely paths in the east, and dark eyes watched him enter hell, and later struggle out. *And keep struggling.* The story of Ban Lohannon was an ugly one. It was nothing I cared to revisit. But I had no choice. My heart was racing and the story was there in front of me, *real* again, as real as it was in those years in Brooklyn when I saw it in my head and lived it in my belly and woke up at night with the muscles in my shoulders and back twitching with fatigue and fear. As if Ban Lohannon had anything to do with me. As if I had any business sweating a story I'd made up myself…

So I shut my eyes. I fought off the mental pictures and concentrated instead on what I could hear and touch and smell. Eventually it worked. I felt my fists open. I grinned at the sights in spite of myself. I couldn't help it. This was a world I'd visited many times, if only in my dreams, and like a kid at a carnival I gorged myself on the scents of grilled beef and fried onions and fresh-baked bread. In a narrow swath of shade beneath the northern wall of the courtyard stood stalls where farmers and artisans sold tomatillos and salt, coarse blue glass and painted pottery, yellow peppers and statuettes of Kalya, Ythedra's guardian angel. A juggler tossed limes in front of an unenthusiastic notary. A toothless old man sat in the meager shade of a jerry-rigged tent, presiding over pyramids of acorn squash and sweet potatoes, occasionally spitting into a bowl he kept at his feet. Two little girls ran past us, chasing a goat.

"You!" said a voice behind me. "Wet nurse!"

I glanced down at my ragged gown. Turned.

The rider was tall and almond-eyed, with a neatly trimmed beard and a foot-long ponytail of raven-black hair. He sat his mount with an insolent ease, guiding the horse with one gloved hand. His attire, which included silver grieves and a burnished silver breast-plate, was spotless and fine. But the left side of the man's face was missing a pie-shaped section of flesh and bone, and his eye socket was empty. His mouth was pulled up in a permanent sneer, as if he was perpetually reacting to some insult he'd never quite learned to live with.

"Move aside," he said. "Before I slice that dress off your back."

He urged his horse forward before I could respond. Behind him marched a column of foot soldiers, grim-faced and tall, maybe fifty strong. They wore steel helmets and breastplates, gray capes and scarlet tunics. As they shouldered past me I could smell the leather of their scabbards and see the dust in their ragged beards. Many carried spears, and what looked like varnished brown gourds on straps around their waists. These gourds had hair, though, and lifeless dark eyes. Gowen told me later that these were the heads of Naztali warriors. The Border Guard shellacked the hollowed-out skulls and used them to hold their *khat*, the waxy leaf they chewed to increase their stamina and sweeten their dreams. Most of the Syrtian soldiers were busy scanning the walls. I'm not sure they even noticed me.

In the middle of the column rolled a sturdy wagon drawn by two blinkered draft horses, enormous beasts with vivid welts across their backs and flanks. The bed of the wagon was covered by a canvas tarpaulin lashed tight over the ribs of a skeletal structure beneath it. Whoever the poor creature confined in the wagon bed was, he rode in the midst of a terrible stench. Townspeople and prisoners alike gagged at the odor of decay and filth that drifted out of the dray.

The wagon driver maneuvered his vehicle to a halt beside the raised wooden platform where, as Gowen explained, the heads got knocked off. As the crowd murmured, the pony-tailed officer who had ordered me out of his way slid off his horse and led several of his soldiers up a set of steps onto the platform. Their heavy boots sounded like thunder on the rough pine planks. Somewhere a dog was barking. Children threaded their way through the forest of legs in the audience, giggling as they squirmed their way to the front. A door at the rear of the platform opened and two Darannan soldiers appeared. A slender old man in a royal blue tunic followed them. When cheers rippled through the crowd, the old man glanced up and smiled. Another pair of guards followed behind him.

"Duke Bryd Drennen," grunted Gowen, swallowing a mouthful of cheese. "I've seen him look better. Dude with the fucked-up face you just annoyed is Tarrant Lef, commander of the Syrtian Border Guard. He took an axe in the head fighting in Emerkest a few years ago. Everyone thought he died. Everyone *hoped* he'd died. It didn't improve his temper any. He's a nasty sonofabitch."

The Duke winced in the midday sun. He was thin and stooped and his lank white hair hung to his shoulders. He did indeed seem ill. As I'd never seen the man before, though, this didn't mean much to me. I studied the draft animals. I nudged Gowen and said, "What do those horses have stuck up their noses?"

"Shut up, Ramirez. Looks like the Duke has something to say."

"Sorry. I was just...I've seen blinkers before. You know. On those horses that pull the carriages through Central Park. Damn nuisance is what they are. Blocking traffic. But never—I don't know—those *nose* things."

Gowen was busy cramming a tortilla into his mouth.

"What are you talkin' about?" he said. "Which horses?"

"The ones with the wagon. See? Like plugs, or something."

Gowen stared harder. "Probably *are* plugs—against whatever that stink is. Never knew the Syrtians to—"

"Those are Syrtian soldiers, then?"

"That's right. In the gray and red. And I've never known the Syrtians to pamper an animal. Unless there's..."

Gowen's face fell. He looked as if he'd been hit with a board.

"Damn," he said.

"What?"

"Goddammit. *Goddammit.* Come on. Start moving back."

"Moving? Why?"

"Just *move*, Ramirez! While the guards are distracted. Keep your eyes to the front."

The dog that had been barking went quiet. Meanwhile, on the wooden platform, Bryd Drennen waved to his subjects. When their applause died down, the elderly duke turned with a sterner aspect to the Syrtian commander. He ran his eyes over the tarpaulin-covered wagon, surveyed the mounted soldiers who guarded it.

"Such a large platoon, Commander!" said the Duke. "You must have a dangerous prisoner. I hope you've got him tied, for the safety of your men."

There was scattered laughter in the audience, along with a few mocking whistles. The Duke extended one hand, granting his guest leave to speak.

Tarrant Lef offered a shallow bow to Bryd Drennen, then turned his back to the old man and spoke directly to the audience of townspeople and prisoners. There must have been six hundred of us gathered in the courtyard. A gaggle of teenagers watched from a nearby roof. Even several of the castle's guards looked on, lounging against the walls of the keep.

"Citizens of Kaer Rhennet!" said the Syrtian officer. "Many of you know me. My name is Tarrant Lef—Captain of the Syrtian Border Guard in this precinct. I bring you news. Word has come from the south of a great victory for our Lord Aln Adrackt. For the Empire of Emerkest, and all its many allies. The so-called Surb Confederacy, that league of traitors and thieves, is no more! We have hanged its leaders at the gates of their cities. We have built a tower of the skulls of their soldiers. As a result, His Most Gracious Majesty Aln Adrackt is now free to direct his attention to the grievances of his northern neighbors: you of Ythedra, the Emerald, who have doubted his intentions for so long, and worked to inflame the wild peoples with pride and anger against him. Toward that end, I take great pride in presenting to you this threat to the very ancient, and so very independent, principality of Daranna."

"Enough chatter, Captain," admonished the Duke. "I don't know that I care for your tone this morning. Do what you came to do."

"We intend to, sire."

"I beg your pardon?"

By way of answer, Tarrant Lef nodded to one of his men. This man barked at another. Together the soldiers drew swords, stepped up to the wagon, and hacked at the ropes that held the tarpaulin in place. One line snapped, and then a second, and another infantryman yanked the tarpaulin from the wooden struts that supported it. I heard gasps around me. A woman beside me dropped a crock of milk and the vessel shattered on the cobblestones of the courtyard. Bryd Drennen stared without changing expression. What stood in front of him had long been a fireside specter, a name to frighten children with. Now that specter had stepped out of the shadows, and the introduction was not encouraging. The urzek stood six feet tall. It had a spade-shaped reptilian skull that tapered to a fanged snout beneath a pair of tiny yellow eyes. Black scales covered the creature's thickly muscled torso and powerful legs.

The urzek sprang from the bed of the wagon, traversed the wooden platform in several quick steps, and sank its teeth in the old duke's neck. With a single savage jerk of its head, the thing ripped Bryd Drennen's windpipe out of his throat. Dark blood doused the urzek's head and chest. The Duke crashed to the platform, one leg thrashing in shock. Then the creature roared, and the earth began to move again. It moved faster than I'd ever seen it.

Tarrant Lef drew his sword and buried it in the back of the nearest of Bryd Drennen's bodyguards. A dozen of his soldiers clambered on to the platform and rushed the rest of the Duke's retinue. Another Syrtian put a horn to his lips and sounded a single shrill note, again and again.

"Cavalry!" cried a Darannan sentry from his post above us. "On the north road! We're under attack!"

A handful of men in the crowd threw off their cloaks to reveal crossbows. The closest to me sighted his weapon, fired, and drove a bolt into the throat of the sentry who'd shouted the alarm. It was a forty-yard shot. The whole thing seemed unreal.

"Search the cells!" shouted Tarrant Lef above the chaos. "He's bald-headed, and wearing a foreigner's clothing! Find him! The rest of you men, to the gates!"

The Syrtian draft horses bolted, hauling the wagon with them. The crowd around me was suddenly a mob, surging every direction at once. I tripped over a discarded bundle of kindling and found myself face down on the flagstones. A sandaled foot ground my forehead into the stone. Another dug into my back. It was Gowen who saved me. He hoisted me up by one arm and dragged me along beside him.

"Next time," he said, "I leave you behind!"

The din of battle erupted behind us: blaring horns and screaming women, the ring of steel on steel. We plunged through an alley at the crest of a wave of a hundred other townspeople, turned at the first side street and sprinted toward a long low building that I recognized, as we approached, as a stable.

A phalanx of Darannan infantrymen cut us off.

"You two!" yelled their leader, a burly man with whorls of dark hair covering most of his torso. He wore leather leggings, but had neglected to put on boots or a shirt. "Fall in. Someone's sounded the alarm. The Duke is betrayed!"

Betrayal was the least of the crimes committed against Bryd Drennen that day. But the soldier didn't seem interested in discussing the matter. He tossed two sword belts at our feet, then turned his attention to the crowd of panicked civilians headed our way. Fortunately, Gowen had developed a limp, and we soon fell to the rear of the detachment. It was only when the last infantryman passed us that Gowen regained full use of his legs. We turned and pelted back the direction we'd been heading before we were intercepted. We cut through the stables and a narrow sally port and found ourselves in the lush pastureland outside the southwest wall of Kaer Rhennet.

"Can you handle a blade?" said Gowen, unsheathing his sword.

"Handle a blade?" I echoed. It didn't matter. The big man hadn't stopped for an answer.

The countryside was calm. Milk cows grazed the tall grass, their tails swishing to keep off the flies. Scythes suspended in mid-swing, two elderly women watched us scramble across the daisy-speckled field, headed for the croplands beyond. *Headed wherever. I'd seen the urzek. I was just running.*

"Syrtian soldiers are attacking Kaer Rhennet!" Gowen called.

The women gaped.

"Syrtians!" I shouted. "Attacking the *city*! Run!"

And the women did run. Unfortunately, they ran in precisely the wrong direction—back toward the walls. Not that they were going to get in. Residents of Kaer Rhennet were now streaming out of the castle through the same narrow opening Gowen and I had used. To my right I spotted a line of Syrtian cavalry. Three hundred yards off when they charged, the lancers covered the ground in a hurry. They drove through the fleeing Darannan civilians like nails through rotten wood, sinking their long spears in the flesh of men, women, and children alike. I was terrified, but I couldn't help watching. Gowen must have felt the same way. We stood at the crest of a gentle ridge, silhouetted against the afternoon sky. *So this is what history looks like*, I thought. It was only a matter of moments before one of the red-caped cavalrymen glanced up, reined away from the carnage, and spurred his horse toward us.

We made it to the nearest cornrow before our pursuer could ride us down. But we weren't safe for long. The Syrtian lancer was closing in. The hooves of his horse pounded the soft earth between the rows as Gowen and I scrambled to find somewhere to hide. I could hear the war horse gaining on us. I could hear it getting closer every second. Just when it felt like I couldn't run any farther, I had a vision of the tip of that wicked lance the cavalryman carried. Almost involuntarily I whirled to keep from feeling it pierce the soft flesh of my lower back and there was the lancer, spear lowered, mouth wide in a scream of triumph. My feet felt like they were nailed to the earth. I realized I was watching my own death, but there was nothing I could do about it.

Just then a hooded figure stepped out of the corn directly into the horse's path. He held a small mirror in one hand and angled it toward the horse. The flash of light startled the animal so completely that it stopped short, pitching its rider forward. The Syrtian cavalryman fetched up at the feet of the stranger. The stranger sank to his knees, took the Syrtian's head in both his hands, and gave it a vicious twist. I heard the snap of the spinal cord from where I stood.

The man we'd met by the river that morning paused to consider the dying rider. He clutched the silver pendant dangling at his chest as he stepped over the body. His dark eyes flashed a challenge.

"The Duke?"

I nodded. Gowen gasped for breath behind me. He started to say something, but the stranger cut him off.

"Pray for him later. Now we run."

Beyond the fields lay the river, and a few hundred yards beyond the river stood the blue wall of the Big Thicket. We ran until we couldn't hear the screams anymore. We ran until I threw up, and only then, in the shadow of the great forest, did we pause to look back. Orange flames burst from the highest of the sandstone spires I'd walked below only an hour earlier. Fire climbed like bright ivy up the trellis of smoke that billowed from the castle.

Kaer Rhennet was called the Rock of the North. It was widely considered to be impregnable. Pride of an ancient people, it stood almost a thousand years. This is how it fell.

Tell anyone who cares.

From the Annals of Ythedra

*S*o eager was Prince Varun to claim the throne of Dar-Annon that he neglected to mourn the brother who had loved him so faithfully. He had his personal flag hoisted over the spires of the White Cities to signal his ascension. Ridwen's counselors were escorted out of their chambers and into the streets. His concubines, devoted protectors of the infirm and needy, were summarily dismissed.

Unfortunately for Varun, several commanders of the Palace Guard had begun to voice their suspicions that the prince's foreign physician had played a part in the murder of King Ridwen. A man named Callan Dysrahi was the boldest of these officers. He warned Varun that the Guard would support his rule only if Varun surrendered the physician for trial. Varun refused. In response, the Palace Guard seized control of Kaer Rhygat and prepared for battle. Messengers pounded north out of the White Cities, headed for Ythedra, where King An's youngest son, An-Nashayel, lived with his mother. The Guard invited Prince An-Nashayel to take the throne, and offered to fight to the last man for him. But at the age of fifteen, An-Nashayel was still a boy. What was a boy to make of the news he heard? And what, more importantly, was he supposed to do about it?

Kaer Rhygat's Palace Guard was made up of Dar-Annon's best men, handpicked veterans of countless Surb border battles and Kusull pacification campaigns. But Prince Varun and the shrewd physician had been busy in the months since they'd met. With promises of wealth and power, they'd recruited supporters among King Ridwen's nobles, and attracted a number of ambitious officers in the regular army. When fighting began, Varun filled the White Cities with soldiers. In these days it was difficult for a man to know who to side with. Was the Palace Guard being disloyal to a legitimate king? Or was Varun unworthy of the throne he was so eager to claim? Many men died without knowing the answer. The weeks of combat that followed paralyzed the capital. Smoke hung like a shroud over the city's spires. Corpses littered the streets, and by the time the first leaves fell from the poplars in the palace courtyard, the Guard and their allies had been reduced to only a few hundred men. But still they hoped Prince An-Nashayel would raise an army to ride on Emerkest, and still they occupied the central keep of Kaer Rhygat—which meant that the White Cities were far from secure.

By winter, Prince Varun had decimated Dar-Annon's armies in his quest for power. But those who still fought for him fought without passion. They found little glory in killing men of the Palace Guard whom they'd once dreamed of calling their messmates. Alarmed by his crumbling support, Varun sent word to the remnants of the Guard. He would let them pass from the Cities in peace, he said, if they left that very night. He insisted that they depart under cover of darkness, so he wouldn't have to look upon their traitorous faces. Battered and hungry, hobbled by half a dozen wounds, Callan Dysrahi looked around him at his exhausted companions. He thought about their frightened families. He gazed once more toward the north—toward Ythedra, where Prince An-Nashayel bided his time—and agreed to the terms.

And so Prince Varun entered Kaer Rhygat, and claimed at last the throne of Dar-Annon. But what satisfied Varun wasn't enough for the scheming physician. When he discovered his protégé had let the remnants of the Palace Guard pass from the White Cities, he grew furious. Some say it was only then that the physician revealed his true nature. As he raged at Varun, he was seen to take the shape of a gigantic black snake, and to fill the room with his coiled flesh. He was a wizard; a shape-shifter; or, worse, a demon. At any rate, that's what some people said. And now no one cared to contradict them.

The survivors of the Palace Guard wandered northwest with their wives and children, heading for Ythedra. They were visited on the third night of their journey by a hermit who promised to lead them safely across the moors.

Instead the anchorite entered the minds of everyone who saw him, casting an enchantment that robbed the refugees of their ability to speak. Then the hermit disappeared. Legend holds that the hermit was actually Varun's physician, cloaked in the seeming of another human form. At any rate, back in Kaer Rhygat, the physician emerged from his chamber. He ordered Varun's newest recruits, Kirikite mercenaries from the highlands east of Emerkest, to track down and slay the survivors of the Guard as they struggled toward Ythedra. The Kirikites were lightly armored horsemen famous for their savagery and speed. They nearly succeeded in wiping out the last defenders of Kaer Rhygat. In the end only a few small bands of men, women, and children escaped the Kirikite riders to make their way across the Straits of Sorrow to Ythedra. From there they wandered far to the north, into the rugged headlands of Fereganth—a country whose very name means "the northern nowhere." And there, for several years, the defenders of Kaer Rhygat disappeared from the chronicles of men.

8

Surrounded

After several hours of walking, even the stranger seemed satisfied we were safe. He didn't say it. He just peeled off his rucksack as he took a last look back along the route we'd traveled. Then he shed his hooded cloak, stretched his neck and shoulders and seated himself against the nearest tree trunk. I lay on my back on the carpet of leaves, so exhausted I had trouble focusing my eyes. My heart was racing. The sweat on my chest and spine was starting to cool. I thought: *So this is what delirium tremens feels like.* I'd been told a hundred times the D.T.s could be fatal. I'd vowed twice that many times to give up the poison. But alcohol was cheap, and easy to get, and I'd been drinking enthusiastically for over a decade. Evidently it was time for my nervous system to pay a few bills. The headache I'd managed to slip out from under that morning was slinking around again on the outskirts of my brain. It was talking crazy, spitting blood, scrounging around for pointy objects to jab into my cerebrum.

And finding them, evidently.

Lots of them.

The Thicket was getting dark. The sky turned from blue to violet as we rested. It was only when my heart started beating normally again that the realities of our situation began to sink in.

Except for the short swords we'd been given, Gowen and I were unarmed. The stranger carried only a wooden staff and whatever he had in his rucksack. We apparently had no food among the three of us, no shelter other than the canopies of the trees. My throat felt like half a mile of bad road. Worse, Gowen and the man who'd rescued us seemed set on resuming their private war. It started innocently enough. The stranger asked for details of the attack on Kaer Rhennet. Gowen told him everything we'd seen.

But Gowen had a few questions of his own. "I guess you think we owe you somethin'. But I see it different. I think you owe *us*—some answers at least. Who the hell are you? And how did you know the Duke was dead?"

"I owe you nothing," the stranger said. "And I don't have any answers. But if you insist on an introduction, my name is Dzerdjik. And I mean to escort Ramirez here to the seer Linnaeth, who lives beyond the Griffin's Teeth in the mountains of Inniskerr."

"Good luck with that, pal."

Our guide smiled unpleasantly. "Luck will have nothing to do with it."

"And the Duke?" said the big man. "How'd you know they killed him?"

"I didn't know. That's why I asked. But assassination is a Syrtian specialty. And Bryd Drennen was too confident in his walls."

Try as I might, I couldn't get a fix on the man. Dzerdjik looked more like a vagrant than a soldier. I saw now that he was older than I had imagined—in his early forties, maybe. He had dark eyes that he only rarely focused on anyone and close-cropped hair that was somewhere between brown and gray but not quite either one. What I'd thought at first was a headband was actually a line of rectangular blue runes tattooed across his forehead. Only his hands showed him to be a man who'd traveled far and hard. They were tanned a deep copper, and ridged with ropy veins.

But Gowen wasn't finished. "What about you, Ramirez? You've got some explaining to do as well. How does our pal here know your name? And why are the Syrtians looking for you? You heard that bastard barking in Kaer Rhennet. The one with the cratered face? Like I told you, that's Tarrant Lef, captain of the Syrtian Border Guard. Biggest butcher in Ythedra. He told his men to search for someone who was bald and wearing foreign clothes. That's you. Or it *was* you, before Dredyat stole your duds. I hate to think where Dredyat is right about now. I kind of liked the little weasel. Lef must have thought Bryd Drennen's prisoners would be stuck behind bars. He had no idea we'd be out on work detail, gathering rocks, or in the courtyard to watch the execution. If you hadn't spotted the plugs in the noses of those horses, we'd prob'ly both be dog meat by now."

"The nose plugs," I said. "What was that about?"

"Horses can't stand the smell of urzeks. Those patches were just torn cloth. Probably smeared with mint, or garlic. Didn't mean nothin' by itself. But after what Happy here said at the river about the Syrtians and urzeks bein' allies, the plugs spooked me. So it… you know." The big man looked away. "It's a good thing you mentioned it."

"You're welcome, if that's what you're trying to say. But that's about all the help I have to offer. I have no idea why Syrtian soldiers are looking for me. And you wouldn't believe me if I told you who I am."

"Try me."

"Ramirez," said Dzerdjik, tossing a small bundle at me. "I figured you might need some clothes. Put that tunic on. I've got boots as well. They'll help you blend in. We'll use that gown of yours to make a false scent trail."

Settling down on his haunches, the stranger gazed up through the branches of the surrounding trees. A few stars were visible in the evening sky. A lone bat rode some silent rollercoaster over our heads and was gone. I shimmied into the new clothes. Pulled on the boots.

"Was there violence where you come from?" Dzerdjik asked me.

"In New York? You could say that."

"More than usual?"

"There's always been more than usual, from what I can tell." Dzerdjik met the comment with a blank stare. It was true, though, and I tried to explain why. The city was suffering. It wasn't just the World Trade Center being destroyed by a bunch of wannabe martyrs who thought they'd be rewarded with a luxury suite in heaven complete with broadband access and unlimited virgins in return for vaporizing a few thousand overworked Westerners. Evil lived closer to home as well. Kids shot up school cafeterias. Fathers raped six-year-old daughters. Body parts—arms, eyes, mismatched feet—were found on municipal playgrounds. Short answer: the carousel of homicides continued. Big. Little. Organized. Random. We locked ourselves in our apartments at night. We closed the curtains and pulled down the shades. What else could we do? Palestinians were blowing up Israelis in discotheques. Israelis were bulldozing whole villages in response. Sunnis burned Shiites, Muslims killed Christians, and African nations fell apart like paper in the rain. It all seemed so pointless. So futile. Most of all, so familiar.

"Ythedra also suffers," Dzerdjik admitted. "Belief is lost, and all the old evils have returned to pollute the land. Urzeks. Draviden. Now even the spiders."

"Spiders?" said Gowen. He spat to one side.

"God between us and evil. The less said of them, the better. I lingered at Kaer Rhennet to find you, Ramirez. To tell you the way to Inniskerr, where you might be safe. But Ythedra grows more dangerous every day. Urzeks are already afoot in this country and I can't send you on alone."

"He ain't alone."

"Even worse," answered Dzerdjik, fixing his glance on Gowen. "You don't strike me as a man of faith, but I imagine even you've heard the legends. About the one who travels worlds? I thought so. You might stand to make a nice profit—"

"Listen, you pompous—"

"Let me finish," Dzerdjik snapped. "You might make yourself a tidy profit if you were to deliver Ramirez, here, to the right people.

So I'll have to take him to Inniskerr myself. Though I have work to do elsewhere."

"Yeah?" I asked. "What kind of work?"

"Alerting the Ganthans to the dangers they face."

Gowen grunted. "The Ganthans, huh? There aren't any Ganthans anymore. None worth the name, at least."

"So you say. You and all your degenerate Darannan race. You'd swear the sky was gone if you couldn't see it."

The big man's eyes darted upward.

"I ain't Darannan," he answered.

"Syrtian, then. Whatever you are."

"My mother was Ganthan—a refugee from that godforsaken country because I was born a runt and my father wanted me dead. She died in a slum in Tull, too poor to pay for her own casket. And if you want to discuss the matter further, you sanctimonious sono-fabitch, I suggest you stand up. Because I'm gonna carve my name on your forehead along with the rest of that mumbo jumbo you've got painted there."

"Your ancestry doesn't concern me," said Dzerdjik, "any more than that bread knife you call a sword. It's your voice that's starting to annoy me. Does it always carry like that?"

Gowen blushed.

"Fine," said the big man. "Run your errands. I'll take Ramirez to Inniskerr, if there is such a place. All I want from you is whatever rations you can spare and ten pieces of Free Cities silver for beer and bread afterward. It's not like I've got anything better to do."

Dzerdjik's voice was sharp. "That I believe. But you're going with me, like it or not, because I'm not going to leave you behind to give away our destination as some Syrtian spymaster digs your eyes out of their sockets. And you'll go without silver, you unshaven clod. And you'll go without beer."

I probably sounded ungrateful. "What about me? I mean, what if I don't *want* to go to Inniskerr, or whatever it's called? Rivendell. Oz."

"I assumed you would."

"Yeah? Why?"

"Because Inniskerr," said Dzerdjik, "is your only way home."

I would like to have contemplated the structural integrity of this statement—its spiky logic, and undeniable appeal, and the way it robbed me of a response. But I couldn't. I didn't have time.

Just then, a branch snapped in the shadows nearby.

———+———

Dzerdjik jerked his hand up to silence us, but it was too late. Torchlight flared in the darkness, gleamed on the steel of drawn swords.

"Strangers! Say if you are friend or foe of Bryd Drennen."

"We are neither," said Dzerdjik. His eyes were black slits. Though he was still squatting, I could see his staff move slightly as he drew it toward him. "Bryd Drennen is dead. He was murdered today, and Kaer Rhennet is cast down."

A bloodstained figure staggered into the clearing.

"LIARS!" bellowed the man. "Stand up and die fighting!"

Dzerdjik rose to his feet as the warrior stumbled toward us. The gaunt man waited till his attacker was only a yard away. Then he swung his staff, striking the attacker's sword arm so sharply that the blade pinwheeled into the air. Before the sword even reached the ground, Dzerdjik whirled and delivered a roundhouse kick to the warrior's stomach, lifting the man off his feet and dropping him as if he'd been shot. Several more figures materialized from the woods. Two rushed to aid the fallen fighter, who was wheezing as he struggled to catch his breath. Another strode toward us. He held a torch in one hand, a broadsword in the other. He was tall and clean-shaven and he wore his red hair loose over his shoulders. A dark gash creased the left side of his neck. His mouth was clenched tight, but his eyes darted over each of us in turn. He too was a warrior. More cautious than the first, perhaps. But clearly more dangerous.

"Who speaks this evil news?" he said.

"I do," said our companion. His voice remained flat. If he was nervous—if he felt, that is, anything like I did—he didn't show it. "I am Dzerdjik, a servant of the Seer of Inniskerr. The Syrtian captain Tarrant Lef betrayed Bryd Drennen. He gained entrance to Kaer Rhennet by pretending to bring in a Naztali prisoner for execution. Once inside, he had the Duke assassinated. Lef's men held the gates as Syrtian cavalry rode in from the hills. Bryd Drennen's son and his Marshal, Atryen Quin, were both absent, along with the Marshal's Outriders, the Duke's best men. From what I could see, the fighting went badly. The city was burning by the time we entered the Thicket."

"Syrtian *cavalry*? The men of Kaer Rhennet are more than a match for Syrtian cavalry."

"The Syrtians do not fight alone."

The man leveled his sword at Dzerdjik's throat. "The Syrtians have made an alliance? With whom?"

"Urzeks," said Dzerdjik.

The red-haired soldier was silent, as if he was trying to remember the meaning of the word. Finally he nodded.

"Then truly," he said, lowering the blade till its tip touched the earth, "we are damned. I am Atryen Quin, Marshal of Kaer Rhennet. The man you just disarmed is my lord Mikel Drennen, son of the Duke." Quin gestured at the dozen dim shapes around him. "And we are all that's left of the Outriders."

9

A Plan

I saw a blur low and to my right and then I was conscious of being airborne. But only for an instant. I hit the earth like a sack full of mud. When I looked up to figure out what had happened, I came face to face with what might have been another dwarf—another *Edward*—except for the creature's grainy hide and glittering green eyes.

"I say they're scouts," said the creature standing over me. He raised an iron hammer over his helmeted head. *Blue troll.* The thought flashed through my brain before I'd even had a chance to send for it. A granite hacker from the Broken Mountains far to the north. *Cave dweller. Enemy.* "I say they're Syrtian scouts and we split their skulls."

"Hold off," said Quin. "If it turns out they're friends of the Syrtians, you can chop 'em into little pieces. But we don't know anything yet, and we've got plenty of enemies already. Lieutenant Teryan, look after the Prince. Teg? That knee of yours okay? You and Alenth bring up the horses. Let me know how many are fit to ride. Then kill the torches. Here. Hand me one of those water bags. The rest of you men split up. I want half of you on perimeter watch, the other half to circulate what's left of the food. No one sleeps till I give the word. And no fires. We have to assume we're being tracked."

The Marshal watched his men scatter to carry out his instructions. Then he turned back toward us. He tossed Dzerdjik the leather bag. He watched as I pulled myself up off the ground.

"Ara," said Quin. "Izgir. Truke tu-Kekh. Follow me. Dzerdjik? Is that your name? You and your friends need to join us as well. I want to hear more."

The woman called Ara stopped in front of me. She was two inches taller than me, with fine-boned Asiatic features and shoulder-length black hair pulled back in a ponytail. She carried a bow on one shoulder, and wore a dagger at her waist.

"Well?" she said. "What are you staring at?"

"Me? No. Nothing," I said. "It's just, you—"

"I *what?*"

"You remind me of someone. That's all."

The woman looked at me like I was something she'd found on the bottom of her boot. Then she turned to join Marshal Quin.

Gowen grabbed a sleeve of my tunic and pulled me toward him.

"She's Sidharan," he said. "Possibly royalty. The dark one the Marshal called Izgir is a Naztali rider. And you already met the troll. *Truke tu-Kekh?* Is that his name?"

"That's not a name. It's a respiratory disorder."

"Goddammit, Ramirez. Was that what Quin said, or not?"

"Ouch. Yes. Something like that. Since when do we hang around with cave apes?"

Closer now. Gowen's breath warmed my ear. "Since the *cave apes* killed their royal family in the name of social equality and signed a truce with the Darannans six years ago. They make the best weapons in Ythedra. Supposedly a big supplier of the Duke, once the Syrtians started leaning on Kaer Rhennet. They buy as much wheat as the farms around Kaer Rhennet can produce, along with wool, beef, and any number of other things you can't find underground. They don't like to be called *cave apes*, by the way. Can't imagine why.

And they tend to distrust anyone they don't know. So if you want to get out of here alive, I suggest you keep your goddamn mouth shut."

We arranged ourselves in a circle beneath a giant sycamore tree. Gowen sat to my left. He was flanked by the copper-skinned Naztali rider, Izgir. Beside Izgir sat the Sidharan woman and, directly across from me, the commander of the Outriders, red-haired Atryen Quin. Completing the circle were the blue troll and Dzerdjik, who was either my captor or my liberator. I hadn't figured out which.

Quin spoke slowly. "As some of you know, we were returning from the Naztali encampment at Three Rivers this morning. We were just a few hours' ride from Kaer Rhennet when Syrtian scouts appeared at the crest of a ridge in front of us. They signaled us to advance. As I'm sure you can understand, Princess, I didn't want the Syrtians to see you and your men traveling with us. News of our alliance with Sidhara was supposed to stay secret for as long as possible." Ara nodded. The Marshal continued. "So I took a dozen men and rode to meet the scouts as the Prince and the rest of the column drew up and dismounted to rest the horses. That's when the Syrtians attacked. They came over the ridge like wasps from a nest. They rode with others—Kirikite irregulars, wild men from the east. There must have been a thousand of them. Tore us to pieces. I'd say we lost three hundred souls today—troll hammermen, Sidharan conquistadors, Naztali warriors, Darannan Outriders. The rest are unaccounted for, scattered to the west, maybe... All of these individuals I was duty-bound to lead and protect." The Marshal looked at each of us in turn, as if we were a jury. "Obviously, I failed."

Ara slid a leather glove off one of her hands. "You fought hard, Marshal. Despite their advantages, it was the Syrtians who fell back. That's the only reason we were able to get to the woods."

The troll nodded. "They outnumbered us three to one, and they knew how to fight. Hell, they even chose the ground. You did what you could."

Only one of the figures in the circle seemed unwilling to absolve the Marshal. It was the Naztali—the raven-haired plains rider. His bony face seemed immune to emotion. The silence was broken by the snap of the branch he held.

"I did what I could," said Quin. "But it wasn't enough. Only a few of us reached the cover of the Thicket. Once we got a chance to catch our breath, I sent messengers north to Naztal, to alert the tribes; to Nat-Alsedra, the troll city in the Broken Mountains; and to our fortress at Dred Thannat in the west to spread news of the attack. After that, my only thought was to use the outskirts of the Thicket to circle around the Syrtian forces toward Kaer Rhennet. It's been a black day. We've lost many of our friends. And now we hear the news this man—this...*Dzerdjik?* has given us. In the morning I'll send scouts to see if what he says about Kaer Rhennet is true. Still, we saw the smoke on the horizon for ourselves, and even then my heart went cold, for many I hold dear live in the city. The Prince was cut deep in our fight with the Syrtians. I've seen my share of stomach wounds. My guess on this one is that the worst is still to come. At any rate, he's in no condition to make plans. But the truth is, neither am I. I'm a soldier. I follow orders. Now I'm out of orders. And I have no idea what to do next."

The blue troll grunted. "That's easy. We fight. We fight till every bastard Syrtian wakes up in hell."

I nodded, thinking: *Trolls will fight anything.* Trolls like Truke tu-Kekh were called *blue* because of the cobalt tinge to their bellies and under-arms, but they were mostly a slate gray, with green eyes and thin black lips. Creators of vast, hive-like cities in the rock beneath the Broken Mountains, they were stubby, compact creatures, rarely over five feet tall, with coarse hides and bony, horned heads. Their upper bodies were thickly muscled (the blue troll, like a gorilla, could rip a man's arm off at the shoulder) and their legs disproportionately short, though also powerful. At close quarters they were fearsome opponents indeed. Notoriously nearsighted, trolls nevertheless had excellent night vision. They were almost impossible to knock off balance, and each could crush a mule's skull with a single swing of the iron hammer he carried. Coax them out of their tunnels and it was a different story. The mountain dwellers were baffled by bright light. They could be confused by rapid movement on open ground and were notoriously undisciplined fighters, easily baited and flanked.

Quin spat. "Truke tu-Kekh, you heard the man. The Syrtians have urzeks."

"So? Urzeks bleed."

Izgir nodded. Though the Naztali's face was lined by years of exposure to sun and wind, his dark eyes glittered. He was probably younger than I.

"They bleed," he announced. "Like the rest of us. Urzeks walk the eastern moors these days, though how they found their way there no one knows. You can kill the creatures with a spear through the throat. Or the eyes. You can kill 'em with a blade in the lower belly, if you're fast enough or foolish enough to get that close. Few men are. These things can snap a man's spine the way we break a branch for the fire. And if urzeks march with the Syrtians, there's no telling what else Aln Adrackt has on his side."

Silence.

"Spiders," Gowen said. "God between us and evil."

"Draviden," said Dzerdjik.

I knew what my companions meant. After all, if I really was in Ythedra, I was the one who had dreamt up these horrors in the first place—dreamt them, drawn them, wrestled them into print. As an eight-year-old I was more terrified of spiders than any kid alive, so it was easy to see where Ythedra's fictional counterparts had come from. But the draviden were worse. They were the so-called Sticky People, worm-skinned lovers of feeble light and stagnant water. In the legends of Ythedra, the draviden were descendants of an accursed race whose blasphemies broke the land in half. Now they lived among the nameless creatures at the bottom of men's night-mares. And waited for us to fall in.

"Do we have a choice?" said Ara. The Sidharan woman studied the faces around her. "I come from far away—far from the shadow of Aln Adrackt. But we in Sidhara have heard the stories of his cruelty. We know what lies ahead for a free people if Emerkest is allowed to expand unchecked. My father has already pledged ten thousand men to Ythedra. This morning, after the Syrtian ambush, I sent a dispatch with one of Quin's messengers. I asked for twice that number. If the messenger gets through, that dispatch will reach Sidhara within a week. My father will send soldiers. And Sidharan conquistadors are not afraid of urzeks."

"That's because Sidharan conquistadors," said Izgir, "have never *seen* urzeks."

I might have missed some of the conversation at this point. I was making a map of Ara's face, from her pale eyes down across her jutting cheekbones to her small, slightly flattened nose and full lips. Did I mention she was beautiful? She talked like a veteran, but she looked to be in her early twenties. In her voice I caught an echo of the precocious little girl she must have been only a few years earlier.

Dzerdjik broke the silence. "There remains the question of where the allied armies are to assemble now that Kaer Rhennet is taken."

Quin reared back. "What do you know about such things?"

"Only what the rest of Ythedra knows," Dzerdjik replied. "The citizens of Kaer Rhennet have big mouths. You, Marshal, rode north with Prince Mikel and the Outriders three weeks ago. You went to Three Rivers to coordinate the response of Ythedra's last free peoples in the event of a Syrtian attack. I also suspect that before you heard news of the fall of Kaer Rhennet, you were inwardly relieved that your column had been ambushed—since you knew violence against your party of emissaries would finally persuade your neighbors of Aln Adrackt's aggressive intentions. Now those intentions are clear."

"Stranger's right," said Truke tu-Kekh. His voice sounded like sand in a blender. This made it difficult to catch the nuances, but his statement seemed to hold both approval and warning. "The Syrtians killed six of my brothers this morning. Six troll hammermen— including one, our commander, who was democratically elected to represent us at Kaer Rhennet. I saw them go down, pierced with spear points, bleeding from a dozen blades. They fought till their last breath, and they killed at least twice their number. Autocracy is a dangerous and outdated practice. It's exactly what allows a clown like this Aln Adrackt to think he can walk over people like we're grass beneath his feet. But sometimes translating political theory into practical opposition is harder than it should be. Now that trolls have been butchered, my people will fight. In this time of distrust and false counsel among the races, maybe bloodshed is what it will take to unite us."

"If bloodshed is all it takes," Ara said, "we're united already. Today I saw men I've known since I could walk—my godfather among them—sacrifice themselves to save my life. *You* didn't kill them, Marshal. The Syrtians did, and I don't see how you could have expected that ambush. Anyway, it's over. It's time to stop talking and start making plans. What about assembling our forces in the Dunes?"

"Or the Near Downs," suggested Izgir.

Quin frowned. "Both of those locations are too far south. The horsemen of Naztal are so nimble they could camp on Aln Adrackt's doorstep and be out of range of his archers by dawn. But our friends the trolls, and the Sidharan legions, traveling with those giant beasts of theirs, are a little slower. If one of their armies were to arrive before the other, it could be cut off by a Syrtian foray from Kaer Rhennet. Assuming Kaer Rhennet really is…"

"Where, then?" asked Ara.

"I don't know," answered Quin. He said the words as if they were another defeat.

"There's only one person who does."

Even Izgir looked up.

"The Seer," said Dzerdjik. "Linnaeth. I was bringing this man—these *men*—to Inniskerr when you found us. Or we found you. And now I think maybe our meeting was more than mere coincidence."

All eyes shifted to Gowen and me.

"Why is that?" said Ara. "And why are you bringing these two to Inniskerr? For sacrifice? They're victims?"

"No more than the rest of us, Princess. The truth is, I know very little about the purpose of my mission, though I can tell you it has nothing to do with sacrificial murder. The task was given to me personally by Linnaeth. This one's name is Gowen. The other one is Ramirez. I chose to travel with them only because the passage to Inniskerr seemed too hazardous for them to risk alone. Now you can take them for me."

"Take them to *Inniskerr*?" said Quin. "What makes you think I'd go within a hundred miles of that godforsaken place?"

"You're already within a hundred miles of that godforsaken place. And where else do you have to go?"

"Back to my people," said Izgir. "That's where *I* have to go."

Dzerdjik shook his head. "The Naztali have been alerted. Better for the group of you to stay together and coordinate a response to the Syrtian attack. You're the only ones who can."

"Makes sense to me," said Quin. "But that means we head for Dred Thannat, on the coast."

"Ah. But the best route to the fortress of Dred Thannat is north-west, through the Thicket, where you'll be able to travel without being seen by the Syrtian cavalry. Inniskerr is practically on the way. And the Seer will have news and counsel, for she is a sworn enemy of Aln Adrackt. Perhaps his only enemy of consequence."

The circle was silent. Only Ara seemed dissatisfied.

"Who are these men?" she said, gesturing toward me and Gowen. "How do we know they're not spies? How do we know *you're* not a spy?"

Dzerdjik shrugged. "You don't. But I assure you, my companions escaped from Kaer Rhennet only today. One of them would be a very great prize to Tarrant Lef and the master he serves. He is important to Ythedra, though I can't tell you why."

"Why not?"

"Because I don't know."

Quin placed a large hand on Ara's shoulder. "I don't think they're spies," he said.

The princess leaned away from his touch. "Again. Why not?"

"The big one," the Marshal said, nodding at Gowen. "If he's supposed to be spying, he's piss poor at it. Coupla months ago he picked a fight with three of my officers in a tavern just outside the castle walls. I had to break a stool over his head to slow him down."

Gowen cleared his throat. "That was you?"

"You put up a hell of a fight, son. I was disappointed when I heard you passed up a chance to serve in the infantry."

"Nothing personal, Marshal. I, uh…I thought it was a table."

"Thought what was a table."

"That you hit me with."

"Maybe next time."

Ara was still suspicious.

"And where else do *you* have to go?" she said, resuming her interrogation of Dzerdjik. "South, maybe? To Emerkest?"

"I travel east. To find the Ganthans."

Quin snorted, staring at Dzerdjik's lidded eyes.

"Then may God guide your steps," said the Marshal, running his fingers along the contours of his jaw. "And let them fall softly. You travel to a dangerous land."

The disciple of Inniskerr spoke softly. "These are dangerous times. The shadows have begun to fall on Ythedra. The night that follows will be dark indeed."

"Then it's true?" said Ara.

It was the question they all wanted to ask. I could tell by the way it hung in the air.

"It's true," Dzerdjik answered. "The Emperor of Emerkest has revealed himself. He is indeed Aln Adrackt, risen from the depths of whatever hell he wandered all these many centuries. The Syrtians do his bidding here and in Emerkest, and have helped him bring death and disease to the rest of the Ninelands as well. Now he is bent on doing what he never could before. Crushing the Emerald. Destroying Ythedra."

"What makes you think he's headed this way?"

As always, Dzerdjik took his time.

"One by one, the prophecies are being fulfilled. The cities on the sea are now under his dominion. Ythedra is divided, and her children have turned from the paths of light. The hole in the world has opened again. Why do I think the Dark Lord is *coming*? That's not even the right question. Look around you. Bryd Drennen is dead. The Rock of the North has fallen, and the chosen emissaries of Ythedra's free peoples are on the run. Make no mistake, Marshal. Aln Adrackt is already here."

1 0

Reveille

*A*ll I wanted was a second chance, but Rachel Chen wouldn't listen. *She dodged into alleys. She darted through the homicidal traffic of Manhattan's broad avenues. I only wanted to talk. I just wanted to look into her eyes and tell her how sorry I was, how stupid I was, tell her I realized finally how right she'd always been—how perfectly, vitally right. You can't just walk away from a woman like Rachel like she comes along every day. Like you'll ever find her again. You can't walk away without losing the one thing no one can afford to lose. I'd lost her years ago. I'd lost her so long ago I'd forgotten how it hurt. Only now it was hurting all over again. Steam rose like ghosts from holes in the manhole covers. Faceless men stood in the shadows. Yellow cabs careened up Amsterdam, scattering the pigeons, and now I saw a figure half-hidden in the steam. Something dark, and moving toward me. Faster now. I carried a sword. I couldn't use a sword, but I carried it. My stomach flipped inside me and I tasted vomit in the back of my throat. I carried a sword. I was hit, I—*

"Ramirez," said a voice. "Wake the hell up."

Gowen's mop of blonde hair was matted with bits of dead leaves and bark. When I shut my eyes again, he stuck a hand in my collar and hoisted my head off the ground. Dzerdjik was gone, he told me. The stranger had departed for the east before sun-up, leaving instructions to guide us to Inniskerr. Marshal Quin and his men were stirring in the green light of dawn, quiet as ghosts, anxious to be on their way.

Atryen Quin appeared behind Gowen. The rangy warrior looked less impressive by daylight. He wore a cap of dried blood like a sarcastic yarmulke. His eyes were bloodshot, and he walked on his skinny legs as if they were stilts.

"What's with *him*?" the Marshal said, pointing at me with his chin. "I gave orders to strike camp. Why isn't he on his feet?"

Gowen burped. "From what I've seen, the man only has three muscles in his body, and two of them are attached to his mouth. So I'd say he's worn out. He didn't even roll out the blanket you gave him last night. He just slept in the leaves like a wounded animal."

Quin tossed us two bricks. They turned out to be biscuits.

"Eat," he ordered, as gentle as a jackhammer. "You'll need your strength. I've sent three of my men south to check out the story your friend Dzerdjik told us last night about Kaer Rhennet. They'll also be looking for fugitives—especially anyone who can ride and fight. We'll leave the horses hidden here and my scouts, with whatever survivors they manage to find, will come back to collect them later. Then they'll ride back along the outskirts of the woods to join the Darannan garrison at Dred Thannat."

"If time is important," I said, "wouldn't it be better to hang on to the horses?"

Quin frowned. "Not the way we're going."

"Which is?"

"Through the Thicket."

Gowen shook his head. "Don't tell me you're taking some drifter with *writing* on his forehead seriously. He doesn't know what he's talking about. And don't tell me this is all we get for breakfast, either."

"You got a problem with the grub," said Quin, squatting beside us, "you can try your luck at Kaer Rhennet. We're headed for Inniskerr. Your friend was right. It's the only plan that makes sense. Inniskerr is more or less on the way to Dred Thannat, and it could be this Seer—whoever he is—can help us. Dzerdjik says he can, any-way, and that's a better offer than any I've heard lately. There's prob-ably a dozen Syrtian patrols looking for us at this point. The trees at least give us cover, though I admit the Thicket ain't much suited for horses. Four hundred miles of forest, north to south. Maybe seventy to the west till we reach the mountains. But the Prince is worse this morning. That means he'll have to be carried. *That* means we'll be moving damned slow, and if we're spotted outside the woods, we'll have to stand and fight. Counting you two, we're twelve men and one woman. We wouldn't last long against the Syrtian Border Guard. Not with their Kirikite friends. And especially not if they've got urzeks."

"Won't they just follow us in?" said Gowen.

"Probably already have. But the Thicket is a tricky place. We'll be safer inside than out. The troll wouldn't do it, but the rest of us buried our armor. We're going to move fast. As fast as we can, anyway."

"On the other hand," I said, surprised to hear my own voice, not to mention the words it was starting to speak. "What about the Tauregs?"

The Marshal pooched his lips. "The Tauregs. Head hunters, right? Forest giants. Dzerdjik mentioned them too. I told him the same thing I'm going to tell you. Keep the bedtime stories to yourself."

"Can I talk about the way you got ambushed yesterday instead?"

For a moment I thought Quin was going to shove his forehead down my throat. I counted six distinct scars on his face.

"You got a hard mouth," he said. "For such soft hands."

"Nice work," Gowen whispered, when the Marshal was safely out of earshot. A blood vessel pulsed at his temple. The whistling sound he made in his nose was worse in the morning. "What with the Duke dead and his son laid up, Atryen Quin is probably the most important man in Ythedra. So why not insult him? Piss him off roy-ally. That what you're thinkin'?"

"Shut up," I explained.

I brushed the dirt off my elbows and neck. I hurt more than I'd ever hurt in my life. Every tendon in my body felt as if it had been torn into a dozen pieces, then reattached to my body with thumbtacks. I was exhausted and dehydrated and still in a state of barely-suspended disbelief. Did I mention the biscuit? It tasted like outdoor carpet. My head was pounding and my nerves were shot. I was a bag of sticks. I was a walking complaint. Like never before, I needed a drink.

The Thicket

We walked single file. In the middle of the column, four Outriders carried Prince Mikel on a stretcher fashioned from oak boughs, a soiled Darannan cape, and strips of horsehide cut from the prince's boots. The Prince had been drifting in and out of consciousness since being wounded in the fight with the Syrtians. Dzerdjik's roundhouse kick the night before hadn't helped matters any. Now the Duke's son was bleeding again. He was also fighting a fever. If it was septicemia, it was going to get worse before it got better—if it got better at all. And since the Prince was almost as big a man as Marshal Quin, carrying him took some effort. Every half-hour the procession had to stop so a new group could take up the load. Eventually even Gowen and I were pressed into service— though only sparingly, since the blisters on my hands and feet had already been noticed by the Outriders.

The seven Outriders traveling with us dressed in the brown and blue cavalryman's livery. There was Teggat, the sergeant, a wiry, capable man with crew-cut fair hair, thin lips and unflinching gray eyes; Rynnit, the unit's armorer, a balding, taciturn coporal with thickly muscled forearms and a fondness for the throwing axes carried by Darannan infantry in generations long past; another corporal, the gaunt Alenth, a shy man with bad skin and a broken front tooth who was said to care more for his horses than for his companions; the freckle-faced brothers, Mahyal and Rhayfe, youngest of the Outriders, much given to practical jokes and private conversation; old Gryel, the company cook, who had followed Quin for twenty-eight years; and Ayrd Teryan, an awkward but energetic young lieutenant with long blonde hair, a crooked nose, and a trusting, unlined face.

I did what I could. If nothing else, carrying the stretcher gave me an excuse to gaze ahead at Ara's neck and slender shoulders. She wore her black hair in a stubby ponytail. She had pale green eyes that seemed to glitter in soft light and a few random freckles on cheekbones that looked like they'd been chipped out of stone. Though she was slightly built, she carried a full pack, along with her elaborately carved bow and a linen bag full of green-shafted arrows, without apparent fatigue. She was clad in somebody's notion of guerilla chic: leather vest and wool pants, with fur-lined moccasins and a belt that held an ornate dagger. But she wore purple silk beneath the vest, and she darkened the rims of her eyes every morning with a tincture of antimony sulfide she kept in her pack.

The Sidharan princess never noticed my fascination. She marched near the head of the column, glancing intently from side to side, pausing occasionally to scrutinize the scrub oak and elm trees around us. It was the first time Ara turned to face the rest of us that showed me why she wore the mascara. Teryan, the young lieutenant, cried out as he stumbled. It was nothing major. He tripped over a root. Still, Ara turned when she heard the cry. Her concern for the kid was obvious. I knew what that look meant, even if it had been a while since I'd seen anything like it directed at me. It meant, roughly: *Don't die on me, you sonofabitch. I haven't even decided what we're gonna name our children.*

Especially after that point, it was a dreary hike. We seemed to be traveling gradually downhill. The Thicket was endless and dark and inhabited chiefly by bugs. It was scored by a network of shallow sloughs, most of which held several inches of stagnant water, and infested with hackberries, mustang vine, and a low-lying bush that looked suspiciously like poison ivy. Swarms of mosquitoes circled our heads, and the earth turned to mud beneath our feet.

And what about my mental state? you ask.

Or even if you don't.

There were times in the Thicket when I just about lost it. I was dizzy and bone tired and I wanted to scream at the trees till I tore out my lungs. I wanted to reach out and rip the skin off the sky to see the face of whatever Creator, Inventor, or chairman of the celestial board was plucking the strings of my senses like an electric guitar. But the bars of my prison were cold. The earth was damp. The sky was out of reach—and after that first day, in fact, out of sight. So there wasn't much I could do but walk. Breathe. Say to myself, *Right, okay, I'm as out of place as a crackhead at a quilting bee but at least I know I'm crazy, so in a sense I can't be completely lost.* I made up my mind just to plant one foot in front of the other. You remember that line from *The Last of the Mohicans?* The waterfall is pounding and Magwa is coming and the Long Carabine says to Madeline Stowe, "STAY ALIVE, no matter what occurs. I WILL FIND YOU!" Rachel Chen and I used to say that to each other. Stepping into a cab. Getting off the subway. It cracked us up every time. But that's what I was going to do. STAY ALIVE. And think. *Why was I here? And where, for that matter, was here?*

Ythedra, evidently. Emerald of the Ninelands.

64,353 square miles of rocky coast and rolling grassland, mountain and forest and mostly fertile earth.

Ythedra. My creation.

But if Gowen was right, I'd missed almost a thousand years of her history. It was like leaving a daughter at the age of three and meeting her again on the day of her wedding. Or, in this case, her *funeral*. Despite the fact that I was the one who'd dreamed up

Ythedra in the first place, my knowledge of the realm ceased with "The Spiders of Dred Siryat," the final installment of my very first comic book series. Maybe you remember "The Spiders." It's the one where Ythedra's armies finally crush Aln Adrackt's invaders. The one where Ban Lohannon and the pathetic prince Varun manage to shove that loathsome cockroach of a wizard king into a pit of his own arachnids. In the depths of that hole Aln Adrackt presumably dies a graceless and entirely appropriate death, torn to pieces by the same oversized spiders he'd used to terrorize others. Fred Astaire shows up to warble a happy tune. A chorus line of dancing ghouls high-kick their way into a Technicolor inferno. Music up. Curtain down. Cue angelic choir. But apparently things had soured since then. This happy ending came without a warranty. It was a Middle East truce. A Hollywood marriage. So had I been sent here to right miscellaneous wrongs? If so, who'd sent me? And what the hell were they thinking? Because let's face it: I'm the sort of man who can't drive a nail into plaster without splitting his thumb. A man who managed to get himself fired from a dream job at Empire Media Arts no one thought he could lose and to lose a woman he never bothered to take seriously and to develop an alcohol dependency with a misplaced patience and perseverance he never managed to bring to bear on any other aspect of his life. A man whose fourteen months on a psychiatrist's couch hadn't managed to alter a single aspect of the behavior the good doctor called severely depressive and borderline delusional. So the thought that I had been sent to Ythedra to *fix* things was oddly awful. I might have laughed, in fact—if I hadn't been swallowing my panic in manly, bite-sized portions. If I hadn't been wrapping my blistered hands in rags that reeked of horse sweat. And if I hadn't been trying to ignore the new emptiness in my belly and the same old emptiness everywhere else.

But there was no sense complaining.

Who would have listened?

Dzerdjik had left instructions that we were to head west till we struck a shallow, swift river. We were meant to ford the river, then make our way upstream along paths that paralleled the watercourse. There would be cairns marking the path to Inniskerr—which was, according to Dzerdjik, roughly forty miles north-northwest through broken terrain. It seemed simple. All we had to do was follow the sun as it slid across the sky. To make things easier, Ara pointed out that a rust-colored moss seemed to grow on only the northern sides of the oaks. *Fantastic*, I thought. We'll be there in no time. Maybe this Seer—this *Linnaeth* Dzerdjik had mentioned—could tell me how to get home. Maybe there was another magical washing machine waiting for me in Inniskerr and I'd finally get a few answers. Possibly even some compensation. I'm generally not shy in these matters.

Just *drunk*.

Gradually, though, the woods grew darker. The moss disappeared, and on the second day of our journey the weather took a turn for the worse. The wind grew chilly. Clouds the color of dishwater massed above the trees.

Izgir made a show of leading our group. The wiry Naztali was the only true tracker among us, he said, and no one argued the point. Quin let him do as he pleased. But soon even Izgir had trouble picking his way through the woods—though, in what I knew was a typical display of Naztali pride, he refused to admit it. Toward the end of that second day of marching, after an hour of argument, Quin sent Lieutenant Ayrd Teryan clambering to the top of the tallest oak. Like the lookout on a whaling ship, the young officer sang out when he spied the sunset. When he pointed, we realized we were headed the wrong way: almost due south. Inniskerr was my passport home. I wanted to get there before, say, Christmas. I was exhausted. I was hungry. I was a barely ambulatory sack of lactic acid and I probably should have kept my mouth shut.

But I couldn't.

"I thought the horsemen of Naztal could read the earth. You can't even read which direction your feet are pointing. You're leading us in circles."

The copper-skinned Naztali stared daggers. "Hold your tongue, white legs. Before I cut it out of your chest and eat it."

"The Naztali I remember could track wind through the snow. So maybe you *aren't* Naztali. Do you know the Song of the Sun? Or the Prophecy of the Seven Stars?"

Izgir cocked his head like a child scolded for a forgotten wrong. The anger drained from his eyes. "No one has known of such things for many years. They're campfire stories. Legends."

"Maybe they're legends now. But they're true just the same."

"That's enough," said Quin. "You two can work this out later."

Out of the corner of my eye, I saw a figure plunge into the woods.

Quin shouted, "Ara! STOP!"

The Sidharan princess ignored him. Teg and Truke tu-Kekh waded into the underbrush in pursuit but found it tougher going. The forest soon spat them back out. They returned a few minutes later, gasping for breath and for suitable curses.

"Girl's likely to end up as something's supper if she's not careful," said the troll, unwinding a skein of brambles from around one of his boots. "Not that she'll make much of a meal."

Quin barked orders. "Gryel, tend to the Prince. See if you can get him to drink. The rest of you men, fan out! Teg. Give me a perimeter."

There was no sign of Ara. We were surrounded by old-growth oaks, massive specimens with trunks the size of drainage culverts. Wind tossed the canopies of the trees, and the limbs above us creaked like the masts of a giant ship. An owl called. Another answered. Night crept into the woods like a fog.

"Lieutenant," said Quin. Ayrd Teryan sprang to attention. "Looks like low ground ahead. We'll camp here for the night. Have the men build a fire. We want her to be able to see us if she's trying to make her way back."

"So we're gonna wait?" asked Truke tu-Kekh.

"All night, if we have to."

"'Cause she's royalty, right? 'Cause her blood flows pure and her piss tastes like lemonade?" The troll stood with his arms folded across his chest. I had the feeling he'd made this complaint before.

Quin sighed. "Not because she's *royalty*. She's an emissary from an allied nation, and the only Sidharan I've managed to keep alive. That means we wait."

"Not too high on that fire, though," I suggested. "Just use the deadfall. As I recall, the Tauregs weren't too fond of folks torching their trees."

I made that universal pantomime of violent death, the forefinger drawn across the throat. Quin stared at me for several seconds. If he'd had a little more energy, he might have rolled his eyes. Or broken my front teeth. But maybe he was listening.

We used only dead branches for the fire.

Ara stumbled back into camp an hour later. In the orange light from the fire I could see she was soaked with sweat. There were scratches on her face and forearms.

"I saw it again," the Sidharan princess said. "A figure in the trees, just…*watching* us. When we stopped, it came closer. As if it was curious. And I went—I tried to surprise it. But it was gone."

"*What* was gone?" said Quin, peering into the darkness beyond the firelight. "And what made you think you could break ranks and charge off on your own?"

"I'm not one of your soldiers, Marshal. I'll do as I choose."

Quin turned to face the Sidharan. "Not if it endangers my men, you won't."

"That's the trouble with aristocrats," said Truke tu-Kekh. "No sense of responsibility. We did away with that disease six years ago."

"I'll handle this, Truke."

"Did away with what disease?"

"Royalty, Princess. Hereditary privilege. Turns out there's an antidote. It's called *democracy*."

"STOP, for God's sake!" Quin turned back to Ara. "What exactly did you see?"

The Princess cocked her head. "I don't know. I didn't get close enough. It was big, though."

"Maybe it was—"

The Marshal glanced up. "Shut up, Ramirez. We've got enough trouble without your fairy tales."

"The Tauregs," I said, "have lived in Ythedra a lot longer than the Darannans. A company of Taureg warriors fought at the Battle of the Standing Stones. You remember the Battle of the Standing Stones, right? When An-Nashayel and the Ganthans pushed Aln Adrackt's hordes into the sea? When the waves broke red on the rocks?"

"*When the waves broke red on the rocks.* You're a poet," said Izgir, through a mouthful of jerky. He said it like he'd found a scorpion in his boot. "I've heard of your kind. The Song of the Sun. The Years of Iron. You're a *poet*."

"No wonder you wouldn't talk about yourself," said Gowen, glancing up at me from where he sat cross-legged on the forest floor.

"I'm a little too fond of actually *eating* to be a poet. I'm a—I'm a *boss*. Sort of. Or I was, before I managed to make some bigger bosses distinctly uncomfortable with my continued existence."

"You lost me again," said Quin. "But who else takes these stories seriously?"

I suppose I was getting excited. Maybe it was the fact that someone was actually listening to me for a change. "That's just it. I know you think I'm nuts. And I admit I can't seem to stop remembering this stuff, which is kind of disturbing. But they're not just stories. As far as you're concerned, they're *history*. I mean, why do you think no one ever goes into the Big Thicket in the first place? The Thicket is almost within shouting distance of Kaer Rhennet. It might as well be on the other side of the planet for all you know about it. What's wrong with you people? Have you forgotten everything?"

"History," said Quin.

Izgir stared at my eyes. "The Song of the Sun," the Naztali repeated.

Only Ara refused to look at me. She was shaking out her bedroll when an arrow slammed into the trunk of the beech tree beside her. The blue shaft embedded itself four inches deep in the wood and quivered there like a living thing. Though the bolt had missed her head by a comfortable margin, the message was clear enough. The princess lunged for her sword, but for what? The Tauregs were only a legend. A myth. *Might as well take a swing at a shadow*, I told her. Then I watched as Ara—lips tight, green eyes compressed to slits— leveled the blade at my heart. As if she had to do *that*.

From the Annals of Ythedra

*I*n *Ythedra, young An-Nashayel had heard enough. Stout and gray-eyed, proud of the wispy beard he'd grown, An-Nashayel ached to return in strength to Emerkest to avenge his half-brother Ridwen's death and claim his father's throne. He told anyone who would listen how he would throw the usurper out of the White Cities and take Dar-Annon as his own. Unfortunately An-Nashayel found himself in command of an army that was barely worth its name. It consisted chiefly of the scattered Darannan garrisons in Ythedra, who had their hands full with marauding black trolls in the west; a few hundred conscripts from the Darannan and Syrtian townships in the south; and a horde of undisciplined Naztali riders, whose ranks swelled or diminished depending on which of its constituent tribes were feuding with each other on a given day.*

The boy's counselors begged him not to invade Emerkest. They urged the young prince to stay home instead. Strengthen his defenses. Let the battle come to him. Rash as he was, An-Nashayel nevertheless recognized the wisdom in their words. He summoned the men of the Darannan garrisons, who abandoned their outposts, including the castle called Glen Kiernan, to ruin where they stood. Fearing an attack from Emerkest at any moment, An-Nashayel's followers set about constructing granite walls around the farming village of Kaer Rhennet, which stood on a bluff overlooking the Talking River. They built well. These walls stood for almost a thousand years before an enemy set foot inside them, and even then the breach was made not through force of arms but by means of treachery and subterfuge.

By this time the inhabitants of Kaer Rhygat called Varun the Autumn King. It was a comment on both his precarious position in the capital and the reports of those privy to the court that the usurper continued to age at an unnatural rate. And though the Autumn King contemplated an invasion of Ythedra, he couldn't get it organized. The White Cities lay paralyzed by civil skirmishes again as Varun's remaining armies clashed with their own supposed allies, Kirikite and Tazgat mercenaries the physician had recruited to reinforce royal authority. Outlying tribes heard of the unrest and began tearing the kingdom apart at the edges. Eventually that portion of the Darannan army that hadn't yet died or deserted was divided into several units and placed under the command of foreign officers. Homegrown soldiers were sent to the borders. The mercenaries were kept in the capital.

Whether Varun approved this measure is unclear. He may never have known of it. The physician who once claimed to have saved the prince had by now rendered Varun a mindless insect, and ruled through this husk with ever less pretense. Not long afterward, the azure banners of Dar-Annon were lowered from the spires of the Red Cities. They were replaced with the pennants of the Standing Snake, black flags emblazoned with the scarlet serpent that was Aln Adrackt's personal emblem.

Ah.

You noticed.

I said 'Red' Cities, not White. In the days of Dar-Annon's glory the sandstone spires of Kaer Rhygat were a majestic ivory, the white of summer clouds. By the time Varun was deposed, though, the fields of Emerkest were overgrazed, and the king's orchards had been destroyed for fuel. Tens of thousands of acres outside the city walls lay barren, and red dust climbed into the winds off the eastern desert men call the Kiln. This dust coated the Cities. Each rain pounded it into the porous stone, until eventually the spires of Kaer Rhygat turned a peculiar ochre-red. Thus, the Red Cities—a name that was to become freighted with nightmare.

Man's Best Friend

Next day the ground got better. The stands of burr oak and black cypress thinned as we climbed out of the lowlands, and we could see the sky again. Only the Prince seemed oblivious to the change. But then he was oblivious to just about everything. Mikel Drennan was a fleshy, fair-skinned man with a barrel chest, a thick neck, and features slightly too small for his face—the kind of man you could imagine had spent his life doing things in a hurry, if not always very well. Now his lips were cracked and he smelled of sweat and piss and the fluids that leaked through the cloth dressing around his abdomen. His men did what they could. The Prince wouldn't eat, but they helped him gulp water mixed with the crushed leaves of a weed that was supposed to help with the pain. Mikel muttered and cursed as we marched. He sang and cried out for his father, the old duke I'd seen murdered at Kaer Rhennet. More than once he asked when he'd be home.

Soon, Quin told him, placing one of his large hands on the prince's forehead. *We'll be home soon.*

The rest of us lumbered along without speaking, stumbling over roots and stray vines as we tried to see more than a few dozen yards into the woods. The arrow launched at Ara had spooked us. It was a good three feet long, fledged with what looked to be turkey feathers, and so deeply lodged in the tree that even Truke tu-Kekh couldn't pry it out. Eventually he just snapped the shaft. We all suspected we were being watched, but whatever was shadowing us stayed far enough away that it couldn't be seen.

Stayed away, that is, until mid-afternoon. As the grizzled sergeant, Teggat, passed out water and rations, a figure emerged from the trees ahead of us.

"No further," it commanded.

Several more figures stepped forward from the woods to our right, holding bows at the ready. They were all over seven feet tall, with skin like stained wood. They wore deer hides stitched in tiny patchwork squares, and their tangled whorls of fair hair looked like birds' nests on their heads. The figures spoke in a coarse, pinched dialect, as if they weren't accustomed to utterance. They were Taureg warriors. The yew bow each of them carried could drive an arrow straight through a man.

"You are entering burial grounds," the figure continued. "This is...not permitted."

"We didn't know," said Ara. She was the only one of us who could speak. "We're trying to make our way west, to the Injured River. To Inniskerr."

"Try again," said the Taureg. "To cross this ground means death."

Ours, I was guessing.

The troll stepped forward. "Says who?"

"Truke tu-Kekh," said Quin. He spoke loudly to reclaim leadership of the group. "These are Tauregs, I think. They live here."

"We have *always* lived here. You dispute this right?"

"No dispute." Quin looked over at the troll, who seemed to be about to say something else. "And we're not here by choice."

The figure nodded. "You are being followed."

"By who?" said Quin. "Or what?"

"By the gray men and their dogs."

"Syrtian *trackers*," spat Izgir, gripping the knife he wore at his hip. "How far back?"

The Taureg paused. "Half a day. Maybe closer. Your trail is fat."

Ara said, "How can we get around your burial ground?"

"Walk north."

"Can you help us? We're almost out of food. And water. And one of us is injured."

The Taureg didn't even think about it. "No," he answered.

"Thank you," I replied.

I could have sworn I saw one of the Tauregs' eyes flicker toward me, as if I had made myself a subject fit for inspection. Then, just as quickly, the interest vanished. The face was empty again—like the rest of the faces watching ours. Empty. *About like our future.* Without another word, the Tauregs turned and strode back into the forest.

"Right," said Quin, surveying the trees around us. He rubbed his silver-flecked beard, bit his lower lip. "You heard what I heard. Unless someone has a better idea, I say we do as we're told. We'll head north. Izgir, keep your eyes open for high ground where we can dig in."

"Speaking of eyes," said Gowen. "Did anyone else notice those bastards winking at us?"

"I saw it too," said the troll. "Damn peculiar."

"It wasn't winking," I said. "The Taureg blink one eye at a time. Helps when they're hunting."

Quin snorted. "Fascinating. We're gonna have all kinda stories to tell if we ever get out of here. But that ain't gonna happen unless we get moving. The Syrtians may be on us tonight."

"If they have dogs," Izgir said, "they *will* be on us. They're not carrying a corpse."

The Marshal's face went red. "The Prince is not a corpse. Are you going to lead us or not?"

The Naztali shouldered past two of the Outriders and started walking north.

Gowen spat on his hands and rubbed them together before he bent to lift the Prince's litter. I tried the same thing.

"They can't keep tracking in the dark," I said. "Can they?"

Teggat tossed his pack to one of the young brothers. He grabbed a handle. "They don't have to *see* anything, son. It's a scent trail. They follow the dogs."

———+———

An hour later we heard the howls, dismal long streamers of sound hung from the ceiling of the sky. In another fifteen minutes the baying was closer and we broke into a trot—or as close to a trot as we could manage, carrying Prince Mikel. There wasn't much high ground in evidence, but dusk was edging in around us and Quin was right, it seemed important to find some place to defend. Half a mile further on, we struggled up out of another muddy ditch, then crossed maybe twenty yards of open ground before we entered a copse of cedar elms. Here lightning had brought down one of the oldest trees. This one had dragged a young beech down with it, and together they created a crude V that pointed back the way we'd come. At the Marshal's command, we settled the Prince and wriggled out from under our packs. We broke the moist soil of the forest floor with two short shovels the Outriders carried, and heaped the loam against the fallen trunks to construct a crude breastwork. We gathered all the deadfall we could find to build a lesser wall behind us.

Ara borrowed Prince Mikel's broadsword and hacked at a young tree.

"I wouldn't do that," I warned her.

"Do *what?*" she said, wiping the sweat from her forehead.

"Kill the tree. The Tauregs don't appreciate that sort of thing."

"Mind your own business, Ramirez."

The voice seemed to come out of nowhere. "He's right, though. We don't. At least here, so close to sacred ground."

The speaker stood just a few yards away. He was small for a Taureg, not much over seven feet, with the sparse reddish beard that marked him as a young adult. As he sized me up, I realized this was the member of the band who had almost grinned at my earlier sarcasm.

"We're trying to defend ourselves," Ara said. "Since you all won't help us."

The Taureg's large head bobbed as he approached. He spoke softly, and just a beat slower than I expected. It was almost as if he was his own echo. I looked at him with what I know must have been ill-disguised fascination.

"I didn't mean to startle you. I'm walking loud. You know. Thought you would hear me. But you'll only make things worse by cutting down these trees. Then you'll have two enemies to fight. Instead of one."

"But your burial ground was...*back there*," Ara protested.

"True," said the Taureg. "But you're near another one now."

The Outriders dropped what they were doing and gathered around, staring intently at the Taureg.

"I don't know who you are," said Quin. "But you're in danger here. You hear the dogs?"

The Taureg blinked one blue eye, then the other.

"I can fight."

The Marshal opened his hands. "I'm sure you can. Why would you want to?"

The young giant was silent, so Quin continued.

"The men chasing us are Syrtians. They control the Free Cities and just about all of southern Ythedra. They're foot soldiers. Vassals of Aln Adrackt, the Emperor of Emerkest. They mean to kill us."

The Taureg considered each of us in turn, as if he was looking for clues. His hay stack of red hair was ornamented with blue and green beads and strips of yellow cloth. "Why?"

"Same reason they kill everyone else," said Quin. "They enjoy it."

Gowen cocked his head. "Moving fast," he concluded, as if he was watching a distant footrace.

"They have four legs," said the Marshal. I watched him size up our defenses. "The Taureg can stay if he wants. The dogs are going to be on us in a matter of minutes. I suggest we worry less about his neck and more about our own. Everyone gets water. Teg, hand out what's left of the biscuits. Lieutenant, I want the Prince *there*, beside that tree. Is he asleep again? Probably better off that way. Put two men beside him, then pick another three to secure the rear. The rest of you, get busy. The more brush we can pile up, the better off we'll be."

———+———

The Taureg finally introduced himself as Usak. He didn't bother to help. He just watched as we scavenged the ground around us, clearing firing lines and collecting fallen tree limbs for our defenses. Eventually the baying of the dogs increased to where it no longer seemed safe to leave the makeshift fort, and the Marshal positioned us behind the piled-up trees. He and one of his corporals, Rynnit, occupied the point of the V made by our barricade. Ara and I stood to his right, Gowen and the troll to his left. Izgir placed himself on the left flank. Ayrd Teryan was assigned to the right. Teggat, Alenth, and old Gryel completed the perimeter, while the young brothers, Mahyal and Rhayfe, were assigned to guard the Prince. Weapons in hand, we stood watching the speechless woods.

By this point, even Usak seemed to have decided something significant was about to happen. He squatted on his haunches just a few feet behind where Ayrd Teryan stood, humming to himself as if he was trying to work out a complicated equation.

I should have been scared. I know that now. Hell. I should have been terrified. What I felt instead was elation, a sort of misguided self-confidence unrelated to anything except my own stupidity. I was nervous, but I liked the sensation. And I enjoyed it even more because I had come to suspect nothing could truly hurt me. Forget the fall of Kaer Rhennet. Forget the urzeks, the Tauregs, the Syrtian Border Guard. I had decided my presence in Ythedra was an illusion—a long and exceptionally vivid nightmare. It's no secret that mood swings and delusional behavior are symptoms of chronic alcohol dependency. Withdrawal is worse. So maybe I was under the residual influence of some really bad chemicals. Or maybe I figured the dream can't kill the dreamer. If I fell thirty stories and hit the pavement, I'd bounce back up. Whatever the reason, I felt indestructible. And less out of curiosity than a desire to prolong my *frisson*, as if it was a fudgesicle on an August afternoon, I turned to Quin.

"What happened to change the Syrtians, Marshal? They weren't always fighters. And they certainly weren't allies of Aln Adrackt."

Quin wiped his long sword with a piece of frayed cloth. He paused for so long that I wondered if he was ignoring me. When he spoke, he stared at the fallen tree trunk in front of him. His flat rasp held everyone's attention.

"For many years, the men of Syrtus were traders and merchants. Not an illustrious people, by any means, but they bore no ill reputation, and no one questioned their fortitude. From their ports in southwest Emerkest they traveled to distant lands to find their incense and amethyst, their emeralds and pearls. But some say they grew too fond of their profits. That eventually they traveled north, and inland, to the ruins of Kaer Rhygat—God between us and evil. You've all heard the stories about that place. In ancient days the sorcerer Aln Adrackt and his puppet, the Autumn King, ruled the Empire of Dar-Anon from the Red Cities. Aln Adrackt's armies were eventually defeated, and Aln Adrackt himself was killed. For six hunred years, the Red Cities lay empty. Until the Syrtians came. In Kaer Rhygat the Syrtians talked to wights—whispering pale men with sightless eyes and hands that felt like ice. The wights made them rich. They guided the Syrtians to treasures no man had seen for centuries: ruby-studded crowns and diamond scepters; silver statues of forgotten kings and golden images of three-headed gods. All the wights asked for in exchange was that the men of Syrtus return, and stay awhile in the ruins, and wander with them in those quiet corridors. So it was that the Syrtians communed with the dead, and with the princes of the dead. They listened, and grew cunning. They learned to *take* what they wanted. They learned to kill. And when the demon who assumed the ancient name of Aln Adrackt crawled forth from wherever in that desolate land he was spawned, the Syrtians were there to hear him. To obey. And to call upon Kaer Rhygat's ancient allies."

"The Kirikites," said Izgir.

"Kirikites. And others. Or so the story goes. Most people in Ythedra don't believe Aln Adrackt ever existed—much less that he walks the world today. I've always been one of them. But now, with the evil loose in the land…"

He didn't have to complete the sentence.

"He's real," I said. "I've seen him."

What was I saying? *Seen* him? Imagined him maybe. And yet it was true. In a shadowed corner of my head or heart I knew I had seen the sorcerer. Not as a story. Not as a legend or a nightmare but as something else. Something closer. More intimate.

I could feel the group's eyes on me.

"Well?" said Gowen. He'd cut himself a four-foot length of oak limb and was whittling the bark to make a handle. I could hear his nasal wheeze from ten feet away. "I don't know if you noticed, Ramirez, but we ain't exactly goin' nowhere."

"Tell," Ara seconded, imperious as ever. Maybe she realized how she sounded. She shrugged. "Maybe it'll distract us from the howling of those damned animals. I can't even tell where it's coming from anymore."

It took me a minute to figure out where to start.

I said: "I'm sure you've heard the name Ban Lohannon." I glanced around at the group. No response. "There was a time when everyone had. He was the adventurer from An-Nashayel's court here in Ythedra who journeyed to Kaer Rhygat at the end of the

Years of Iron, many centuries ago. He wrote a series of long and progressively less comprehensible poems about the trip. It was Lohannon who said the sorcerer was born a scholar's son in the city of Quaiant, far to the east of Emerkest. Aln Adrackt was a slender, exceedingly beautiful child who grew up to be a respected physician. Because of his skills and social position, he was able to cultivate appetites that lesser men couldn't have concealed. Despite his advantages, though, these appetites—a fondness for the skin of children, a taste for the blood of adults—were eventually discovered by citizens of the community. Not by important citizens, who heard the rumors, and shook their heads, and locked their heavy doors against the night. But by the city's poor, whose children were the ones he victimized. Formalities meant nothing to such people. They met one night beside the grave of the young physician's latest victim and decided to take justice into their own hands. When the townspeople came for him, though, Aln Adrackt had disappeared. The frustrated mob destroyed his house instead. By the light of dawn they found evidence in the ashes of horrific practices indeed: human sacrifice, and ritual mutilation, and traffic with dark powers who ruled in lands unknown to the living.

"But by then Aln Adrackt was miles away, wandering in the mountains of Melkennek where even brave men refused to travel. Some say the demons he served had warned him of the mob that was coming to kill him in Quaiant. There were rumors that Aln Adrackt went to repay these powers by offering himself to them as an apprentice. What is known for sure is that Aln Adrackt soon attracted followers to his home in the barren lands west of the city—disciples who worshiped him and lived to carry out his will. As you might expect, this will was warped. It was set on acquisition of more men to sacrifice to the dark ones he served, more children to debase, more gold to buy more men. Over the years, his powers grew. Through occult study he became a necromancer, granted influence by his dark masters over the living and the dead, able to touch the minds of men and bind them to his. A rash of settlements sprang up in the mountains of Melkennek, consecrated to the cult of Aln Adrackt. Neighboring princes sent legates. Tributes were paid. Melkennekite priests traveled far and wide, attracting still more recruits for the bizarre rites practiced in that black kingdom.

"Aln Adrackt's reign in Melkennek was ended by a wizard from the island of Induikh, in the seas far to the north. Nihreth Wyn was a solitary, gray-eyed man who rarely spoke. But he was also a consort of the storm goddess Kalya, a fierce and unpredictable deity who lived in the highest peaks of Induikh. Nihreth Wyn was captured— or *allowed* himself to be captured—by a band of Melkennekite soldiers as he made his way through Emerkest. Eventually he was taken before Aln Adrackt himself, who thought nothing of tearing the medallion from the prisoner's neck. This was a mistake. Nihreth Wyn was not given to finery. He had no great wealth. But he too walked under the protection of immortals, and he too had learned to speak the secret names of stones and stars, wind and water. Nihreth Wyn's medallion burned Aln Adrackt like an acid, leaving his right hand a ruined stump. That's how the battle started. The two wizards fought for days. They spoke enchantments. They wove spells of fire and frost as they grappled in a dozen different shapes through the halls of Aln Adrackt's central temple. It is written that in the end they contended as cyclones. The great temple shook and fell around them, and they both died beneath the piles of shattered stone—though neither was ever found. After the temple collapsed, a ferocious wind blew through that unhappy land. Some say it was the storm goddess herself, come to look for her fallen favorite. Lightning shattered the dark altars the sorcerer had raised up in defiance of natural law and the revelations of all that is holy. Then everything went quiet. It was as if a curse had been lifted from the hills themselves, like a veil from the face of the dead.

"The Melkennekites were helpless without their leader. Their slaves rose up against them, and the dance of their liberation was violent and merciless. Fortune hunters from the nearest cities rode hard and empty-eyed into that land of crypts and temples and butchered worshippers and servants alike as if they were rabid dogs, unclean to the touch. And many of the black-tongued priests were captured alive but they were least fortunate of all because they were the object of tortures devious and cruel, among them a procedure whereby molten lead was poured down the throats of men and women alike in order to purify with some awful torment the polluted waters of their very souls. In their last moments of consciousness they called out to their sorcerer lord to save them, as he always promised them he would, from the hands of the ignorant and uninitiated. But their lord never came, and the words of his abandoned acolytes were bitter, and their deaths without grace. And so Aln Adrackt passed from the sight of men. But not for long. At least, not for long enough."

My companions weren't silent for long.

"Horse shit," growled Truke tu-Kekh. "It's like the Council says: Superstition is the mask of autocracy. What does this jumped-up conman *look* like?"

"Now, you mean? It's hard to say. Aln Adrackt learned long ago to alter his appearance. He could appear as any one of us if he wanted. As an animal. As a cloud. Or in his true shape, which was no longer very attractive even in the days when Ban Lohannon saw it."

"His true shape?" said the Taureg.

Now it was my turn to hesitate. My mind was filled with a jumble of images. Faces. Figures. Stairways and doors. But somehow the images weren't imagined. They were *real*, like memories, and my skin went cold as they flashed in front of me. When I came to my senses, the blue troll was standing beside me, tugging at my left ear with his outstretched hand. Strike that. *Claw.* It grated like sandpaper.

"Ramirez?" said Truke tu-Kekh. "You heard the kid. What's this mud sucker's true shape?"

"Enough," said Quin. "No more stories." The howls of the Syrtian dogs echoed off the hardwood trunks, rolled over us like waves.

"Getting closer," said Teryan.

"Good. We need them to come before we lose the light. Izgir? Any advice?"

The Naztali spoke without turning his head. "The Marshal wants *my* advice? Fine. The Syrtians use two types of dogs. The trackers are vicious but slight. The mastiffs, the fighters, are larger. More dangerous. Keep them in front of you. And—"

"Over here!" shouted Gowen.

"And go for the kill," said Izgir. "Because *they* will."

Branches snapped a hundred yards off. Now closer. At fifty yards we could hear the barks and snaps of individual dogs. Their high-pitched whines—whines of appetite, frantic and unnerving—were all around us. I glanced sideways and saw Ara mumbling to herself. *A prayer? An admonition?* I was wondering if I knew any prayers when the pack crashed out of the trees in front of us, moving at a dead run. The trackers were slender fawn-colored animals that resembled greyhounds. They had wicked, wedge-shaped skulls, and they darted like schooling fish. But the mastiffs were huge. They were gray and black, and muscled like horses. They had heads the size of cinder blocks. After the long pursuit, their jaws and shoulders were draped with white lines of saliva.

Izgir buried an arrow deep in the lead dog's throat. It kept coming.

I felt my stomach sneak into my mouth.

"Jesus," I said. "They're just *dogs*. Don't—"

Ara loosed the string of her bow. One of the slender hounds skidded into the leaves, its jaws snapping as it pawed at the shaft embedded in its eye. Two more of the tracker dogs leapt up on our tree-trunk wall and launched themselves at Izgir.

Shouting.

Confusion.

The dogs were everywhere. They scrambled up over the fallen elm and bellied beneath it—ten, fifteen, thirty of the creatures flashing wicked teeth, lunging and snapping and driving us back. Quin split the skull of one mastiff with his broadsword, but another dog was on him in a breath. Rynnit buried a hatchet in the cur's shoulder. Quin got a grip on the dog's head, twisted hard, and snapped its neck. Then the Marshal went down, pinned by two more of the animals.

Gowen swung right and left with his rough-hewn club. He connected with solid *whoomphs*, like a man beating a rug, and the smaller dogs yelped and squealed as he struck. Truke tu-Kekh sang a profane battle hymn as he carved a path through the pack with his iron hammer. I saw him kill three canines with as many swings, crushing skulls, shattering spines. Izgir leapt onto the back of one of the largest animals and shoved his long knife completely through its throat. Without even checking to make sure the dog was dead, he picked himself up and threw himself at another. But just a few yards away, one of Quin's soldiers shrieked as he defended the Prince. It was impossible to see what was happening in the writhing knot of human and animal flesh. I wasn't sure I wanted to know. Because beyond the melee stood trees. *Dogs can't climb trees.*

I'd only taken a few steps when a hundred and forty pounds of mastiff slammed into me. I felt a sharp pain in my side and I did the only thing I knew how: I jammed my hands between the spikes of the dog's collar, looped one elbow over its shoulder like a cowboy wrestling a calf and held on for dear life. I smelled the rank pelt of the Syrtian cur. The froth of its jaws speckled my cheeks.

"Ramirez!" It was Ara, sprinting toward me. "Hold on!"

The Sidharan hit us at full stride and the dog went down with me pinned beneath it. Ara plunged the blade of her jeweled dagger into the beast's belly, screaming as she fought through the heat of its blood and spilling entrails. I tightened my grip. The dog yelped and thrashed, but it had nowhere to go. Ara worked her knife up into the animal's chest, thrusting deep to puncture its heart. The dog gave a low-pitched grunt, as if of release, and collapsed.

When the creature went limp I lay beside it, panting, trembling, raking dead leaves with my fingers. As I tried to sit up I felt a flame in my side, just above my right hip. I reached back to rub the skin and brought back a palm full of blood. *My blood*, mingled with dirt and the dog's yellow snot. And then I watched the world spin again.

It was official.

Illusion or not, Ythedra wanted me dead.

Wall of Dogs

My companions killed twenty-one dogs in the fight and another four immediately afterward, when Izgir slit the throats of the animals too badly wounded to run. But there was no cause to celebrate. The Taureg, Usak, had lost a chunk of his calf, ripped from the bone by one of the tracking dogs that failed to notice the Taureg was just an observer. Teggat's neck and left shoulder were punctured and bleeding. Gowen's scalp was torn. Quin had half a canine tooth buried in his outer thigh, and old Gryel had broken his elbow, though he couldn't remember how.

Still, they would live to fight again. Prince Mikel Drennen was dead. Eleven dogs lay around him. Their blood mingled with the blood of the soldiers—the young brothers, Mahyal and Rhayfe—who had failed to hold them off.

Ara didn't care to look. As we tended to the bodies of the fallen soldiers, the Sidharan princess wandered around the skirmish site, yanking arrows from the carcasses on the forest floor. I was puzzled when I saw her duck behind a twisted oak. A minute later, a lone man appeared at the edge of our clearing. He wore the slate and scarlet Syrtian livery.

"Dog handler," hissed Izgir. He sprang up on the fallen tree trunk and started toward the enemy.

The Syrtian shouted a curse, then turned to run. He didn't see Ara till it was too late. The flat of her bow caught him on the right temple and the Syrtian crumpled in mid-stride. By the time he regained his senses, he was bound at the wrists and ankles by lengths of coarse troll twine.

——+——

Quin nodded to Izgir, who removed the gag.

"Listen up, you Syrtian whore, because I'm only going to say this once. Answer my questions and you walk out of here. Lie and I'm gonna to cut you into a dozen pieces. And then," said the Marshal, gesturing back over his shoulder toward the blue troll, "I'm gonna let my friend have a turn."

Truke tu-Kekh was leaning against the fallen elm. He looked on dispassionately as he ran a calloused hand over the handle of his battle hammer. The troll's weapon was an evil thing, a massive lump of iron forged deep beneath the earth and mounted on a three-foot shaft of mountain oak reinforced with metal bands. The hammer had two faces. One was blunt, for smashing shields and skulls. The other was honed sharp like an adze, for gutting and scraping. On top was an eight-inch spike, a point designed for dealing the death blow in crowded quarters as the trolls surged forward over their fallen enemies. The whole thing was matted with blood and fur.

The Syrtian was a hollow-cheeked man with stringy dark hair and more nerve than sense. Still, his cheeks seemed to sink further into his face as he considered Quin's threat. A thin line of green drool leaked from one corner of his mouth. It was *khat*, Gowen explained, the resinous shrub cultivated in the southlands as a stimulant. Syrtian foot soldiers chewed it habitually. It eased aches, elevated spirits, increased the flow of adrenaline. In larger amounts, it produced hallucinations—and, occasionally, delusions of invincibility.

"You ain't gonna see another sunset anyhow," the handler mumbled.

"That's right," said Quin. "We're dead men. How far back is your column?"

"Three hours. Maybe less."

"How many men?" Quin demanded.

"Forty," said the Syrtian. "Forty-five. More than you."

"We've got another ten on patrol."

"Like hell you do."

"Archers?"

"None worth the name," the prisoner admitted. "But it don't matter. Aln Adrackt is coming. He'll turn your crop lands to dust, your rivers to mud and ash. Surbiss. Morab. The Inkavidians. They all learned. Don't prepare to die, Marshal. Anyone can die. Prepare to *suffer*. That's the only thing he's gonna leave you."

"Speaking of Aln Adrackt..."

When the Syrtian snorted, Quin hit him so hard that I felt the handler's blood freckle my face. The bound man coughed up a wad of *khat*. It landed on his lap.

"Where *is* he?"

"You want to know? Fine. I'll tell you where he is. He's crossed the Strait. He's in Ythedra, and his army outnumbers the leaves on the trees. Heading north, is what they say. Coming this way. Nothing can stand against him. *Nothing*."

"Why?"

"Why what?"

"Why is he here? He's got half the world under his thumb, with most of the other half not worth claiming. He controls the Free Cities already. What does he want from Ythedra?"

The handler glanced down. He chuckled. Started laughing.

"What does he want? What have you *got*?"

Quin shook his head. "I've heard enough. Go back to your captain. Tell him we travel under protection of the Tauregs who rule this forest. Tell him he's in grave danger if he continues to follow us."

"Tauregs," said the Syrtian.

"Like that one," said Quin. He nodded toward Usak.

The Syrtian squinted his hoptoad eyes. "*That one* looks like he'd fly off in a high wind. Never heard of 'em."

"You will. Izgir?"

The Naztali pulled the handler's head back by his dirty hair. He placed his long knife against the Syrtian's throat.

"What are you doing?" said Quin.

"Justice," said Izgir.

"I was asking if you had any questions, not if you wanted to slit his throat."

Disbelief was etched on the Naztali's face. "You're letting him *go?* This piece of worm shit?"

"You heard my promise."

"Your promise means nothing to a Syrtian, Marshal. The Syrtians have no honor."

"I realize that," said Quin. He stepped behind the dog handler and sliced the twine that bound his hands. "But I do."

The Syrtian smirked as he scrambled to his feet. He found the wad of *khat* he'd been chewing and reinserted it in his cheek. Though he paused as if to shout another curse, one look at Izgir's dark face changed his mind. Muttering to himself, the handler stumbled into the trees and disappeared from sight.

"We trolls have a saying," said Truke tu-Kekh, watching the man's back. "*Never give gifts to a snake.*"

Quin tried to sound matter-of-fact. "We were lucky the dogs got ahead of the soldiers. Got too far out and wouldn't come back. Syrtian tracking squads always attack with their dogs. That handler probably won't live to see dawn, once his captain catches up to him."

"Those dogs," I said. "They were so thin."

Izgir breathed out through his nose. "Starved. That's how the Syrtians train 'em. Start 'em out hunting children. Naztali children. My brother was seven years old when the dogs killed him. What we found to bury could have fit in a boot. And these—these *Syrtians*— are the sort of men Bryd Drennen allowed to butcher Naztali warriors inside the walls of Kaer Rhennet. The sort of man you just let go, Marshal."

Quin and the Naztali stood toe to toe, their eyes locked in anger. The old feuds of their peoples seemed to be summed up in their stares.

Quin's voice was calm, but iron-edged. "As I told your elders when we met in council, rulers don't always get to rule the way they want. Bryd Drennen put up with the Syrtian demands because he had no choice. Kaer Rhennet was too weak to stand alone, and the Naztali wouldn't pledge to fight beside us. The Duke is *dead*, goddammit. His *son* is dead. Is that not enough for you? Maybe you should save your venom for the people who are trying to kill us."

"Agreed," said the troll, laying a rough hand on Izgir's waist. The Naztali refused to return his glance. Truke tu-Kekh looked back beyond Quin. Teg and Teryan had taken up positions behind their commander. The gruff sergeant held a short sword. The blue troll flexed his fingers on the handle of his hammer.

I tried to act like I mattered.

"Where I come from, the Spanish trained their dogs to track and kill Indians. Women. Children. Whoever. The dogs did such a good job, the King of Spain recommended they be given full military pensions." There was no reaction. "Not one of Western civilization's brightest moments, I guess."

Ara showed little interest in the feud. "How long till the Syrtian infantry shows up, Marshal?"

Quin exhaled, turned away from the Naztali. "You heard the handler. He said they were three hours back. Assuming he marked the trail right—"

"And if he told the truth," Izgir said. The Naztali wandered over to where his gear lay at the base of one of the trees.

"Yes," said Quin. "And if he told the truth, that's how long it'll take. Might as well break out the food. Eat. Rest if you can. Ramirez, why aren't you taking care of that wound?"

"I'm fine. It's not deep."

"Deep doesn't matter. It's the infection that's dangerous. Clean it."

"I will," I said. But I waved off Ayrd Teryan's offer of water. *Don't show the hurt*, I warned myself. *Don't show any more weakness*. Maybe Ara will forget to mention to the rest of the group how you ran for the hills when the dogs showed up. Maybe Ara will forget, period. And maybe you still have a shot at living the whole thing down. Like Lord Jim, for example. With a brand new boat full of pilgrims.

"But shouldn't we keep moving?" said Gowen. Dried blood covered his face like a mask. Usak was trying to doctor the big man's scalp. "I mean, now that the Prince...?"

"No sense moving. It took us long enough to find this poor excuse for a defensive position. Better we meet the Syrtians here on our terms than somewhere else on theirs. Teryan, take first watch. I want everyone else to rest. They won't attack while it's dark."

"Why not?" I thought Gowen's question made sense. We could move faster now that we didn't have to carry Prince Mikel. Maybe we could lose our pursuers in the woods. "Why won't they attack in the dark?"

"Old military secret," said Quin.

"Yeah?"

"Hard to see."

Quin laughed so hard that he nearly stabbed his own foot. *The tension's getting to all of us*, I thought. But only at first. I looked closer at the sword-scarred Marshal. I studied his empty eyes and slack features and I realized he'd drifted beyond fear. He'd subsumed it in his fatigue and maybe also in his shame for his part in the loss of his Outriders and the foreigners in his care. Now he waited for death with a calm that chilled me.

He caught me staring. Usak sat on the ground nearby, tending to his injured calf, but aside from the young Taureg we were out of earshot of the company.

"My wife lived in Kaer Rhennet," Quin said, pushing his stringy hair out of his face. He spoke so softly that I had trouble hearing him. "God knows where she is now. The Duke and his son are dead. Most of my men…" He shrugged. "So I'm a man without a family. I'm a commander with no one to command. There's nothing left for me in Ythedra. And you want to know what, Ramirez? I'm gonna wait right here to claim it."

"Fantastic. A soldier with a death wish."

The Marshal settled himself against the fallen tree trunk and leaned his head back. "You want to leave, be my guest."

"Leave? How can I *leave*?"

"Just scale these majestic walls. Then you can run to your heart's content. I've noticed you're pretty good at it."

The Marshal closed his eyes. The muscles in his face drooped and his jaw dropped open. In the last light of dusk I saw the hollows of age in his cheeks and noticed for the first time the silver hair amidst the red at his temples. Just then he startled himself awake, glanced around, reached for his sword. I saw confusion in the soldier's eyes. Quin was getting old.

I pretended to look elsewhere as he collected himself.

"But it's not like it's hopeless," I said. "Right? I mean, I really need to get home. Can't we fight our way out?"

Quin surveyed the body of the lifeless Prince Mikel, now covered with a blue Outrider's cloak. He shook his head. His voice was as thin as a blade.

"We're finished," he said.

The Syrtians caught up with us at midnight. It wasn't a surprise. We saw their torches through the woods. We heard the yelps and whines of their few remaining dogs and heard their sergeants calling out orders. Finally we heard the soldiers them-selves as they tripped on roots and stumbled over branches in the shadows. There was a series of shouts, and then the torches went out.

They set the fire at dawn.

1 4

Conflagration

I recognized the smell from my childhood in south Texas. I thought of autumn bonfires and high school football games, of migrating geese and my mother singing along to Selena in the kitchen as she made *masa* for the holidays. But the situation changed fast. Tendrils of acrid black smoke drifted toward us. We heard the sizzle and pop of green wood burning and finally we saw the flames themselves. They climbed up out of the smoke into the canopies of the trees. They licked at the pale dawn sky. The fire was directly behind us, and moving our way. In front of us was the bulk of the Syrtian platoon, waiting for us to break cover.

Gowen rubbed a bandaged hand through his mop of blood-stained hair. His eyes were swollen with fatigue.

"Marshal," he coughed, "I don't know about you, but I'd rather take my chances fighting."

Truke tu-Kekh nodded. The troll was clearly unaccustomed to inactivity in the face of a threat. He squatted behind one of the fallen trunks, staring out at the woods. He snapped dead branches into progressively smaller pieces.

Another several minutes passed. The smoke grew so thick that I lost sight of the Outriders on our right flank. The heat broke over us like a wave.

"What does the pride of the Darannan cavalry have to say?" said Izgir. He was cleaning his knife by plunging it into the dark soil, then yanking it back out. "Any plan?"

Quin locked eyes with his sergeant. Then he turned toward Izgir. "I wish it hadn't ended like this," he said. "The Duke was never your enemy. And neither am I."

The Marshal glanced back over my head at the fire. He wiped his watery eyes and stood up. By way of command, he drew his long sword from its scabbard and stepped around the fallen elm into the clearing.

"For Bryd Drennen," he said. "For the PRINCE!"

Fifty yards away, the gray-clad Syrtians also stood. It would be an easy victory after all. They'd flushed their quarry. They could see how few of us there were to fight.

Fingers flexing on the haft of his iron hammer, Truke tu-Kekh joined Quin. Like all trolls, he had a large, horned head, a face like a peach pit, and a set of jagged teeth that didn't quite fit in his mouth. Because their enemies were generally taller than the trolls, the mountain dwellers wore armor on their shoulders and chests but little below their waists besides their wool trousers and a pair of hobnailed boots. Truke's helmet was fashioned of iron, inlaid on each side with granite tiles and topped with a horsehair plume that increased his height by almost a foot. Thickly muscled but stump-legged, trolls had a waddling gait that was inefficient on open ground. But this wasn't open ground. I had a strong suspicion Truke tu-Kekh would find the fight he'd been looking for in these woods. His *last* fight.

The Syrtian line started forward, the infantrymen beating their swords against their shields as they advanced. One of the soldiers screamed a challenge and the rest answered, their voices guttural and low. It sounded like a rumble emanating from the earth itself.

Gowen and Izgir stood up. Ara rose as well, an arrow nocked in her elegant bow.

"Hold!" barked Quin. "Ara and Izgir—take your shots now, while you can."

Usak, meanwhile, seemed to have divorced himself from the situation. Unlike the rest of us, the Taureg had seemed to relax when he smelled the smoke.

He looked over at me. Blinked one eye.

When I turned again to face our attackers, I saw a Syrtian infantryman gaze down at the green shaft sticking out of his stomach. Then he sank to his knees, clutching his wound. His open mouth made no sound. A second bolt split his forehead and slammed him backwards onto the forest floor. There were more arrows now— messengers too swift to be seen. The air sang with their errands. And a line of Taureg warriors materialized from the grove around us, silent as mist on a northern lake, firing their long yew bows as they came.

"Bad idea," said Usak. "Burning the woods."

1 5

Salve

Only a few of the Syrtians tried to fight back.

These unlucky souls were cut down where they stood, knocked off their feet by the wicked shafts of the Tauregs or pinned to the trunks of trees like butterflies on a bug catcher's board. The rest of the gray-clad soldiers turned on their heels and fled into the Thicket. The Tauregs strode wordlessly after them. Disregarding Quin's shouts, Izgir and Truke-tu-Kekh hurried to join the pursuit.

But there was another danger to face, and this one wasn't going to be as easy to fend off as a company of panicked Syrtian infantrymen. The fire that had eaten the underbrush behind us now gnawed at the hardwoods, roaring like an animal as it gathered heat and speed. It seemed like a bitter reprieve to have escaped the swords of the Syrtians, only to see our temporary refuge burn around us. We'd have to gather our dead and start running again.

Before Quin could give the order, though, the clearing began to fill with Taureg women, fur-clad giants with blue eyes, copper skin, and enormous manes of fair hair wrapped in loops around their shoulders. The women set to work with axes, hacking at the stand of yellow pines that stood to the south of our clearing. Usak explained that the women were creating a firebreak in case the wind were to shift to the north. But the greater risk, Quin argued, came from the fire's possible spread to the west. Usak only pointed. As we watched, the shallow ditch that bisected our clearing began to fill with muddy water.

"These channels run all through the forest," the Taureg explained. "My people dug them centuries ago. When there's a fire, we divert water from springs in the area and channel it where it's needed. Not much wind today. The fire won't live long."

"But how can you——? I mean, these women are cutting down the trees, right?"

Usak nodded.

"And cutting down trees," I said, "is a *bad* thing."

"Not all the trees," said Usak. He led me a little distance into the forest. At the top of a low ridge he stopped and pointed into the branches of a sycamore forty yards from where we stood. In its canopy I could just make out what looked like a lean-to built across two of the largest limbs. Green ribbons drifted and scissored in a whisper of wind. "After death, a Taureg is left to the gods in the arms of a tree. Away from the earth. Alone with the sky——what we call the mouth of heaven. Desecration of these graves is punishable by death. And setting a fire where it can *spread* is a desecration."

"Because...." I began.

He nodded.

"It would——"

"Be a desecration," he said.

Despite the fact that he was bigger than an elevator car, there was a curiously boyish quality to Usak. He grinned, and I found it hard not to grin back. It was so hard, in fact, that I failed. The Taureg held up his webby hand as if he was about to take an oath. I did the same. He stooped a bit. He reached over and locked his fingers with mine, and I found myself folded in his embrace. He smelled of sweat and mud, wood smoke and tree bark. It was like hugging a wigwam.

———+———

It was another three hours before the fire burned itself out, hemmed in by standing water to the north and west and the fresh-cut fire break to the south. By this time, several of the Taureg men had wandered back into the clearing.

Foremost among them was a warrior who stood eight feet tall—not counting his thicket of tangled hair, which rose another foot and a half above his narrow head. His skin, the furs he wore, and even his teeth were brown, which made his sky-blue eyes all the more striking. Though there seemed to be no muscle on his bony frame, appearances in this case were misleading. The Tauregs were strong enough, as the Syrtians had discovered.

Quin spat in his palms and tried to clean the soot off his face. Then he bowed to the forest dwellers.

"You saved our lives," he said. "Thank you."

The Taureg leader remained impassive. "The gray men were warned, just as you were. Our resting places must not be disturbed."

"So we see. But I'm afraid one of your people is hurt. It was the dogs. You'll want to tend him yourself, I imagine."

The Taureg stiffened. "You mean the boy. Usak. He has chosen his path."

"It's not bad," grunted Usak. He shook his spindly leg as if to demonstrate. "I can travel."

Quin frowned. "Travel? Travel *where*?"

The young Taureg glanced down. "With you, Quin Marshal. If you allow it."

"It's Marshal Quin. And what you want is impossible. We don't have the grub, for one thing. Gryel?"

The old cook spat. "No grub."

"The Tauregs," I said, seeing the disappointment in Usak's eyes, "are a valuable ally. And I'm willing to bet Usak here knows the way to Inniskerr better than we do. I would welcome him, Marshal."

"You'd welcome a flood if it could float you out of these woods." Quin glanced at the Taureg chief. "No offense intended, but it's our understanding that the Tauregs have no allies. The oldest stories among our people—stories that I find myself recalling more often these days—tell us that the silent ones never leave their home in the Thicket."

"*Seldom* leave," said the Taureg. "But you speak truly when you say the Tauregs are no man's ally. Still, we carry a salve made from the red root that grows in the western woods. Since none of us is injured, we have no need of it. Take the medicine for your wounded. You may bury your dead as you see fit. We will dispose of the others. The earth is always hungry."

The Taureg chief tossed a leather satchel at Quin's feet. Then he turned and headed back into the trees, followed by several of his kind.

"Real friendly," said Gowen.

"He was being as courteous as he knew how," Usak responded. He watched as his people dispersed, heading in several different directions. "The Tauregs speak as the trees, not as the flowers."

"You know this leader?" asked Truke tu-Kekh.

"Not well." Usak looked at his hands. "He's my brother."

"And the salve?" I said.

"That's right. You said you were bitten. Let me see."

I pulled up my tunic.

"What? What's wrong?"

"We should have dressed this last night," said the Taureg.

"It's not that bad."

"Trolls," said Truke tu-Kekh, "have a saying. *An unwashed wound is like an unwatched thief.*"

"You're killing me with these sayings, man. I'm fine. It barely hurts."

Usak pursed his narrow lips. "It will."

1 6

Fever

We buried Prince Mikel Drennen beneath a massive elm, side-by-side with the young brothers who'd died defending him. Quin murmured an awkward blessing. He and his few remaining men sliced their foreheads and cheeks with Teggat's dagger, and trails of blood snaked down their faces to mingle with the dirt and debris in their beards. Then the soldiers sank to their knees and joined Quin in a warrior's farewell—a song for the afterlife, mournful and slow.

Truke tu-Kekh led us back to our makeshift fort.

"Damn shame," he said. "They were good men."

Ara nodded. "They say Mikel would have been the first ruler of Kaer Rhennet the Naztali could understand. Losing him is a blow to the free peoples."

Izgir hadn't bothered to attend the service. He sat on one of the fallen tree trunks, fletching an arrow. "The man was headstrong. Quick to draw the knife. Like a Naztali. He might not have had the wisdom of his father—or what the Darannans call wisdom—but he fought like a lion. He deserved a better death. Quin says he loved the Prince like he was his own son. If he's a man, maybe he'll remember this wound. Maybe now he'll fight."

"Now?" said Gowen. He put a foot up on the tree where Izgir sat. "What do you think he's *been* doing? And are you gonna keep pouting for the rest of the trip? 'Cause it's startin' to get under my skin."

"Hold off," said the troll. "I've heard this argument already."

"No, I ain't holdin' off, and this ain't about *you*."

"I know that. But it's not about Bryd Drennen either, when you think about it. It's about a social system, hereditary autocracy, that treats government as a personal privilege rather than the prerogative of a sovereign people fully capable of governing themselves. No troll will ever serve a monarch again. The Naztali are essentially nomads. No kings. No princes. We can respect that. God only knows what these tree people do. Taureg. Are your laws imposed from above or generated organically, by the will of the governed?"

"What laws?"

"Never mind. I don't imagine our peoples' paths will cross anyway. But Kaer Rhennet, with its ancient houses, and Sidhara, with its gold-flecked nobles, are always going to be threats to a society like ours."

Gowen hissed in disgust. "Horse shit—whatever you said. It ain't about governments. It's about common sense. Everybody here knows if the Naztali and the Darannans could have patched things up a decade or so ago, Ythedra wouldn't be in the fix it's in now. Instead every Naztali I've met has to relive every goddamn injustice ever done to his race since the world began, with the result bein' nothin' ever gets done. And most of those injustices involve Kaer Rhennet. But I got news for you, Izgir. You too, troll. Kaer Rhennet is most likely a pile of ashes right about now. You gonna keep hatin' a pile of ashes? I ain't the smartest individual in the world. I know that. And God knows I ain't a flag waver. But I've been in the Free Cities, which are about as far from free as you can imagine, and I've seen Tarrant Lef, and I know the Syrtians and their dogs are the least of our worries if Aln Adrackt is headed this way. So why don't you try to look a little further than your own goddamn noses for the next few days, huh? You think you could handle that?"

You'd think a rant like this would set everyone off all over again. I don't know why it didn't. Maybe it was exhaustion. We were head, heart, and bone tired. Or maybe it was respect for the men who had died beside us. At any rate, the tension in the air dissolved. Izgir wandered off into the woods, nursing his private resentments. Ara cleaned her arrows with a piece of dirty cloth. And I settled back into a pile of leaves and tried to forget who and where I was.

———+———

As if.

———+———

We resumed the journey to Inniskerr that afternoon. No one said it, but the Prince's absence made the trip easier. It also helped to know we were walking with someone who knew the way. Usak hustled us through the Thicket as if he was following sidewalks. Our loose-limbed guide supplied us with food he retrieved from larders known only to the Tauregs. We dined on slabs of cured venison seasoned with berries and nuts, on mushrooms and dried cherries and an orange butter Usak described, vaguely, as "acorn paste." Not that I had much of an appetite. By evening of that first day I burned like a furnace. The wound in my side had started to weep yellow pus. I spent the night shivering, dreaming of fire. My legs felt like railroad ties. I emptied two goatskins and still couldn't drink enough water.

We struck the Injured River near noon on the third day. Here the water came foaming full-throated out of the mountains, boiling blue-green over a series of limestone shelves. Ara plunged in ahead of the rest of us. She was just about to start swimming when the Taureg beckoned her back.

Her green eyes blazed as she wallowed back to the bank. "We were told," she shouted, "to head north! After we crossed the river! Am I the only one who remembers Dzerdjik's instructions?"

Usak sidestepped the challenge. "Your friend probably said to cross because it's the easier route. The trail on this side of the river is dangerous, but it's also shorter. The mountains ahead are called the Griffin's Teeth. I can lead you through them."

"Dangerous?" said Gowen. He'd taken off his boots. Now he sat rubbing his blistered feet with bandaged hands. It couldn't have been comfortable. "Dangerous *how*?"

"Mountain lions. Quicksand. Dead souls that steal breath from the living."

I lay down on the gravel of the riverbank and stared at the sky. Storm clouds in the west were churning silver and black, but the sky above us was clear.

"Besides," said Usak, addressing Quin, "Ramirez's wound is getting worse. He needs stronger medicine. Linnaeth can help him, but he might not make it to Inniskerr if we cross the river and take the long route."

Quin stepped in front of me. "Ramirez? You listening?"

"Whichever way. Let's just...*go*. Okay? Where are you?"

"Can you walk?"

"I'd rather put a saddle on Gowen and ride, but—"

"Can you *walk*?" Quin demanded.

"I heard you the first time. *No se*. I don't know."

The Marshal pinched the bridge of his nose between his left thumb and forefinger. "Idiot's half-dead already. Lieutenant?"

Young Teryan snapped to attention. I'd always had trouble with obedience. This guy was making me sick. This guy or the staphylococcus that had rezoned my stomach for residential development.

"Sir."

"Any idea what he's talking about?"

"None whatsoever."

"Keep him moving. Get him off the *ground*, for starters. Kick him. Drag him. Carry his sorry ass if you have to, but don't don't let him fall behind. Understand?"

"Understood."

"Good," said the Marshal. "And don't let me hear him complaining again. Lead on, Taureg."

———+———

I'm sure Usak knew what he was talking about when he said the east bank was dangerous. Still, for most of our journey through the Griffin's Teeth, the biggest hazard we faced was the route itself, which climbed up through an eroded terrain of narrow ridges, deep ravines, and hidden sinkholes. The vegetation was mostly scrubby junipers and madrone trees, with a few century plants studding the landscape like green anemones on a barren sea bottom. We scrambled for cover whenever chunks of crumbling limestone came cascading down the slopes around us. Izgir and Quin searched the heights for signs of ambush, but Usak assured us the slides were random, a fact of local life like mud in a marsh or falling tree limbs in the Big Thicket. We didn't see any mountain lions, but there was plenty of quicksand, black quagmires created by run-off trapped in the ancient dust amid the stones. And as for dead souls: we heard them. At least, we heard *something* speaking in the canyons at night. It was a high-pitched wail, by turns angry and anguished, as if the mothers of a spectral, long-dead race stood massed at the edge of forever, mourning their lost children. It was probably just a vagrant wind howling through the rock, we agreed. Wind could do that. Make those sounds. The keening of regret. The discordant dominant sevenths of anger. But not even Truke tu-Kekh ventured away from our campfire till the sun reappeared over the cliffs, and the first thing we did each morning was give thanks for the blushing sky.

———+———

It was almost dawn on one of those chilly nights when I finally spoke to Ara. A fingernail moon was sinking in the west, but a dusting of stars still glittered above us like tiny diamonds in a sea of black. We were the only ones awake. The princess was pulling last watch. I was pushing my luck. I hoisted myself into a sitting position, attempted to straighten my spine. I know I winced. I may have cried out.

The princess crouched in front of me, her green eyes probing mine.

"A Sidharan man," she said, "would be ashamed to make a sound like that."

"*Any* man would be ashamed to make a sound like that. You think I'm proud of it?"

She glanced out into the darkness. "Or to run from a fight."

I laid myself back down on the rock. "Okay. Fine. I knew this was gonna come up. I'm a coward, all right? I've never used a sword in my life. And I've never even *seen* a Syrtian attack dog, much less had to fight one. So thank you for saving my life. Now leave me alone, so I can keep screwing it up by myself."

I could deal with contempt. More difficult was the sight of Ara draping her cape over my legs.

"Keep you from freezing to death," she said. "Whatever the Seer wants you for in Inniskerr, I presume you're wanted alive."

"That's better. For a minute there I suspected you had a heart."

She shrugged. "Funny."

"Funny? What's funny?"

The princess almost smiled. "So did I."

She stood and padded to the edge of the firelight to look back down along the trail we'd come up. I was waiting for her when she returned.

"Tell me," I said. She was listening. That's all I cared about. It took me a while to think up a question. "What is Sidhara? I mean, what's it like?"

Ara used her moccasin to rearrange the embers of our campfire. A few sparks floated skyward. I watched thoughts drift across her face like shadows of clouds on an open field.

"It's a country of cliffs. Of high pastures, and stone walls, and wind-sculpted trees. My people are shepherds and artisans. Traders. Fishermen."

"Of what stock? Those used to be Darannan lands—though I suppose there weren't many Darannans in them when your people arrived. Where did the Sidharans come from?"

"From Erillith. The migration started four hundred years ago. Now there are cities all across Sidhara. Many temples. Three palaces. We are a diligent people. Sidharan traders sail to ports all over the world. As many ports as are still open for trade, that is. And not crawling with disease."

I lifted my chin to the wind-pitted landscape around us. "And you found it in your hearts to feel for Ythedra?"

"In our hearts, no. We found it in our heads. Aln Adrackt doesn't see borders. He wouldn't see ours."

"Ah. And the Sidharan emperor thought it best to stop him at a comfortable distance."

"Is there something *wrong*—?" Ara glanced around, calmed herself. "Is there something wrong with self-interest? My father is a wise man. He says Ythedra lies like a stone on the grave of evil. When the stone begins to tremble, we have to hold it down."

"I'm sorry. I meant no disrespect."

"Aln Adrackt's agents are afoot in our land as well as in Ythedra. Everywhere they buy the weak, and preach dissent, and whisper of the witch king's powers. We have to stop him. We have no choice. And neither do you."

"Don't be so sure of that," I said.

She studied me for so long, I started to blush.

"Where are you from, Ramirez?" she asked. "And if all you want to do is run away, why are we here with you?"

"I'm not running away. I'm not from Ythedra, and I never asked to be here—despite the fact that at least half of what I see looks familiar and I seem to know the history of the place better than any of the folks who've actually inherited it. As to where I *am* from, how can I say it? You take the Earth exit and hang a right at New Jersey.

And finally, as for why you're here with me, I have no idea. I'm just glad you are."

"It's a difficult trip," she offered.

"That's not what I meant."

Ara gazed at the red horizon. A minute drifted by like a sagging balloon. "Do you miss your home?"

I started to speak, then paused. That's the trouble with honesty. It takes time. Especially if you're out of practice.

"I don't know. I'm not exactly royalty. And where I live doesn't sound much like Sidhara. People don't trust each other anymore. The cities are dirty. The forests are gone. Kids kill each other for a new pair of shoes."

Ara frowned. "Aren't you one of Gowen's people?"

"Gowen doesn't *have* a people. He said something about it to Dzerdjik when we first met up. I eventually got the whole story out of him. You know how he gets that sour look whenever someone mentions the Ganthans? Turns out his mother was a Ganthan who ran away from her clan because Gowen was born sickly and her husband wanted him dead. Claimed he'd never be a warrior. But Gowen's mother wasn't buying the whole survival-of-the-fittest thing. She left the mountains when Gowen was just a few days old and managed to evade the women they sent to drag her home. They ended up on the coast, in Tull, and she died there, from what sounds like a combination of pneumonia, malnutrition, and simple exhaustion, on his eleventh birthday. The city was hard on them. They had no friends. No family. Not even a home they could call their own. When she died, she left him that copper key he wears on his bracelet. It's a talisman of his mother's family in Fereganth. He says he's always wanted to go back there and hold someone responsible for his mother's death. He just, I don't know—got *distracted*. Best I can tell, he makes a living as muscle for various loan collectors. I take it he drinks. Which is, you know, not necessarily such a bad thing. But then he gets to feeling sorry for himself. Calls people names. Gets furniture broken over his head."

"He fights like a bull. We're lucky to have him." She lowered her voice. "Though he could use a bath."

I had to laugh. "I'll let you try."

"Who was she?" she said.

For the first time, I noticed Ara spoke to me with her face angled away from mine, averted as if she was expecting an insult. I wondered if she had any idea how attractive she was. That shock of midnight hair. Those river-green eyes.

"Remember?" she added. "The first night you saw me? The person you said I reminded you of?"

A gust of wind collapsed the glowing skeleton of branches and brambles in the fire. Which was just as well. It was my turn to stammer. Dawn was wading through the darkness to the east and I could see the broken teeth of the mountains surrounding us. I breathed in, breathed out, wondered if I could tell the story. I realized Ara shared yet another attribute of the woman I remembered. It was the fullness of her eyebrows that made her look fierce. Take that away and her face was gentle, open, almost forgiving.

"Rachel Chen was her name," I said. "We loved each other, I guess. I know I loved her. But I walked away from it. After her father blew his life savings starting a second comic book company, he and Rachel had nothing. We saw each other for a few months. She wanted me to say something to her I just didn't know how to say. Finally she got tired of it. She got tired of me. She left me alone with my fifteen-year-old single malt scotch and a drawer-full of designer chemicals, which wasn't so bad since my life was pretty much over anyway, and one night I switched on the news, hoping to see that I'd jumped off the George Washington Bridge, when this dwarf named Edward stepped out of my closet. I was attacked by giant frogs under the command of something that looked like evil incarnate. I know that much. Then things sort of get mixed up in my head and I wake up in a dungeon at Kaer Rhennet. Now I'm sitting in the baddest set of badlands I've ever seen with a woman who'd rather eat a fistful of dirt than look at me any longer than it takes to—I don't know—*aim*—trying to figure out a way to impress her that doesn't involve, like, strength, courage, or intelligence."

"I'd say you were eloquent, Ramirez. If I had any idea what you were talking about. You have no children?"

"Always thought I'd get around to it."

Ara shook her head. "And Rachel? Couldn't you go to her now?"

"As a matter of fact, I can't. Rachel is dead. She was hit by a drunken investment banker in an Audi—a sort of carriage—dragged seven blocks down 10th Avenue and pronounced dead on arrival at St. Luke's. I'd cry about it if I could. If I was a human being, for example."

Ara tossed a couple of twigs into the embers. We watched as they warmed, twisted, finally caught fire. I rubbed at the skin of a blister on my left palm. In only a few days my hands had become unrecognizable. My knuckles were scabbed and raw. Litle crescents of filth lined my fingernails.

"She was Sidharan, your Rachel?"

"There are no Sidharans where I come from. But her people were similar, I guess. Anyway, I apologize for staring at you."

Ara's eyes held an oddly wistful expression. "If that's your only crime, I forgive you."

"It isn't. I know you think about Quin's lieutenant. And I also know he doesn't seem to notice."

Now *she* was blushing. I'd have expected it sooner from one of Quin's cavalrymen.

"But that's him," I said. My heart was beating at roughly twice its normal rate. I felt like a teenager again. Clueless. Awkward. Exposed. "I notice. I can't seem to stop noticing."

I shoved my pain down into my stomach. I had just touched Ara's cheek with the back of my hand when a percussive snort split the silence. It was Gowen. He'd awakened himself with a particularly loud snore. He sat up and looked around.

"Everything okay?" he said.

Just then the sun eased its forehead over the horizon, as if it wasn't quite ready to see what the day had to offer. Ara turned away from me. The pain in my side came racing back, and the world went red again.

From the Annals of Ythedra

*T*he cellars beneath Kaer Rhygat were deep and extensive. In the days of King An they were used to house the treasures of Dar-Annon: linens and silks, emeralds and gold, stockpiles of salt and grain and iron ore brought from the furthest reaches of the Ninelands. Now these passageways were dark, and harbored only evil: twisted things that even the hardest Kirikite mercenaries found it difficult to speak of. Few who entered those cellars as prisoners came out alive. None came out unscarred.

Though proclamations forbade it, Darannan citizens had been filtering out of the Red Cities since the siege of Kaer Rhygat began. Many were captured or killed. But those who escaped the Kirikite patrols fled across the Strait of Sorrows toYthedra, where Kaer Rhennet stood in defiance of the evil in Emerkest. Such defiance the old physician could not abide, for his ambition was an ocean, and his hatred for men inexhaustible. He was a consort of the unclean. A shape-changer. A mind-eater. And his name, he now revealed, was Aln Adrackt.

The time of Aln Adrackt's wars against the peoples ofYthedra are called theYears of Iron.The Kirikite andTazgat riders who carried the red flags into Ythedra were swift and brutal. They were armed with their master's spells of protection and stealth, and many of An-Nashayel's warriors darkened green fields with their blood. But in the eighth year of the wars,Ythedra's fortunes seemed to improve. After a series of minor battlefield triumphs,

An-Nashayel found himself in control at last of Ythedra's southern coastline. Rumors circulated that Kaer Rhygat was in ruins. That the sorcerer's troops had rebelled against him. That the sorcerer himself had gone back to his hell, and Emerkest lay empty. Inflamed by pride and his lust for vengeance, the young prince began planning an expedition to reclaim the lands his father had ruled.

It was at this time too that the poet Ban Lohannon set out on his own for the Red Cities. Ban Lohannon had distinguished himself at court as a creator of odes to the heroics of others. Now the young man—short and slight, with curly brown hair and thick lips he tried hard to keep from pursing when he was nervous—decided it was time to do something worthy of a poem himself. He went in search of his fortune in what he presumed would be the deserted capital of Emerkest. He intended to arrive before Ythedra's legions and load up as much treasure as would fit on the back of two mules. What he found, however, was elements of an enormous army that Aln Adrackt had deployed in the moors to smash Prince An-Nashayel's advance on Kaer Rhygat.

What he found, in other words, was a trap.

The Race to Inniskerr

It was Izgir who spotted the scouts. We followed the line of his leathery arm and spied two Syrtian infantrymen watching us from one of the rocky hills across the Injured River.

"Damn," said Gowen.

"What is it?" Truke tu-Kekh's eyes were useless at this distance. "What do you see?"

Izgir spat to one side. "Syrtian scouts. There. By the biggest of those rocks. And they've seen us."

Ara was unimpressed. "So? We're a match for two Syrtians."

The Marshal stepped up beside her. "They ain't out for a picnic, Princess. Bound to be a unit nearby. How far is it to Inniskerr?"

The Taureg thought about it. "Half a day, if we move quickly."

"And can we? What's ahead of us?"

"More of the same," said Usak. "But the terrain gets difficult on their side too. And you see how wild the river is here. Inniskerr's the nearest point where they can cross."

Quin was already moving. "Then we'll have to get there first."

I stumbled along with Outriders on either side of me. Sometimes they supported me. At other times they dragged me along with them. I thought a lot about the sun. I kept seeing this enormous yellow-orange object that started out in the sky where it was supposed to be and then came closer and closer until it was directly over me, at which point it turned into an egg. The egg broke and a yellow yolk of light dribbled down over my brain, and for several minutes afterward I saw everything in sepia tones. I couldn't explain it. I couldn't stop it. But it wasn't all oblivion. Occasionally my senses would clear and my nausea would ebb and I'd realize where I was and what we were doing. I had no idea how many Syrtian soldiers might be stalking us. It was better not knowing. It was better just *doing*, shoving one foot ahead of the other, forcing myself up the steep hills. Lunch was venison jerky and a few blackberries. By four o'clock that afternoon the sun was slipping out of the sky but we could see greener land ahead. And finally we saw *them*, half a mile away, paralleling our progress on the far side of the river. At the head of a column of Syrtian infantrymen strode several dark figures.

"Urzeks," said Quin.

We froze where we stood. The word was like a punch in the gut.

"Can we make it?" said Ara.

Usak nodded. "Inniskerr's just over that next set of hills. But Quin Marshal—"

"It's '*Marshal Quin*,' all right? Marshal. Quin. But *what*?"

The Taureg looked grave. "Inniskerr may not be what you imagine."

"It's got to be better than being caught out in the open." The Marshal forced himself into a weary trot. He stopped when he realized that only his few remaining Outriders were following him.

"Goddammit," he said, stalking back toward the rest of us. "Ramirez, what are you doing?"

"Leave me," I said. "I'll catch the bus."

"Get his arm."

"Lend me a token, somebody? I can't—"

Just then, in the midst of my delirium, as I imagined there might actually be a Metroliner arriving soon to schlep me to Inniskerr, 34th Street, and all points west, I slid into a period of utter clarity. The world slowed to a crawl. I saw my companions as if I was holding them under a microscope. Usak seemed genuinely worried. The lanky Taureg squatted beside me. He placed the back of one of his hands on my forehead, gauging the strength of my fever. Izgir was enraged at this waste of time. He scoured the far bank of the river as if he could kill with his eyes. I imagined him thinking, *Let's shove this waste of a good pair of boots into the river and save our own skins while we can*. But seeing Ara shake her head hurt me worse than the hole in my side.

Loser, she was thinking.

Weakling.

And of course it was true. I could admit it. I'd grown accustomed to my cowardice. I could stand all the insults. I just couldn't stand them coming from her.

"*Vamonos*," I said.

I pulled myself to my feet.

———+———

Gowen and Ara hustled to catch up with Izgir, the Marshal, and most of the Outriders. Usak, Teryan, Gryel, Truke tu-Kekh and I brought up the rear. It was obvious I was the one holding us up. I was endangering the group, but there wasn't a lot I could do about it. I knew we had to make it to the gates of Inniskerr and I was stumbling as fast as I could, given my fever and what felt like a flathead screwdriver stuck in my ribcage. I stopped to heave up what little I had in my stomach, which was trying hard to climb up out of my throat. My companions stopped with me. I ran a few more steps and nearly passed out. We watched the figures ahead of us disappear over the grassy ridge, turned our heads almost in unison and saw our pursuers—gray-clad infantrymen, naked urzeks—scrambling over the loose rock on the opposite bank of the river. No one said a word. No one had to. The Syrtians were going to beat us to Inniskerr.

———+———

Usak and I crested the first ridge just as Quin and the others started up the second slope. They waited for us at the top. Disappointment welled up within me as I looked down at the kingdom of Inniskerr. In the narrow valley below us stood a few ramshackle huts, an empty corral, and a tiny stone cottage with a tiled roof. Another range of dark mountains reared up beyond the valley, promising hard travel to anyone foolish enough to enter them. I heard one of Quin's men curse under his breath.

"Might as well defend this ridge," the Marshal wheezed. "Or fall back into the highlands."

Ara shook her head. "Maybe not. I like the look of that cottage. They won't be able to torch it, anyway."

"Bald ridge. Stone hut. Don't suppose it makes a hell of a lot of difference. We can't run much further anyway. Teg, Alenth. All of you. Drop everything that doesn't have a blade and get to the cottage. Now!"

The company started down the slope. At one point I slipped and skidded several yards on my knees, nearly impaling myself on my sword in the process.

Usak helped me up. "Almost there," he said.

As we hurried over the last two hundred yards or so of level ground toward the hut, the Syrtian platoon scrambled down the far bank toward the green river. The waterway was wider here, but a chain of rocks made a path across it.

When I glanced ahead, I noticed an old woman standing at the door of the cottage. She wore a shapeless blue gown and, on her left forearm, a set of black bracelets. She shook her head at our approach, as if we were unwelcome guests. Then the woman turned her head to watch our pursuers. Seeing them approach the far bank, she stepped out of the doorway and padded toward the river. Ara veered off to intercept her, but the woman held up one hand.

Though she didn't shout, I heard her words clearly.

"No, child," she said. "Stay back."

Once we reached the cottage, there was nothing for us to do but watch. The woman left the near bank and made her way across the river, stepping gingerly from stone to stone as the Syrtians approached. She halted when she reached midstream. Shortly after that, I heard what I can only describe as a faint melody. The woman was humming as she waited for the urzeks. The fact that I could hear her from this distance was, I later found out, a form of her magic.

The Syrtians and urzeks hesitated as they neared the waterway. They slowed from a bloodthirsty sprint to a mystified trot, and finally a cautious walk, as the soldiers realized the old woman who barred their way was unafraid.

Breathing hard, a Syrtian officer barked: "Stand aside, witch! This is the Emperor's business—and none of yours."

"Bold words, captain. But this is my home. And your presence here is most definitely my business."

"Send the urzeks," said one of the soldiers.

"Kill the crazy bitch," shouted another.

The woman was silent. A stray breeze swirled her loose robe, whipped strands of her snow-white hair around her face.

The Syrtian commander's features flushed redder. "Stand *aside*, damn you!"

No answer. Two hawks circled high in the purple sky.

When the officer nodded, the largest of the urzeks lumbered forward. Its tiny eyes glittered, and its dark tongue flicked cautiously at the cool air. When the creature slipped on a loose stone, it lost its grip on its battle-axe. The weapon splashed and disappeared into the current.

No one said a word.

Enraged, the urzek picked itself up and lurched across the next two rocks to where the woman waited. It swung hard, backhanded, with its left arm.

The tiny figure caught the blow with one hand.

Caught it.

Held it.

The old woman lifted her other hand. She stared into the urzeks's eyes and continued to hum. Only at some point it wasn't *her* humming anymore. The sound was coming from the river. Then it seemed to come from behind me, as if a small storm had sprung up in the valley. Finally the sources merged and the river was singing and the sky and the rocks were singing too and all in the same low key. The air grew heavier. I swallowed to clear my ears. Then everything was vibrating, resonating together, and a skein of pale blue lights pulsed like a small star in the woman's raised palm. The star disappeared briefly, and when I saw it again it seemed to be shining from the urzek. From its eyes, and open mouth. Then the world went white, and we—Gowen, me, *all of us*—shielded our eyes against the light and noise.

The world fell silent again. The urzeks's left foot remained where it had been before the blast, still gripping one of the stones. The rest of the creature was spattered across the faces, chests, and shields of the Syrtian platoon.

A moment later the woman crawled out of the water. Gowen and Ara broke from our group, scrambled down the riverbank, and helped her to her feet. Gowen later told me that her grip was cold but strong. Surprisingly strong. The woman herself weighed as much as a wet towel.

Ara sank to her knees before the sopping figure.

"I assumed...people said the Seer of Inniskerr was...a *man*."

The woman twisted her long hair into a ponytail and wrung it like a towel. River water doused Gowen's boots. A faint smile played on her lips.

"People," she said, "can be unkind."

From the Annals of Ythedra

*B*an Lohannon sent all six of his carrier pigeons to warn Prince An-Nashayel of the army that lay in wait for him. Only one of the birds arrived, but it was enough. An-Nashayel didn't call off his invasion immediately. He was too frustrated for that. But what with sending out scouts to confirm Ban Lohannon's reports, and massing more men and boats to meet the expanded threat, the arrival of winter wrested the decision from him. There would be no conquest this year. It was the worst winter of the young prince's life. It was also the luckiest. Had he advanced across the channel, he and his army would surely have died in the moors of Emerkest, and the hopes of a free Ythedra with them.

Lohannon had several reasons for continuing east. Greed, as he later admitted. Stupidity. A need to make a name for himself. But he was also urged forward by voices he heard at night that wouldn't let him sleep. The voices invited him to travel further. They promised great things. They promised him fortune and glory. Slipping into the loosely guarded Kaer Rhygat was easy enough. Getting out proved more difficult. In weeks of wandering through dark regions below the palace, the wayward poet located uncountable riches and untellable horrors. He even found the walking corpse that was Prince Varun, now a babbling, empty wreck. Then Lohannon was himself captured by the sorcerer's disciples and separated by pain from his soul. He became a prisoner of the Dark Lord, and the things he saw were evil indeed.

Ban Lohannon nearly died in those underground cells. Maybe he should have. But his greatest work was already done. And when Aln Adrackt, tired of feeding the huge army he kept in reserve, launched a final assault across the Sea of Stones the following spring, An-Nashayel was ready for him. The armies of Emerkest were defeated at the Battle of the Standing Stones, where the free peoples of Ythedra united at last. Darannan foot soldiers fought beside Taureg archers from the forests of the west. A horde of Naztali riders harried the enemy's flanks. And the tattered remnants of King An's Palace Guard marched from their stronghold in Fereganth behind seven enchanted swords, which shone like sunlight on cold water and brought terror to the armies of Emerkest. The battle raged for four days, and many men died on the sands of those black beaches. But in the end the armies of Ythedra crushed Aln Adrackt's invaders and put an end to his tyranny.

Prince Varun was called many things. The Autumn King. Betrayer of Brothers. The Death of Dar-Annon. By now, though, the names seemed ridiculous. Each was like an elaborate vase for a withered flower, or a grown-up's coat on a sickly child. The former king wandered the palace halls like a harmless ghost, ignored by the sorcerer's lackeys. But Varun still retained some semblance of himself, a vestige of the consciousness he'd owned when he was still just his father's beautiful second son. And most of all what he had now was a hatred of Aln Adrackt. For using him, obviously. For causing him to destroy what he'd wanted so much to rule.

One night not long after the sorcerer's armies were destroyed on the shores of Ythedra, Prince Varun unlocked the cells that held Aln Adrackt's slaves. He was trying to lead—what? A jailbreak, maybe. Some kind of pathetic rebellion. But broken bodies make for feeble rebels. The captives mostly stayed in their cages, huddled in their own blood and filth, unable or unwilling to think about freedom. In fact Ban Lohannon was the only man who followed Varun as he proceeded deeper into the cellars, down a dozen black stairways into chambers quarried long before mortal memory. In what felt like the center of the earth, closer to hell than to open air, was a huge subterranean vault. It was dark and hot and its jagged ceiling looked as if it had been scratched out of the granite from below. There was no floor, only a maze-like pattern of ridges that rose out of the abyss. A stone's throw into the vault stood a figure silhouetted by the light of a single torch: Aln Adrackt.

Ban Lohannon had heard of this place. Anyone still in Kaer Rhygat knew of its existence, though few had seen it. This was the portal to the underworld where Aln Adrackt prayed to his dark masters. This was Anek Sapyr, the Spiders' Gate.

Fighting his fear, Lohannon watched from a position of concealment as Varun made his way across the rock toward the physician. Aln Adrackt turned to face him. There was an argument. Lohannon heard the voices but found it difficult to make out the words. Finally Varun drew a knife and leveled it at his enemy. The sorcerer laughed. He raised one arm and the knife leapt from the prince's hand. Varun stumbled forward anyway. He wrapped his thin arms around the wizard's chest.

Varun's attack was over almost before it began. Aln Adrackt spoke, and the stick figure before him collapsed to the cavern floor. What happened next was almost too bizarre to be described. Aln Adrackt crouched over Varun's motionless body. With one hand he made several small circles above the prince's chest, chanting to some twisted god of emptiness and despair. Before long a stench began to emanate from Varun's corpse. A black haze drifted up from the dead man's mouth, hovered in the still air, and then began to coalesce into a shape. A human shape. And this shape, in sharp contrast to the form that had birthed it, was clearly alive—and clearly struggling against the monster that had called it forth.

———+———

Lohannon was never sure why he followed Varun in the first place. Partly it was curiosity. Partly it was because he sympathized with the muttering prince, ruined and so utterly deceived. But present too in this muddle of emotions was a desire to protect Aln Adrackt, sovereign of the dismal realm that kept Ban Lohannon alive—to keep him from harm and thereby gain from the sorcerer some small boon or privilege.

The horror he saw now drove such thoughts from his head. Ban Lohannon was himself again, whole again, and convulsed with disgust for the reeking world around him and the evil thing that stood at its center. He crept toward the two figures, uncertain of his own intentions even as he moved closer. Fortunately, the sorcerer was distracted. He was so engrossed in his incomprehensible witchcraft that he didn't see Ban Lohannon until it was too late. Lohannon picked up the knife Varun had dropped and drove it deep into the flesh at the base of Aln Adrackt's skull. Holding the weapon, Lohannon ran the sorcerer off the rocky shelf into the Spider's Gate.

———+———

Aln Adrackt was no longer a man. This much is clear. But he still occupied a human form, and the human form has weaknesses. And though the sorcerer could, generally speaking, make short work of any Ythedran warrior, he had the same problems any mortal might experience in a pit full of spiders the size of horses. Ban Lohannon never forgot the shrieks that came from that hole. He stood trembling as he listened, unable either to advance or to flee. It was only when he saw a long, stick-like leg appear above the edge of the pit that he remembered how to move. Another leg appeared, and now a monstrous head—wet with blood, and containing a set of six gleaming eyes. The eyes fixed upon him. The creature pulled itself up and out of the pit and started forward. Trembling, Ban Lohannon slung the corpse of Prince Varun over his shoulder and scrambled back the way he'd come. Varun was little more than skin and bone, but Lohannon was weak with hunger too and he struggled with the weight of the emaciated corpse he carried. He heard the monster scrabbling across the rocky floor behind him, hissing as it came, getting closer each second. Just when he thought he could run no more—when he could have sworn he felt the nightmare thing's hot breath on the back of his neck—he found a niche in the cavern wall that was too narrow to allow the spider to follow. He ducked inside and followed a narrow seam deeper into the rocks, hoping against hope that he could find his way out of Aln Adrackt's dungeons.

The task took weeks. He buried Varun in the darkness and stumbled out of the ruins of Kaer Rhygat a broken man, skeletal and bearded, wrapped in a robe of filth and wearing a crown of scabs. He needed another month to traverse Emerkest, cross the Straits of Sorrow to Ythedra, and make his way north to An-Nashayel's stronghold at Kaer Rhennet. His welcome there was brief. For though he was hailed as a hero for alerting Ythedra to Aln Adrackt's trap, the Years of Iron were finally over. No one wanted to be reminded of them. And no one quite believed the mad tales Ban Lohannon told of the hell beneath the Red Cities.

An-Nashayel gave the ruined poet a pension. He also gave him a small but handsome house on several acres of farmland, located not coincidentally many miles from the walls of Kaer Rhennet. It seemed like everything might turn out all right for the man. But Ban Lohannon carried the curse of Kaer Rhygat inside him. The poison festered and spread and he grew sicker with each passing season. He wandered the woods and fields of the region like a restless ghost. His hair grew long and tangled. He seemed oblivious to rain and snow, and children called him wight, or fiend, because he walked the woods with unseeing eyes and a face that was twisted in pain. And one day Ban Lohannon disappeared. It was rumored for many years afterward that he was aided in his escape from the land of the living by the magus Nihreth Wyn, a consort of Kalya, the goddess of storms, who watches over the world and grieves for its torments. But no one could say for sure. And there came a day, as there always comes a day, when no one really cared to ask.

Ban Lohannon was dead. His songs went unsung. His story was forgotten. And his memory sank from human consciousness like a stone falling to the bottom of a deep, dark lake.

The Face of the North

"Quickly!" said the Seer, as she hustled Gowen and Izgir toward the cottage. Again I heard her as if she was standing beside me. "They'll be coming soon. Urzeks are too stupid to stay scared for long."

With this, she shooed us into the rough-hewn structure we had hoped to defend. A slab of granite the size of a refrigerator lay beside a hole in the earth.

"Underground, if you please."

It seemed like a good idea to do as she said. Usak was the only one who had trouble folding himself to fit in the aperture. It was a problem Linnaeth solved, he later explained, by placing a foot on each of the Taureg's broad shoulders and forcing him down like a cork in a bottle. I was only a few steps into the tunnel when I heard the granite slab slide back into place above us, sealing the entrance. Another noise followed this. It was someone dusting off his hands. Or, in this case, *her* hands.

"Who's down there?" Linnaeth called. "Who's first?"

"I am. Danny Ramirez."

"There's our first mistake. You, troll. Can you hear me?"

"I can."

"You have a name?" said the Seer.

"I am Truke tu-Kekh, a citizen-soldier of Nat-Alsedra; a tender of the northern quarries…"

"And a delver in the earth's deep places. Your kind are known to me, comrade. Long live the Council of Equals! Take Ramirez's place at the head of the line. He sounds unwell. You'll want to follow that third set of steps that leads off to the right, then bear to the left as you descend. And try not to lean forward. Take a tumble down here and it'll be a good long while before you come to a stop."

We hadn't gone far when more noises came echoing down the tunnel. From above us came muffled thumps and crashes, punctuated by subhuman shrieks. I heard the nasal whistle of Gowen's breathing. I heard the beads in Usak's hair rattling, and I heard the anxiety in Marshal Quin's voice. "Madam," he said, "is there any level ground here where we could turn and fight? A defensive position? I hate the thought of being taken from behind in this pit."

"Don't worry about our visitors, Marshal. None of them will find anything pleasant in these tunnels. Quite the contrary, I suspect. And they certainly won't find *us*."

Linnaeth's laugh was an eerie tremolo that seemed to be amplified by the granite walls. It was exactly the sort of sound I could have done without hearing in the confines of that subterranean maze. I felt myself starting to sway. Fortunately Truke tu-Kekh, whose customary ill humor had been melting away as we descended, turned to steady me.

"We trolls," he announced, "have a saying."

"Oh, screw your saying."

Someone chuckled in the darkness behind me.

———+———

Eventually I could see again. The walls of the tunnels were veined with a phosphorescent mineral that glowed a brighter green as we descended. Still I mouthed a silent thanksgiving when the stone steps ceased, the passageway flared, and we entered an enormous cavern. The chamber was the size of a football stadium, with a roof two hundred feet over our heads. Carved into the walls around us, and reaching as high as I could see, was a staggering array of terraces, stairways, turrets and bartizans. We were standing in the courtyard of an entire vertical city. Weak as I was, I gaped nevertheless at the sights above and around me. It was as if an elaborate palace had been turned inside out, so that all its finery faced in on itself, buried beneath countless tons of rock and dirt. The entire vault was lit by irregularly spaced torches, the most distant of them glittering on the far walls of the cave like winter stars. Sprays of amethyst and quartz rose above us, and dozens of huge stalactites, cobalt and coral and cherry-red, drooped overhead like strands of melting rock. From the tips of the stalactites dripped slow streams of fresh water that pooled in depressions in the cavern floor. A group of three deer stood at one of these pools. They raised their heads to study us, then resumed their drinking as if we were only a troublesome dream.

Usak and Gowen supported me as we walked a few yards further. The roof of the cave soared higher. "This will do," said Linnaeth, gesturing toward a jumble of straw pallets on a level section of the cavern floor. A hundred small candles placed in niches of the rock lit up the space. No stalactites here: the roof of the cavern was dark, but it glowed with a silver tint. In the distance we could see a tiny white crescent. The air between us and the glowing figure seemed to move. I shivered when I realized what we were standing under.

"Above you is the lake the black trolls called *Keela Inythedrat*," the old woman said. "The Eye of Ythedra. Purest water in the world, they say. Possibly the coldest as well."

Quin rocked his big head straight back on his neck.

"But—what keeps the water…up there?" he said. "As opposed to, you know, *down here?*"

Linnaeth regarded him blankly.

He chuckled. "Never mind. How's the fishing?"

"Awkward, from this angle. But I assure you there's nothing to worry about. The lake has promised to stay where it is. Lay down your packs. I've got food enough for a whole tribe of Tauregs. You. Ramirez. And you with the elbow—your name? Gryel? Blessings to you, friend. And anyone else who's injured or sick—I want you right here."

For once there was no argument among our unruly group. We unbuckled our sword belts and eased ourselves onto the pallets. After she retrieved several lengths of wood from a cord stacked between two rock outcroppings, Linnaeth kindled a fire. Not with her hands or anything. This time she used straw and a candle. We gave her plenty of room.

Her disciples arrived without a word. Though they were women of various sizes, shapes, and skin colors, it was nevertheless difficult to tell them apart. They had close-cropped hair and nails. Each wore a loose green gown and, suspended from a leather necklace, a circular silver pendant. *Just like the pendant Dzerdjik wore*, I reminded myself, recalling the servant of Inniskerr who had helped Gowen and me escape the massacre at Kaer Rhennet. A woman with hazel eyes and chapped lips knelt beside me to look at my wound. The others bowed to Linnaeth, then laid out a meal. There were loaves of dark bread and bowls full of honey. There was butter and jam, a white cheese shaped like a land mine, bushels of apples and figs and several jugs of a milky thick cider. Gowen grabbed the largest loaf of bread and ripped it in half, like a telephone book. Usak helped himself to a fistful of blackberries. This left only a few. He had a big fist.

Only Truke tu-Kekh seemed disappointed.

"What's the matter, troll?" said Linnaeth. "Not enough nightshade? Sisters, see if you can dig up an eggplant or two for our friend. I'm afraid we're fresh out of skinks. Ramirez, I'm surprised you made it. It looks like your eyes are about to fall out of your head. Our physician reckons we have less than twelve hours to control your infection. She's mixing a poultice. In the meantime—"

"A *what*?"

"A poultice. Medicine. In the meantime, you should eat as much as you can and drink more than you want. Of the water, that is. Stay away from the cider. That goes for you too, young Taureg. Your kind have a weakness for this stuff. I'd rather not have to strap you to a rock, but I'll do it if I have to."

Usak frowned as he pulled back his cup.

I was more persistent. "Immune system's not used to your Ythedran bacteria, I guess. Still trying to get adjusted. If I could just get a swallow or two of that, uh...the alcohol might actually help."

"One cup," said Linnaeth. "And only because you look like you died a week ago. I told you to eat. Not to simper."

Linnaeth's assistant returned and applied a reddish paste to my wound. It smelled like boiled cabbage. As she wrapped a strip of cloth around my midsection to hold the dressing in place, Quin told the story of our journey. The Marshal rubbed a hand over the muscles of his jaw as he described the ambush of his column on the South Downs. Once again he shouldered all blame for the disaster. Once inside the Big Thicket, he and his band of survivors worked their way south, hoping to make it to Kaer Rhennet. They met up instead with Dzerdjik, who advised travel to Inniskerr and consultation with the Seer. But it hadn't been easy. Quin analyzed the Syrtian pursuit. He talked about our fight with the dogs and thanked God for the Taureg intervention, faltering only in his depiction of the deaths of Prince Mikel and the Outriders who fell beside him. He described our trek through the Griffin's Teeth and the race to Inniskerr.

But Linnaeth had grown somber at mention of the Syrtian dogs. Long after the Marshal finished his story, the Seer stared off into the middle distance. The candles around us guttered and died. Old Gryel fell asleep. Occasionally a drop of cold liquid would land on somebody's shoulder, or head, and we'd glance up at the body of water suspended above us. The moon had disappeared. Still Linnaeth meditated, as if she could conjure up for herself visions of all we'd told her, of the evil spreading like a flood-swollen river across the land. I may have nodded off at this point. The fever was back. I felt myself falling, though I was already seated.

The old woman startled me when she stood. It was clear our audience was over.

"Rest," she said, as she turned away from us. "Rest while you can. I have news to share with you after you've slept, and God knows you'll need your strength."

The End of Days

When Linnaeth returned, she held a candle an inch from my eyebrows. "Come," she whispered. "We need to talk." Talk. Yes.

Major understatement.

Despite my exhaustion, I was prepared to discuss at least one topic immediately—namely, the prospects of getting me the hell out of Ythedra. But Linnaeth was already walking. I wrapped a coarse blanket around myself and followed her, threading my way through the bodies lying around me. Gowen was snoring. The man could sleep anywhere. Truke tu-Kekh had wedged himself under a low shelf of rock and dozed facing outward, as if wary of attack. Marshal Quin and his men slept in two neat rows, but Ara lay face-up a few feet from the rest of the group. Her lips were slightly parted and she had one arm extended, as if to call out to a friend. As I padded around her I felt a brief but unmistakable desire to climb under her blankets and press myself against her narrow back. To whisper her name. To be someone again. But the Seer kept walking. She led me to a set of uneven steps carved into the face of a bus-sized boulder. I climbed the steps behind her and found myself standing in a shallow depression atop the rock.

Three more candles burned here, and the cool air smelled of cinnamon and sandalwood. I found a sentinel, too. He bared his teeth when I appeared.

Linnaeth spoke to the dog as if he were a child. She stroked the ruff of fur at his throat and soon the creature lowered itself onto the granite, though his eyes remained fixed on my face.

"How long have I been sleeping?" I asked. The words came out as a croak.

The woman eased herself down into a sitting position. She beckoned me to join her.

"Two days," she answered. "You're still dehydrated and more or less beat up, but our poultice seems to have stopped the spread of the infection. I think you'll be fine. Maybe better off, in fact. The Marshal says you've lost some weight."

"Most of that was my sanity."

Linnaeth smiled. "That may help. I have a letter for you. Maybe we should start with that."

"Looks old," I said.

"A few months by your time. Decades by ours."

I opened the envelope and pulled out a wrinkled sheet of Red Chief notebook paper. Brown crayon is tough to read by candlelight. As best I could decipher, the letter said:

Ramirez—
End of days approaching fast but if you're reading this you're as safe as anyone can be. Trust Linnaeth and take a hint if she drops one. STAY PUT. Nothing personal dirt bag but Earth breathes better without you.
Edward
P.S. Steer clear of Naztali women, they kick like mules.

Linnaeth plucked the note from my hand and carefully refolded it. "I know who you are, Ramirez. I know of your chronicles of this land. And I'm prepared to return you to your home."

"My home," I echoed. "I'm glad you mentioned that. My home is New York City. On Earth, that gruesome little galactic wart this letter wants me to stay away from. I don't mean to sound ungrateful, Lin—Sorceress…whoever you are."

"I've been called many things. Goddess. Angel. Crazy bitch. You will find it difficult to offend me."

"Thank you. I think—"

"Though not impossible."

"Got it. I think I'll call you *ma'am*, for now. I just wish someone would tell me what the hell's going on. Put yourself in my place, right? I'm minding my own business, boozing myself into oblivion, when reality as I know it opens its raincoat and starts shaking its private parts in my face. It gets worse. A dwarf stuffs me into a washing machine and hits the STUPEFY cycle and I wake up some place that claims to be Ythedra and promptly stumble into the path of a Syrtian army that's trying to stick a sword through my head. Among others. So I humor myself. I run. I sleep. I get eaten by dogs. My side's feeling better. It's my mind that's like, slamming itself against walls. And what's this *end of days* stuff? One minute my *chingon* guardian dwarf sends me to an alternate reality half a universe away and tells me not to bother calling home and the next you say you're gonna send me back? Like, *Hey, Bon Voyage, next stop Manhattan?* I'm sorry. I know I'm a little out of control here, but…I mean, *come on.* This has all been pretty damn weird."

Linnaeth gestured behind her toward a tear-shaped gap in the wall of the cavern. It was one of a dozen hollows that pockmarked this section of the cave. A crude rope bridge connected the rock we sat on with the aperture.

"The passage to Earth," she said, "is just beyond this bridge."

"Nice. Rope bridge. Earth. Seems simple enough. Forgive me for not just, you know, *exiting Ythedra via rope bridge.* But believe it or not, I've got a few questions. Number one: How could you possibly know who I am?"

The Seer drew a deep breath and gazed into my eyes. I wondered if she was trying to find something in there resembling a soul. I was tempted to tell her not to bother. The Seer of Inniskerr was a small woman, maybe five foot four, with a longish hooked nose and whorls of fine white hair at her temples. She walked with a studied infirmity that came and went depending primarily on her mood; she could dart like a fish when she needed to. Old age suited her. She liked it. She practiced it. She improvised in its clawlike grasp. Her eyebrows were full and set low on her brow, giving her an intense, almost disapproving look that only lasted until the next time she laughed. Then she pursed her thin lips and her blue eyes sparkled with interior light and you felt like doing a handstand to keep her amused. Her stature was the smallest thing about her. Her smile was a sudden summer. She was her very own atmospheric disturbance.

"Tell me," she said. "Why do you think you're able to talk to your companions?"

I had to think about this one. "The Common Tongue. Good question. I mean, I've been aware I was using it since I woke up in the dungeon at Kaer Rhennet. Or sort of using it. There are a lot of concepts that just can't be expressed in anything but English. *Oxycontin*, for example. *Car bomb. Methamphetamine.* But I didn't think to ask why I could speak the Tongue at all. It just seemed to happen, like everything else in my life these days."

"As you said: *weird.*"

"Yes and no. Where I come from, we've been aware of the possibility of other worlds—of *parallel universes*—for a long time. Our holy people have always said things like, 'My father's house has many rooms.' Physicists talk about it in terms of *multiverses* and *Hubble volumes*, terms that sound impressive until you drill down and find out they're just as vague as anything the theologians are saying. They wonder if folds in the fabric of space might allow for instantaneous travel between two points otherwise separated by these incomprehensibly huge gulfs of time and distance. In fact *wormholes* are pretty much a stock in trade for folks in my line of work: post-pubescent omnipotence fantasies with generous helpings of feminine flesh and exotic weaponry. I'm just not sure how I could 'remember' something I never knew in the first place. The Common Tongue, for example."

Linnaeth nodded. "I know you think of yourself as Ythedra's creator. Your friend Edward told me that the one time he was here. Does that surprise you? That Edward was here? Maybe it would surprise you more to learn that Edward is an angel. One of the First-Created. You left Earth a little over a week ago. You entered this world near Kaer Rhennet and were found by one of Bryd Drennen's people. These are troubled times. Word spread quickly about the strange man who'd turned up in a pasture, wearing outlandish clothing and mumbling words no one could decipher."

"That would be *English*."

"*Enklish*," she repeated. "They threw you in jail. One of my scouts heard the rumors. He knew I was expecting you. Bald head. Dragon tattoo on one arm."

"So he tried to kidnap me."

"Yes. Well. He's a gifted man, Dzerdjik, and a devoted disciple. But his methods aren't terribly subtle. At any rate, I suppose I should tell you Nihreth Wyn was also a disciple of mine many centuries ago, when that most blessed of mortals wandered Ythedra. You remember Nihreth Wyn? Ban Lohannon went looking for him after he'd returned to Ythedra from the dungeons of Kaer Rhygat. Unfortunately, there wasn't much to be done for Mr. Lohannon. The poor man was a wreck. And after he helped Ban Lohannon end his existence here in this world, Nihreth Wyn traveled west. Here, to Inniskerr, where he told me goodbye. Nihreth died of his own will, Ramirez. He was poisoned by the same darkness Ban Lohannon carried inside. I could have kept him longer. I had kept him for many centuries already. But my desire started me on the path to what you see today, and I think he grew ashamed of that as well."

I stared up at the shimmering ceiling of the cavern, trying to remember the legend. "There was a story about Nihreth Wyn," I said. "Even in Ban Lohannon's day it was an old story. Most called it a myth. Something about a storm goddess who fell in love with a man and traded her immortality to keep him alive."

Linnaeth glanced down at her hands. "Fell in love with a man. Achingly, stupidly, uncontrollably. But even with all I could give him, Nihreth grew tired of the world. The best always do. Only the worst continue to want it. The worst they call Aln Adrackt, after dim and half-remembered stories of the dark lord who came from the east and harrowed Ythedra in the Years of Iron. But even those stories are inadequate. Because what walks in Ythedra now is a demon of infinitely greater power and malice, though he may indeed have taken the form of Aln Adrackt."

"So tell 'em. Tell *me*. What's happening? And why?"

Linnaeth paused. As she ruminated, I studied her features. Through the curtain of her silver hair I glimpsed patches of pink scalp, and green veins in her temples that looked like sluggish rivers on a tropical map. Her eyes were the purest blue I'd ever seen.

"Think of it this way," she said. "When spirit is strong, it invades matter. It makes meat into men. Summons souls from the sewers. But when spirit is weak, matter imprisons imagination. Just as it has yours. The Enemy has captured your children, Ramirez. Your monsters. And he's making them real."

"Laser," I mused aloud, remembering my last night on Earth. The cyborg's attempt on my life. The battle at Belvedere Castle. "He sure seemed real. But why would they be after *me*?"

"Your creations want you dead because you still exercise a degree of control over them. By killing—or, as Edward put it, 'crossing'— you, they take the last step toward *being*. Unfortunately, it's not just your creations. Soon there will be war on every mountain in the mind of God. Every evil thing has joined to fight what remains of good. Demon against angel. Villain versus hero. Satan fighting the Giver of Life."

"But *why*? Why is evil rising now?"

"Because it can. The balance of thought and deed has shifted. People in your world have finally accepted, as people have here, that all the ordering mysteries, the creeds and faiths, are just sto- ries. They don't realize there's no such thing as *just stories*. Stories of good *are* good: create good. Just as stories of evil—of violence, chaos and betrayal—beget evil." For the first time I noticed the iri- descence of Linnaeth's white robe. It shimmered peach and plum in the flickering candlelight. "Despite his powers, the thing we call Aln Adrackt is only a follower of the Common Enemy. He feels the call. He senses the gathering on Earth, and he aches to join it. But you're the fly in the ointment. Because once you leave, I'll destroy the portal. He'll be trapped in Ythedra forever."

I chewed on a thumbnail. "But why was I sent here in the first place? I mean, if my coming here means Aln Adrackt can escape?"

"Good question. Maybe you're the traveler of worlds."

"The traveler of worlds?"

"It's a prophecy," she said.

"Yours?"

"Hardly. I lack the gift."

"I thought you were the Seer."

"I can see the present pretty well. I can see the past just about perfect. I'm not so good at the future. The *traveler of worlds* was foreseen many years ago by one of my...I won't call her a *disciple*, because that would imply she actually listened to me on occasion... one of my *guests*, we'll say. She dreamt that the evil of Emerkest would rise again. Ivizele was just a girl when she was brought to us. Seven years old, and even then it seemed as if her abilities were starting to fade, although she was helpful with the weather, now that I think about it. At any rate, she left us at the age of fifteen to marry a halfwit baker's apprentice she met on a visit to Dred Thannat. Spent her life making muffins and raising six children— happily enough, she claimed—and we didn't hear from her for many years. Finally, very late one night, her eldest son brought us a parchment with a few lines of verse written on it in some sort of handmade ink. Blueberry, maybe. Our little prophet was dead. It was the wasting disease. Seaside towns are subject to that sort of thing, you know. You end up coughing your lungs straight out of your mouth. But Ivizele had written down her last visions for the free peoples to ponder, and we have dutifully done so for the last forty years. Unfortunately, we're not the only ones. Word of her prophecies has spread through the Ninelands."

"Well?"

Linnaeth's eyes returned to mine. "Well what?"

"What did she say?" I persisted.

"Ah. The part that concerns you went like this: *Within your lives the sky grows dark. Ythedra again will learn to pray. The storm will tear tall towers down. The Dark One comes but not to stay. Tomorrow soon will be unfurled by he who travels between worlds.*"

"As in, travels between my world and this one?"

Linnaeth shrugged. I took a deep breath, let it out.

"Here's a stumper for you," I said. "What if I don't want to leave Ythedra?"

Her smile vanished. "Don't be an idiot."

"How is that idiotic? If what you say is true, Earth is on the brink of apocalypse. My foster parents were hardshell Baptists. From *Texas*. Believe me, I know what the end of the world is going to look like. The angels who were cast out of heaven at the beginning of time are going to rise up from Hell to fight God's armies. The oceans will turn to blood. Stars will go dark and people will die by the billions, like insects. The Bible says the good guys are gonna win, but I've always wondered if that particular ending was tacked on for recruiting purposes. And don't forget, there's already a bunch of very unpleasant comic book characters back home who may or may not be real and who may or may not be in league with the forces of evil but who definitely want me dead. And that's assuming I'm actually still sane. I mean, the alternative is that I'm a crackhead who stepped in front of a bus and suffered major closed-head trauma and I'm dreaming all this. Or that I just went plain ol' paint-licking crazy and as soon as I leave here I'm going to spend the rest of my life sucking thorazine lozenges and supplying some grad student in clinical psychiatry a whole lot of copy for a very strange dissertation. Living on the Upper West Side is aggravating enough as it is. Why would I want to go back?"

"Same reason you wanted to leave Ythedra in the first place," said Linnaeth.

"You're going to have to explain that one to me."

"Have you ever wondered how you came to dream this land? To know its peoples and places so well?"

"Imagination, I guess. That's how I make my living. I'm—"

"Not imagination."

I shook my head. "What are you saying?"

Linnaeth gave me a wan smile. "Think. I'm saying you've been here before. I'm saying you know this place's history and legends and language so well because Ythedra is your home. I'm saying your name…"

I stopped her with an open palm.

"My name," I said.

Her eyebrows rose like trade show curtains.

A whisper was all I could manage. "My name is Ban Lohannon."

My Heart Is a Cartoon Bullet

Linnaeth picked up a candle and held it in front of her as she led me off the rock onto a narrow ledge. We padded along the ledge for a few yards, then entered a cave and started up a flight of stairs carved into the stone.

"You suspected it," she said.

"Not until just now. You know. When we seemed to think it at the same time. I remember growing up with the feeling that I didn't belong where I was. I mean, from the time I was five years old. Feeling I was like, *alien*, in a sense I could never quite figure out. But show me a kid who's never felt *that* way, right? Especially a kid who wants to draw comic books. Eventually I stopped questioning it."

"The feelings were real. Centuries ago, you wandered into the dungeons of Aln Adrackt. He kept you alive. He made you *his* in that world beneath Kaer Rhygat. The stories say you killed him, finally. But he never really let you go. And to save you, Nyhreth Wyn sent your soul far from this world. Sent you very far indeed."

"Not far enough, evidently."

"True," said the Seer. "Edward and the others transferred you here without knowing what—without knowing *who*—you would face. But I'm prepared to set things right. Nihreth sent you away once. I will honor his promise. I'll return you to your home."

"That's big of you."

Linnaeth whirled to face me. "Don't mock me. As Ban Lohannon, you did much to help Ythedra in a time of need. Nihreth was grateful to you, and the debts of my friend are my debts as well. But you must go soon. As long as the portal stays open, Aln Adrackt has an open road to Earth, where he can join the final battle. Is that what you want?"

"I don't know," I admitted. "Why can't I stay here and help stop Aln Adrackt before he gets the *chance* to travel to Earth? That would be the best thing, wouldn't it? Rallying the Naztali tribes? And the armies of Sidhara?"

"She's beautiful," said Linnaeth. She tilted her head, as if to allow me a chance to confess, and though my heart ricocheted around in my chest like a cartoon bullet I remained quiet. "I've talked to Ara several times. Each time I've been impressed by her intelligence and courage. But I've also seen that she loves someone else. The Darannan lieutenant. Her eyes practically shout it."

"I don't know what you're talking about."

"You know exactly what I'm talking about. This isn't the time for schoolboy infatuations, Ramirez. Every minute you're here, you add to the menace. Go back to where you came from. Fight there, on earth, where a world still hangs in the balance."

Linnaeth was walking again.

I shook my head, struggling to stifle my annoyance. "But what if I really *am* the traveler of worlds? The hero foretold in the prophecy. I mean, who else could that be?"

A laugh, this time. Not a cruel laugh, but a laugh just the same. "It's a valiant thought. And frankly it isn't one I expected to hear from you. But it's clear you were damaged by your contact with Aln Adrackt far beyond what I expected. Even through all the years and distance, his touch has been heavy on you. You're in no condition to help anyone."

"Maybe I haven't had the chance."

"Tell me this. Whose side are you on, Ramirez?"

"My side, I guess."

"*Your side.* Did you explain that to Ara before she killed the dog that attacked you? Or to Usak, before he left his people to lead you here? To Quin, who wouldn't leave you behind? You were hallucinating for a good part of the journey to Inniskerr, so you can't be expected to know. But there's been talk among your companions already that you might be the traveler of worlds. Not everyone agrees. Two of your company have told me that the last time you lost consciousness on your way here, the Naztali advised Quin to slit your throat and leave you for the urzeks. The Marshal refused. For a man who claims to be on his own side, you seem to have had a lot of help so far."

What could I say? She was right. Without my companions, I'd have been dead several times over. As we walked, I ran a hand through my week-and-a-half's-worth of beard. We passed a series of candle-lit chambers that had been carved from the rock. In one of them I saw three women kneeling on the floor, eyes closed, apparently meditating. In another, two men were watering hundreds of small plants. A middle-aged woman with close-cropped red hair passed us. She saluted Linnaeth by touching her middle fingers to her forehead, lips, and chest.

"Are things really that desperate?" I asked.

"I'd say impossible. Aln Adrackt is too strong for anyone to stop."

"But there has to be something we can do. Uniting the free peoples, like An-Nashayel did before. Refusing to quit. And finding the Ganthans. Though some of the Outriders don't seem to believe the Ganthans even exist anymore."

"I've heard that too," said Linnaeth. "But they're wrong. It's not that the Ganthans don't *exist*. It's just that they're not the same people they once were. They've been fighting each other so long that they may have lost the ability to use the Seven Swords. I'm not sure I believe in them in that sense either. Do you?"

I surprised myself with my certainty. "Of course I do. I know what they did to end the Years of Iron. If I *am* Ban Lohannon, if *part* of me is, then I made the Battle of the Standing Stones possible. I was the one who alerted An-Nashayel to the armies waiting for him in Emerkest and kept him from crossing the Strait of Sorrows. Instead he waited for the sorcerer to invade Ythedra, and when he did, the Ganthans came carrying the Swords before them. They fell like a landslide on the sorcerer's legions. Those swords can't be destroyed. I don't know how it could be true—I mean, I've seen some strange things, but I'm still not sure I believe in magic, and there's nothing more magical than enchanted iron mongery. But I know it happened. They're difficult to rouse, and they require strength to hold, but—"

"But nothing," said Linnaeth. She stepped out onto a shelf of rock where we could look back down at the floor of the cavern. She lifted her chin, and a thousand torches flared to life around us. Her right hand strayed to the circular silver pendant she wore around her neck. "You're right. Nihreth Wyn added something powerful to those blades. It was foolish of him—of us—to do it, but you know the story. We mixed the metal of the Seven Swords with my blood. The blood of a goddess. An angel. If they still have the swords, the Ganthans are dangerous, and Aln Adrackt knows it. That's why I sent Dzerdjik to warn them. And then there's the prophecy. *The traveler of worlds.*" She smiled to herself. "I despise prophecies. They never mean what you think they mean. Do you want to be a hero, Ramirez? Do you believe in yourself enough for that? Do you believe in what we're fighting for?"

"I don't know."

"Then we're off to a peculiar start. And you understand, I hope, that even if you defeat Aln Adrackt's armies, it's not the same as beating him."

"What if you helped us?" I asked.

"Good God. I *am* helping you. But it makes no difference. Aln Adrackt is no longer a sorcerer. He's merely the vessel for something worse—a demon that has taken his physical seeming for a purpose I cannot yet divine. If we meet, he may destroy me. It may be his hour. And the strangest thing is, I'm not sorry. I've been here a long time. I've seen my worshippers in every corner of the Ninelands flourish and die, gather again, lose the spark that shone from their eyes. I've seen the gray-gowned Rufayans wandering the Sacred Mountains like mournful ghosts. I've watched the Mevlevi dervishes of the Tower of Winds make their bent-kneed prayer rounds in the rain. I remember the face-painted Liaps of Souli and their three-legged queen, dauntless in the face of the Black Horde of Domjuk. I can still hear the harmonies of the Pomaks of the Rhodopian Plateau. How they perfumed the air with their hymns! And how frequently I walked unseen among them! I've borne witness to the ceaseless circus of humankind: to rises and ruins and suns and moons and songs that died in the darkness. I have looked upon God's children and loved them all through ages past numbering and their own slow decline and death, and I'm tired. My bones are turning to stone. My songs are the lamentations of buzzards. But if your heart is here, Ramirez, I'll guard the passage for as long as I can. I'll only destroy it if there's no other choice. So go east. Find the descendants of King An's Palace Guard. Bring the Swords. And the Emerald may shine another day."

"And if I screw it up?"

Linnaeth exhaled lightly. I couldn't tell if what came next was a laugh or a strangled sob. She lifted her right hand and traced a circle around the cavern. As her hand moved, every light in the vast chamber winked out, and we stood again in darkness.

Into the East

"Some of us," Linnaeth declared, aiming her eyebrows at me, "have been awake since early this morning, discussing what the Marshal calls *tactics*. We've come up with a plan."

We were seated around the little fire ring, which held nothing now but a layer of ash. Above us the lake bottom glinted like blue steel. Women in green gowns moved wordlessly among the rock outcroppings, laying out clothing and provisions in neat little bundles. It looked like someone was getting ready to leave. It made sense. Atryen Quin's limp was gone. Old Gryel had a fresh sling and a poultice for his broken elbow. Gowen had rinsed the caked blood out of his hair, and Izgir had been given a fresh tunic to replace the one he'd lost to the dogs. Even Truke tu-Kekh seemed rejuvenated. I would be sorry to see them go.

The Seer's gaze swiveled toward Usak. "It's been my experience that not all the Tauregs require fourteen hours of sleep. In general they are an industrious people, masters of woodcraft and waterway alike. They have lately supplied my disciples and me with several excellent birch-bark canoes. Using two of these boats, Quin and his men can travel down the Falling River to Speckled Bay. It's less than a two-day trip when the creeks are running, as they are now, and Dred Thannat is an easy hike from there. I don't need to remind you that with Kaer Rhennet destroyed, Dred Thannat is the last fortified outpost of Daranna. It's an ancient place, not as well kept in these latter days as it should have been. But it has ribs of granite, and it must be held."

Quin sat up a little straighter. "It will be held. The question is only for *how long*. Ramirez, when I reach the fortress, I'll send men and horses to meet you at the ruins of Glen Kiernan."

"Glen Kiernan?" I said, glancing up from a slab of brown bread.

The Marshal scowled. "The Seer said you were going to try to get the Ganthans to join us in our fight against Aln Adrackt. I confess I have no idea what makes you think you can find the Ganthans, or even why you'd want to, since we know your friend Dzerdjik is already on the same mission. But Linnaeth agreed with the plan. She's going to supply you with rations, blankets—the lot. And you've got volunteers"—he nodded at the rest of the group—"so you start today. Like I said, I'll send horses."

I tried to stay calm. It was one thing to dream up a comic book's worth of heroic bullshit. I could do it with my eyes shut. This sudden insistence on reality had me spooked.

"I'm afraid you've got the wrong idea," I said. "My talk with Linnaeth was purely hypothetical. You know: *Could. Would.* Possibly *should.* Not necessarily *can* or *will*. I'm not saying I hate the idea. Theoretically, it makes good sense. But as I think you mentioned, I have no concept of how to find the Ganthans, or even how to get to Fereganth, which—"

"Which is Izgir's job," said Quin. "The fastest way to Fereganth is through the Greensea. He'll guide you."

"Provided you can find your way out of the Thicket," said Linnaeth. "That happens to be Usak's assignment. You can start as soon as you finish breakfast. The journey to Fereganth will be dangerous. You'll have to cross lands that are now within view of the enemy. You'll circle around the Silent Marsh, of course, but the Copper Mountains are almost as inhospitable, and the Ganthans do not welcome strangers. It's true Dzerdjik is on a similar mission. I'm counting on him to help you when you arrive. But remember:

he went with a warning. You go with a plea. Dzerdjik could only talk about the alliance of the free peoples. You—all of you—can *demonstrate* it. Ythedra needs the Seven Swords. It's up to you to get them."

The old woman's eyes seemed to hold me in place. There was no use trying to get out of it. I realized I was going.

"Meanwhile," she continued, "my disciples send unhappy news. Aln Adrackt and his army are on the move. Last reports put them two days south of the Step, moving north. Kaer Rhennet is now a Syrtian barracks. The villages in the highlands east of the castle have been razed, and their inhabitants enslaved."

"You're certain of this?" said Quin.

"I hear what I hear."

Though the Marshal said nothing in response, the glance he exchanged with his men spoke volumes. Seeing Quin's disappointment, Linnaeth turned her attention to the Sidharan princess.

"And child…"

"I'm not a child."

"Of course not," said the Seer. "Forgive me. Trouble has come to your homeland as well. Your father is fighting rebels in the capital province. Rebels funded and controlled by Emerkest. He fights successfully, by all accounts. But he has few men to send you."

Ara started to protest, but something about the woman's words convinced her. "Then he'll send what he can."

"He's in considerable danger, Princess."

"As are we all."

Linnaeth touched Ara's slender wrist. "Perhaps you're right," she said.

But Ara turned away, and in the candlelight I saw silver streak her cheeks. I wanted to shelter her beneath my buzzard wings. Bury her enemies. Lick up her tears. All I could do was watch.

Maybe she was trying to distract us from our grieving comrade. At any rate, Linnaeth spoke briskly.

"You'll start," she said, "by following me through the tunnels under these mountains. When we surface, we'll be close to one of the little creeks that feed the Falling River. That's where we'll say goodbye to Marshal Quin and his men. Not far from their departure point is the head of a trail leading into the Thicket. Usak will guide you from there—and guide you with a happy heart, I suspect, for no Taureg is altogether comfortable underground. Autumn has arrived. The nights will be cold, but these capes and blankets should help. Be sparing with the food we've packed for you. Once you leave the Thicket, you're not going to have time to hunt or forage. In four days' time you'll meet up with a group of Marshal Quin's Outriders at Glen Kiernan. They'll bring horses. After that you'll be on your own, and with any luck the next face to take an interest in yours will belong to a Ganthan war wolf."

"Some luck," said Gowen.

The Seer took a deep breath and let it out slowly. Her blue eyes gleamed.

"A word about our enemy," she said. Now her voice was like distant rain. We leaned forward to take it in. "If you still harbor doubts that he exists, dismiss them. He is real, and he is powerful, and he will take your lives and souls if you give him the chance. Aln Adrackt is no longer a man, though we call him such. His mortal form is occupied by something that for ages past has roamed the cold places of hell, seeking to return to the realm of light. This *thing* is a creature of terrifying appearances, noontime nightmares and spinning rooms. He's a mind-poisoner, and working through his proxies and familiars he has caused more death and suffering on this planet than any disease or disaster. It's just the opposite of what we seek in Inniskerr. The men and women who live with me here don't want to cloud anyone's minds. We want to change the world. We want to grow it. To *shape* it. I have a gift. I can gather forces from the earth and the air and they will dance for me. But mine is not the only gift here. Nor is it, in normal times, the most valuable. Among my disciples are healers, and cultivators, and makers of intricate devices. I've sent most of them away. I've dispatched them from this place like a child blows the seeds from a dandelion. I hope that out there, in quiet corners of the Ninelands, maybe even in corners of Emerkest itself, our shared knowledge will take root and grow—even if it takes another hundred centuries for this world to shake off the ugliness that grips it now. Even if no bright angel stoops from the mountaintops to catch the tears of those who grieve."

Gowen made as if to stand. Linnaeth raised a finger to stop him. She gazed around the circle at each of us in turn, from Izgir on her left to Quin on her right.

"One warning," she said. "You'll need to watch Ramirez. He is of special interest to our enemy, and the demon will certainly visit his dreams. Keep him in sight. Don't let him lead you from your course. He will suffer greatly, in ways that may not be apparent. But he suffered before, many years ago, and the tendons of his heart were tough enough to keep him whole. Perhaps they will be so again. My friends, be kind to each other. Share yourselves. Speak no evil thing."

<hr />

We climbed for hours. Sometimes we had to duck, or crouch, and we crawled through the tightest spaces but we never stopped making our way upward. Twice I felt my ears pop. Once I had to ask my companions to stop so I could catch my breath. But this was only for a moment. I knew I was stronger—stronger not only because my fever was gone but also because my body had purged itself of its crippling chemical debt load. It was entirely possible my liver was functioning again. My muscles were reintroducing themselves to each other, shaking hands over fences, entering into various sorts of cooperative treaties. I couldn't help feeling encouraged. Once I even had the pleasure of catching Izgir when he slipped backwards on a spill of gravel.

"Steady," I said.

He shook off my hand.

<hr />

When we finally emerged from the flank of a windswept mountain it was mid-afternoon, overcast and cool. We stood above the tree line, but other peaks of the Griffin's Teeth rose around us like sentinels, snagging stray clouds. Thirty minutes' descent down a set of rocky switchbacks brought us to stands of spruce and aspen and a giggling spring at the head of a narrow valley. Two canoes lay upside down beneath the trees.

"The water deepens," Linnaeth instructed Quin, "just a few hundred yards downstream. I could put in here and float just fine, but grown men are considerably more ballast than a bag of sticks, so I suggest you portage the boats down beyond that bell-shaped rock. See it? Another creek meets this one just beyond, and a third not far below. You'll be fine from that point on. The snowmelt is long gone, but we've had rain. You'll hit the Falling River by nightfall. It runs all the way to Speckled Bay. Enjoy the trip. There's work to be done at Dred Thannat, and I suspect you'll have your share of it. Understand?"

Quin managed to work up a rueful chuckle. "I'm used to taking my orders from someone with a deeper voice. But yes. I understand, and I'll obey. God bless you, lady. And to the rest of you: Safe journey. We'll meet again at Dred Thannat." He put a big hand on Gowen's shoulder. "Bring a friend," he added.

Quin and his Outriders slung their packs and swords over their shoulders, hoisted the boats between them and began picking their way down the near bank of the stream toward deeper water. The gray-eyed sergeant, Teg, was the only one who looked back. Ara waved. I knew why she was watching, but I wasn't worried. Lieutenant Ayrd Teryan was walking out of my life. Ara would be my constant study.

By the time I turned around, Linnaeth was sixty yards up the trail we'd followed down the mountainside.

"The Thicket," said Usak, starting in the opposite direction, "is this way."

Still I held back.

"Linnaeth!" I called.

The Seer turned. When she saw me, she bent and picked up a stone the size of a softball. She flung it out over the ravine with a swift backhand motion. As I watched, the stone turned into a dove, and fluttered off into the trees.

The voice came to me as if she was standing three feet away.

"Believe, Ramirez!"

"Believe in God?" I shouted. "The God of car wrecks and cholera? The God who killed Rachel Chen? And let me make the mistake of leaving her?"

"That's right! The God of tapeworms and pine forests! There is good and there is evil and they do not continue always in balance. One is not the pre-ordained successor to the other. To uphold good requires your belief in its importance."

"Belief in *what's* importance?"

"Creation. Life. Reverence. Awe."

"You sound like a faith healer."

"Your faith could use some healing," the Seer said. She looked like a moth against the massive backdrop of brown rock and gray sky.

Now I was whispering. It didn't matter. She heard me just the same.

"I don't go to Sunday school anymore, if that's what you mean."

"No, and you no longer draw, or paint, or dream. You drink, according to Edward. You swallow pills to help you sleep and you choose your female companions according to price."

"Never pay retail, right?"

"I know you hurt," said Linnaeth. "But remember, Ban Lohannon found something to keep him whole in the cellars of Kaer Rhygat. Even in the darkest nights he found something that fed him, kept him hoping, kept him alive. I pray you find such sustenance."

"I'm scared," I admitted.

"You should be. Stay close to your companions. I've watched them and found them strong. Lean on them."

"I will."

"And open yourself."

"Wait for me! I'm coming back!"

"I will pray," she whispered, "that you do."

The Seer of Inniskerr resumed her climb up the narrow path. I turned to join the group. I thought I'd have to hustle to catch up, but they had barely moved.

"Sorry about the yelling," I said to Gowen.

"What yelling?"

"Back there. When I was talking to Linnaeth."

The big man waved his hand as if he was warding off gnats. "Knock it off, Ramirez. You didn't say a word."

2 2

Glen Kiernan

The northern reaches of the Big Thicket were easier to get through than the boggy lowlands to the south. Here the trees were mostly spruce and lodge pole pine, salted with stands of aspen and silver birch. Even the slightest breeze tickled tin chimes the Tauregs had hung high in the timber, so that at times it seemed as if the forest was singing. Rabbit, squirrel, and deer abounded, and the rapping of woodpeckers provided counterpoint to the bright tones of the chimes.

We sipped cold water from springs Usak could have located in his sleep, and we rested each evening on beds of pine needles. It was obvious the Taureg loved this country. He woke up grinning. Though the leaves of the aspens were yellowing on their stalks, and in the mornings our breath steamed around our heads, it was a heartening time. It was a time to enjoy the measured tramp of our footsteps, a last chance to think about today instead of tomorrow and the dark things that waited for us there. Izgir followed close on the heels of the Taureg, listening intently to the lessons Usak dispensed on reading the runes of the forest: how to find game and where to look for water and what the thrushes said when they scolded each other. Occasionally the two of them would disappear into the woods, returning in an hour or so with a few choice pieces of fat pine. They'd hand the aromatic slivers of wood to one of us with instructions to add it to our pack so we'd have fuel for fire during our travels in the Greensea.

Gowen and Truke tu-Kekh also gravitated together. Truke talked; Gowen listened. They both liked to stop occasionally to bash the branches off a tree trunk with Gowen's club, so Ara and I were left to each other's company by default. We hadn't spoken since that chilly morning in the Griffin's Teeth—mostly, I hoped, because there hadn't been time. Now as we chatted again we approached each other with humility and small gifts of deference. We talked about our homes. We talked about how the woods had looked where we grew up, about the biggest storms we remembered and the way summer clouds turned themselves into pirate ships or dragons' heads to entertain daydreaming kids. When the conversation slowed, she asked me about Ythedra, and why the past had come back to devour the present. I didn't need much encouragement to tell her. In fact it was a relief to start the story, to re-live scenes I always thought I'd imagined but now felt myself reclaiming as something more intimate and infinitely more difficult.

And so I began. I told the story of the physician Aln Adrackt—of his devotion to the dark arts and his battle with Nihreth Wyn in a land two oceans away. I recounted the several marriages of King An of Dar-Annon, and listed the three sons born to him as a result. I explained how Aln Adrackt presented himself at the gates of the White Cities a decade and a half later, claiming he could heal the unfortunate Prince Varun. I told as best I could of the seduction of Varun and the long years of war that followed, of the victory and eventual decline of the Darannans in Ythedra and, finally, of the despair and self-destruction of Ban Lohannon, whose bizarre ramblings were believed by no one.

When I finished, I glanced up at my companions. We'd stopped walking just about the time in my story when Callan Dysrahi led the battered remnants of the Palace Guard out of Kaer Rhygat, headed for the Straits of Sorrow and Ythedra beyond the gray sea gate. Now the entire troop—Truke tu-Kekh and Usak, Izgir and

Gowen—stood or sat around Ara and me. Even the sparrows were quiet. It felt like the Thicket itself was listening.

"No one?" said Ara.

"No one what?"

"Believed him? The man who escaped from Kaer Rhygat?'

"Maybe his sisters. He had six. At least they said they believed him when they tried to comfort him. But Ban Lohannon was plagued for the rest of his life by dreams of his wanderings in Aln Adrackt's dungeons, and by visions of the creatures that crawled in the holes beneath Kaer Rhygat. He died young. By his own hand."

"By—?"

"He killed himself, Princess. In the presence of the wizard Nihreth Wyn, he begged for release from his guilt and fear. The wizard presented him with several vials of a solution of morphine. Lohannon waited till he was alone, then drank them all at once. He wrote a note to his sisters that said he'd found a way to free himself from the pain once and for all. But Ban Lohannon was wrong about a lot of things in his short and mostly unsuccessful life. And he was wrong about that too." I considered my audience again. "Or so they say."

We lingered for another ten minutes, each of us lost in our own thoughts. Gowen chewed a hunk of the hardtack we'd brought from Inniskerr. Usak rolled a leafy sprig of some local plant between his long fingers, then sniffed at the residue. Ara sat with her arms encircling her knees, her emerald green eyes affixed on some spot in the woods, or the past, or the world to come. There never was a more beautiful woman.

Finally Izgir made a show of adjusting his pack.

"Might as well," said Truke tu-Kekh.

So we gathered our belongings and resumed the journey. But as we moved through the forest, I couldn't help but notice something. Not that it *bothered* me. I'm just saying. No one said a single word, good or bad, in remembrance of Ban Lohannon.

Glen Kiernan was once a formidable stronghold, a vital link in the chain of Darannan outposts that ran from Kaer Rhennet to Dred Thannat. Now it was little more than a jumble of moss-covered limestone blocks on the eastern fringe of the Big Thicket. As we stumbled out of the woods, several Darannan cavalrymen emerged from the ruined outpost. I recognized their leader immediately. It was Ara's favorite, Ayrd Teryan, come back to haunt me. When he shucked his helmet, his blonde hair streamed out behind him in the breeze like some personal pennant. Ara did a quick about-face when she spotted him. She pushed one hand through her dirty hair, rubbed at her grimy cheeks.

Izgir was in no mood for pleasantries. "The horses," he said.

"Through here," Teryan responded, swallowing his grin. He should have known better than to expect kind words from the Naztali. The kid led us through a grove of beech trees into a scrubby clearing. The herd considered us with grave disdain. A half-dozen Darannan soldiers lounging in the shade glanced over at us with just about the same expression. But Izgir kept walking. He freed the hooves of the nearest horse from its hobbles. He sniffed the animal's sweaty spine, then smeared the sweat on his own face. Shedding the fatigue of our long days of slow travel, the Naztali leaped up on the startled mare, squeezed once with his heels and galloped the animal in a circle around us. The Naztali are a squat, unlovely people, but they ride like they were made for the purpose. Izgir's raven hair gleamed in the afternoon sun. His single scream echoed off the encircling trees.

"Show-off," grunted Gowen.

When the Naztali reined up only inches from Teryan, the younger man took a grudging step backward.

"What news, Lieutenant?" said Izgir.

Teryan steadied himself. "Two of my men returned from the south this morning. They spoke with some of those who flee Aln Adrackt's army. No man has seen a force like this before."

"Tell," said Ara.

Teryan exchanged a nervous glance with his second-in-command, a heavy-set sergeant who was missing two of his teeth. The sergeant nodded.

"Fifty thousand Syrtians," said the young lieutenant. "Along with an entire company of urzeks. Kirikites, with their humped beasts. Atarian riders. Piryat mobs. And spiders, no telling how many, in iron cages."

"How close?" Gowen asked. I hoped he wasn't as scared as he sounded.

"Several days from here. At least a week from Dred Thannat. But it's worse than that." The young officer peered southward, as if he could see all the way to the enemy's camp. "That dog handler we caught was telling the truth. Aln Adrackt himself moves with his army. I'd say we have no time to spare."

Izgir flicked a clot of mud from his horse's mane. "And I'd say you're right. Better get moving."

"Sir?" said Teryan.

"Saddle your horses and go. Get back to your commander."

Teryan's face turned red.

"I'm sorry, but…"

"Sorry? For what?"

"Marshal Quin has assumed command of Dred Thannat. The district's Council of Farmers and Tradesmen has vested him with all authority, military and civil. His word is law. He gave strict orders that my men and I were to accompany you to Fereganth."

Izgir's dark eyes flashed. "Your Marshal's not in charge here, Lieutenant. I am, and we don't need *you*. As we are now, we look like refugees." The Naztali paused to survey the rest of us. "Maybe worse than refugees. With you and your soldiers riding with us, we'd look like an armed patrol—which is exactly what the Syrtians are watching for. Best for you to get back to Dred Thannat. We're going to need every hour you and your Marshal can buy."

Teryan looked down, folded his arms across his chest. Finally he appeared to give in.

"I'll get there as soon as I can," he said.

"Good," said Izgir, fighting his mount as she sidestepped in the face of a sudden breeze. "And do me a favor, Lieutenant. Tell your Marshal Quin that if Dred Thannat falls before I get there, I'll piss on his Darannan grave."

2 3

Blood

My nightmares started on the hills of the Near Downs. That's where I first dreamt blood. Smeared on cinder-block walls. Puddled on cement floors.

It's also where I first dreamt the voice.

His voice. The voice of Aln Adrackt.

It said: *You want to go back?*

Even in my confusion I couldn't help wondering which was worse. That faint, insinuating whisper? Or the fact that I recognized it. That I turned toward it.

"I want—" *Blood.* A child clung to the legs of her mother. A man dragged her off. I remembered this scene. I wrote and lavishly illustrated it in one of the very first issues of my comic book *Laser Kill*, then presented it for the delectation of America's youth.

Now it was real.

Want to go back? To your home? To this?
Stay with me, Ramirez.

Blood. On the wall. On the girl. The man held her down, forced himself in.

You wish to return?

Eventually the girl stopped screaming. She stopped making any sound at all.

You stayed with me once. The things you saw are with you still.
They have left you fit for nothing else. You're mine, Ramirez.
Run wherever you want. Every road will lead you back.

When I woke up, my clothes were clammy with sweat. Only my mouth was dry. I felt for the earth and waited for my heart to slow.

Ara stood over me, frowning. "Ramirez. Are you all right? Is it the fever again?"

"No, not…I'm *fine*. Really."

I tried to stand, but I didn't make it. Ara lowered herself to one knee to help me. This, of course, made matters worse. *Was I ever going to do anything right? Was I really as helpless as she had to see me?*

"You're flushed," she said. "Lie still."

"Careful, Princess. I'm a commoner. You'll get your hands dirty."

She shook her head as she walked away. I hoisted myself into a sitting position, nearly collapsed again. The rest of the group watched me as if I was an insect trying to wriggle out of its skin. I wrapped up my bedroll. I choked down a biscuit and some water. Following Izgir's lead, we saddled up and headed east. It was a mushroom-colored morning, cool but humid. Having spent so many days in the woods, the grassy hills around us seemed too quiet to bear. It was as if the world was empty. Several times I turned to look back the way we'd come. The Thicket was just a blue shadow on the horizon. But I wasn't really looking for things I could see. I'd always suspected what was back there. On even the brightest days in Brooklyn, some part of my mind or my soul knew I had been violated, had been *polluted*. Increasingly I had come to feel that the agent of my destruction was behind me, and watching my every move. Now I knew something else. Now I knew it was coming after me.

2 4

The Greensea

For four days we rode the Greensea, the vast sprawl of prairie that stretches from the foothills of the Broken Mountains south to the Step and east to the edge of Ythedra itself. Wild rye and cap weed stood knee-high as far as the eye could see. The tall grass rolled and swayed in what seemed like a constant wind. Grasshoppers sprang up alongside us, and tiny larks rose and circled overhead as we passed. The sky was immense. One day we counted three separate storms in various quadrants of the heavens, swaying indistinct curtains of steel gray and black, periodically lit from within by lightning. Sometimes we saw columns of smoke as well, particularly to the south. In ordinary times we might have investigated. Instead we sought out seams in the earth, avoiding the high ground for fear of being spotted by whatever Syrtian or Kirikite patrols were afoot in the land. We paused to water our horses from the muddy arroyos, to eat a cold meal at noon and stretch our aching legs. For most of our journey the autumn sky was a washed-out blue, fading imperceptibly into the gauzy white of cirrostratus clouds to the north. The mornings were chilly, maybe fifty degrees, and the wind was the only one talking.

Izgir set the pace. It was the way of the Naztali to keep moving. Even on the longest expedition he carried no baggage, only a jumble of goatskins for water and a tent of boiled antelope hides to shield him at night from rain or snow. Every warrior owned as many ponies as he could breed, borrow, or steal. On longer journeys he took four or five of his favorites. They were transportation, obviously. But they also served him as currency, as company, sometimes even as sustenance. If water was scarce and there was no game to be found, the rider could suck milk from the teats of the mares. In worse circumstances he might pierce a vein of a younger horse and lap the blood as it flowed. The Naztali could ride for a week with nothing else to eat.

The rest of us did what we could. The air smelled of dry grass and good soil and the sweat of our animals. By the second day of our ride I was so sore I could barely walk. It wasn't the horse's fault. I had been given an ancient bay mare with a spray of white hair in her mane. *Wind Sister*, they called her. She put up with me as best she could, only growing fractious late in the afternoon, when she tired. Not that I blamed her. Izgir reckoned we were making fifty miles a day.

———————

We bivouacked that evening near a brackish brown puddle that smelled like wet pennies. Usak sniffed it and frowned, but our choices were limited. According to Izgir, this was the best water we were likely to see until we'd made our way through the Silent Marsh. We boiled the liquid, filled our bags, took our chances. There wasn't much talk around our feeble campfire. We chewed another ration of the dense biscuit we'd brought from Inniskerr and listened to the sky running its fingers through the grass around us. A pair of mourning doves called back and forth. The western horizon was a mass of billowing clouds, pink and purple and red, like smoke from some unseen celestial fire.

"Sleep," Izgir instructed me, after we'd laid out our bedrolls. "I'll take first watch, and wake you when the moon comes up."

"I'm not tired," I said.

"No?" The Naztali eyed me skeptically over one knee. "You *look* tired."

"Spend enough time on a sofa and your muscles forget what they're made for. I'm doing better. How far is the Marsh?"

"I can smell it from here. We'll be in it by nightfall tomorrow."

"You've been there before?"

"Once."

"And? It used to be an evil place."

Izgir had turned to me, ready to speak, when he noticed Ara. She was awake and listening.

"It's not pretty," said the Naztali, his voice thickening. "But it's passable."

I held my tongue as Izgir banked the fire. The stars above us swarmed closer. *Were they my stars?* I wondered. *Earth's stars?* Aside from the Dippers and Orion's Belt, I'd forgotten the constellations. Never known them, in fact. Astronomy was just one of the several thousand things I'd always wanted to commit to memory but failed to pay attention to as I reached for my wallet or my bottle or settled to sleep on the hood of somebody's car. There wasn't much use in gazing at the heavens in Manhattan anyway. Ground light swallowed the spectacle. *But learning to fly? Or to dive? To run or raise kids or to read hieroglyphics? Couldn't I have done something besides what I'd done? Been someone besides a purveyor of spatter punk? A merchandiser of massive head trauma and stylized carnage?*

"That's Ell-Eret," said Izgir, gesturing with one hand. "The Eagle. My people's guide. You know his story?"

"I guess I should. But I don't."

"I won't bore you. It's all about buzzard demons, and ravens who talk, and a god who wears the sky as a cloak."

"I'd like to hear it."

"Another time. To tell it now, so far from home..." Izgir tossed a scrap of bark on the embers of the fire and watched as it flared up. He stared at his boots. At his hands. "If I were there now, I'd be listening to hunt songs by a center fire, trying to think up a few new lies before it was my turn to sing. I'd watch my wives making plans for me. My sons would beat each other with sticks. Later I'd walk out in the fields to talk to my ponies. The stars would distract me and I'd wake up the next morning at the feet of my favorite mare. I'd feel her breath on my face."

I looked over at the Naztali to confirm he was the same man I'd come to know and distrust on our trek through the Big Thicket. He was still staring into the fire. In the flickering light I studied his high cheekbones and long, flat nose.

"What about you?" said Izgir. "Where would you be if you weren't here?"

I said: "In the past, I guess. Before my life fell apart. I'd be sitting by a fire, like you. Listening to Billie Holliday singing *Night and Day* and looking at lights across the Hudson River. Apartment lights. My substitute for the constellations. Drinking a glass of red wine and touching a woman's hair."

"Any particular woman?"

"Aren't they all?"

Minutes passed before the Naztali spoke again.

"Few days back," he said. "I wanted to leave you for dead."

"I get that a lot."

The Naztali grunted. "The world is closing in on us. The only thing I know to do is to cut it open. To fight. And sometimes... maybe...I fight the wrong people."

It was an extraordinary admission. I couldn't help wondering why I was the one he'd chosen to make it to.

Izgir glanced at our companions. Ara was asleep.

"And I lied," he whispered.

"About what?"

"About the Marsh. It's a dangerous place. A nesting place of the worms."

"The draviden," I said.

"In the Darannan stories, yes. They're called *draviden*—the *damned*. When I was a boy I heard a poem. It went, *Sticky people, white as...*"

"*Tendon white,*" I said.

"You know the poem?"

I recited my answer.

> *They're sticky people, tendon-white.*
> *They never knock. They cannot shout.*
> *A slender flame will drive them out.*
> *They're sticky people, spawn of night.*
> *Damp as April's darkest grass,*
> *cold as mist on morning glass.*
> *They're sticky people, tendon-white,*
> *and you will know them by their touch.*
> *First a little. Then too much.*

Izgir cocked his head at me. "How could you know a—?"

"Ban Lohannon wrote that poem a long time ago. He knew plenty about the draviden. They're cold-blooded things, more like slugs than human beings, but with faces that look vaguely like ours. They have viscous skins and underbellies, and because they're partial to rotting flesh they paralyze their victims and store them in burrows, immobilizing the bodies limb-by-limb and laying their eggs in the necrotic tissue. When the young ones hatch, they eat the living flesh of their hosts. You hadn't heard *that*, I bet."

"We know their ways. They're more common in this country than ever before."

"And you want to go on?"

"No choice. To the south is more marsh. Probably worse. We could detour north, but that would put us two days further from the pass into Fereganth. Time is our enemy now."

"Then we go through the Marsh," said Ara. She lifted her head from her bedroll. A thick lock of hair hid her eyes.

"You sleep lightly, Princess," said Izgir.

"You were speaking of matters that concern me. Why shouldn't I listen?"

"You heard what I said?"

"I did."

"And still you vote for the Marsh?"

"So we'll post double guard."

"The blueblood's right," grunted Truke tu-Kekh. "For once. We'll post double guard. We can handle *slugs*."

"Jesus," I said. "Is anyone asleep?"

"Not me." Usak sat up to join the conversation. Even sitting, the Taureg was taller than Truke tu-Kekh. That left only Gowen. He made grizzly bear sounds as he slept.

"Why do these draviden threaten travelers?" asked Usak.

"No more questions," said Izgir, pointing at the gangling giant. "Get some rest. Ramirez, it's your watch. Tired yet?"

"To tell you the truth, I am. But I'll—"

"Then you won't mind company. I heard about your dream last night. I'll watch with you."

We sat together another two hours. When Truke tu-Kekh took over, I felt calm enough to close my eyes. The dreams this time weren't of blood but of sky. I was flying. I glided over stone villages and black beaches, over miles of the lushest farmlands I'd ever seen. Finally I swooped lower to enter a glade of pine and oak and spruce. I threaded through stands of trees, past blue jays and scarlet butterflies, black squirrels and whitetail deer. I could see every stem of grass, every aster and daisy and goldenrod, as if I was looking through a magnifying glass. And finally I looked up at the hips and slender shoulders of a woman who was bathing in a rock-rimmed pool. I lingered on the ridges of her vertebrae, moved up across the smooth nape of her neck. Recognition pierced my heart like a needle. It was Rachel Chen. It had to be and it couldn't be but this was a dream and in dreams you don't ask questions, you just ache.

Rachel, I said. *Rachel, we have to talk. I know I occasionally act like I'm in control of myself but it's a shameless lie and inside I'm as empty as a broken promise. I can't stop thinking about you, wanting you, wishing I'd been smarter. I can't stop w anting that innocence in your eyes—a sight so strange it took me all these years to recognize it.*

I tried to move, to circle around her, but I couldn't. It was as if every one of my movements rocked me off balance and set me drifting again. I tried harder, swam against tides in the air, finally touched Rachel's shoulder. Something happened with that touch. She stiffened and turned toward me and what I saw wasn't Rachel anymore. It was a mockery of the woman I loved, a monster who wore Rachel Chen's face as if it was a shrunken shirt. I heard laughter above or behind me and I knew who it was without thinking. I knew I'd been tricked and could be tricked a thousand times and I remembered Rachel was dead, a corpse, and as far away from me now as the smallest star at the edge of an unnamed galaxy. *Lonely?* said a voice. I screamed and screamed again. I screamed till Gowen's rough hands woke me and I stared at the sullen sky. It was dawn. My cries had roused crows from their roost in a copse of cottonwoods nearby. The black birds wheeled twice in the chilly air. Then they gathered close to become a unit, a single entity, before they swooped low and beat a ragged course south.

———+———

An hour later we buried the ashes of our campfire, gathered the horses, and broke camp. Ara tossed me a wallet-sized biscuit. I took a long gulp from my water bag. We resumed our journey to Fereganth just as it started to rain.

The Dirty Veil

In the eastern moors the grass lost color, fading from green to yellow and finally to a dreary brown. Even the sky grew dull. Low clouds crawled out of the south and inched their way across the heavens like giant snails, heavy with rain and fog and leaving glistening puddles in their path. The sun was a distant white eye behind a dirty veil. And here we found the debris of war: discarded boots and abandoned handcarts, a dead mule, a broken drum. Early that afternoon we crossed a barren ridge and nearly stumbled over a band of refugees, wide-eyed filthy things who watched us approach with a look that suggested night creatures surprised by the sun. The exiles led a spavined horse that carried blankets, cooking gear, and a flimsy blue chair. They also had an ox. The animal dragged a makeshift travois, on which rode a pregnant woman and several white chickens.

"We come from Tull," said the leader of the group. He was a teenaged boy with an infected eye and a nasty wound—possibly a sword-slash—across his neck. Tull was one of the Free Cities, a coastal metropolis that was for many years known to harbor elements hostile to Emerkest. "The Syrtians left it burning."

"And they left you alive?" asked Izgir. If he was moved by the plight of the people he saw in front of him, he didn't show it.

"Some they kill. Others they don't. They say there is plenty of time left for killing. The Dark One is in the land. And..."

"And what?"

The refugee looked around at his companions. "He has opened the gates of hell."

Ara tossed the boy two loaves of the bread we'd acquired at Glen Kiernan. Ignoring Izgir's glare, she told the kid to lead his group west toward the fortress called Dred Thannat, where what remained of the Darannan army was gathering to defend Ythedra. The boy's response was polite but skeptical.

"Ythedra," he repeated, as if the name was already a distant memory. His eyes were fixed on the bread.

———+———

I understood the kid's doubts. I was fighting a few of my own. As we rode that day, my thoughts made slow circles. Should a man have to pay for the sins of someone else, I asked myself—even if that someone else was really *him*? How many people could have resisted the ugliness Ban Lohannon saw in the cellars beneath Kaer Rhygat? How many times did he—*did I*—hurt men, women, and children in an effort to keep myself alive down there? I hadn't known the people around me. They were prisoners, *slaves*, brought in from whatever far-off land Aln Adrackt was bent on destroying, marched the hundreds of miles to Kaer Rhygat for his edification or amusement or simply to gratify the desire he felt to degrade and disfigure whatever or whoever was out there and obedient to any god or government other than him. The dungeons were a sort of factory. They manufactured despair. It made no sense, but in some perverted way this factory kept Aln Adrackt's empire alive. They fed its grotesque belly. They nourished its million mouths. And I knew that all the while I was in there, under Kaer Rhygat, part of me was horrified by the rotting flesh and stench and misery. Part of me wanted to be free again, to breathe fresh air, to drown myself in the nearest lake. What sickened me was knowing too that another part of me (*greater? smaller?*) was adapting. Changing. Enjoying the fact that I was surviving while so many of the sad, luckless people who joined me died in pain, out of sight of the sun. I was no better than them. I might have been worse. And yet I lived while others died. This was the difficult cargo. The sleep killer. Destroyer of dreams. And this, too, I owed to Aln Adrackt, who had managed to poison my life even in another world.

———†———

We saw three more bands of refugees struggling north that day, three knots of maybe a dozen people each, mothers and daughters, old men and infants. They seemed to wander not knowing themselves where they were heading but heading there anyway with as much as they could carry because there was nothing else for them to do. Unwilling to advertise the odd composition of our group, only Izgir would ride to meet the dispossessed. *Go to Dred Thannat,* he'd say. *Seek refuge at Ythedra's last hope.* It was unclear whether anyone actually followed his advice. Probably they kept heading north, into the trackless expanse of the Greensea, though Izgir was unable to predict how his people would treat such intruders.

Late that afternoon, as we neared the desolate fringe of Silent Marsh, Izgir cantered out to meet another small band. This one looked like it was made up of Darannan refugees—possibly survivors of the destruction of Kaer Rhennet. He was fired at as he neared the group. Though the arrows fell pitifully short of their targets, Izgir reined his horse around and spurred back toward the rest of us.

Gowen asked what accounted for the attack.

"Maybe they're *hungry*," said the Naztali.

But we learned why only an hour later, when we came upon a shallow wash where human bodies lay naked and obscene on both slopes. They had been butchered by unartistic hands and desecrated thereafter—torn apart by the less culpable teeth and claws of creatures who couldn't know the laws vouchsafed by men and broken almost from the moment of their utterance. Flies zipped past our heads toward the banquet of bodies. When the wind shifted, we gagged on the stench blowing over the field.

Truke tu-Kekh noticed the black arrow lodged in the ground a few yards away.

"Syrtian Border Guard," he said. "Tarrant Lef's men."

Mostly it was Usak who seemed stunned by the sight. The Taureg looked to each of us for an answer. His eyes held genuine confusion.

"Women. Children. Does it make no difference to these people who they kill?"

No one spoke. We reined around the corpses and continued on our course toward the Silent Marsh. The fens lay dark and uninviting in front of us, stretching as far as we could see to the north and south, and in the distance the Copper Mountains rose like the humps of some ungainly creature surfacing in a misty sea. On the far side of the mountains lay our destination. *Fereganth.* Home of the fabled Seven Swords, and the unruly people who owned them. It wasn't a heartening destination. But this was only fitting.

It wasn't a heartening trip.

"RIDERS!" Ara hissed. "At least two, due north. Headed this way."

The princess was right. I followed her gaze and saw tiny figures silhouetted against the dull sky. Ara pulled her bow from her shoulder and nocked a long arrow. The blue troll swiveled to free his war hammer from where it was lashed behind his saddle.

When the figures were still three hundred yards off, Izgir raised his right arm and sent a high-pitched shout out over the prairie. The riders raised their hands in response as they spurred their mounts toward us. A half-dozen ponies cantered behind them.

"Naztali," Izgir announced, nodding to no one in particular.

The two Naztali warriors dressed as he did, in an eccentric combination of furs and hides, with stone and silver bracelets rattling on their forearms. Their dark hair billowed behind them in the breeze.

"I am Chayak," said one of the riders, reining up only a few feet from us. It was clear he spoke only to Izgir. The rest of us weren't worthy of his attention. "Son of Lirin, of the Barrows Clan. This is Jhia, son of Tamir, also of the Barrows."

"I am Izgir son of Aakil, Chief of the Two Streams Clan. My hands are empty."

The Naztali riders considered each of us in turn, still alert for threats.

"Brothers," said Izgir. "You're troubled."

"Izgir son of Aakil is known among our people. He is a fierce warrior, zealous in defense of Naztali lands. He does not consort with outsiders. It is at his summons that we are preparing to leave this country."

"Preparing to leave this country," Izgir said, stiffening in his saddle, "so you can ride to join the Tribes at council. Because Izgir and his companions were ambushed on the Downs two weeks ago by Syrtian and Kirikite cavalry. Because Izgir watched as five of his brothers were butchered by the Syrtian riders, and took vengeance on his attackers by sending seven to darkness. Because Izgir sent word to his people of the Shadow King's return to this land, a threat more deadly than any Syrtian patrol or troop of renegade trolls, and because Izgir signed this message in blood, daring his Naztali brothers to take up the bow in defense of their homelands. I am Izgir, son of Aakil. I am the man who called you to war. If you wish to test me, pull your knives now, for I have no time to waste making wind with my mouth."

Jhia bowed his head. "Forgive me, brother. Truly you are the one called Hawk in the northlands. But these—?"

"These are my..." The world seemed to wobble on its axis. The strangers shifted in their saddles. "These are my friends," said Izgir. "And my concern. What are two warriors of the Barrows clan doing so far east in these dark days?"

"Patrolling. Watching for Syrtian incursions. Kaer Rhennet is..."

"Destroyed," said Izgir. "I know. I wish the words were lighter."

"Now the Syrtians kill many of those who flee the southlands, and leave them for the birds. They even kill Ganthans. A party of our scouts found six bodies near the East Barrows a week ago."

"Then truly Tarrant Lef is growing bolder."

Chayak shrugged. "The Ganthans we found were only children. Tarrant Lef has never been afraid to kill those who can't fight back. But his soldiers are sloppy. They lack discipline. And the undisciplined make mistakes."

Jhia raised what appeared at first to be a string of crabs. I looked closer and realized the objects were human hands, burnt black by the sun of the plains. The Naztali took the hands of their enemies as prizes—and to keep the dead from seeking vengeance on them in the afterlife.

"The Syrtians," Chayak added, addressing us with a professorial air, "are a filthy people."

"What news of the tribes?" said Izgir.

Jhia said, "The Council has sent word we'll fight. The tribes are gathering in the north. Ride with us, brother!"

Chayak added: "Surely you're not heading east?"

Izgir shrugged. "I've ridden the Marsh before."

"Not lately, I think. The worms are thick in the Marsh, and even here the land is sick and smells of death. We must report in the north tomorrow evening, but wait a day. We'll send men to ride with you."

Izgir slid off his horse. "None of us can wait even an hour. What's left of the Darannans are gathering at Dred Thannat, their fortress on the western bay. The tribes need to ride soon to join them. The Shadow King is on the move. More I cannot say. Nor can I go north, but I will see you when the earth shakes, for the battle to come will pardon no true Naztali."

"Well said, Izgir son of Aakil. We'll bring the message."

"But before you do…" said Izgir.

The two Naztali turned back to face him.

"Where are the antelope?" he asked. "I haven't seen a single herd."

"Few to be seen. The Syrtians take more every year. And now, with the animals being pushed north, many will die this winter."

"This fight," said Izgir, "has been a long time coming."

"Too long," said Jhia.

"I ask a favor."

"Done," said Chayak.

"Lend me two of your ponies, for I tire of riding this Darannan nag with the mouth made of stone."

The Naztali braves chuckled together, considering the offending horse as if she were a wayward niece. Chayak dismounted. He slipped the bridle off his pony's head and said, "This is Feather, whom you honor by accepting."

The second warrior scanned the horizon before he too dropped to the ground.

"This is Goat," he announced, bowing to Izgir. "He will not stumble."

"I am the one honored," said Izgir, executing the same shallow bow. He breathed into the nostrils of each animal in turn. "I'll treat them as I would my own. And I give you in exchange this cow, whom the Darannans call Cloud."

"Cloud," said Jia, stepping forward to take the reins. "He'll do to pull a travois."

The Naztali riders transferred their gear to new ponies, then remounted.

Chayak's smile faded. "Now, brother, do us a service in return."

"Only if you ask it."

"Lend us your woman," said the Naztali, "for we have been almost a month on the Greensea."

Izgir laughed again. Louder this time. He glanced back at Ara as he spoke.

"That I cannot do. She's not mine, I'm happy to say, nor any man's. She's a Sidharan princess. And she's learned to use the bow."

Ara never twitched. She simply stared at the Naztali men for several long seconds. I could hear the swish of Wind Sister's tail.

Chayak broke the standoff by pulling his horse's head around. "Then we'll civilize her another time. Avoid the Marsh if you can, Izgir son of Aakil. Sleep lightly if you can't."

———+———

As we watched the tribesmen gallop back over the grasslands, Izgir spoke to the Naztali ponies as another man might speak to his children.

"I could not choose between the two of you," he said, "while your masters looked on. But you, Feather, smell like one of my wives—so it's you I'll burden for now. You, noble Goat, I will save for the mountains."

For once the Naztali was in great high spirits. Even Ara smiled at Izgir's flirtation with the two beasts. In this damp unholy place we welcomed every laugh we could find. They died out soon enough. It was raining again.

2 6

The Marsh

Silent Marsh is a vast expanse of wetland criss-crossed by ridges of sodden earth. The ridges were once hilltops. Now they seemed to be nothing more than fuel for some monstrous mechanism of decay, an agency of malice bent on consumption of even the earth that contained it. As we rode into the Marsh a shifty, insubstantial drizzle moved with us, collecting on the hoods of our cloaks, beading on the manes of the horses. There was no sound but the suck of hooves in the mud, no sign of animate life beyond the grackles that occasionally beat past us overhead. Along the ridges, clumps of choke weed and spindly hackberry trees huddled together as if for safety's sake against the grasp of whatever nameless thing might rise from the depths of the bogs. The air itself seemed tainted with the stench of rot and secret wounds.

That afternoon, the air grew colder. The sky cleared and the Marsh glistened like an open sore in the weak sunlight. During this break in the weather we could see a low line of black battlements on the horizon to the southeast. These were the ruins of Craigh Glzak—at one time, millennia ago, the imperial city of a people who ruled Ythedra centuries before the name of Dar-Annon was ever uttered. Even when Ban Lohannon was alive, no one could recall what blasphemies committed by the wizard kings of that ancient race caused the earth itself to shudder and split, dragging the lands around Craigh Glzak so much closer to hell that the rivers running out of the Copper Mountains had nowhere to go. Cultivated fields became swampland. The city swam in its own waste. Perhaps the answers were written in a history moldering in the library of some priest-built tower deep within Craigh Glzak. If so, the answers would surely stay unread. Whatever their former glories, the hulking ruins of the city were now the obscene center of the Marsh, its rotting heart, and a lair of the draviden who lived in the dark waters of this spiritless region. No one had ever visited Craigh Glzak and returned to tell what glories, or horrors, survived within its age-smeared walls.

———†———

Izgir led us. As if to make up for his humiliation in the Thicket, he kept his eyes fixed forward—always, it seemed, two ridges ahead of where we rode—and refused even to answer our questions. Still, by late afternoon it became clear we weren't going to reach the Naztali's stated goal, which was getting through the Marsh in one day. There were too many dead ends, too many barriers of deep water and treacherous mud. The realization didn't help Izgir's mood. He was too hard on himself. We'd have been lost a dozen times without his guidance, and despite the delays, the Copper Mountains loomed larger. We'd get there, we told ourselves. Sooner or later, we'd get there. But finally even Izgir despaired of breaking free of the fens by dark. Muttering to himself, he led us through several acres of muck and sickly vegetation toward the highest ground in sight, a hump of brown earth between two stagnant sloughs. The water here was nearly black, coated with an iridescent goo that broke the light into ugly rainbows. Truke tu-Kekh lowered himself off his horse to examine the substance.

He did this, oddly enough, by taste.

"Some kind of tar," I said. "As if mud wasn't enough."

He started to answer, but had to wrestle his reins back instead. The horses were acting strangely. They pulled at their bits, and shied at the slightest movement of weeds in the wind. The troll took it personally.

"This is no place for games," snapped Izgir, riding back to calm Truke's skittish pony.

Say what you will about the Naztali. They know horses. It took Izgir just a few seconds to coax the animal back into line.

———+————

We made it to the hummock with just enough light left to make camp. As the sun went down in a reddish haze, painting the edges of the few clouds that hung high in the sky, Izgir unpacked the fat pine we'd carried with us from the Thicket. With embers he'd saved from the previous night's camp, he and Usak managed to kindle a fire. We hobbled the horses directly outside our circle of bedrolls, and fed them what little bread we could spare. They weren't going to get much else. Even the rangy Naztali mares declined to eat the nettles that speckled the hillside.

"Pay attention," said Izgir, returning from his patrol around the campsite. "We...wait. Where's the troll?"

He was right. Truke tu-Kekh had disappeared. There was a panicked tone to our shouts. Maybe that's what amused the troll, who reappeared from the reeds at the base of the hill, smirking in spite of himself. His left hand and lower lip were coated in the black goo that floated on the swamps around us. It looked as if Truke had found a new source of sustenance. It wasn't anything I wanted to share.

"We'll watch in pairs," Izgir resumed. "Ramirez and I first. Then Gowen and Ara, and Usak and Truke tu-Kekh in turn. I said before this is no place for games. We all know what lives in the Marsh. But the draviden are scavengers, not hunters. As long as we stay together, we'll be fine. If you see anything, any of you, wake the rest of us. Show your weapons. We want them to know we'll fight. And whatever you do, don't leave the fireside."

"Why not?" said Usak.

"The worms can't stand a flame. It's our best defense. Anyone who's not on watch had better turn in. There's nothing to see."

He had that much right. Though a three-quarter moon eventually appeared amidst the high clouds, it merely silvered the mist gathering on the waters around us. Soon it was difficult to make out much of anything beyond the glow of our campfire.

For obvious reasons, I tried not to sleep. First of all, I was on watch. Izgir swore to himself as the fog curled around us, and I hated to think what he'd do if he caught me dozing. Second, there were the nightmares to deal with. They were worse than a day in the saddle—and more fatiguing for the fact that the burden they left me with was psychic. My shame. My doubts. My growing fear. So I fed our feeble fire and drew dragons in the air with a glowing ember till my watch ended. By the time Gowen and Ara relieved us, I was out of excuses. I wriggled into my bedroll. I pulled my cape up over my chin and lay gazing at the Sidharan princess as she polished her bow. Once, when she cocked her head to listen to some far-off sound, our eyes met. We stared at each other for several seconds before the princess stood, drew her gilded dagger, and walked into the mist. Gowen stood too. I was just about to wake the others when Ara moved back into view. She shook her head, and Gowen relaxed. False alarm. Nothing to worry about. I tried to rest without actually closing my eyes. I thought about Ara. I thought about her freckles and her throaty laugh and about what it would be like to stay with her in Ythedra. Eventually, though, the exhaustion of the last several days dragged me down. The walls of my mind began to melt. I stood by myself in the darkness. I barely heard the whispers. But I couldn't stop listening.

"What do you want?" I said.

Only what you want for yourself.

"You're testing me."

I tested you long ago. Back
when you were stronger than you are today.
Now you carry a sickness inside you
darker than anything these idiots you travel with
have ever seen. I taught you, Lohannon.
Back when you learned to walk with me.
Walk with me again. Take what you want.

"And what do I want?"
There was a hiss of breath behind me. I felt my skin crawl.

What you want is to linger in this world
where you belong.
You can't save anyone, Lohannon.
You can't even save yourself.
Your dreams are dirty, and
you corrupt everything you touch.
I know how lonely you've been.
I'll give you a chance to cure that.
Take it. Stay here and rule a world.
Rule the woman. The Sidharan.
Rule with me.

"I don't want to rule anyone. I can't—"

You can have anything you want.

"And if I don't stay?"

Come, Lohannon.
Come and join me again.

I tumbled through images: the wing of a raven; a glimpse of white mountains; Kaer Rhennet burning like a bonfire. Empty desert and then the hulking stone ruins of the Red Cities, scarlet in the last rays of an evening sun. But I went further this time. I dived through a broken window into Kaer Rhygat itself. I glided down corridors and stairways into the dungeons of Aln Adrackt. The horrors there—the broken men and their sobbing women; the things that came for the children at night; the spider pits and human soups—refused to stop. I walked again among those instruments of pain. I heard the tortures. Worse. I *watched* the tortures, and I held my tongue for fear that I might be next. All the while I was aware of a second voice, only a murmur at first, but growing in intensity and volume until I could hear myself repeating variations of my panicked mantra, saying, *Oh my God, Oh God*, shouting now, and whispering or praying *Oh my God this is not who I am and if it is don't let it be. Don't let me be! Don't—!* I screamed, shook myself, tried to hold on to something solid but couldn't.

I was alone again.

I lay on my side in a shallow puddle, breathing hard, listening harder. *But listening for what?* I tried to collect my thoughts. I was cold. I was shivering. But there it was again. *The sound.* This was what I was listening for. Something was creeping toward me, hissing wetly and whining with hunger or pleasure. I grabbed a handful of weeds. My mind said *move* but I could barely sit up. By moonlight I saw a horse standing a few yards away from me, half-hidden by mist. It snorted, as if smelling something unpleasant, then went pounding off through the mud. Voices were calling in the middle distance and I tried to answer but couldn't. Only my eyes still worked. What I saw made me wish I'd kept them closed.

The draviden glistened in the silver light. They had empty dark holes where their eyes should have been, and as they approached they whispered to each other in a language of rasps and clicks. I tried to scream. The best I could do was a sort of moan that felt like it was being scraped out of my lungs. The creatures dragged me by my legs toward the marsh. Tall stalks of switchgrass seemed to swallow us up. More draviden lifted themselves out of the muck. I smelled rotting flesh and counted two, three, now five of the monsters gathered around me. They bent me backwards over a clump of reeds and pinioned me at the shoulders so I had to look up. Then the largest of the creatures leaned over my throat. It bared two sets of tiny, sharp teeth, and at last a shriek exploded out of my rigid body. The dravid paused. It placed its smooth palm over my mouth and cocked its head as if to listen for movement. Satisfied there was none, the creature bent toward me again and coughed up a milky liquid that spattered over my throat and chest. It was the draviden venom, a nerve agent that attacks like some monstrous variant of atoxin-a, causing mental confusion and almost instant paralysis. The fluid was warm compared to the flesh of the creatures that held me. It only stung for a second. Then I felt my my skin go numb as the poison seeped into my bloodstream. I could feel it spreading through my body like the concentric circles of a splash in a pond. It was the predator's edge: the more frightened the victim, the harder his heart worked to pump blood through his veins, and the quicker the toxin took effect. And my heart was pounding like a motorcycle piston—which meant that soon I felt nothing at all.

Maybe you've been scared before. Startled. Anxious. Jumpy. What I experienced was categorically different. As the draviden watched, I struggled to keep myself breathing. I knew what came next. Immobilized, barely conscious, I'd be hidden away in a muddy burrow beneath the banks of the marsh. There I'd subsist for a period of perpetual night as a semi-comatose meat locker, being eaten alive from within by the larval forms of what can best be described as walking maggots.

I felt my body being pulled through the mud.

We reached the water's edge.

Then, in my final seconds of anything close to a normal life, I saw the face of one of the creatures collapse like a rotten pumpkin. The dravid fell like a puppet cut from its strings. Truke tu-Kekh stepped forward and drove his war hammer deep into the neck of another worm, screaming in a tongue I didn't know and yet understood perfectly.

At first the slugs retreated, fleeing Truke tu-Kekh and his deadly hammer. But Truke's successful charge almost got him killed. He lost his footing as he drove the worms into the swamp. The mud sucked at his boots. It swallowed his hammer, and in a heartbeat the *draviden* were on him, pulling at his chainmail sark, his chitinous arms and heavy helmet. For one horrible moment Truke tu-Kekh disappeared beneath the churning water. Then the troll clawed his way back to the surface, gasping for air and lunging to tear whatever he could touch. As I watched, he jammed the fingers of his right hand deep into the eye socket of a worm, grasped the back of the creature's skull with the left, and ripped the soft head off its body. Still screaming, he lifted the grisly white orb up over his own head and smashed a crater in another worm's face.

But more draviden materialized from the mist. As Truke tu-Kekh was pulled down a second time, I managed to pick myself up out of the muck. I clenched my fists. Concentrating as hard as I ever had in my life, I forced myself to take a step. I felt like the goddamned Tin Man. My arms and legs barely moved.

"Help," I croaked. "Truke! I'm…"

I fell. Ten yards away, a friend was fighting for his life. I couldn't even control my toes. I grabbed a handful of mud and tried to pull myself closer. Truke had found his hammer. He struggled to free it from the grasp of three worms. Two more were pulling him down from behind. The troll roared in frustration and rage.

"Outriders! TO ME!"

A lean figure leaped over me and hurled itself into the tangle of flesh around the blue troll. Two more, then a third, followed close on the first figure's heels. Everything around me was mist and motion, splash and curse and scream. I saw silhouettes clash and reel apart, blades trace arcs through the fog, bodies drop and fail to rise. Gowen staggered past me, wet-legged and wild-eyed, brandishing his oaken club. He disappeared in the mist. When I felt myself being dragged again through the mud, I thrashed like a fish in a net.

"Ramirez!" said a familiar voice. "It's *me*."

Usak helped me to my feet. He supported me as I hobbled back to our campsite.

Minutes passed. But not for hours.

"Are they coming?" I said. "Can you hear them?"

"Nothing. I can't even hear the fighting anymore."

"What happened? Where'd everyone go?"

Usak cast me a sidelong look. "They went looking for *you*. Don't worry. I'm not leaving. Are you hurt?"

"Leaving?"

"We should stay here with the packs. Make—"

"Re-establish a base camp," I said, drawing myself up, aware even as I said it of how ridiculous the phrase sounded. But I had to say something. "I'll get the fire going. And I wasn't worried about you *leaving*. Do I seem that helpless?"

"I didn't mean to offend."

"I'm fine. Just a little...terrified."

The Taureg nocked an arrow in his bow and settled onto his haunches, listening intently to the muffled cries and commands that started to drift out of the night. As my strength returned, I struggled to rekindle the campfire, feeding it the last of our firewood. A north wind had begun to filter through the fog. It tore holes in the curtain of white and helped keep the embers glowing. A few minutes later we heard shouts nearby, then the irregular squilch of footsteps coming toward us from the Marsh. Usak drew his bowstring back to one ear, prepared to loose one of his long Taureg missiles. As peaceable as the kid generally was, the sight of him now reminded me of just how formidable an enemy his people could be. He sighted along the shaft of the arrow, but it was Gowen, covered in tar and blood, who emerged from the mist. He carried a spluttering and equally filthy Truke tu-Kekh across his shoulder. Izgir and a grimy Outrider bore a limp body between them, and two other Darannan soldiers

supported Ara as she staggered back to our camp. Yet another soldier dragged the blue troll's hammer.

When the limp body was laid beside the campfire, I recognized
the blonde hair.

It was Lieutenant Ayrd Teryan.

"Drowned him," said Gowen.

I am not a good man. This much is clear. I have made bad
choices in my life, and they have made me in return. I have not
loved God—or anyone else, for that matter—with my whole heart.
I have neglected to recycle, conserve, or compost. I've pissed on
my friends and ignored my fans and I threw away the only woman
I ever felt any lasting desire to be with—*possibly because I felt a lasting desire to be with her.* I have happily surrendered my capacity for
independent decision-making to a collection of molecules I bought
from a two-bit gang banger named PeeWee. My mind is a sewer.
My soul smells worse. Don't tell me profanity isn't a language. I am
not a good man.

Ara pressed her face into her hands. I heard her sobbing. And
grief is ordinarily contagious. But facets of this particular tragedy
sparkled in my head. *Get a grip,* I told myself. *Hold everything. Think
for a minute! This rosy-cheeked sonofabitch of a lieutenant is about as
definitively out of my way as a rival can be. Aln Adrackt promised me this
chance at Ara and damned if the Ol' Conjurer hasn't come through 1000%.
Have to shake your hand buddy. You done me up right. Dead dude. Grieving
squeeze. Hell yeah…Na na na, gonna have a good time! Hey hey hey…*

I can't explain why I dropped to my knees.

I am not a good man.

"Straighten his legs," I told one of the Outriders.

Dead dude. Stray squeeze. Hell——

Or maybe I *can* explain. Linnaeth's words. Ara's pain. The life of my eternal soul.

"His——?" said the soldier.

Dead dude stray squeeze what are you hey man what are you what are you DOING?

I said: "His *legs*, goddammit. Lay them flat. And hand me your cloak."

I am not a good man. But I wadded the cloak and placed it under Ayrd Teryan's neck, forcing the lieutenant's head up and back. I scooped the filth from the kid's mouth with my index finger. Then I moved his tongue out of the way, placed my lips on his, and blew into his lungs. I centered my hands on his sternum and pressed down hard. Repeated the process. And again. I was vaguely aware that Izgir tried to stop me. It was Truke tu-Kekh, back on his feet and as irascible as ever, who yanked him off. Gowen stared at me like I'd lost what was left of my mind and maybe I had but even though the fallen lieutenant's skin felt like ice I just kept pushing. I thought, *Jesus, let him live. Let me live, let us live, let somebody live. Deliver us from evil, from anvils, from faulty warranties, bleeding hearts, broken backs and poison sacs for Thine is the power, the passion, the microwave oven, whatever you want Lord, take it, it's yours, just let him live...*

Ayrd Teryan coughed, and an ugly mixture of mucus and last night's supper dribbled down one of his cheeks into the grass. The Darannan lieutenant opened his eyes. He dug his fingers into my hips. Truke tu-Kekh bellowed his approval.

Only Izgir was unconvinced.

"What brand of witchcraft is *this*?" he demanded, grabbing a handful of my hair. "What have you done?"

"Let me go," I said. "It's not—well, I don't know. I suppose it *is* a sort of magic. But anyone could do it."

Izgir stuck his face an inch from Ayrd Teryan's nose. "Darannan. Can you hear me?"

"I hear you," said Teryan, before he retched again. Ara wiped a clump of tar from the lieutenant's forehead. He looked like a seabird caught in a tanker spill.

When his coughing subsided he lay back, exhausted.

"Where am I?" he mumbled.

"Welcome to the Marsh," I said. "You're back in the land of the living. For the time being, anyway. The draviden may have more to say about that. We got a blanket for the kid? Feels like the wind is picking up."

But two of us were no longer listening. Holding the young officer's hand in hers, Ara stared at his face as if it was about to fade away. Ayrd Teryan opened his eyes. He looked up at the princess. And this time he kept looking.

"Wait a minute," growled Truke tu-Kekh, who had drifted to the edge of the circle of firelight. "I hear something."

Izgir finally glanced away from Teryan. "Not likely. The worms attack the unprepared. We've seen the last of them tonight. And by mid-day tomorrow we'll be on the moors."

"Sure about that?" said Gowen.

His voice sounded wrong. We all looked up.

At first it seemed as if there was only one of the draviden, standing motionless a few yards from our camp. This was disturbing enough. Izgir was right. Legend held that the worms were antisocial. They lived skulking solitary lives in the swamps, avoiding the light of day and feeding by night on fish and eels trapped in the marsh by the tides. Only occasionally were they known to travel inland, and even then they avoided confrontation. It was rare that one even allowed itself to be seen. But something had changed. This dravid was unafraid. The creature was a glistening, grayish-white, manlike in limbs and features but hairless and at least partially translucent. Green veins were visible beneath its skin, which was covered with a film of slime. The dravid's dark mouth bristled with tiny teeth. It seemed to be *smelling* rather than watching us.

As the mist cleared, we could make out another of the monsters standing behind the first. Then another, a few feet further down. Finally we saw the rest of the hillside. It was covered with the pale unholy things. They stood facing us with eyes that reflected no light at all.

It didn't help to see the blue troll retreating.

"Must be a *hundred* of the bastards," said Gowen.

"More," said Truke tu-Kekh, as he pushed past Gowen toward the fire. In the darkness his eyes worked better than ours.

"Form a circle," said Izgir. "Weapons out. And get the lieutenant on his feet. If we can hold out till dawn, we may have a chance."

The nearest of the draviden stepped closer. Like some segmented larval thing, more distant portions of the glistening mass around us moved closer in turn.

"Where's my club?" said Gowen.

"Right here," answered Truke tu-Kekh. The troll knotted a blackened rag around the cudgel and rotated it over the embers in our fire pit. Muttering to himself, he got down on all fours and blew. A slender flame appeared and guttered out. Almost as quickly the rag itself flared up, giving the troll a crude torch.

"Who's with me?" he said.

"We're *all* with you," said Ara. "What are you talking about?"

Truke tu-Kekh glanced around at the rest of us. He started to say something, but thought better of it.

"Never mind."

"Truke," said Gowen. "Stop. What are you—?"

Too late. The troll turned and sprinted down the hillside toward the mass of draviden that faced us. The creatures shrank from the flame, retreating back into each other to make a path for the charging troll. We saw Truke tu-Kekh enter the ranks of the worms and for several seconds we lost sight of him, obscured as he was by the darkness and ragged fog and the re-forming mass of glistening creatures.

Gowen set out to help, to do what he could, but Izgir caught him by one arm. It was no use.

Then the torch reappeared, flaring as it arced up over the swamp. Ara closed her eyes. We all knew it. Without the flame, Truke wasn't going to last long with the worms.

Hell.

None of us were.

Fifty yards away, the torch fell back toward the Marsh. It hit the dark water with a flat smack, and we heard the blue troll's battle cry as the draviden closed in around him. It sounded desperate, doomed. A chill shot up my spine.

"NO!" shouted Gowen, breaking free of Izgir's grasp.

Just then, starting at the spot where the torch had landed, the world caught fire.

———†———

Fingers of flickering light raced across the waters of the Marsh—stretched out, doubled back, and intertwined, filling the night with a lurid orange glow. We could see worms caught in the flames as the fire spread over the swamp. They thrashed as they burned. They shrieked in their agony and the sound of it was like fingernails on a sky-sized chalkboard, grating and high-pitched and multiplied a thousand times.

The draviden in front of us stood as if ensorceled, watching the weird arabesque of shadow and light before them. That was all the time they had before Gowen slammed into the mass of bodies around Truke tu-Kekh. He knocked five of the sluglike things to the ground and set about crushing heads with the troll's hammer. Izgir and the Outriders were just behind him. They slashed at the confused throng of worms, sliced into the creatures, lopped off limbs and hanks of fibrous flesh. Even I screamed for vengeance as we charged to free our friend. But it wasn't a fight for long. As the heat and glare intensified, the worms fled from us, retreating over the hillside into waters that hadn't yet been touched by the conflagration. A few feet away, one of the creatures pulled itself out of the mire onto shore. Flames covered its lower body, and the worm hissed in agony until Ara dispatched the creature with an arrow to the forehead.

Truke tu-Kekh lay on his back, unable to move, paralyzed just as I had been by the venom of the worms. But there was a gleam in his green eyes. Ara clasped one of the troll's rough hands in hers. He took a shallow breath, then coughed most of it back out. The flames rose like solid walls on two sides of our little island, and the shadows of our huddled figures darkened the troll's face. Exhausted, immobilized, Truke was nevertheless still with us. He held up a finger that was coated with the muck he'd scraped out of the swamp.

"*Karj*," he croaked, in his guttural troll tongue. "Oil. The Marsh is full of it."

2 7

The Offer

Ara and Gowen blamed themselves. They'd heard something moving in the mist and left the fireside to investigate. Maybe they'd gone a little too far from the flames. The draviden must have crept into camp just then. The foul creatures doused the fire, grabbed whoever they could—*me*, as it turned out—and beat a hasty retreat into the reeds that lined the swamp.

Fortunately, Ayrd Teryan hadn't turned back when Izgir ordered him to do so at Glen Kiernan. "I divided my patrol," the young officer said, knuckling soot from his eyes. "Sent two men west to report to Marshal Quin. The rest of us…you know. *Followed.* In the evenings we bivouacked close enough to keep an eye on your camp, and stood watch till dawn. Last night we saw your fire disappear in the fog. But then, just before it became impossible to make out much of anything, I saw something strange. Saw, or maybe imagined— I wasn't sure which. Shadows in the mist…slugs…those *things* we fought. I woke my men and we rode toward where we'd last seen your fire. For a while I was afraid I'd lost my bearings. Finally we stumbled onto your campsite. They must have heard us coming. We saw figures disappearing into the marsh, so we drew our weapons and went after them."

Gowen nodded. "The worms must have dropped Ramirez in the confusion."

"Unfortunately," I said, "they came back. It was Truke tu-Kekh who saved me. Truke and that hammer of his."

Izgir spoke with his customary bluntness. "Lieutenant, you were dead by the time we got to you. But your men fought well. Like *Naztali*. We lost no one. The woman is hurt, but she says she can ride."

"Because I *can*," said Ara. She was clearly annoyed by her relegation to third-party status. "Usak? That salve?"

"Right here."

"Good," said Izgir. "We've found the horses, so we'll start at sun-up. If we can *see* the sun through all this smoke."

"And Teryan?" said Gowen. "He's coming with us, right?"

"No. Teryan will return to Dred Thannat. I know you want to ride with us, Lieutenant. I would too if I were you. But once we clear the Marsh, we'll be out of danger. You would best serve Quin by riding back with news. The Naztali are gathering to fight Aln Adrackt."

"How many Naztali?" said Teryan. "When will they come?"

Izgir gazed westward. "If all the tribes decide to fight, Quin can count on ten thousand warriors. I don't know when they'll ride, but if what I fear is true, Aln Adrackt will set out soon from the ruins of Kaer Rhennet. Retrace your steps to the edge of the Marsh, then make your way northwest through the Greensea. Carry this amulet as a token of my protection, and you'll pass safely through the Naztali patrols. Return to Dred Thannat, as you promised me you would, and deliver my message."

Teryan nodded, but Izgir wasn't through. He looked off through the haze at the eastern sky, which was starting to pale. "At Glen Kiernan I told you to give your Marshal a message."

The lieutenant blushed. "I remember. But—"

"I want to add to it. Tell him I see now that the Darannans are not my enemy. Tell him...to hold on."

Half an hour later, dawn turned the waters around us a deep purple. We watched Teryan and his men ride off into the smoke, and we stood there several minutes after the little troop had disappeared. Part of it was fatigue. Maybe another part was reluctance to say farewell to friends in such a desolate place. When Izgir finally roused us with a curse, it was as if a spell had been broken. We saddled the horses and prepared to move on. But Ara watched long after the rest of us had turned away, and afterwards she rode with her chin on her chest, as if nothing that lay ahead could offer her any consolation.

———+———

We left the Marsh that afternoon and entered a stretch of blighted lowlands. Beyond these barren fields stood treeless hills, and beyond the hills loomed the Copper Mountains, western boundary of Fereganth. The lower slopes of the peaks were an appropriate rust-brown, but halfway up we could see a band of red and yellow-leafed aspens that stood like a wall at the border of the diseased land we traveled. It was said that on the eastern side of the mountains the world grew comely again, graced by miles of forest and upland fells that ended at the cliffs of the Sea of Storms. We hoped it was true. It was difficult to imagine beauty here.

We were silent as we rode. The only sounds were the creaks of our saddles and the rhythmic *thunks* of the horses' hooves on the withered turf. We'd crept out from under the pillars of inky smoke that hung over the swamp but it seemed as if we traveled still beneath a less visible pall. It was as if, having evaded the physical perils of the Marsh, we had not quite escaped its poisonous spirit. Maybe we carried it with us in the oil and soot that caked our skin and hair, making us look like refugees from some primitive refinery of hell. Or maybe hope took too much effort. At any rate, we did the only thing we knew how. We put the sullen miles behind us.

By now the duties of camp life were routine. Late that afternoon we found an arroyo protected from the wind rolling down off the mountains and bisected by a rocky creek. We unpacked our bedrolls and our single cook pot and dug out what little food we had left. Izgir watered and hobbled the horses. Truke tu-Kekh inspected the perimeter of our campsite, war hammer cradled in his thick arms, while Ara kindled a fire. Gowen and I fetched and boiled water for coffee. For the first time I could remember, the big man had nothing to say. Usak divvied out our final rations of Linnaeth's pemmican and hardtack. We drew straws for the sequence of guard duty shifts and laid out our bedrolls for the night.

———+———

I was changing the dressing on my wound when Ara found me. She stood twenty feet from where I sat wrapping a fresh strip of linen around my waist. The dog bite was an afterthought now. It hardly hurt. I don't know how long Ara waited for me to notice her, but when I did, she met my gaze and held it. A few minutes later I followed her out onto the moors. A cold moon was rising over the Copper Mountains, and from far off I heard the thin howl of—what? *Wolves*, I guessed. It had to be wolves.

Ara waited for me just beyond the crest of a gentle hill.

"I want you to have this," she said. I looked down at her emerald-studded dagger. It was the knife she'd used to save my life from the dogs in the Big Thicket. "For what you did last night. Helping the—helping *Teryan*. My father gave it to me. It's very old. Very fine. The inscription along the blade is said to be magical, though no one has ever been able to translate it for me."

She placed the weapon in my open hand. Maybe it really was enchanted. Even now, in the dim light of hard stars, I thought I saw a gleam of white flash from the metal.

"It's beautiful," I said. "Are you sure you want...?"

The princess unfastened her cloak and let it fall to the ground. Beneath it she wore a soft leather vest and a pair of linen breeches. She was as slender as a seedling oak. Her scent was half sweat, half perfume. She smelled so good, I almost sank to my knees.

Her breath made clouds in the night air. "I don't do this happily. But I do it nevertheless."

"I'm a little confused."

With a speed that stunned me almost as much as the blow itself, she slapped me square in the face.

"Don't mock me, Ramirez."

"I'm not..." I protested. "How am I *mocking* you?"

She looked like she might hit me again.

"Is this a joke? Or some weird ritual thing? You don't have to do this, Princess."

"In my country, it's said that a life is worth a life. You saved someone who is dear to me. I...what?"

"Let me get this straight. This is ending your life?"

She paused. "That's not what I said."

"It's what you meant."

"You don't want me?"

"I want you more than I want my next breath," I confessed. A gentle breeze filtered through her dark hair. Even the wind wanted to touch her. "But you still don't have to do this."

Ara lowered her eyes. "This is uncharacteristic of you, Ramirez. Almost..."

"I know. Almost *something*."

She gave me a sad little smile.

I looked up at the peaks to the east, which were etched in silver against the night sky. From back at camp came the nicker of one of the horses. "Would it be so bad, though? I mean, I don't want to be a penance. It's just—can't you see yourself with me? Even for a minute?"

Her eyes wandered. "I'm old, Ramirez. I'm afraid."

"You're not old," I said.

"My sisters married before they were twenty."

"You're not your sisters."

"I know. I just...I wonder if I've waited too long. And now—"

"Now you think you've found someone."

"Found," she said, "and lost again. You were in love once. Don't you remember how that feels?"

I put one hand on her shoulder. Of course I remembered. I carried the memory like a stone in my stomach. Ara looked into my eyes and eventually she nodded. I picked her cloak up off the damp ground and draped it over her shoulders. My heart was doing a frantic dance inside me but I gave her one chaste kiss on the cheek before she turned and made her way back to camp. And then I just stood there. I stood there and I listened to the howls float over the moors, up into a sky where long fingers of cloud gripped the moon like they were about to pluck it from heaven and hide it where it would never be seen again. I could hear the wolves distinctly now. It was just like the writers always said. They did sound lonely.

Amateurs, I thought.

Fereganth

We met up with our friend Dzerdjik the next morning. Linnaeth's disciple couldn't tell us much. He sat in a puddle of his own congealed blood in the center of the trail, impaled on a wooden stake. The dead man's hands were lashed behind him, and his head was thrown back as if he was trying to spit the shaft at the clouds.

Izgir slid off his horse and walked stiffly toward the body. The Naztali paused. He reached as if to touch the corpse, but thought better of it. What was left of Dzerdjik's skin was a rotting patchwork of green and gray.

"Been dead a week," said the Naztali. "Maybe more."

"And he was the one who was going to prepare the way," said Ara. "Is this something the Ganthans did?"

Izgir shook his head. "Spike through the body. Another through the skull. This looks more like Syrtian work to me."

Truke tu-Kekh spat. "Sonsabitches had their fun with him first. Half his face is missing. His eyes…"

"Birds." Izgir pointed with his chin at a scrubby tree that stood a few yards off the trail. A dozen vultures perched on the branches, watching us assess their handiwork. They didn't make a sound. But neither did Ara. The Sidharan dropped to the ground and nocked an arrow in her bow. She took her time sighting. Then the string sang and she sent the shaft straight through the heart of one of the filthy creatures. It didn't even have a chance to raise a wing. The rest of the flock scattered into the sky.

"They took his pendant," said Gowen as he dismounted. He was right. Dzerdjik's silver circle, the medallion that had flashed so brilliantly on the banks of the Talking River, was missing.

"Gowen," I said.

The big man didn't answer.

"Gowen, what are you doing?"

"What does it look like I'm doing? I ain't gonna leave him like this."

Eventually we joined him. Using knives and short swords, we gouged a pit in the stony earth. We pulled the stakes from Dzerdjik's corpse and buried him in his awful crouch, piling stones on the grave to keep the animals out. There was nothing clean enough to say. The Copper Mountains seemed to be inching closer, like the teeth of some giant predator bellying toward us. A lean wind prowled the valley, and the path we were following disappeared into the highlands.

"Welcome to Fereganth," muttered Truke tu-Kekh. "Ass end of nowhere."

———+———

Welcome.

Right.

Welcome to a land littered with rocks the size of houses, where stands of wind-withered trees dotted the mountainsides and the mouths of caves yawned in the cliffs that towered over the trail into Fereganth. At least we *assumed* it was a trail into Fereganth; Izgir was following the tracks of horses that had passed this way a few days before. Our watchfulness stemmed only partly from fear. The Ganthans never attacked from ambush. They fought in broad daylight, with their pipes keening and their voices raised in song. Rather, we watched because so few travelers from the lowlands had ever seen the sights of this far-flung region. When we returned to the west, if it came to pass that there was a west to *return to,* our accounts would fuel a thousand fireside stories.

We spotted four elk, a lumbering black bear, long slopes of purple heather. We crossed creeks as clear as gin, little ribbons of pure water wriggling down the mountainsides. At one point, as we traversed the highest ridge on our route, we looked back to see clouds moving like a silent tide over the land we'd just left. We were several thousand feet above sea level at this point. The sight was explainable. Still, the effect was eerie, as if someone was trying to erase any hope we had of turning back.

The further we rode, the more my companions seemed to avoid me. It wasn't dislike. I mean, as far as I could *tell*, it wasn't dislike. It was more like they were trying to give me a chance to prepare for whatever colossal feat I'd been sent to Fereganth to perform. I had never said what that might be, of course. So maybe they figured my *modus operandi* was a secret. Maybe they figured I was wise beyond my appearance—not unlikely, when you thought about it—or that I possessed strange and incomprehensible powers, like Linnaeth. I'd managed to resuscitate Ayrd Teryan, after all. I had to smile about that one. It was the first thing I was proud of doing in...*what?* Frankly, it was the first thing I could remember. And it must have seemed epic. But beyond a little mouth-to-mouth, my miracle-making abilities were severely limited. I had been counting on following Dzerdjik's lead. The fact was, I had no idea how to persuade the Ganthans to leap with the rest of Ythedra into what might well prove to be a suicidal war. The notion that Truke and Izgir and Gowen suspected I *did*—that they thought we had some urgent and well-defined purpose for entering this desolate land—only increased the pressure.

So I told the story partly to calm my own stomach. I related what happened when the last of King Ridwen's decimated Palace Guard straggled northwest away from the Red Cities nine hundred years earlier. It wasn't a pleasant journey. The refugees were despondent and bone-tired. Many were close to starvation. And they were attacked so relentlessly by Aln Adrackt's Kirikite mercenaries that only a few score guardsmen and their families lived to cross the Strait of Sorrows to Ythedra.

"The Guardsmen who survived the crossing," I said, "always despised Prince An-Nashayel for not returning to Emerkest to break Varun's siege of Kaer Rhygat. Swearing an enmity with An-Nashayel's followers that was almost equal to their hatred of Aln Adrackt, they traveled into these unforgiving lands, which we still call *Fereganth*, or 'the Northern Unknown.' Aln Adrackt's enchantment robbed them of speech, so they could no longer converse, and they wandered hungry and sick through the dismal lowlands and marshes of eastern Ythedra, heading north toward the Copper Mountains and the rugged coastline beyond. In the mountains they were befriended by the wizard Nihreth Wyn. The old man took pity on the ragged outcasts. He had lived for generations with little or no contact with the world of men, but from the pictures the Guardsmen scratched in the dirt it dawned on him that the wizard who had driven these refugees from their homes in Emerkest was his own ancient enemy, Aln Adrackt. Nihreth Wyn disappeared for several weeks. When he returned, he presented the wanderers with seven swords. You've probably heard that mixed with the metal of these swords was the blood of Kalya, the Storm Goddess, the Face of the North. It was an alloy that made the blades invincible in war against evil. The Guardsmen were grateful to the old sorcerer. He brought them food as well, and taught them where to find water and game. They would have followed him in conquest and adventure. They would have followed him anywhere. But Nihreth Wynn asked for nothing in return. In fact he soon vanished, leaving no man able even to recall where his dwelling once stood. Hindered by Aln Adrackt's spell of speechlessness, the Guardsmen—the people we now call *Ganthans*—learned to communicate instead with the wolves they found in this land. They trained the animals to aid them in their hunts and wars, and even when they could speak again, some of the Ganthans communed more easily with their wolves than with other men.

"Linnaeth says the Ganthans have created a culture of warfare and testing, incorporating as legends many of the feats of their ancestors in the keep of Kaer Rhygat during Prince Varun's siege. The Ganthans do not surrender. They learn from an early age that death in battle is preferable to life in peace, which is in any case harsh in this bleak land, and that cowardice is not an option, since those who display it are executed by a committee of Ganthan women.

"In these dark days no one, not even Linnaeth, knows how many Ganthans there are, what their customs may be or how they worship their gods, if indeed they have any. The Ganthans have forgotten much of what made them civilized in centuries past. They are a wild people, quick to anger and impossible to pacify, filled with ancient rage for wounds that other men have long forgotten."

Ara nodded. "Hey," she said. "Can't wait."

"I can," said Gowen. I may have been the only one who heard him. Fingering the copper key he wore on his wrist, the big man surveyed the mountains around us like a man returning to a prison he thought he'd long ago escaped.

2 9

Kaer Dinock

The first dwellings we passed were rough-hewn stone houses with sod roofs but no chimneys. Many were decorated with dried octopus carcasses, nailed with legs splayed out like crude sunbursts on the walls. Children stared dirty-eyed from the open doors of the low-slung structures, and gathered in twos and threes at the side of the trail to observe our passing. The Ganthan women were a sturdy, unkempt lot, much given to spitting. They looked almost as hard as their men, who wore untended beards, braided hair and, despite the autumn chill, nothing but leather boots and dark woolen kilts.

At last a red-haired man carrying a freshly killed deer over one shoulder deigned to speak to us.

"Where can we find the leader of the Ganthans?" said Izgir.

I might have tried a greeting of some sort.

The hunter paused to sample a finger's worth of the deer blood trickling down the side of his thigh. "Which Ganthans?"

The Naztali shrugged. "Of all Ganthans."

"You can't."

"Of *any* Ganthans, then," Ara said. "We're not choosy."

"I can see that." The Ganthan shifted the weight of the carcass on his shoulders. He gazed above and beyond us, as if he'd stopped on his way home to ruminate on a change in the weather. The breeze had freshened. I could smell the sea. "The leader of the Knife Mountain Clan lives two hours from here, in the longhouse called Kaer Dinock. Callan Rahiel is his name. He know you're coming?"

"We bring news," said Izgir.

If the Ganthan cared to hear what was happening in the world, he hid it well. "And what's *this* thing?" he asked, pointing with his beard.

"His name," answered Gowen, "is Truke tu-Kekh. He's a blue troll from the Broken Mountains far to the west, and a very great warrior."

"Looks like a turtle without a shell. Does it bite? Can you eat it?"

Truke tu-Kekh fingered the shaft of his war hammer. "You can try," he said.

The Ganthan flashed a carnivorous smile. He was missing two of his upper teeth, and a waxy, crescent-moon-shaped scar disfigured his forehead. "Got my dinner. Another time, Mr. Troll."

"Any time," Truke tu-Kekh said, "would be fine."

The red-haired man chuckled. "Ready to meet your maker, little one?"

"If it meant I wouldn't have to keep looking at your women, I'd consider it."

Gowen coughed so hard that he nearly choked.

"Big mouth," said the Ganthan. "For a turtle."

"My voice counts as much as anyone else's, if that's what you mean. It's called democracy. By the way, which ones *are* the women?"

The Ganthan wasn't smiling anymore. "Ride on," he said to Izgir, though his eyes were fixed on the troll. "While you still can."

By the time we reached Kaer Dinock, late that afternoon, a gaggle of Ganthan men and boys followed us. They were accompanied by a dozen gray wolves, gaunt golden-eyed creatures that trotted loose-limbed through the trees alongside the trail. Two boys advanced from the mob to take our horses. Izgir patted Goat's neck as if to say good-bye. A pockmarked man with maybe three strands of black hair on his head opened the door of the longhouse and peered out at us. He winced at the daylight. When he stepped back, leaving the door ajar, we ventured inside. The place stank of wood smoke and sweat, and it was hard to see through the haze. Squinting, I made out brown bearskins on the floor and various well preserved heads—moose; shark; mountain lion—mounted on the walls.

"They told me what was coming," said an elderly man at the far end of the room. He was shirtless but partially wrapped in a deer hide robe. His eyes were gray, and a shock of snow-white hair fell to his shoulders. Two younger men sat on the floor beside him. "They said a Naztali scavenger has ridden into our land. They said he is leading a yellow woman, a stick man—this giant, who barely fits under our roof beams—a troll, and two Darannans. I said, *Are they refugees, or simply fools?* Now that you're here, I can see you're not refugees."

A half-dozen men lounged on the floor around us. No one laughed.

"We are neither," said Izgir. "We are envoys from the free nations of Ythedra. We're looking for Callan Rahiel, chief of the Knife Mountain Clan."

"You've found him," said the Ganthan in the deerskin robe. He had a face like the prow of a ship: all forehead, nose, and chin. White sideburns extended down to almost his jowls. He pulled at a long wooden pipe and let the smoke leak from the corners of his mouth. "Now what?"

Behind me I heard the shuffle of boots on the stone floor. More men were arriving. I wanted to turn around, but I kept my eyes fixed forward. Izgir's voice thickened: "The nations of the west are menaced again by the dark lord the Darannans call Aln Adrackt. We call him the Shadow King. His creatures, the Syrtians, are taking our lands and killing our people."

Callan Rahiel was silent, so Izgir continued.

"We are gathering for battle with the Shadow King and his armies. But we need more men. We have come to ask you to help us drive this threat back into the sea, just as the Ganthans helped to turn him back once before." Izgir glanced at me. *Right?* his expression seemed to say. I nodded. The Naztali cleared his throat, then continued: "At the Battle of the Standing Rocks…"

"Stones," I prompted.

"At the Battle of the Standing Stones. When the waves broke red on the rocks."

The room was silent.

"Why?" said the old man.

"Why? Why *what?*"

"Why have you traveled so many miles to lie to me, Naztali?"

Izgir took a step forward. "The Naztali do not lie."

"Only when they move their mouths. Give up your tricks. We know of your true plans. And of your attacks. Your people recently killed a hunting party of our young men not three days' ride from here, on your eastern fields. We heard it took two dozen of your tribe to kill them. Only six of them…"

"Whatever you heard. Whatever you—"

"Silence! These were not men armed for war. They were children tracking game. The Naztali butchered them and left them to waste in the wind. We care little for the lands outside our own, but even we have heard of the stories the Naztali tell to justify their attacks on Syrtian subjects in the Greensea, fireside tales of the Enemy who stole Emerkest, now awakened to walk the earth again. It doesn't seem to occur to anyone that Aln Adrackt is *dead*, defeated by the might of Ganthan war craft many centuries ago. It has been my experience that the dead know their places. Why you come here talking alliance with us, bringing this collection of scarecrows and hobgoblins, is beyond my reckoning. So don't insult me with your lies. And keep the ghost stories to yourselves, for your time on earth is growing short."

Izgir bowed slightly. "Callan Rahiel, grant me one request. Tell me who has filled your ear with these falsehoods."

The old man scowled as he relit his pipe. Then he glanced up and beyond us.

"I did," said a voice just behind me. "Though they're hardly falsehoods."

I turned to see a disfigured face, lank dark hair, and one expressionless eye. It was Tarrant Lef, Captain of the Syrtian Border Guard. The big man's fist drove me to the floor.

3 0

Waking a Legend

Tarrant Lef wasn't alone. As we faced Callan Rahiel, a dozen Syrtian soldiers had filtered into the longhouse and taken up positions among the Ganthan men behind us.

"Kill them, Callan," the Syrtian commander said. "Kill them as repayment for the death of your son."

The old Ganthan nodded. Rough hands grabbed my tunic and hoisted me back up. A dozen swords were leveled at Izgir and Truke tu-Kekh. Ara was backhanded when she tried to resist.

"Take them to the shore," said Callan. His voice sounded more tired than angry. "Cut their throats. Leave them for the waves."

The Syrtians shoved Truke tu-Kekh and Usak toward the door.

"Callan Rahiel!" I said. "Wait! Listen to me. We've come to wake the Seven Swords."

All movement in the room ceased. I knew I'd taken a fool's chance. It was the only kind we had left.

"I know you and your people are frightened," I continued. "You're frightened because you've forgotten the swords that led the Ganthans to victory over Aln Adrackt in the Years of Iron. But those swords were real. And they can lead you again."

Tarrant Lef burst into laughter.

"Pigshit stories," said the Syrtian commander. "And an insult to the warriors of Fereganth, if you'll allow me to say it."

Whoever was holding me from behind tightened his grip, squeezing until it felt like my shoulders were being ripped out of their sockets. I felt my face flush with anger, heard my tongue take off on its own. "How an insult, if it's true? The insult is that this Syrtian dog is allowed to speak in the house of Callan Rahiel, whose ancestors fought the Autumn King when he tried to take Kaer Rhygat."

Callan stood. His face was bleak. *About like my future*, I concluded. "Let him go!" he commanded. "What do you know of the Swords, scarecrow?"

"I know each sword lives if taken up to battle evil. It lives in the hand of the warrior it's chosen and makes him *more than one*. It binds him to the spirit of every Ganthan who ever defied Aln Adrackt in the streets of the White Cities or boarded the storm ships of the Niyarrin where the islands are ice or battled whales in the Sea of Clouds and lived to sing about it over a fire at night. Where are they, men of Fereganth? Have you lost Nihreth Wyn's gift to your fathers? Where are your swords? Why don't they sing for you anymore?"

Chaos erupted around me. I felt a sharp pain in the small of my back and I fought to stay on my feet. Callan Rahiel raised his arms for quiet, but even that didn't work at once. At the same time, I struggled to recall more of the stories I'd heard about Nihreth Wyn's legacy to these unruly people.

Callan Rahiel glanced around at the Ganthans in the room. "Are you mocking us? The swords have been silent for centuries."

"Maybe they've been silent because you haven't fought for anything *worthwhile* all these centuries. You've been battling yourselves. Taking each other's women. Stealing Naztali ponies and Niyarrin gold. What work is that for the defenders of Kaer Rhygat? Take me to the *swords*, Callan! Take me to them, Guardians of Ridwen, son of An, Emperor of Dar-Annon! If you fight the Syrtians, you fight Aln Adrackt again. You—"

Tarrant Lef's voice was insistent. "Callan, why do you listen to this nonsense? You have pledged fealty to the Emperor of Emerkest. He doesn't appreciate disloyalty."

"We have pledged ourselves to no one," said the Ganthan elder. "And the stories are not nonsense."

"He talks treason," said Lef, "and I'll finish him now!"

Two Ganthans intercepted the Syrtian captain as he lunged at me, blade in hand. As they pinned his arms, pulling his doublet tight against his chest, I saw a pendant flash in the firelight. *Dzerdjik's silver circle.* His eye met mine, and I could tell Tarrant Lef knew I'd found him out. The Syrtian captain had impaled Dzerdjik and left his corpse for the birds. He was probably the one responsible for the deaths of Callan Rahiel's son and his hunting companions as well.

I said, "Take me to them, Callan! Take me and your best men. Fight the Emperor of Emerkest, if that's what Aln Adrackt calls himself now, and we'll hear the swords speak loud and clear."

Tarrant Lef shouted to be heard over the buzz of voices around us. "This is madness, Callan! Let ME kill them, if you won't!"

The old man stared at his hands. He surveyed the elderly men who sat around him and waited until the noise in the hall subsided. "You will be sorry, scarecrow, if you are wrong. The silence of the swords is a wound that pains the men of Fereganth even in our dreams. Some of the weapons have been...*lost.* Others are broken. But we shall see what is left. We'll see it now, in the Cairn of Winds."

Outside, as we blinked in the gray-green light, I heard Tarrant Lef tell his men to leave us our weapons. The command struck me as odd. Why would the Syrtians want to leave us armed? I had visions of an unprovoked attack, of the Syrtian soldiers butchering us on the hike to the Cairn of Winds on the pretext that we'd struck one of their men or tried to escape. So I unbuckled my sword belt and let it fall. Ara seemed to sense my misgivings. She laid her bow in the dirt. Usak relinquished his bow as well, and Izgir gave up his dagger. Last to comply was Truke tu-Kekh. The war hammer landed with a solid *thunk* on the stony earth. I knew what he was thinking. *So what if Ramirez drops his sword? He doesn't know how to use it anyway.* But I might as well have tied my friends' hands behind their backs. They were defenseless. On the other hand, what if I was wrong? The whole scheme was flimsy. *Find the Seven Swords. Gawk at the Seven Swords. Admire the Seven Swords. Then what?* I suppose I was counting on jogging some sort of collective memory to rouse the Ganthans. I didn't know how to do it or if it would make a difference if I could. But we weren't exactly holding aces. If my idea failed, we'd only die a few hours later, and maybe a little more slowly. That we *would* die was certain. The only question seemed to be who would be given the task of dispatching us, Syrtian thug or Ganthan warrior.

———+———

The Cairn of Winds stood high on the face of the largest crag in sight, an anvil-shaped mass of granite that hung out over the churning surf of the Sea of Storms. As we started up the narrow footpath toward the Cairn, I saw shirtless, kilted Ganthan men hustling from their scattered huts to catch up with us. By the time we'd walked a mile out of the village, scores of the clansmen followed along behind Tarrant Lef's armed escort. The number of witnesses must have made the Syrtian captain's task more difficult. He surely wanted to kill us as quickly and unpleasantly as possible, but I figured that almost as strong as Lef's desire to see us dead would be his urge to see the fabled Swords—if only to gauge the prospect of claiming them for Aln Adrackt. Or for himself.

Callan Rahiel, on the other hand, wanted us alive. An unprovoked attack might trigger the old man's wrath—and possibly endanger the alliance between Emerkest and Fereganth. So Tarrant

Lef had little choice but to follow along, biding his time, as the sounds of surf and sea gulls swirled around us.

———+———

The Cairn was an unadorned fortress, the first structure the Ganthans built when they arrived in the land beyond the Copper Mountains, unable to speak and fearing pursuit from Emerkest. Constructed of black granite on the uppermost heights of a bluff, it was a formidable stronghold: a compact collection of vertical walls built in a semi-circle around a rectangular stone keep that backed to a cliff. The final hundred yards of the trail were brutally steep, and zigzagged through knife-sharp outcroppings of rock. My heart pounded hard by the time we reached the Cairn's ramshackle gate. Though the air was chilly, my back was slick with sweat.

Bearing a single torch, Callan Rahiel led us into the dim keep, through frigid halls and down a flight of cracked stone steps to a cavernous empty chamber.

"Open the casements!"

When two Ganthans did as the old man ordered, the Sea of Storms stretched out below us like a sheet of liquid steel, accented with rippling lines of whitecaps. Wind stirred the tattered battle flags hung on stanchions around the room. In one corner lay a pile of battered iron and bronze shields. And on the wall opposite the windows, I saw the swords.

We all moved, more or less together, to get a better look. It wasn't a pretty sight. First of all, there were only four swords. To make matters worse, the blades of three of them had been snapped or hewn in half. Their iron handles were wrapped in the withered remains of what had once been leather, and dimpled at the hilt with empty jewel sockets. The jewels weren't missing. They'd never been there. Weapons forged by Nihreth Wyn always had such empty sockets—a statement in opposition to the embellishment and empty pomp of Aln Adrackt and other, less dangerous enemies. To the casual observer the only thing unusual about these swords was the quality of the blades. It was most apparent in the one weapon that remained unscathed. Stout and straight, the blade shone as if it had been forged earlier that day.

Chiseled in the wall above the weapons were these words:

> *We are Snake destroyers,*
> *Nihreth's hammered flame.*
> *Draw us not in anger,*
> *Sheathe us not in shame.*
> *Justice is reborn here.*
> *Vengeance is its name.*

"So it's true," said Truke tu-Kekh, shouldering his way to the front of the group. He spoke the words as if they were an accusation. "In the Broken Mountains we thought the Seven Swords of Fereganth were simply a legend."

"Legends are never simple," said Callan Rahiel. He padded to the wall, lifted the single intact sword from its mount, and held it before him as if it were a newborn child. He slid his thumbs along the grooves of the haft. He turned to me. "Are they, scarecrow? What would you have us do now?"

A Ganthan warrior shoved me toward the old man. "Speak!" he said.

I glanced at the sullen faces surrounding me. My heart was pounding so hard, I had trouble standing still.

"Swear," I said. The word came out as a whisper. I raised my voice. "Swear you'll fight Aln Adrackt."

Callan Rahiel was still admiring the sword. He didn't even look up. "Aln Adrackt is long dead," he said. "The men of Ferganth do not fight shadows. Nor will I promise to fight the Syrtians. We have no quarrel with them, and we welcome their counsel, at least until the Naztali can be punished for their crimes."

Then I did a colossally stupid thing. I stepped forward and reached for the sword. Callan Rahiel stared hard at me before he let me wrest the weapon from his grasp. The blade was remarkably light.

"Then you," I hissed, "are a FOOL! This sword isn't a child to be coddled. It's not an idol to be fondled and clucked over and hidden away like a Syrtian's bauble. It's a *weapon*. It's a demon killer, and it wants the blood of Aln Adrackt!"

———+———

That's right. Shouting.

———+———

What else could I do? My Exhibit A had become an embarrassment. It wasn't *doing* anything. I scanned the weapon from hilt to tip. I was searching for a clue I'd overlooked. I needed a rune. A glyph. An on/off switch. *Anything.* I had nothing. Everyone knew it. In my frustration, I hurled the weapon across the floor. Gowen watched the weapon fetch up at his feet.

"Enough!" said Tarrant Lef. Before I could react, the Syrtian captain's saber sliced through the flesh of my left arm.

Callan Rahiel looked on impassively as Tarrant Lef brought his blade up over his head to finish me. But the scarred captain halted at the height of his stroke. Something beyond me had caught his eye. As if obeying a silent command, we all turned toward Gowen. The big man held the sword I'd discarded. Now, though, the weapon looked different. It was like looking at sunlight on a mountain creek. The metal seemed more *visible*, somehow, more real, than anything around it—as if the rest of the world was blurred in its presence.

Gowen spoke softly. "Drop the sword, you half-headed bastard."

Tarrant Lef laughed. It was a forced, high-pitched sound.

"What sort of trickery is this?" he demanded. "KILL him!"

A burly Syrtian infantryman swung at Gowen, who parried high with the luminous Ganthan blade. The Syrtian cutlass shattered. Fragments of metal rang like coins on the floor, and even Gowen looked puzzled. The last of the Seven Swords seemed to shimmer in his hands. The room was silent.

I watched all of this from the flagstones, cupping a palmful of my own blood. Ara and Usak were beside me before I'd even figured out what happened. The Syrtian captain seized the nearest Ganthan and pulled him close. The captive was a boy, maybe twelve years old. He had curly dark hair and he was missing a front tooth. Tarrant Lef held his blade against the boy's throat.

"Callan!" cried Lef. "Keep your men away from me. Sergeant! Get that sword!"

But the Ganthan elder moved too fast. Callan Rahiel had already stepped to where the weapons hung along the wall. Now he paused before one of the broken blades, plucked it from its stanchion and measured the weapon in his hands. Still studying the steel, about two thirds of the blade's original length, he leveled the sword at Tarrant Lef. There was no glimmer of enchantment in the metal of this sword. But maybe it didn't matter.

"Brothers," said Callan Rahiel. "Stand back."

"Don't be stupid, old man. You want to lose another son?"

Callan took another stride forward. He studied the boy's captor with a curiously blank expression.

"I said *stop!*" shouted Lef. His captive writhed in his grasp, and the Syrtian captain squeezed his neck tighter, forcing the boy's chin up. The kid was cooler than I would have been. Still, I could see the doubt in his eyes.

"You hold a man of Fereganth," said Callan Rahiel. "He feels no fear."

"Wrong. His heart beats like a bird's."

"You lie," said the old man, staring now at the boy. "He is my son."

When Callan took another step forward, Tarrant Lef drew the edge of his blade across the boy's throat. Dark blood fountained into the air. The kid tried to scream but couldn't. He slumped to the floor, both hands holding his throat. His legs thrashed as if he could run from the wound. Usak moved quickly to wrap his tunic around the boy's neck. Dazed by the horror of the moment, I saw without immediately recognizing it that the boy wore a bracelet. And on the bracelet was a copper key.

Callan Rahiel's cry was awful. I felt a chill in the long room as his voice swelled in a scream of pain and revenge. The Ganthan's broken sword flashed as he lunged at the Syrtian commander, burying the blade in the cavalryman's chest with a sound like bamboo snapping. Tarrant Lef's knees buckled, and he slumped to the floor. He stared at the man who had killed him. Callan Rahiel stared straight back.

"Coward," said the old man.

Then the world fell apart.

Syrtian soldiers slashed frantically against the unarmed clansmen of Fereganth, who pressed forward regardless of hurt, regardless of fear, tearing at their enemies like animals. Though the Syrtians were members of the Border Guard—a tough, elite unit—the Ganthans had just seen one of their own murdered in cold blood. And the clansmen had help. Gowen's sword flashed like winter lightning in the chaotic chamber. Izgir snatched up Tarrant Lef's bloodstained saber and threw himself into the melee, attacking the Syrtians with his lifetime of accumulated hatred. A few of Tarrant Lef's men tried to surrender, but it did them no good. When the fighting ceased, not a single Syrtian drew breath. Broken bodies littered the stone floor like leaves after a summer storm.

———+———

Callan Rahiel knelt beside one of the dead. For almost an hour, he traced the contours of his young son's face with his fingertips. When one of his people offered to help him up off the floor, he brushed the man's hand from his shoulder.

"What does it mean?" I asked the Ganthan who'd tried to help. I said it loud enough so Callan Rahiel could hear. "That bracelet. The one his son wears."

The man I asked appeared to think about the matter, but he didn't answer. Another Ganthan spoke instead. "It is the emblem of his family. And nothing to discuss today."

"Gowen," I called.

The big man sat slumped against the wall beside the chamber doors. Most of his face was shaded by his mop of unruly blonde hair. His beard was streaked with sweat and gore.

"What do you wear on your wrist?"

Gowen held up one arm as if it took all his strength. He peeled his sleeve back to almost his elbow.

"I see it," I said. "Tell me what it is."

"You know what it is. A key."

"Right. But what kind of key?"

"I don't know. A copper key."

The room went silent. Callan Rahiel looked up. He studied Gowen the way an astronomer might stare at an uncharted planet.

"That key," he demanded. "Where did you get it?"

The big man drew his legs up against his chest. "It was my mother's. She left it to me when she died. And don't go gettin' any ideas, old man, 'cause it ain't coming off."

"When did she die? Of what cause?"

"They said it was a fever. I think it was hunger. And heartbreak. It was only a few years after she ran away from you people."

"She ran away," said Callan Rahiel, staring down at his hands, "just after her child was born."

Gowen sat up straight. "How did you know that?"

The old man bowed his head. "Because her name was Diersa. She was my sister."

My wound was bloody but shallow. Tarrant Lef had managed to cut an inch-wide strip of skin from my left arm, but he hadn't hit an artery. Usak scavenged a tunic and ripped it into several long swaths. He cleaned the cut, then wrapped the cloth tightly around my bicep. I flexed to check that the bandage fit right. I looked up to see Callan Rahiel standing in front of me.

"It was all a lie," I said. "The alliance with Emerkest...the stories of Naztali attacks...whatever else Tarrant Lef was telling you. It was all a trick. Aln Adrackt is alive again. He's taken Kaer Rhennet and we suspect his next target is Dred Thannat, the last Darannan fortress in Ythedra. Once he's crushed the Darannans, he'll come for you. For the Ganthans. For the people who beat him once before, centuries ago. But he's stronger now. And not even the sword that remains will save you if you try to stand alone."

Callan Rahiel squeezed his eyes shut, as if he was searching his head for a vision of what to do. Then he found it.

"Throw the Syrtians into the sea!" he cried, with a confidence I hadn't heard before. "Then let us bury our dead, and give thanks for their strength. You. Gowen. I want words with you. Nethred: have our kinsmen bring enough wood to fuel a fire in every chamber of the Cairn. Sound the horns. Send word to the clans that every man of Fereganth who can fight is called to join us here—every warrior with his wolf, and ready for battle. We are called again to face the evil that destroyed the homeland of our fathers, and the last of the swords forged by Nihreth Wyn has awakened to fight with us. Two days hence, we march for Dred Thannat. We go to battle in the west, where many blades will swim in blood." Callan Rahiel considered his son where he lay pale and cold on the stained stone floor. One of the boy's hands was open, as if he was reaching to touch his father. The old man's voice thickened. "And mine, I promise you, will be one of them."

3 1

The Siege of Dred Thannat

A nd so the enemy came to Dred Thannat.
There were Syrtian regulars, of course. Rangy and profane,
hungry for plunder, legions of slate and scarlet-clad infantrymen
made up the backbone of Aln Adrackt's army. Their flags, black
gonfalons bearing the crimson emblem of the Standing Snake, made
a garish forest above the pike-bearing soldiers.

Hordes of Kirikite riders, yellow-skinned mercenaries from the
deserts of Emerkest, served as the army's scouts and light cavalry.
They carried circular shields and painted scimitars. Ranged alongside them were platoons of Kyrd engineers, thin-lipped masters
of the scorpion, catapult, and siege engine; Syrtian dog handlers,
with their packs of tracking hounds and armored mastiffs; Atarian
renegades with filed teeth and tattooed faces; Niyarrin pirates,
strangers to the word of god; the Azhirim, white-haired, scythe-
wielding riders from the plains of Ezkahrrak, who called themselves the consorts of Death and rode to war in masks of bronze
and slate; chariot-driving Kusulls, black warriors under saffron
flags, destroyers of a dozen southern cities; cold-handed Fegrians,
wielders of delicate nets and heavy maces, who wore jewelry fashioned from the bones of their foes; Surb slaves with seared stumps
where their tongues once wagged; and hulking Piryati, the hairless,

heavy-browed mountain-dwellers who devoured the flesh of their own kind and fought with clubs the size of horses' legs.

Beyond the bivouacs of these predatory tribes lay the fireless encampment of the urzeks. And beyond even the dark precincts of the urzeks stood the scarlet tents of Aln Adrackt and his draviden, the walking worms that shrank from sunlight, and the iron-barred cages of the wizard's giant spiders. All told, Dred Thannat's attackers numbered sixty thousand men, beasts, and creatures beyond accustomed category, a host of stone-eyed marauders and nightmare figments scraped from the furthest realms of the far-flung Ninelands and drugged, beaten, and bribed into a single devouring organism. This army worshiped half a hundred gods. It made sacrifices to imperious shadows. It traveled on *khat* and whatever it could catch and kill. It was massive. It was hungry.

And now, finally, it was *here*.

Atryen Quin slapped his palms against the stone of Dred Thannat. He figured he had a week to live. A week at best. When he'd finished reflecting on his fate, a scream was heard on the fields above Speckled Bay—heard from the walls of the fortress all the way to the siege lines of Aln Adrackt. It was the battle cry of Atryen Quin, Marshal of Kaer Rhennet, who faced his teeming enemy with eyes that burned and yet were cold.

3 2

Reinforcements

As Quin peered out over the army besieging Dred Thannat, I stood watching a ragged line of Ganthan warriors straggle out of the Silent Marsh into the Greensea. It wasn't a pretty picture. Knots of bearded, half-naked clansmen carrying axes and heraldic shields marched beside their shaggy packhorses. Their wolves ranged alongside the column like shadows in the grass, quiet as a midnight breeze.

Earlier the Ganthans had sung battle hymns and played their pipes, and skeins of wild music had swirled like storm clouds above us. Now the excitement of the enterprise had faded. I heard only creaking leather, clanking cook pots, the desultory banter of the men around me.

Callan Rahiel was too old to walk. He rode an ox instead, with his axe lashed to the horn of his saddle and one of Nihreth Wyn's broken swords resting on his lap. His back was bent. The muscles of his chest lay flaccid above a scarred stomach, and his cheeks had taken on a sunken pallor as the march wore on. But he refused all offers of food, and spoke to no one. He rode with his face set to the west.

Gowen slogged along behind him. He carried the last intact sword of Nihreth Wyn in a battered blue scabbard draped over his shoulder. The Ganthans customarily walked to war and so, he told me, would he. It was now known by all that Gowen was a nephew of Callan Rahiel. This made him a man of prestige, if no particular rank, among the Ganthans. The copper key he wore on his wrist was a talisman of the Callan clan, direct descendants of Callan Dysrahi, Keeper of Kaer Rhygat and the Defier of Aln Adrackt so many centuries before. Gowen's mother, Diersa, was Callan Rahiel's youngest sister. She'd fled Fereganth twenty-four years earlier when her husband decreed that Gowen, a jaundiced, colicky newborn, should be left exposed on a nearby mountainside until death. It was the custom. In Fereganth, only the strong survived. Gowen's father was long dead. He'd drowned while fighting the Niyarrin in a pointless and mostly forgotten coastal raid many autumns past. He was a brave man, Callan Rahiel said, and not without honor. It seemed he preferred to leave it at that.

———+———

I still ached from the wound I'd received from Tarrant Lef, but I wasn't about to wait behind. I had reclaimed Wind Sister and I was happy to ride. Those first days, Usak watched over me like a pterodactyl wet nurse. Periodically he passed me a flask of brackish water fortified with a bitter herb Izgir had scratched from the earth. The Taureg watched as I choked it down. Ara and Truke tu-Kekh rode in silence beside us.

We'd rested in Fereganth and had a chance to eat our fill. Just as at Inniskerr, the respite helped. I could see my companions felt better. Physically I was recovered as well. My dreams had let go of me at last and I slept for most of two nights. But the break in activity—a forced break, really, as the Ganthans gathered at the Cairn of Winds, pledging themselves to the fight against Aln Adrackt—had left me time for reflection. Too *much* time, maybe. I felt more alone than ever as we followed the Ganthan army down the narrow trails that led out of the mountains. Much had come back to me since

that night in Inniskerr when I'd remembered or discovered my former life in Ythedra and sometimes the grief and discomfort were so
sharp that I gripped the pommel of my cracked saddle to keep from
being overmastered. My friends feared some contagion was working within me and so it was, but this illness was rooted deeper than
blood or bone and susceptible to no salve or philter. Up until he
remembered himself at the Spider's Gate, Ban Lohannon had done
all he could to stay alive in the cellars of the Red Cities. He—I—*we*
had survived while others died. In that sense I had walked with Aln
Adrackt. Because I had not fought him, I'd *served* him. And yet the
lowliest animal gifted or possibly cursed with self-awareness knew
at least what I was struggling to realize: that no loss is complete
until assented to. And if any thought preserved me from the dismal
pull of my own despair as we waded a second time through the rolling plains of the Greensea, it was that I had to take it back, take *me*
back, look that dark thing in the eyes that promised everything and
say *I won't, I can't, I never did.* The time for redemption had come.
Either I took it now or I was going to keep on lapping at the poison. Either I killed Aln Adrackt or I lived with him inside me till he
dragged me down to madness and self-murder again. *Confrontation.*
Renunciation. Struggle. It all sounded fine and silvery. But the truth
was, I didn't know if I could do it.

Any of it.

I wasn't the only one who was preoccupied.

Usak was riding a Ganthan plow horse, a tremendous beast
with a head like a paving stone, but the Taureg seemed to be no
more comfortable than he'd been on our trek to Fereganth. He
gazed at the sights around him as if he was trying to catalogue them
for future study. It was hard to say if he approved. He was a shy
man—a shy *boy*, really, despite his size—and he seemed to grow
quieter with every hour he aged, every thought he wrestled. Truke

tu-Kekh by contrast got louder as we re-entered the Marsh. He reminisced about how he'd set the fire that burned the swamps to black and still smoldered in the blasted lands around us. He followed up with asides on the inevitable corruption of hereditary rule and contrasted monarchical government with the virtues of a stringent egalitarianism. The young forest dweller listened without comment. He shook his head at the stench and the scorched contours of the land and refused to look at the vultures that fought over the last charred remains of the worms killed in the flames. It was the morning of the sixth day of our march when we discovered Usak was gone. He'd slipped away during the night. Izgir tried following his trail, but concluded it was too old, eight hours at least, to be worth riding further.

"Three guesses," I offered.

Truke tu-Kekh nodded. "Headed back to the Thicket."

"It's not his fight," added Ara. "You can't blame him."

Of course we couldn't blame him. Usak had grown tired of life outside the woods. He was sick of the butchery he'd seen and possibly daunted as well by the prospect of the slaughter yet to come. Though I was disappointed the wide-eyed Taureg had left us, I wished him well. At any rate, there wasn't much time to dwell on departures. We were marching hard for Dred Thannat. The question was, *were we marching hard enough?* I cursed every tedious mile. I found myself watching the horizon. Far west of the Copper Mountains, beyond the curtain of smoke that hung over the Silent Marsh, beyond even the endless swale of wind-tossed grassland that made up the Greensea, a crumbling fortress held what little breath Ythedra had left.

We're coming, Quin, I mumbled.

We're on our way.

Hold on, goddammit.

A Suitable Afternoon

A week later, Quin stood puzzling over the plume of black smoke rising above Aln Adrackt's camp. At this distance he couldn't tell whether it came from the camp itself or from the northern outskirts of the Thicket just beyond. *Surely not*, he thought, *from the Thicket*. Why would the sorcerer pick a fight with the Tauregs before he'd even captured Dred Thannat? On the other hand, what could it mean if the smoke was coming from the camp? What could Aln Adrackt be burning? It was a thought that didn't bear pursuing. The Marshal shook his head. Even Speckled Bay seemed sepulchral this morning, ashen beneath a colorless sky. A slight wind still blew from the sea, and he could smell salt water and rain in alternating gusts. But the breeze also held hints of human decay—a scent that would no doubt become a stench before evening. Not that he would be here to smell it.

This, Quin suspected, would be his final dawn.

"Marshal? You wanted to see me?"

Quin didn't have to turn. He knew the voice. "Lieutenant Teryan," he said. "I left orders that I was to be awakened as soon as you returned. Was I unclear?"

"Sir," said the younger man, a blush creeping into his cheeks. "You hadn't slept for days. I thought my report could wait."

"So you took it upon yourself to let me sleep."

"I did. And…"

"And what?" Quin demanded.

"I heard about your wife, sir."

Quin clamped his jaw shut. Alone in his quarters the previous evening, he'd wept again at his failure to save the woman he loved. She'd been sent in front of one of Aln Adrackt's first assaults, roped into a line of slaves and civilian prisoners driven at spear point toward Dred Thannat as a sort of human shield for the Syrtian infantrymen behind them. Now she lay dead at the base of the fortress's east wall, another lump of cold earth for the elements to reclaim. How could a man presume to save a continent when he couldn't even protect his own wife? Quin tried but couldn't bring to mind pictures of happier days: of her auburn hair and hazel eyes and the white hands she'd always felt were too big. He just kept coming back to the sight of her dying in the mud with an arrow lodged in the base of her neck. Of course she would have wanted him to do his duty. She was prouder than he was of his triumphs as a commander of the Outriders. This only made him feel worse. Once as the early morning hours wore on he picked up his dagger and pressed it to the pulse in his wrist, thinking of the release that lay beyond resistance. It would have been simple enough—not even painful—to make the quick incisions lengthwise along the inside of his forearms. This would open the arterial canals. All he'd have to do then would be to watch the life leap out of his veins. At some point he'd grow weak enough to sleep, and that would be it. The end. *Simple.*

But then he thought about who would monitor the defense of Dred Thannat's southern wall in his absence, and how the supply of fresh water inside the fortress was dwindling, and how many good men he'd lost the day before. Good men who'd been counting on him. Who had followed his orders till they couldn't follow them anymore. He opened his eyes. With a swift, negligent toss he buried the dagger deep in a plank of the wooden floor. He slept like a stone for almost nine hours. When he woke up, he was thinking clearly again.

"I see," the Marshal conceded, climbing the steps toward what was left of the castle's southeastern bartizan, "the walls are still standing."

Teryan followed. "Still standing, sir. There's been no movement in the enemy camp since midnight. I think we may have discouraged them."

"Don't bet on it. Any report from Captain Olwyn?"

"He says we're at three hundred and forty dead, with another nine hundred or so wounded—though at least half of those can still fight.

Quin frowned at his subordinate. It was mostly to keep up appearances. The numbers were better than he expected. He had almost a thousand men left.

"What about the rest?"

"The rest?"

"You know. Women and children?"

"I don't know, sir. I didn't ask."

The Marshal let his head rock back on his neck so he could look at the sky. He heard a high-pitched whine a few inches away and realized it was probably an arrow that had just missed his skull. He stepped behind the nearest merlon, pulling Ayrd Teryan with him.

"*Ask* next time," he said. "Any other news, Lieutenant? Any problem getting back through the lines?"

The young officer bit off a yawn. "No sir. It was like you said. The shore road is only lightly guarded. We came in with the rain just before dawn and weren't spotted till we were within a hundred yards of the sally port. We sounded the signal and made a run for it, and Corin's archers managed to bring down a few of the enemy. But I'm afraid there's not much news. We still can't get past the Kirikite patrols to make contact with the Naztali."

Quin beat a one-handed tattoo on the battlements.

"The Kirikites. They know what they're doing," he admitted. "I shouldn't have sent you. But we're running out of options."

"Izgir said the Naztali would come," said Teryan.

"We just don't know when, is that it?"

"Not yet, sir."

Not yet. Quin searched for sarcasm on his lieutenant's features. He noticed also that Teryan had so far weathered the siege without a scratch. Only his bloodshot eyes testified to his fatigue. *Not yet.* Quin didn't know whether to be grateful or terrified in the face of the younger man's optimism. He still wasn't sure, either, what to make of the stories Ayrd Teryan had carried back with him from the Silent Marsh. *Danny Ramirez had brought him back from the dead. The blue troll saved them all by setting the Marsh on fire. And maybe unlikeliest of all: a Naztali warrior had praised the valor of a Darannan Outrider.* Quin wished he had a few hours to ponder the strange events populating his world. But he knew he wasn't going to get them. He placed a hand on Teryan's shoulder.

"Tell my cavalry officers I need to see them immediately. Then find a piece of unoccupied floor, place yourself on it, and shut your eyes. That's an order, son."

"Yessir."

"And after that—after you've slept…report back to me. I need an adjutant. Someone to be my shadow. My memory, too. Think you could handle that?"

Teryan seemed to grow another inch. He saluted. "I'd be honored to try, sir."

Quin almost smiled as he watched his lieutenant hurry down the steps toward the courtyard. He'd been like that once. A boy, aching to be a man, and confident the men around him knew what they were doing. What a blow it was to *become* one of those men. To know it was only you, after all—only you, with all your faults and weaknesses—who was making the decisions that meant life or death for a city. For a people. For a continent. The Marshal's ragged army of citizen-soldiers had fought better than anyone could have predicted against the waves of attackers that crashed against the walls of Dred Thannat. But now a good part of his garrison lay dead or wounded. The walls were being smashed into gravel, and the worst of the battle was yet to come.

Quin had figured all along that Aln Adrackt would send his most expendable forces into the assault first, using his Syrtian regulars only after the fortress's defenses were thoroughly battered. He'd save the urzeks for the final onslaught, thus preserving the aura of invincibility around his most fearsome followers even as he risked them least. Quin had copied the tactic on a far more modest scale. He held in reserve two platoons of Dred Thannat's mounted guard—elite soldiers commonly held in former days to be almost the equals of the Outriders of Kaer Rhennet in martial discipline and skill. But Quin was no longer a cocky lieutenant. He had to face facts. The drizzle had let up, and the breeze from the bay was drying his carefully nurtured bogs. Relief wasn't coming. Teryan was doubtless correct about the stillness in Aln Adrackt's camp. But the lull was ending. From where he stood, Quin could see Syrtian infantrymen forming ranks again, mixed with mobs of the club-wielding Piryati. Behind them milled the black figures of urzeks. And an hour later, as the barrage of stones intensified, driving Dred Thannat's defenders off the battlements, Aln Adrackt's armies advanced. There were no cheers or shouts now from either camp; there was only hatred and fear. When the first line of attackers neared the castle, Quin's archers fired blindly from their positions in the courtyard, aiming high over the southern wall to rain missiles on the living tide. Some in the advancing army fell. Many others kept coming. They anchored their ladders in the bloated bodies of their fallen comrades and started to climb. Quin's defenders dropped stones on the attackers, smashed the top rungs of their ladders, sheared off the faces and fingers of those who climbed fastest. Any attackers who made it over the battlements were thrown into the courtyard below, where a battalion of farmwomen surrounded and dispatched the enemy with cleavers and pitchforks. The women hacked and stabbed with a ferocity even the Marshal found unnerving. They emerged from these huddles dripping with blood, their faces masked in scarlet. This was Quin's own planned atrocity. It was a violation of every article of the code of warfare he'd studied and lived all his adult life. But his life, he reflected, was over. He didn't want to think about the horrors that awaited anyone taken alive by Aln Adrackt's omnivorous horde—especially anyone female. Better to go down fighting. Better to die quickly in battle than face the slow death of the captured.

"Sir!" said a voice behind him.

It was Ayrd Teryan again.

"I thought I told you to get some sleep."

"We can't hold the south wall much longer."

"Why not?"

"They're sending in urzeks. The men are panicking."

"Urzeks? Now? Why now?"

"Don't know, sir."

"Maybe they're getting anxious. We can kill urzeks, you know. They do *die,* regardless of what the stories say. Listen. Send for the archers, and tell them to deploy in the courtyard. Once they're set, sound the horn for retreat. We've got to get everyone off that wall and into the courtyard. And send word to Captain Olwyn that I need men in the bartizans at either end of the wall. They've got to be ready to re-occupy those positions. They've been drilled in this. They'll know what to do. Now go!"

Teryan was running by the time his commander finished the sentence.

Quin swayed where he stood, lost in thought. Then he snapped to attention. For several minutes he threaded his way through the chaos on the southern parapets, urging his soldiers on, directing reinforcements, stopping to extract a fragment of stone from the cheek of a beardless conscript who'd probably never held a sword before the siege started. The kid couldn't have been older than fourteen. He wept with the pain. Quin tried to think of something to say, but events cut him off. The south wall was in peril. Hearing the horns behind him sound the signal for retreat, he raced down the steps of the battlement toward the courtyard. Several of his men sprinted from their positions to follow, joining the Marshal behind the throng of archers in the courtyard. But the archers weren't alone. A crowd of ordinary men and women had gathered as well. Some held scythes. Others brandished oyster knives. Quin didn't have time to order them back to safety. In only moments the abandoned bulwarks teemed with advancing Syrtian soldiers, who stopped only to cheer as they leaped or climbed off the walls into the fortress itself.

"Captain Corin?" said Quin.

"Sir?"

"Now."

"First rank! Loose!"

Thirty Syrtian soldiers fell.

"Second rank! Loose!"

It was one line, then the next, then the third, as the first two ranks of bowmen nocked new arrows and aimed. When the first urzeks reached the battlements, they poked their narrow heads up, clambered over and hesitated when they saw the men firing at them. Quin's archers laid down a withering barrage. Two urzeks stumbled, then another. But others kept coming, infuriated by the five, now eight, now ten shafts protruding from their chitinous hides. Quin noted that his bowmen needed anywhere from one— in the eyes or the throat—to a score of arrows to drop the beasts. But drop them they did. And now, as Quin's archers seemed to turn the tide, as the urzeks could no longer raise their misshapen heads above the fortress wall without being struck by several arrows, Quin ordered a charge.

There was neither discipline nor logic to the advance. Darannan men and women simply swarmed forward together, overwhelming the few Syrtians who tried to resist, clubbing and slashing the wounded urzeks and driving those who could still move back over the wall.

But it worked.

Quin sensed opportunity for the first time since the siege began. He felt his blood race in his veins as it had when he was thirty years younger. With his broadsword he sliced through shield and armor, flesh and bone. Men fled before him. He buried his sword in the throat of a wounded urzek and leaned hard on the blade as filth spurted from the dying freak's mouth. He'd fight till they dragged him out by his feet, he vowed to himself. The battle would live on as legend. He pounded up the steps to the palisade of the southern wall, ready to fend off the sea itself. Then he looked out, and almost collapsed.

Another several thousand of Aln Adrackt's troops—urzeks and Syrtians, Kusulls and Piryati—stood in dark columns, ready to advance. The sheer numbers chilled Quin's heart. As he watched, they started forward. Like columns of ants. Like a wind-driven storm. Quin wiped the blood from his cheeks. He stared down the line at his panting, gore-spattered comrades. Only a few stared back. Their eyes were dark with doubt.

Fatigue and thirst and adrenaline had tightened the muscles in Quin's throat. His voice felt like a knife in his neck. But he knew he had to say something.

"Defenders of Dred Thannat," he croaked. "Hold your positions! For Kaer Rhennet! For the Emerald!"

Hold your positions. Hell. He wasn't even convincing himself. The situation was no longer desperate. It was hopeless. Quin was aware of the distant cacophony before he realized what it was. The squeal of Naztali horns. The *basso profundo* of blue troll drums. And another sound.

Gongs.

Whistles.

Quin squinted out over the plain. His tired eyes burned as he tried to focus. What he spied was as strange and marvelous a sight as any Darannan soldier had ever seen. It was Naztali riders in a long, irregular battle line. And weren't those the Sidharan colors, red and green, beyond the Naztali? It took him several moments to figure out that what he saw bearing these colors were the legendary gray monsters of the West—house-sized beasts with long, ropy snouts. High above the earth floated Sidharan observation balloons, green orbs suspended in the sky like giant raindrops, signaling the movements of the enemy back to communications officers on the ground. The Marshal stumbled twice as he scrambled up to the bartizan. He heard himself making sounds and was unsure if they were sobs or laughter. Farthest off, barely visible across the battlefield, a phalanx of blue trolls advanced on Aln Adrackt's right flank. Ever the tactician, Quin tried to calculate the new balance of power. Impossible as it seemed, the trolls appeared to number in the thousands. Closer to the fortress, the Naztali and Sidharan forces together made another division and a half. The Marshal's excitement faltered. Maybe it wasn't enough. What was he thinking? *No way it was enough.* Still, it was all he would get.

It was a chance.

"They're COMING!" Atryen Quin screamed to his men, with all that remained of his breath. "Naztali horsemen, like a wave! Blue trolls! Conquistadors! They're all here!"

There were men around him who had no idea what he was talking about. There were men around him who lacked the strength to see beyond the tips of their swords. But their commander's frenzy was contagious. Quin's exhausted defenders echoed his joy. Confusion rippled through the ranks of the attackers. As those in the vanguard looked back to see their comrades turning to meet the new threat, the assault on Dred Thannat slowed. Quin's men fought harder. Syrtians and urzeks, Piryati and Kusulls—all of Aln Adrackt's awful might—began to fall back.

Quin called to his captains: "Clear the barricades! Cavalry, mount up!"

Watching his enemies run from the walls of Dred Thannat, the Marshal's first impulse was to ride directly into the ranks of those who were retreating. He would lead a sortie to harass the enemy and kill any stragglers, then return to the safety of the fortress. But as his men hurried to the stables—returning, mounted, to assemble in the courtyard—Quin changed his mind. From his perch he'd spotted a detachment of Syrtian lancers galloping through the ruined fishing village below Dred Thannat, within sight of the fortress's southwestern wall. It was low tide. The Syrtians probably intended to ride along the shoreline and around the fortress, then spur up the narrow trail to the headlands and attack the Naztali force on its undefended right flank. This was something Quin knew how to stop. The Marshal's riders were mounted and ready. Their horses danced with nervous energy as the last of the barricade behind the south gate was disassembled. Quin sent a platoon of his archers to the southwest wall in case the Syrtian force should turn back. Then he sprinted down to the courtyard and grabbed the reins of his charger from the skinny kid who stood holding them. *Skinny kid.* He was going to have to start thinking a little differently. The man holding his horse was a lieutenant of Kaer Rhennet's toughest cavalry unit. It was his new adjutant, Ayrd Teryan.

Quin couldn't help it. He chuckled.

"Shadows are supposed to follow," he said. "Not lead."

The horse was a huge sorrel that stood almost seventeen hands. Quin hoisted himself into the saddle.

"Captain Olwyn!" he called.

"Sir!"

"You have the fort."

Quin reached out and snatched the flag of Dred Thannat from the corporal who held it. He gazed up the pole at the pennant: a fortress of gray, surmounted by three ivory stars emblazoned on a sea of midnight blue. Quin studied the tower on the flag as if it were Dred Thannat itself, battered and undermanned but still standing. Then he nodded.

Teryan again. At his side.

Quin reined the sorrel close with his free hand. "Remember how to ride one of these things, Lieutenant?"

"I'll watch you, sir."

"You do that."

———†———

The battered gates swung open and Quin and his horsemen thundered out of the courtyard. They rode sixty yards over corpses and rubble toward the northeast corner of the castle. Here the Marshal's cavalry veered west and charged at the Syrtian column.

The first gray-clad riders were just clambering up onto the head-lands from the beach below. Quin spurred his big horse until the wind screamed in his ears. He was ten paces in front of his men, wielding the flag of Dred Thannat like a lance, when he slammed into the nearest Syrtian cavalryman. He almost broke the man in half. The shock of the Darannan onslaught unmanned the Syrtians. A score were driven over the cliffs of the headlands onto the jag-ged rocks below. Others died where they fought, or turned and fled back down the steep path to scatter haphazardly over the sand of Speckled Bay's dark shore. Those who returned the way they'd come rode directly into the sights of Quin's archers. The Marshal learned later that fewer than half of the Syrtian lancers who'd rid-den out to flank the Naztali made it back to their lines. Quin lost three riders and a single horse.

But he'd also lost time. Reining up as he watched the Syrtians scatter before him, he turned to find the route back to Dred Thannat blocked by resurgent throngs of urzeks and Piryati. He was trapped outside his own walls.

"Follow me!" the Marshal called, spurring his horse in a wide arc around the enemy infantry toward the Naztali lines. The Naztali, Sidharan, and troll armies had pulled back to regroup after their suc-cessful charge, lest their forces be dissipated among Aln Adrackt's hordes.

Quin waved the bloody Darannan pennant as he approached. A Naztali chieftain galloped to meet him.

"You've seen the urzeks?" Quin said.

The Naztali spat. "One dragged my shield bearer down, horse and all. They're demons. My warriors are…"

Scared out of their wits, thought Quin. But then he remembered the thin skins of the Naztali. He bit his tongue. "Your men fight like lions. But we could use some help. Send word to the Sidharans that we need their great beasts—"

"*Elephants*, they call them."

"Send word that we need their *elephants* over here on the right. They may be a match for the urzeks."

"I'll tell them. We came without the chance to plan, Marshal. We knew of your struggle."

"And our children's children," Quin recited, not wanting to engage in the Naztali chieftain's tallying of accounts, "will sing your names to their sons. But first we need those elephants."

Barking orders, the Marshal ranked his horsemen in three units: two for deployment, one to be held in reserve. Now, at ground level, Aln Adrackt's forces seemed more imposing than before. Even counting the beleaguered garrison within the walls of Dred Thannat, the armies of Ythedra faced several times their own number. Having recovered from their shock, the enemy seemed more confident. They sent up disorganized shouts of threat and derision as they dared the outnumbered Ythedrans to advance. Many of the urzeks held severed Naztali heads. A few twirled the heads by the hair, then heaved the grisly projectiles out over the swath of grassland that separated the armies. Terrified, but unwilling to admit it, the Naztali refused to commit. Meanwhile the Sidharan elephants lumbered behind the lines toward Quin's position on the Ythedran right flank. They were still being positioned when, to the beat of bone drums, Aln Adrackt's armies began to advance. Quin winced when two of the elephants broke formation and trotted out across no man's land toward the enemy.

Halfway there the creatures slowed, as if bewildered. One gathered grass with its snakelike snout. The second, a smaller animal, pressed its face into the flank of the first. Neither elephant noticed the group of reptiles advancing upon them. The urzeks swarmed the nearest pachyderm. Swinging their huge axes, they peeled red swaths of flesh from its head and flanks. The smaller elephant seemed not to comprehend what was happening, even as the urzeks turned their attention to it. Screaming in fright and pain, the animals quickly fell beneath the onslaught.

Quin shook his head. Not only were the elephants ill disciplined. Despite their size, they were easy marks for the urzeks.

"Lieutenant," he said. "We may be pulling back. Tell the men—"

"Marshal, wait."

"Now, Lieutenant."

"But sir. *Look.*"

Quin turned in his saddle. He watched with morbid fascination as a third elephant, an enormous bull, lumbered free of the Sidharan lines. This animal trumpeted too—but not in pain, Quin noticed, and not in fear. The bull simply ran over one urzek, crushing the freak's skull beneath its huge feet. A second lizard lunged and was knocked flat by the elephant's trunk; the bull then seized the reptile, lifted it, and slammed it down again. The urzek lay without moving. Now other elephants advanced, urged on by the *mahouts* perched high on their backs. The beasts trumpeted wildly to each other, their frond-like ears raised in alarm and anger, and the Sidharan infantry surged forward to support its animals.

Despite the elephants' strength, Quin recognized in their disorganized movements the portents of defeat. He spat to one side, loosened the reins of his sorrel, and heard, finally, his lancers' shouts. He'd expected exhaustion and gloom. These cries carried neither. They were screams of defiance. Of outrage, and contempt. Quin glanced up. The wind was shifting. Now it blew from the north. At his back. *Maybe I'm the timid one*, the Marshal thought. *The exhausted old man, wishing for warmth at the foot of a fire. Ready to admit defeat because he's too tired to suffer it.* Quin's premonition of doom changed shape. He felt instead exhilaration at the confusion of the day, an unexpected but fully formed conviction that a world spinning out of control was a world that he, or any man, could shape for himself. He laughed out loud. *Elephants!* He'd never even seen one of the odd animals before. Now he was feeding off their strength, their example. *We're following elephants!* Quin's blood raced inside him like a flood-swollen stream. He felt tears on his cheeks. He tore his helmet from his head and shook his red hair out over his shoulders. He was ten feet tall. He was lightning in a summer sky.

The big sorrel capered and pranced in front of the Ythedran lines.

"Ayrd Teryan!" Quin shouted, so loud that all his men could hear.

"Sir!" responded the startled lieutenant.

"Has there ever been a better day to DIE?"

The stallion reared. Quin spurred hard and the horse sprang toward the forces of Aln Adrackt, ranked in numberless waves, advancing like a woodland fire. He gave no order. No order was needed. This was a fight for land and kin, for blood and air and life itself. This was the sight of shadows moving in the still of night, the crash of breaking doors, the rush of awakening rage. Behind Atryen Quin, Ythedra charged. Rain blew in from the bay, and a stiff wind snapped the cruel flags.

Chasing Disaster

I woke up that morning shivering and sore and still several miles from Dred Thannat.

I'd spent the night surrounded by mountain dwellers. Long-haired and heavily bearded, careless of their manners and appearance, the Ganthans were a glamorless lot, clearly the product of a hungry land. One had lost an eye. Another was missing two fingers on his left hand. Together they shared an assortment of scars and facial craters that would have done a Marine battalion proud. Occasionally one of their loose-limbed wolves would enter the circle of firelight to acknowledge its master, receiving a bone or a scrap of gristle and an affectionate cuff on the shoulder in return. In general, though, the wolves kept their distance. I never quite got used to the eerie golds and greens of their eyes flashing from the shadows around me. They were a sort of animate security system, restless and constantly vigilant. Even I, a nominal ally, never got close enough to touch one of those magnificent animals.

My sleep was empty. I dreamt no dreams of destruction. I hid from no demons in my head. Yet my sense of foreboding was, if anything, worse. I knew there was something ugly waiting for me just beyond the horizon. But I also knew it was too late to jump off this particular train. In order to cleanse Ythedra, someone was going to have to rid it of Aln Adrackt once and for all. Linnaeth had spoken of a Traveler of Worlds who could destroy the sorcerer. Or not. The prophecy itself only promised that the traveler would reveal—or possibly *create*—the future. Unfortunately, there was no guarantee as to what that future might look like. The traveler of worlds had to be me. But who was I to do such a thing?

And what weapons did I have?

——+——

Most of the Ganthans drank themselves to sleep. But the next day, as dawn broke gray over the grasslands of the Near Downs, the mountain dwellers shuffled through their preparations for the march to come as if Aln Adrackt's ancient enchantment of speech-lessness had settled over them again. The alcohol was only partly to blame. Sobriety held additional horrors. The Ganthans were war-riors of vaunted courage and obstinacy. They considered retreat unthinkable. Still, they valued their lives, and they weren't stupid. Everyone knew that an army of enormous size and strength waited on the plains ahead. It was rumored that we would see battle before noon, which meant that by evening many of us—quite possibly *all* of us—would litter these lowland fields like fallen leaves, food for the earth, never to see friends or family again. The men around me folded their bedrolls and checked their weapons as if these simple tasks might be their last. A few wolves padded wraithlike through camp, but even they looked anxious. With two strangers I shared a breakfast of cold rabbit and hardtack.

Then we headed west.

Gowen found me not long after the march began.

"Ramirez!" he shouted. Apparently he'd given up the notion of walking the whole way. He was leading a horse, and he was talking as he approached. "I passed Truke tu-Kekh and the others about a quarter mile up the line. They're looking for you. You all right?"

"Arm's better," I replied. "But I'm damn sick of rabbit."

Gowen took a minute to catch his breath. He was sweating beneath a layer of rust-speckled chain mail. "I haven't seen you in days. What'd you think of the Marsh? A little different from the first time we crossed, eh? Not even a sign of the worms."

"Too bad. I was ready for 'em this time."

"You heard the news? Two of our scouts reported back last night. Dred Thannat's still standing. But Aln Adrackt is camped just south of the fortress in numbers too large to count, and the Naztali are nowhere to be seen."

"What about the Sidharans? And the trolls?"

"No sign of either force. They could be out there, but we're cut off to the northwest by Kirikite patrols and we can't push any further without givin' ourselves away."

"They'd *better* be out there. We'll have to wait for them, right? I mean—"

"I don't think so. Hear the cheers?"

"Hard not to. What's going on?"

"Word is out. We fight alone."

"Your people," I said, "are crazier than I thought."

"My people," Gowen said, studying the warriors around us. We heard the skirl of pipes and a thousand voices took up a Ganthan battle hymn, ancient and unappeasable. A grin gathered at the edge of Gowen's mouth. Then disappeared.

"You don't have to do this, Ramirez. You or Ara or Truke either. This is a Ganthan fight. You can still bow out."

"Bow out. Right. You mean tuck my tail between my legs and run. And believe me, I'd consider it. If there was any place to run *to*."

Gowen shrugged. "Ythedra has a lot of corners. I'm sure you could find one out of sight of this wizard."

"You still don't know who we're fighting, do you?"

"Only what I've heard."

"Aln Adrackt is a *name*," I said. "A borrowed name for an ill-fitting form. Beyond Aln Adrackt—*beyond* him, *beneath* him—is something that doesn't die. That can't be beaten. And can't be hidden from."

Gowen scanned the horizon. "Maybe so."

"And you still want to fight?"

"I do." The big man pulled Nihreth Wyn's sword from its make-shift scabbard. He sighted along the length of the blade. Out here in the middle of the grasslands, beneath a lusterless sky, it looked like any other weapon. "I still want to fight. Because I've been thinking. What if there's something beyond the Ganthans too? Something beyond you and me and Quin and his Outriders that's, you know… *good*. Something heroic and bright that doesn't die either. And what if Aln Adrackt can't hide from *us*?"

I couldn't help it. I laughed out loud.

"A philosopher," I said. "I should have known. Though I have to say, you hid it well."

Gowen grinned. "Stay behind me. You and the others. I'll protect you for as long as I draw breath."

The big man wrapped me in a bear hug, lifting me up off the ground in his powerful arms. I smelled sweat and fear and the oil in his hair. I couldn't help it. I hugged him back.

Once More into the Breach

Three hours later the sky was a rapid caravan of clouds. The breeze had picked up, and crows circled above us like cinders in a whirlwind. The forward elements of the scattered Ganthan column paused at the foot of a treeless ridge. At the crest of the ridge, a dozen scouts stood silhouetted against the clouds. They waved their arms and shouted, but I couldn't make out the words. I had rejoined my companions by now. They looked as nervous as I felt.

"The Naztali *will* come," Izgir insisted.

"The Naztali are *here*!" barked a Ganthan warrior, bounding past us up the hill. "All the armies are here!"

Izgir called after him but got no response. Around us, men stripped bridles and blankets from their pack animals. Some asked comrades to lash their axes to their palms with strips of deer hide, the Ganthan warrior's method of ensuring his hands could not be used for surrender. Others smeared their faces and torsos with bear grease, or sliced themselves with their own weapons so their first injury would come neither as a shock nor at the hands of the enemy. And a few men crouched alone near their packs, spilling their guts in the grass.

Izgir, Truke tu-Kekh, Ara and I set about freeing our horses. It was harder to say goodbye to Wind Sister than I had expected. But my friends were waiting, so I said a simple thank you, gave the animal a slap on the rump, and hustled up the slope. Ara got there first. I was last to reach the ridge, to gaze out across the valley toward where Speckled Bay lay like a gash on the western horizon. My pulse danced like a drunken punk in the ballroom of my wrists. Before me lay the battle. I saw men and machines, horses, trolls, flags of all colors, smoke and flames, clouds and rain. Seagulls wheeled in the sullen sky, and Sidharan observation balloons hovered high over the lines. We arrayed ourselves on a promontory looking southwest across the South Downs. Dred Thannat stood three miles away, perched on a ledge above Speckled Bay as if it was just about ready to jump. Even from this distance it was obvious that the fortress was in trouble. The tallest of its spires spouted flames like bright flowers.

To our right stood the armies of Ythedra. Nearest us were several companies of blue trolls. They were arrayed beneath gigantic red flags in several loose lines of hammermen, punctuated here and there by commanders riding black bears. Beyond them marched an army of precisely arrayed Sidharans, spit-and-polish perfect, spear points bristling at a forty-five degree angle from their ranks. And beyond even the Sidharans rode a Naztali horde on their rangy ponies, fluid as mercury, sudden as a summer rain. But directly in front of us stood the legions of Aln Adrackt. We could see Syrtian infantry and Kirikite cavalry units, urzeks, and what I later learned were Kusull and Piryati irregulars. Half a mile behind the undulating phalanxes of pikes and shields, half-hidden by an ugly haze, was a city of midnight-tinted tents, each emblazoned with the Standing Snake of Aln Adrackt. In the distance we could see the blackened remains of the northern fringes of the Big Thicket, all scorched hills and barren stumps.

"Times like this," said Gowen, "you need a poet."

I turned to find the big man gazing over my shoulder toward the battlefield. He had been joined by Callan Rahiel and a dozen of the old chief's kinsmen. The Ganthans and their wolves had formed a line along the crest of the ridge. They stood contemplating the carnage below.

"He's got to be in those tents," I said, pointing. "Right? Could he really have been stupid enough to set fire to the Thicket?"

Gowen shook his head. "Probably easier to be stupid when you've got an army behind you. Let's hope the Tauregs take it personally."

"There's something else, too," said Ara. "The cages. You see?"

"No, but I'll take your word for it. For the spiders, I guess."

"With any luck," Gowen said, "we'll die before we get there."

"There are too *many* of them," said the princess, pointing out what we could all see for ourselves. "Syrtians. Piryati. Kusulls. It's like trying to count trees in the Thicket. Even with the trolls and the Sidharan army beside us, an attack would be suicide."

"I think even the Ganthans are starting to have doubts," I added. It was true. All along the line I saw men talking to the earth in front of them.

"Too late for doubts," said Izgir. "Look. The Syrtians are sending reinforcements right, behind their lines. The left flank of the troll army is about to be crushed. Gowen. Callan Rahiel. Send messengers to—"

Truke tu-Kekh grabbed Izgir's arm and yanked the Naztali around. "Wait a minute. What'd you say about the trolls? What's happening down there?"

"The trolls are in trouble. They're being flanked. We need to get—"

Izgir didn't have time to finish. The blue troll launched himself down the broad slope like a raindrop off to contend with the sea. Halfway down the hill, he raised both arms and screamed, "Nat Alsedra! We are HERE!"

And it worked. The spell of stasis broke. Truke tu-Kekh's cry was echoed by an army. Men surged past me. Callan Rahiel drew the broken sword that had slain Tarrant Lef and leveled it at the

distant ranks of Aln Adrackt's army. Izgir shrieked as he started
forward. Bagpipes wailed in the wind, and our fierce songs sailed
again. The Ganthan line advanced.

———+———

We were greeted by a low-pitched, croaking cheer from the
blue trolls. Half a mile ahead, the Syrtians aligned themselves in a
broad defensive phalanx. The scarlet emblem of the Standing Snake
writhed on a hundred black flags behind the enemy's lines, and a
forest of pikes was leveled at our hearts. But there was no sense
concentrating on my imminent dismemberment. Instead and for
no good reason I remembered riding to Ed White Elementary on
an April morning many years gone. Spider webs glistened with dew
in the grass of the empty lots around my house. Mexican primroses
held themselves like cups to catch the sun. Bikes were bikes in those
days: noble Stingrays with iridescent banana seats, low-slung Huffys
modified for combat with electrical tape girding forward-flung
handlebars and broomstick lances lashed to the frame. Baseball
cards were still just diving boards for dreams, and heroes (Green
Lantern, Neil Armstrong, Almighty God) lived in the ranch-style
split-levels of our hearts. Buggy Wagner kicked a football through
a window once and there was hell to pay on account of Old Man
Hyde shot salt pellets at the kids who climbed his trees and Angie
Graves had eyes so blue you could fly a kite in them of course I
never did I never even tested the wind but I drew her watching
me as John Elway, me as Wolverine, I drew every freaking wonder-
ful thing in the world like airplanes Jesus killer whales Cal Ripken
Comanche braves tornado funnels pumpkin pie the beads of summer air condensing on an ice-cold glass of Jesus Christ I was scared
did kids still eat Pixy Stix? Was this really dying? I would like to have
shaved. Only now we were running. Ara shed her rucksack without
breaking stride. Izgir stumbled once but found his feet and a pack

of wolves darted through our line, galloping toward the enemy. A hundred yards from the Syrtian position, Callan Rahiel bellowed, "For the WHITE CITIES! For DAR-ANNON!" and all our voices thundered back. I followed the old man into the shield wall. I heard the dank defiance of steel meeting steel. Then the armies roared together, and the cry was deafening and profane.

———+———

You've seen the movies. They get these scenes just about right. The noise is like a subway train rumbling through your cerebrum. Men shove and stumble over each other and grunt and say things that make no sense even when you can make out the words. Arrows sizzle in the air around you and people are pierced in the stomach or shoulder, cheekbone or foot. They twist and fall. They reach out. Bend over. Spit blood. One difference is, when it's for real, it doesn't stop. You think, okay, *Battle scene. Climactic roar. Head shot. Action. More action. Dramatic Slo-mo action. Head shot. Pan. Cut to victorious star.* Only this scene kept going. On my right I saw a Ganthan hatchet split a Syrtian soldier's forehead in half. Wolves dragged down a flailing enemy sergeant, and a Syrtian pike snapped off in a Ganthan warrior's rib cage. Gowen stood ten yards in front of me. Gowen, only more so. The affable layabout I'd come to know and just about trust seemed to have been transformed. Now he stood like a lone tree on an empty field, hacking at the enemy around him, bleak and terrible in the bright light of his blade. Many of the foe advanced to try him. All went wordless down.

But heroics were one thing. Numbers were another. All the courage and desperation in the world couldn't change the fact that we were hugely outmanned. Though we gained ground, I suspected the advance only increased the chance we'd be engulfed by the much larger organism that was our enemy. And while it was true that everything I'd ever learned about battlefield tactics could have fit in a dime bag, even I knew an assault force was supposed to safeguard its flanks. It was also supposed to keep a body of men in reserve to buttress a sagging line or punch up a crucial advance. The Ganthans had made no such plans. As far as I could tell, the Ganthans had made no plans at all. As the afternoon wore on, our momentum slowed. Gowen's blade still flashed like the scales of a fish in a murky pond, but the Ganthan line was faltering. For the first time that day I found myself moving backwards, tripping over lifeless bodies and shattered pikes. So far I had advanced behind my comrades, keeping as low as I could, wondering with increasing optimism if I might make it through this portable madness with full use of my spleen—whatever full use of a spleen entails. My sense of well-being turned out to be misplaced. Probably it stemmed from the simple fact that I couldn't see what stood beyond the Ganthans in front of me.

Turns out, there was plenty.

The Piryati counter-attack stripped me of protection. These semi-human giants haled from the mountainous deserts of Emerkest. Not one of them stood less than seven feet tall, or had any more hair on his bulbous head than a five-lined skink. Huge and misshapen, the Piryati brandished wooden clubs studded with spikes of iron and shards of stone. The Naztali, unfortunately, did not. Izgir took a wicked blow to his left shoulder and spun to the ground like a rag doll. The enemy was *everywhere*—in front of us, in back, on both sides. Ara screamed as she slashed left and right with a short sword she'd picked up on the field. Callan Rahiel hacked deep into the chest of another attacker but as quickly as he did, he was dragged down from behind by two Syrtians. I saw men come to his aid, but the scene was too chaotic for me to make out much else. I had trouble enough on my hands. Izgir was struggling to regain his feet. As his Piryati attacker brought his club up over his head to finish the Naztali, he was struck by two wolves. The Piryat bent beneath the onslaught and a third animal leapt up on his back. Then the Piryat was down, thrashing in the jaws of the creatures, and a spray of blood filled the air. Another Piryat came to his aid. Before the newcomer could drive off the wolves, though, Truke tu-Kekh swung his hammer. He caught the hairless brute just above one of his knees. The Piryat collapsed like a burning barn, shrieking in pain, and the blue troll promptly buried his mallet in the crown of the Piryat's smooth skull. The blow made a sound like a pumpkin hitting cement. Even in the middle of the battle I could hear the slurp of suction as Truke yanked the hammer back out.

Intent on his bloody work, Truke never saw the axe that split the seam of his iron helmet. Black-skinned, naked, reeking of blood and stagnant water, an urzek bellowed over Truke tu-Kekh's motionless body.

Only a few yards away, Izgir struggled up into a sitting position. He nocked an arrow in his bow and buried the bolt in the urzek's red throat. In theory it was a perfect shot. Only this wasn't a strategy session. The urzek reached up and snapped the arrow shaft as if it was kindling. When Izgir's second bolt glanced off the creature's shoulder, the urzek lifted its axe and stepped toward the fallen Naztali. This was just about the point where my mind disappeared. I leveled my sword in front of me, sprinted at the creature, and— *nothing*. Might as well fight a tank with a toothpick. The monster deflected my sword stroke with one arm, knocking me several feet backwards with the other.

In one sense, though, my attack succeeded. I was now the urzek's quarry. Panting with fear, I braced my sword in front of me. The urzek struck it from my hands. I tried to move back, but I slipped in a puddle of mud and landed on my spine. I looked up to see a silver blade blazing like a second sun.

"You want BLOOD?" Gowen screamed. "Take MINE, if you can!"

Man and beast lunged. Gowen parried the urzek's roundhouse blow, then whirled and drove his sword deep into the creature's abdomen. The sound of the monster's agony was ungodly—an ear-splitting wail that drowned out everything else within a thousand square feet. The urzek sank to the ground slowly, its eyes wide, as if it couldn't believe its own pain. But Gowen wasn't finished. He yanked the blade out, reared back, and lopped off the lizard spawn's head with a single stroke. Around us, the men of Fereganth roared their approval. One warrior snatched up the obscene trophy and carried it with him into the fray. Others piled in behind him. The Syrtian line gave ground. I sensed the enemy was as tired as we were, that the battle could be won if only we could keep pushing. But we needed more warriors. We needed *fresh* warriors. Let's face it: we needed a miracle.

It was Ara who spotted it.

"Look!" she gasped, pointing south, far to the left of the Syrtian ranks. Beyond Aln Adrackt's teeming lines, on the gentle hills where the blackened stumps of what had once been forest stood, I saw figures like trees. Only *moving*.

"The Tauregs!" shouted Izgir, following my gaze. "Usak has brought the Tauregs!"

A cloud of green arrows darkened the sky. For the first time a cry of lamentation rose from the armies ranked against us, as the Syrtians realized *they* were the ones who had been flanked. Fear flickered in the eyes of our enemies. And the Ganthans staggered forward again, advancing over the bodies of the enemy dead and singing songs of sun and blood.

———†———

Truke tu-Kekh's green eyes were open, but unfocused. He seemed unable to speak.

"Got himself knocked cold," said Izgir, cradling his injured arm at his side. "See? Split his helmet. Crushed one of his horns. But trolls have been known to live through worse, and I don't think there's a thicker skull in Ythedra."

"Maybe one," I observed, glancing up at the Sidharan princess.

Ara rubbed the heel of one hand through the line of blood that was worming its way down her forehead. "I'm fine," she said, kneeling beside us. "Can he *walk*? We can't just leave him here. There's no telling how the battle will turn."

As if to underscore her warning, a mass cry of triumph or alarm sounded from the front of the fight.

"We may have to carry him," I said. "Izgir. Can we get this chain mail off? It's gotta weigh fifty pounds."

"Of course," said the Naztali. "We—wait a minute. Truke?"

His eyes fixed on Ara, the troll seemed to recollect who and where he was. He felt for the wound on the back of his head. He tried to hoist himself up.

"Not so fast," said Izgir. "You okay?"

"Been better," the troll grunted.

We helped Truke tu-Kekh to his feet. He took one look at his ruined helmet and tossed it aside. Ara found his iron hammer lying nearby and carried it with both hands to the impatient troll. I understood his eagerness. Even I could feel the charge in the air. History was alive around us. Together we hustled to rejoin the Ganthan advance. The ghosts of the Thicket were emerging from the darkness of legend. The word spread like wildfire.

The Tauregs had come.

———+———

Aln Adrackt's first line of defense—his legions of Syrtian pike men, with their reserves of hairless Piryati and a scattering of urzeks throughout—had crumbled. Only a few segments of it still resisted the Ganthan advance. But the disintegration of that first line brought us in sight of the second, which was headed toward us. Naturally the Ganthans surged forward to meet it. But the wizard's armies were no longer attacking. In fact, the Syrtians we could see were running for their lives. It only took me a second to figure out why. *The spiders.* Their torsos were camel-sized, and covered with coarse black hair. Each face had four yellow eyes set in a roughly trapezoidal pattern above a beaklike mouth, and radiating out from the thorax were eight slender chitinous legs. Most terrifying of all was the *speed* of the spiders. Their bodies never seemed to move, even as the creatures' legs raced across the grassy earth toward us. There were dozens of them. *Scores of them*. And they were headed our way.

———+———

Now the world made no sense at all. It was impossible to see who led and who followed. It was hard even to know which way to move. A few Syrtian regulars turned to fight the spiders. Others thought only of escape. These men plowed into the backs of their comrades, some of whom were still trying to ward off Ganthan swords. Syrtians and Piryati were fighting each other, fighting the few urzeks who tried to hold them in place, fighting simply to wedge themselves through the Ganthan lines to avoid the night-mares behind them. But the nightmares moved too fast. Soon we were face to face with the monstrous things. They leapt and tore at anything and anyone in reach. You had to keep your feet; getting knocked down meant you might never get back up. Dangling from the fangs of the nearest spider was a sickening mélange of arms and legs, held together by the viscous white toxin the creatures injected into their prey. Beside me, Ara and Izgir strained to find clear bow shots—a nearly impossible task, given the mass of men around us. Farther forward, Gowen was buried by an eddy of the human sea and disappeared from sight. It was hard to speak of heroes now. Even among the Ganthans there were warriors who ran from the arachnids, and there was no way to blame them for obeying what every instinct screamed was the right and proper course of action. This was the hour of Aln Adrackt's triumph. In the midst of the blood and terror there was no hope of salvation left us, no con-solation even in the valor of our fight. All we had was our fear. But some of us—*enough of us*—remained. No one warrior accom-plished much. Probably the boldest ended up dead. But the gradual accumulation of sword slashes and arrow wounds took their toll. The spiders bled, and a creature that bled was a creature that could die. Near where I stood, a Ganthan warrior managed to sever the end of a chitinous leg with his axe. A Syrtian archer drove an arrow deep into the same creature's forehead. It hesitated, its mandibles clicking furiously, then staggered off at an angle from its attackers. This was the cue for a dozen men to fall upon the spider, hacking and thrusting till the monster spouted greenish-black ichor from its wounds. Truke tu-Kekh stood in the middle of the crush, swinging his hammer whenever he could get close to a target, bellowing with anger and panic and desperation, smashing the spiny black limbs. The story repeated itself a hundred times across those fields. Slowly the spiders weakened. Men gathered in circles around them, darting between the spindly legs to slam their blades into the glabrous underbellies, screaming through gouts of gore and filth.

——+——

There was little rejoicing when the slaughter was done. The unimaginable carcasses lay smashed and eviscerated across the South Downs, eyes, legs, and mandibles intermingled with the mangled and bloody corpses of men and wolves. Maybe the foremost emotion among us was disgust. Fused with it now was a grim ambition to put an end to the grotesque violence of the day. There was still combat off to our right, where a cadre of urzeks held several Kirikite and Kusullian companies in place. Now, though, the Ganthans stormed in to attack from *behind* the urzeks—joined in this thrust by Taureg archers and by a number of the Syrtians and Piryati who'd at first defended Aln Adrackt's own eastern flank.

"The sorcerer's army," said Ara, gazing at the battle with a clinical eye, "is a beast without a head. I swear to God, it's breaking up."

Incredible as it seemed, she was right. We could all see it. We watched riderless Kirikite horses rear and bolt on the rolling hills where only a few hours before the banners of the Standing Snake had seemed untouchable. A line of Syrtian foot soldiers threw down their swords and raised their hands in surrender. The battle still whined and shrieked, but its outcome was no longer in doubt. Aln

Adrackt's military machine—his horde of disparate tribes, united by brutal discipline and a desire for spoil—was falling apart. There appeared to be no one in command. It might have seemed like a time to celebrate, except for two things. First, I was too tired to celebrate anything other than the gradual decrescendo of my own heart. And second, I knew our triumph was hollow. The sorcerer had yet to show himself. This meant he was out there, somewhere, and still so dangerous that any assumption was folly. Nothing was won while Aln Adrackt remained alive. Nothing, I reminded myself, could *ever* be won.

Smoke from the Big Thicket drifted over the battlefield, burning my eyes, smearing the afternoon sun that had finally broken loose from the clouds. Elsewhere on the Downs, rain was falling. The sky was a patchwork of light and dark, swirling gray and mottled blue. The killing continued. I drank water from a dead Ganthan's canteen and closed his eyes to thank him. I crossed myself. Spat. Turned to find my friends.

Council

By evening we'd made it to the sorcerer's tents.

Dominating the encampment was Aln Adrackt's personal pavilion, a massive scarlet and black structure complete with fanciful turrets and towers. It was a Ganthan warrior who finally took an axe to one of the canvas panels and hacked through the dense fabric of the walls. There was a score of interior chambers. Some were filled with helmets, swords, and shields. Others held liquor and foodstuffs in various degrees of preservation. Though we found several stacks of brass and wooden chests, the types of chests that might have held coins or jewelry, they all turned out to be empty. At the very center of the labyrinth we stumbled upon a scene—and a stench—that sent some of the strongest men among us reeling back along the paths they'd come. Gathered around a stone fire pit sat a congregation of royal corpses. The emirs, warlords, and chieftains of the many tribes that made up the sorcerer's army sat slumped in iron chairs. Their bodies were cold and stiff, as if frozen, and their eyes had been clawed out of their heads, apparently by their own hands. Their retinues of warriors lay behind them, throats and bellies torn open and the flesh within partially devoured. Entangled with them lay a number of the slug-like things we'd fought in the swamps—draviden, deliquescing in puddles of the vile fluid that filled their veins when living.

There were additional horrors found in the tent city. A room full of human skins, hung from the ceiling to cure. A room that a dozen men entered and from which none ever reappeared, though the chamber seemed empty. A room where dreams danced in bottles, and children were held in pens.

And other rooms, with other nightmares, that do not bear repeating.

———+———

Ultimately the battle for Dred Thannat disintegrated into a series of running skirmishes spread out over several square miles of the South Downs. The only clear enemy was a dangerous but rapidly diminishing contingent of urzeks and Kirikites, who fought hard and without quarter but who were gradually cut off from all assistance. Now elements of the various Ythedran armies—Darannan and troll, Sidharan, Ganthan, and Naztali—mingled in what had been the enemy's stronghold. The congregation made for strange sights. Riderless Sidharan elephants wandered across the trampled grass, foraging for their supper and frightening the rangy Naztali horses. Half-naked Ganthan warriors liveried in blood embraced Sidharan generals wearing yellow silks and polished steel. Raven-haired Naztali riders clasped hands with crew-cut Darannan infantrymen and muttering, ape-shouldered trolls. A forest of tattered Ythedran flags drooped in the calm of evening. Even the air was exhausted.

Not all the news was good. Casualties were high, especially among the Ganthans. Callan Rahiel lay dead, slain by an urzek axe midway through the battle. His followers declined to mourn the man. They spoke instead of his valor. He'd fallen leading his kinsmen. He'd died a warrior. Besides, they added, nodding at Gowen, he had a nephew to carry on his line.

Only one force was absent. This was the Taureg army, which had retreated into the smoldering ruins of the Big Thicket almost as soon as Aln Adrackt's reserve force of urzeks was defeated. The only Taureg to be seen in the aftermath of the battle was Usak. He wandered into the derelict camp by himself. Moving with that odd, bobbing gait of his, he was almost attacked by a group of bellicose blue trolls before Truke tu-Kekh could set matters straight.

"He's a Taureg," Truke told his gawking comrades. "Lives in the forest. Anarchist, as far as I can tell. Anyone touches tree boy, he answers to me."

Atryen Quin's nose was broken. He had a four-inch sword slash on his right forearm and a pike wound in either thigh. As was generally the case, he managed to take command of the ragged congress around him without even trying.

"I say we burn the tents before sundown," he counseled, as a Sidharan healer attempted to bandage his arm. "We've checked them all and there's no sign of the sorcerer. The only draviden we've found are dead, most of them cut to pieces by Aln Adrackt's own men—probably when they started letting those damned spiders out of their cages. Looks to me like the draviden and the spiders were disciplinary devices, used by Aln Adrackt to keep his conscripts in line. The Syrtians might have been more scared of the damn things than we were."

"Were?" said one of the Sidharan commanders. His question was met with nervous laughter.

"Or are. True, there may be a few dozen spiders out there. Urzeks as well. It's hard to say what might be loose on the Downs tonight. But we're talking about the remnants of a beaten army. The Naztali will track them down."

"And what do we do," demanded a troll, "with the Piryati and Syrtians who helped us *fight* the spiders? Some of them even joined the Ganthans in that last assault."

Quin shrugged. "We're not going to be able to sort out the ones who helped us from the ones who didn't. Reports say they're headed south. All of them. I say let 'em leave. They can't even trust each other anymore. Their leaders are dead, victims of a sorcery I can't pretend to explain. Without anyone to lead them, they're no longer a threat to Ythedra."

There was a murmur of agreement among the officers.

"What about the wizard?" I asked. I was several yards away from the Marshal, and I had to shout to make my question heard. Half the congregation turned to stare at me. I didn't care. I was still confused by the sorcerer's absence from the scene. It didn't make sense. "Aln Adrackt. Has anyone thought about sending out scouts?"

"Already done," said Quin. "I've got men riding south and east as we speak. But it may be too late. The cooking fires in the big tent are cold. Izgir reckons the wizard's been gone for days. Well before the final assault began, at any rate."

"Gone?" said Ara. "Gone *where*?"

Gowen gazed south. "Headed back to Emerkest, I'd bet. Back to save his hide."

"No," I said. Quin was addressing a group of trolls, so my companions and I were left to counsel ourselves. "It doesn't make sense. Why would he have left *days* ago? Before the battle even started."

"Maybe he knew he'd lose," said Izgir, rotating his injured shoulder. "They say he can see the future."

"I don't think so," I answered. "If he could see we were going to win, why would he have invaded Ythedra in the first place?"

"Maybe it didn't matter to him who won the battle," said Ara. "Maybe just getting us all here—doing *this*—was his victory."

I lifted my eyes to take in what she was looking at. Fires glowed on the grasslands around us. Bonfires, fueled by the corpses of our enemies. There was no choice. Burying the thousands of men and animals whose bodies littered the Downs would have taken weeks.

"I see what you mean," I said. "And maybe *why* doesn't matter anymore. I think he's headed for Inniskerr. It's his only chance."

"His only chance for what?" asked the princess.

"To get out of this alive. To get out of *here* alive. Look, it's a long story, but Aln Adrackt is beaten in Ythedra and I've got a feeling he's on his way to Earth. I've got an even worse feeling that maybe this entire war was a pretext for him. A way to get this far north in the first place."

Truke tu-Kekh had occupied himself with a rind of hardtack biscuit. Now he squinted up at me.

"Earth?" he said.

"My home."

My companions exchanged glances.

"And you get there," said Ara, "through *Inniskerr?*"

"There's a portal in the cavern. A sort of...look. I know this doesn't make a whole lot of sense, but there's a door there that leads to the place I came from. It's a kind of magic. Big magic, from what I understand, and not necessarily healthy for children and other living things. Linnaeth was going to destroy it once I used it to travel back to where I belong, but now...I don't know. Aln Adrackt may have gone there to escape. To get to a completely new world, *my* world, and to start this insanity all over again. Linnaeth might not be strong enough to hold him off. She told me so herself. So I need to get to Inniskerr, and I need to get there fast. Gowen, I could use your sword."

The big man was still carrying his weapon. He nodded as he held it in front of his face.

"You can have my arm along with it. I'm going with you."

"So am I," said Izgir.

"I'm in," said Truke tu-Kekh.

"You're not going anywhere," I told the troll. "You need to have someone look at that skull of yours."

"I'm *in*," said the mountain dweller, his emerald eyes flashing. Two passing trolls paused at the sound of his voice, then started toward us. Though they had no idea what Truke tu-Kekh was arguing about, it didn't seem to matter. Like trolls anywhere, they were ready to take the matter outside. Unfortunately, we were outside already. I looked to my friends for support. None was offered.

"Fine. If a three hundred-pound reptile can't knock some sense into you, I don't suppose I'm going to be able to. We'll ride Naztali ponies. And we'll leave tonight. In fact we'll leave right now, if Usak will lead us."

The gangling giant had been loitering at the edge of the group, diffident as always, a picture of adenoidal uncertainty. But he proved he'd been listening. "I was hoping you would ask. There are trails through the northern edge of the Thicket, and shortcuts only the Tauregs know. We can make it to Inniskerr in less than three days. With luck we can reach the mountains before Aln Adrackt, and warn the Seer he's coming."

I felt a hand on my shoulder.

"I can smell a conspiracy a mile away," said Atryen Quin, looking less confident than he sounded. His voice was a chain dragged on asphalt. "And this one stinks. Tell me what you're plotting, or I'll have you locked up in what's left of Dred Thannat faster than you can spit."

The Marshal gazed southwest as he listened. When I finished, he said, "I'm coming. I can arrange for provisions."

"You're coming? You've got—"

"I've got men who can take over for me at Dred Thannat, and I'm ready to ride. As ready as a man in my condition can be, I suppose. But first I have to say a goodbye. Go ahead, if you need to start now. I'll catch up."

"Go," said Izgir, holding up one palm as if in benediction. "We won't leave without you."

Quin gave him an amused glance. "I can tell you one thing, Naztali. *You* certainly won't."

Several officers of the various military commands gathered around us. They studied Izgir's face with a strange intensity.

"Someone has to coordinate the operations of Ythedra's armies," the Marshal explained. "Mop up any renegade urzeks. Safeguard the refugees on their way back home. Your name has been mentioned."

"My name?" said Izgir. "By who?"

The group's attention swiveled to Quin.

"By me."

Izgir seemed unable to believe what he was hearing.

Quin chuckled. "You always hated diplomacy. See how long you last without it now." The Marshal grabbed Izgir's right hand and raised it above his head. "Gentlemen! He has agreed! To lead the council of a united Ythedra, I nominate a great warrior of the Naztali tribes. I give you Izgir, son of Aakil of the Two Streams Clan!"

A raucous cheer erupted around us. Izgir appeared to want to say something, but he couldn't quite get it out. It looked as if he'd lost his chance. A gaggle of Ganthan and Sidharan officers crowded around him, peppering him with questions and requests.

Quin winked at the rest of us.

"We'll meet here," he said, raising his hoarse voice over the din, "at moonrise. Three hours, give or take. Bring a horse."

As the others scattered to prepare for the journey, Ara lingered beside me.

"What about me, Ramirez? Why are you ignoring me?"

I gave the princess my best thousand-yard stare.

"And stop pursing your lips," she said. "You look like a priest."

"I'm ignoring you because you're not coming."

"Not coming? Why not? I can—*look at me*, dammit." Ara grabbed my elbow and yanked me around to face her. "I can ride as well as anyone. And I can fight a hell of a lot better than you."

"I agree. But that's not the point. You're not going because I don't want you to, and that's all there is to it. Go find that lieutenant of yours."

"He's fighting urzeks with the Sidharan cavalry. Quin saw him. He's alive. That's all that matters."

"Go home then," I said. "Help your father."

"I can do that after—"

"I don't want you with me, Princess."

"That's a lie."

She was right. I tried to memorize her green eyes and vaulted cheekbones. The blood had dried on her scalp and forehead and just about half her face was going to be one big bruise by morning, but she was still stunning, still that disarming combination of vulner-ability and bravado.

"Maybe it is," I said. "But there's no way to get back from where I'm going. Stay with your people. Stay with Teryan. I should have stayed with a woman once, and I regret that I didn't. I'll always regret it. If you owe me anything, stay."

Ara gazed toward where Truke tu-Kekh stood waylaying Naztali warriors, haggling for their spare horses. The sun was a violet glow on the horizon. Two Sidharan conquistadors passed, carrying torches. When a tear rose in the corner of Ara's eye, my resolution shattered like cheap glass. I struggled to patch it together. *Don't beg, Ramirez. Not now. Not when you're about to do something right for once in your miserable life, not easy, not pleasant, but right in a sense you used to know and maybe still could. Stiffen that upper lip, Sergeant Major. Ythedra expects every gin jockey to do his duty.*

The Sidharan princess leaned close. I smelled the blood on her skin and the thicker scent of her coarse dark hair. She wouldn't meet my eyes. She kissed me gently—once on the chin, once on the lips—before she turned and walked away. Before I could change my mind—as I probably would have. Before I could embarrass myself.

I never saw Ara again.

The Portal

Stars through the trees: grains of gold in a sea of black. Sunrise.

Galloping, now, through a valley spangled with asters.

Parched sky of autumn. A chill in the air.

Shadows lengthening.

Another night.

I can't remember much of that final ride, but I know we struggled with our various wounds and with exhaustion of body and soul. I know also that not all of the aches slowed us down. Gowen had lost his kinsman Callan Rahiel in the battle. It was the first link he'd ever known to an extended family he never expected to meet. Now it was gone. Usak's people, the Tauregs, were still calculating the ranks of their dead and the extent of the damage to the Thicket. And we learned before we left Dred Thannat that Atryen Quin had seen his wife killed by Aln Adrackt's archers in the mud at the base of the walls of the fortress. At times when I caught the Marshal's eye I sensed his heart would have to stop beating before his appetite for vengeance subsided.

But it was obvious we'd figured right. Aln Adrackt was ahead of us. I could feel it in the pit of my stomach. It was a concrete dread, a sort of neural poison that grew stronger every hour. In the dark small hours of the morning as we stumbled along, half-asleep, we heard thunder rumbling in the south. At times the earth seemed to tremble, and we saw pulses of white light flash and dance in the mountains around Inniskerr.

"Something's happening up there," said Quin. "But I'll be damned if I know what it is."

"Storm coming?" said Gowen.

There wasn't a cloud to be seen.

"Could it be the Tauregs?"

Usak reined up and sat looking southeast. He shook his head. "Most of the Tauregs will be home by now. Far from Inniskerr."

Quin took his feet out of the stirrups and extended his legs. "Still makes no sense to me that the wizard would have allowed his army to torch the Thicket. The one thing guaranteed to buy him another set of enemies. If he's as smart as people have always claimed, he must have known how the Tauregs would respond."

"His army never touched the Thicket," said Usak.

"Hell. *Somebody* touched it. That fire burned thousands of acres, from what I could see. Not sure it wiped out any burial grounds, but—"

"It did," said Usak. He turned from us and gave his horse a flick of his heels to resume the journey. "My people are stubborn. Sometimes they need provoking. I set the fire."

———+———

We made it to the vale of Inniskerr at twilight on the third day of our ride. Since there was no way to know if we'd be back, we unsaddled the horses and turned them loose. Then we filed into the stone cottage where we'd first seen Linnaeth. The granite hatch lay in pieces, partially obstructing the aperture it was meant to guard.

"Looks like someone got here before us," growled Truke tu-Kekh. He tossed his saddle into a corner of the narrow room.

Quinn lit one of the pine-pitch torches we'd brought. Pausing only long enough to check each other's eyes, we started digging out the fragments of rock that barred our entrance to the tunnel. One piece was so large we had to re-enlist a couple of the horses. We rigged a harness and lead line and, together, man and beast, finally managed to shift the stone. Once this was accomplished, we lowered ourselves into the darkness.

———+———

I had no idea how to find Linnaeth. I only knew we had to move quickly. Something was urging me on, telling me to go, and go *now*. I probably would have taken my chances wandering blindly, in fact—and spent the rest of my life scurrying like a trapped rat through those underground corridors. But I didn't have to. Truke tu-Kekh remembered every step of our previous visit as if the route was etched on his eyelids. Without hesitating, he led us through dark passageways deep into the phosphorescent glow that burned in the maw of the mountain. We found evidence of struggle as we neared the cavern. Smoke and dust choked the tunnels. There was a stench in the air as well. It was the same smell the courtiers of Dar-Annon noticed centuries ago as they loitered outside the door of Prince Varun's chamber in Kaer Rhygat.

It was the smell of death.

The elaborate vertical city carved into the cavern had been destroyed. The rock walls stood pocked and smoking, with only traces of their filigree of elaborate architecture intact. Several of Linnaeth's acolytes lay on the rough floor. There were men and women both, still clad in their homespun frocks and tunics, unmarked saved for the coronas of blood caked around their eyes and ears. We checked the bodies for signs of life, but they were all cold. The Seer was harder to locate. After several minutes of searching, I found the tooth-shaped rock she'd led me to on the night we talked about Edward and angels and the fate of Ythedra. There, just beyond the uppermost step, Linnaeth lay on the pitted granite, barely breathing. By her side sprawled two of her dogs, badly broken, now stiff in death.

Truke tu-Kekh shouldered past me. He put his clawed hand on Linnaeth's forehead. He called her name.

It startled us all when she replied.

"It's not done," she whispered. Her sapphire eyes were pooled with tears.

Quin clasped one of Linnaeth's thin hands between his own large palms. "We came as soon as we could. We rode the whole way."

"So did he. On the wings of a crow."

"Where is the bastard?" said Truke, peering into the shadows around us. "Is there nothing we can do?"

Linnaeth managed a feeble smile. "Not much, I'm afraid."

She turned her head slightly, gazing at each of us in turn as if to memorize our features. She seemed to be amused by our clenched panic. "What news do you bring me?"

"Good news," said Quin. "The wizard's armies are defeated."

"It's true," said Gowen. "The Syrtians have been crushed."

Linnaeth nodded as if she'd suspected as much. Finally she looked at me. "Aln Adrackt will go to your world, Ramirez. Where things..."

"The battle?" I said. "It's started?"

"It started long ago. But your home is in trouble. The Dark One is stronger than anyone imagined."

"Still," I insisted, "there's a chance. Right?"

The Seer was quiet as she looked at me. I sensed she was trying to classify what I'd just said. If it had been the troll staring at me, I would have guessed he was attempting to recollect an appropriate cliché. But if Linnaeth managed to recall some helpful aphorism from the many she'd heard in her thousand centuries of existence, she must have thought it unhelpful to repeat.

"Yes," she offered. "The stories."

The Seer pressed her right elbow against the rock and tried to sit up. But this proved too difficult, or too painful, and Quin helped to ease her back down.

"I hurt him, you know. I hurt him badly. We fought for days through these caverns. He won. But he's..." Without taking her eyes from mine, Linnaeth passed me something that felt like a pencil. I looked down at a slender glass cylinder. It was three inches long and weighed next to nothing. The substance inside was clear at rest, but opalescent when jarred even slightly. It moved like mercury.

"What is it?"

"Softly," she said.

"Shhh," Gowen scolded. "*Rest*."

"My blood, Ramirez. A good part of what little I have left. If you see a chance, use it. Mix it with his. It will destroy him."

"Mix it?"

"With *his*," she repeated.

Quin scanned the shimmering ceiling of the cavern before he looked back at her. "Something tells me you're not just a seer," he said.

"Clever man. I am of the *eloihim*, God's first-created. In former days I was called Kalya. Storm Goddess. Face of the North. The evil thing you fight is one of the Fallen—one of those who rose up long ago in defiance of God's will and was cast out of heaven in retribution. We have been expecting their return. Now it has begun, and I am truly sorry for you. All of you...That you are here to see it."

Linnaeth's skin was now a translucent white, the veins in her forehead the green of slow rivers. Her lips moved once more, but no sound came out. A ring of pale fire danced in the air above her chest.

"I have one more request."

"Anything."

"One only. And you must promise to do it."

"I swear," said Quin.

The Seer gazed up at the ceiling of the cavern. She raised herself to a sitting position and touched the skin between her collarbone and the soft skin of her neck with one finger.

"Take the sword," she said. "And kill me."

———+———

I couldn't have done it. I couldn't even have *thought* it. It was strange, because I'd built my career on depicting random homicides in as many pixels as possible. Now, when requested to participate in one, my stomach turned at the prospect. We argued about it. We agonized. We apologized. But Linnaeth insisted, so finally the Marshal took Gowen's sword in both hands and ran it into the Seer's flesh, his eyes squeezed shut so he wouldn't have to witness his participation in this assisted suicide. The Seer only screamed once—at the instant the steel entered her body. After that, the blade's path seemed to be unhindered by muscle or bone. The Marshal pushed, and felt no resistance, and finally he stood there holding nothing but the unadorned hilt of the weapon as if the enchanted alloy had somehow been absorbed into Linnaeth's prone figure. Quin hung his head as if he'd done something he'd be ashamed of for the rest of his life.

The slender flame above Linnaeth's chest flickered out. Then her breathing ceased, and the Seer was gone. I leaned down, hesitated, kissed her cool cheek. *Hoped you'd be here to help me with this*, I thought. I placed the little vial of blood in the waist pocket of my tunic. Then I glanced up toward the cavern wall that stood fifty feet away. At almost eye level, just beyond the light of our torches and the furthest stretch of the rope bridge, a dark hole yawned in the rock.

The portal.

I took a deep breath. When I looked up at my friends, I found them staring at me. They made such a pathetic picture that I laughed in spite of myself. Usak with his long jaw and outlandish crown of hair. Quin, his cheeks hollowed out by weeks of desperation and rage. Truke tu-Kekh like a child's nightmare vision in gray and blue, his canine teeth gleaming in the light of our torches. Gowen with his blonde beard full of breakfast and cavern dust.

"Look," I said. "It's been a long time since I've had anyone to say goodbye to. So the thing is, I haven't had a whole lot of practice. All I can say is, there are people in the place where I come from who are in a whole lot of trouble, and it may be my fault. So…I don't know what I can do. I just know I should *be* there."

Quin folded the Seer's hands on her chest. His touch was gentle, just as it had been with Prince Mikel in the Thicket.

"Don't explain," said the Marshal. "Go. You'll be remembered here."

Ah, said a voice. *Remembrance. The beggar's consolation.*

The words seemed to come from everywhere at once. We reached for our weapons, straining to see through the gloom and smoke of the cavern. This turned out to be unnecessary. A towheaded boy stood on a shelf of rock only a few yards from us. *Had he been there all along?* I couldn't say. All I knew was that he was naked, and perfectly formed, but for the extra set of nipples set low on his chest. It was the voice that gave him away: sarcastic, cozening, sliding back and forth between promise and threat. It was the voice of Aln Adrackt. The voice I'd heard in my dreams, in this life and in another.

They still don't know who they're talking to, do they? Ban Lohannon. Wizard's Bane. Uniter of Nations. Funny, isn't it? However you're remembered in Ythedra, on Earth you're just a middle-aged drunk with a bad stomach and no one to listen to your complaints.

I tried to speak, but the words wouldn't come.

But I remember you, Ramirez. Lohannon. Whatever you're calling yourself. And I assure you, you made a very big mistake in coming here. Why didn't you stay with your princess? Her lieutenant is dead, you know. Lost his skull to an urzek's axe. You really should be by her side.

Quin advanced to stand beside me. "That's a lie. Teryan's alive. I saw him before we left. And *you*, wizard. You're the one who's made the mistake. Your army is destroyed."

My army?

The boy laughed.

I am my army!

But as he said this, his body shimmered and shook like a dying flame, and I saw a darker face beneath the smooth skin. Another face, on the head of a snake. The boy's feet melted and spread like paste over the rock he stood on. Then, as if it was a dream, everything was normal again. The figure stood undisturbed.

"You're hurt," I said. "From your fight with Linnaeth."

Linnaeth is dead! I saw her begging you to put her out of her misery. It doesn't matter. She's mine. As are you all. But you first, Lohannon. For the time you've cost me, you'll serve a hundred lifetimes in hell. You remember that hell, don't you?

Suffice it to say that I did.

Most moments I dealt with the fact. But now the past came seeping into my soul like back-flushed sewage. It was the presence of the sorcerer. *The stench. That voice. His eyes most of all.* Whatever his outward seeming, the eyes of Aln Adrackt remained emotionless and black, with depths that spoke of emptiness eternal and unremitting. I looked into those eyes and the world rolled off its pediment and went clanking off into an alley where I didn't care to follow. The boy seemed to grow, to swell to the size of the cavern itself, so that finally all I could see were those vacant eyes in front of me, *around* me, opening to take me in. Aln Adrackt held up a fist, then opened it, slowly, as if he were releasing a delicate wish. Instantly he began to change. His limbs thinned and stretched as his torso rose and receded from us until his body was a web suspended from the cavern walls, braced by his arms and legs. A tiny black-beaked head laughed at us from the center of the freakish structure. Our torches flickered out, a scalding wind screamed around us, and now the wizard was a *hundred* wizards, standing beside and above and among us and then just one again but the size of a thundercloud, his black eyes open like doors made of midnight. It was then that the demon inside Aln Adrackt revealed itself. It was huge—beyond the size of any earthly creature. Its dark skin crawled with lakes of flame. Above lusterless eyes its head was crowned by a tangled nest of horns, and its feet were cracked and bleeding hooves. The thing reared up to its full height and stared down at us as if we were ants. I heard Gowen scream. I saw him clutch his skull and I knew we were lost at last, utterly forsaken, and that madness was the only home we'd ever know.

But at just that moment the demon disappeared, and the blonde boy stood in his place. He stared at a spot high on the cavern wall behind us. Truke tu-Kekh raised his hammer. He'd taken a first step toward our enemy when Quin caught him by the collar.

"She's back," said the Marshal. We turned our heads to follow Quin's gaze.

Linnaeth stood on a narrow ledge of the cavern wall, a hundred yards above us. Her face was a glowing mask. She looked younger. Stronger.

I glanced back at the cavern floor. The Seer's body was gone. *Linnaeth, I underestimated you. Again. And maybe Aln Adrackt has, too. Maybe he waited around here thinking the fight was over. Maybe he didn't know that the sword held your essence, your blood. He waited for us to arrive so he could amuse himself, recover his strength before he traveled to Earth. And maybe that wasn't such a great idea.*

Linnaeth raised her voice in song. It was clear and high and unlike anything I'd ever heard before, an anthem so piercing and inevitable that even the dust in the air around us seemed to dance to it. The old woman ascended with her song, literally rising until she was suspended halfway between the roof of the cavern and where we stood. At first Aln Adrackt seemed confused. He peered harder at his enemy, and at last a thin smile appeared on his face.

You tried that once already, whore! Before I left you for dead!

Only now Linnaeth's voice grew louder. Around her a cloud of white light expanded like a star in the chamber. The first stone was a small one—hardly enough to distract us. But the rocks got bigger. A score of dagger-like stalactites smashed themselves to rubble only a hundred feet away. High above us, through the dust and glare, I saw the bottom of the dark lake churning. Linnaeth's song intensified, and we winced at the rising harmonic wail.

"This whole cave," shouted Quin, "is about to come *down!*"

The slender boy that was Aln Adrackt took a step backward, his attention focused on the water above us.

Linnaeth threw her arms back and lightning coursed through the cavern. The strike knocked us down. We heard a keening shriek and saw a wall of flames where Aln Adrackt had stood. The singing stopped. The dust swirled like a curtain and it took me a moment to make out that beyond the fire, a dark figure was dragging itself along the rope bridge toward the entrance of the portal. Rocks started falling again. With them came the first gouts from the lake above us: long ropes of cold water pounding the floor of the cavern.

Linnaeth's voice rang out through the roar of the collapsing cave.

"Ramirez! Go while you can! The rest of you, GET OUT! Now!"

With this, the Seer disappeared.

———†———

We hoisted Gowen to his feet. Strands of snot and blood hung from his nose and mouth, but he was conscious, and he whispered that he understood our words. He seemed to be able to travel. Another shower of stones—*closer, this time*—indicated that travel might be a good idea. Fingers of water came crawling along the cavern floor toward us.

"Listen, all of you. You heard her. This place isn't going to hold up much longer."

"I know the way," said Truke tu-Kekh.

"What about Linnaeth?" said Usak. "We can't leave her."

My voice was as loud as I could make it. "Linnaeth can take care of herself. Just get *out* of here! And promise me one thing. Gowen. Quin. All of you. Go to Emerkest. Take an army and destroy Kaer Rhygat. Once and for all."

Gowen nodded. Usak laid a huge hand on my shoulder. The faces around me belonged to people I'd never seen only a few weeks earlier. Since then they'd become my dearest friends. My *only* friends. And maybe they felt it too: the certainty that we would one day regret this speechless parting, this swallowing of what should have been said. But there was no time. I turned away from my companions. Stooped like a GI running for a helicopter, I scrambled up the rock and set out across the rope bridge. I threw myself into the shadowed cave without once looking back.

And then, of course, I fell.

3 8

Homecoming

I felt the usual shocks of adjustment. Nausea. Dizziness. Despair. Smoke rose from the charred remains of trees around me. I hoisted myself up off the damaged earth and tried to stand. My eyes lost focus. I reeled to my left, tripped over my own feet, landed flat on my back. I couldn't tell what was worse: how I felt, or what I'd just seen.

Because Aln Adrackt had made it through the portal too.

It was little consolation that he looked worse than I did. He wasn't a child anymore. His dark eyes leaked pus. His mouth was a toothless shell. Swaths of his skin were streaked with a scabrous gray mold, and his face had begun to flake away from his skull. Between his withered legs he dragged half of another form—the form of that beautiful boy he'd been on Ythedra, hanging like a stillborn fetus. He held one arm at his side and moved sidelong, as if the right side of his body was paralyzed. But he was alive. And alert. And now, unfortunately, he realized he had company.

It took every ounce of strength I had to struggle to my feet. The demon's breath rattled in his throat as he extended his left hand toward me. On his middle finger he wore a strange little ring, a band of polished black metal with an inch-long spike protruding from it. He took another step.

Lohannon! Your heart is still empty. Your world is in flames, and the woman you wanted is wasting in hell.

I looked up as I backed away from him. The heavens were veined with lightning, elaborate networks of white light flashing fully formed across the expanse of sky like tiny capillaries in a vast living organism—and just as quickly winking out. *You're about to die here. You wanted this...thing, and now you've got him and you haven't got the slightest idea what to do next. Think of a barbed bon mot for the road,* I told myself. The road to hell. The path I paved with my neutral intentions. When the world was a joke. Before I was the punch line.

Come taste. Taste my blade, and join your whore.

We were no longer alone on the scorched field. Around us, shadows watched. The dull orange of distant fires filled the sky. I turned my head and two things happened at once.

First, I glimpsed the ruins of Belvedere Castle. I realized I stood on what had once been Central Park's Great Lawn.

And second: Aln Adrackt tried to kill me.

I grabbed his arm as he forced his spiked ring closer to my eye. I felt the coiled strength inside him. I felt a hatred capable of poisoning worlds, and I was afraid. But I met his gaze and didn't blink, and I touched at that instant something deeper than my fear. It was *anger*. Anger at the ugliness around me and all the waiting obscene mouths. Anger at the smoldering trunks of oak and elm and beech on what had once been green earth and the realization that without even noticing when it happened I'd lost everything clean and stippled, wind-blown and rain-soaked, everything I could have smelled and touched and tasted once but no longer could and never would. My right hand slipped to the sheath I wore at my side. I wrenched Ara's jeweled dagger free and shoved it into the demon's belly. Aln Adrackt opened his mouth to scream. Nothing came out but the odor of his own decay. And still he pressed harder, forcing that wicked little spike to within an eyelash of my right pupil.

Did you really think it would be so easy? That you could think pretty thoughts to open my veins? Ythedran magic won't work here. This is the world of force and fulcrums, Ramirez. Motors and missiles. The center of the circle!

I heard a bone snap. *My* bone. A finger, cracked by the creature's gathering strength. I fought for the life I had more than once tried to throw away. I fought with everything I could bring up out of myself. But my mind started drifting. Falling. Whatever. It was just that Jesus it hurt and I thought God I've let you down and never realized what I had and truly I regret my idiocy but it's all too late, just let it end let it end let it please let it please let it...

Remember this, worm, when you think on your failures. When you think of the evil you loosed on your world. We are gathering like locusts, all of us, and we will drag your angels from the thrones they stole from us at the beginning of time. Our thrones! Think of the lives I'll take. The souls I'll eat. Your return to Ythedra led me to this place, fool. And now I'm going to KILL!

"So am I," said Atryen Quin.

His sword split the demon's skull in two. He nearly took one of my shoulders off with it. Black fluid oozed like oil from Aln Adrackt's broken head. His right eye rolled upward, and he gasped as if beholding the judgment of heaven itself.

"But my wife never would have," Quin said, trembling with rage. "And this is for HER, you blood-sucking freak."

Pieces.

More pieces.

Tears smeared the Darannan Marshal's face. Still he hacked at the corpse of Aln Adrackt, hammering till its thin bones were shattered and the rancid dark liquid pooled at our feet. Finally Quin cut furrows in the Earth itself. He reared back, disgusted by his own dark work, exhausted from the days of desperation and grief that had brought him to this strange red place and delivered him to this ecstasy of rage.

He locked his eyes on mine. He took a step toward me and fell on his face.

I didn't have time to help him. I knew what would happen before I actually saw it. It was like a nightmare, unstoppable and awful and somehow completely logical. The fluid that had drained from Aln Adrackt began to seek itself. It began to reconstitute, forming little lakes that rolled together to form bigger lakes in turn. The severed pieces of flesh floating in the pools gravitated toward each other. He wasn't dead. *It* wasn't dead. Whatever it was, Aln Adrackt was coming back. That's when I took the glass vial from the pocket of my tunic. I'll admit it. I hesitated. Even now I felt Aln Adrackt's hold on me. I wondered if the stain I carried inside me would let me do it, wondered as I had wondered a thousand times before if I was more a part of that blackness than of anything else I'd ever know. I held the vial up anyway. I held it up over the crawling remains of Aln Adrackt and I snapped the vessel in half. The liquid glimmered purple and blue as it fell to the earth. At the instant it met the demon's essence, the air made a retching sound—a deep-throated, rasping *KKACHOOM*—and the world went white. All sound stopped, and color blanched from everything around me. It was as if time ceased to exist. It was as if the universe had turned itself inside out to purge this unwholesome thing from its guts. Then the night returned, and I heard the hiss and sizzle of burning earth. The remains of the demon were gone.

Aln Adrackt was dead.

Again.

Strange Days

R eader, I carried him.

Atryen Quin is a big man. *Linebacker* big. And I was stronger from my stay in Ythedra but still it took everything I had to haul the Marshal out of the Park. I looked back once to see the luminous eyes that had watched my feeble waltz with Aln Adrackt circling the ground where the demon had fallen. A glance was all I needed. I quickened my steps. Soon the fires ended and as my mind cleared I entered a thicket that was green again and through the trees I made my way toward a mountain range of apartment buildings. Finally I staggered out into the avenues of the living city itself. Taxicabs prowled the cement canyons. Couples walked arm-in-arm in the autumn air, their mingled breaths making mist below the streetlights.

I laid my friend on the cracked sidewalk as gently as I could. Then I collapsed beside him.

"Welcome to the Upper West Side," I said. And then, because he couldn't hear me: "You dumb sonofabitch."

That's how Atryen Quin—commander of Ythedra's Outriders; Marshal of Kaer Rhennet; the Traveler of Worlds foretold in the prophecy—ended up in Manhattan. I didn't ask him, but he came just the same. He stumbled across the rope bridge just seconds after

I did, as the cavern of Inniskerr cracked and sagged and the cold pure lake fell in upon it. It was Quin who told me the story of the bloody siege of Dred Thannat. We talk about it less than you might imagine. For our own separate reasons, Ythedra is for both of us a world that hurts too much to recollect. We hope our friends made it out of the mountain. We hope Linnaeth still lives—or, if she doesn't, that her disciples will find a way to heal that injured planet. We could speculate forever, but speculation is all it would be. So we don't bother.

We just hope.

Besides, we have other battles to fight. I remain a fugitive from my own creations. I realize there's a sense in which this is true for all of us. Every man creates his own most dangerous pursuers. One of mine just happens to be a cyborg named Laser. He has a cannon grafted to his ulna that can fire toroidal plasmas at speeds of seven thousand meters per second. He can also see in infrared and, last time I checked, run forty-six miles per hour.

But there are consolations. For the first time in my life, I know I'm not alone. In the ruins of some mind's forever, we have found each other. We the survivors. We the hunted. We who ride empty E trains at hours of the night even the rats find odd and wander Water Street searching for word from the First Born in spray paint on the cinder blocks. Now we live in two worlds. In one we walk among you. We drive your courtesy vans and sort your recycling. We hold the door, as Quin does, for elderly residents of the Beth Israel Retirement Village. He's learned about ten words of English. He tells folks his accent is Slovakian. The gig doesn't pay much, but he occasionally gets to run off a bunch of crackheads, which he finds enjoyable. And with that utter absence of irony available only to longtime veterans, he says he likes the uniform. He's taken to riding an old Triumph Thruxton he found on Craigslist. He eats too much beef jerky to stay healthy for long, and he's developed an interest in ice hockey. But it's just as well he's fitting in. As you might have guessed, he can't go back.

None of us can. Once you've seen the world beneath this one, it's impossible to ignore it. Quin and I have become spiritual conscripts, subject to constant call-up in the conflict that is gathering as I write this and you read it and as you sleep and eat and dream. Long nights linger like lesser forevers but we fight on. "Believe," we mumble to ourselves before each battle, as the Fallen One masses his demons on fields that might one day be Earth. And we do believe. We believe in promises and pelicans and oatmeal and oak trees. We believe in the dance of sunlight on cold mountain creeks and the lullaby of wind through cottonwood leaves and the intricate staccato poetry of Louis Armstrong's trumpet. It's strange to find ourselves at war. It's strange to be who we are. Then again it's strange, as Jeff Mangum once sang, to be anything at all. Is it this world? *Your* world? I only know what I see. Life goes on. The struggle continues. Beside you. Beyond you. In the gap between earth and sky, the hole behind night and day, Atryen Quin tosses his broadsword palm to palm. The archangel Michael stands at the front of our ranks, his gaze the color of sun striking ice. With us are cartoon legions, seraphim in armored cars, hermits manning howitzers. They're all here: all the heroes. Lou Gehrig. Aquaman. Joan of Arc. Sleep tonight, reader. But think of us out here, besieged, fighting for everything you should hold precious in your pitted hearts. I know those hearts. I owned one. I own one still. Our homes and help lie buried, but we'll fight till we no longer stand. Then we'll pray that one more terrible and beautiful will storm at last, and we'll watch the oceans rise to kiss His hand.

TO BE CONTINUED IN
BOOK TWO OF
THE CHRONICLES OF DOOM:
THE DREAM OF THE RED CITIES

www.ingramcontent.com/pod-product-compliance
Lightning Source LLC
Chambersburg PA
CBHW030028180626
46810CB00001B/267